MW01616429

PROXIMATE CAUSE

CAUSE

DAVID PRITCHARD

Proximate Cause

Copyright © April 2014, David Pritchard

No part of this book may be reproduced, transmitted, downloaded, distributed, or stored in or introduced into any information storage and retrieval system, in any form or by any means, whether electronic or mechanical, without express written permission from the author, except by a reviewer who may quote brief passages for review purposes.

This book is a work of fiction, and any resemblance to any person, living or dead, or any events or occurrences, is purely coincidental. The characters and story line are created from the author's imagination and are used fictitiously.

Cover Art Copyright & Design by Indie Designz

CHAPTER ONE

MILLER WALKER SLEPT IN HIS north campus home, while the man who wanted him dead rode in the passenger seat of a truck just a few blocks away.

It was far too early on a Thursday morning for anyone without very good reason to be driving around Walker's neighborhood in the first place, even if that neighborhood was situated in Austin, Texas; a college town known for its perpetual late night music scene. But what was more out of place in this modest enclave had anyone been awake to notice, was the vehicle itself. It was a very expensive and well-appointed jet-black Chevrolet Suburban with windows tinted as dark as the exterior paint; the kind one might expect Secret Service personnel to be driving when surrounding a presidential motorcade.

The truck's bottom half would have been obscured by the layer of low-hanging fog extending a few feet above the pavement, if not for its bumper-mounted fog lights cutting a glowing amber path through the soup. The density of the haze had been increasing over most of city since midnight, thanks to double-digit Texas humidity that had enveloped the central Texas region for the past week.

Now on its third pass through the neighborhood, the truck slowed to a crawl just up the street from the Walker house. Never quite coming to a complete stop, it paused long enough for the passenger to step out and gently push the door closed. Easing around the corner, the vehicle accelerated on its way out of the neighborhood.

Thor watched as the truck disappeared back into the haze. Silently, he moved away from the dimly lit corner and crossed the street. This was by no means his first trip into the neighborhood. He had been watching the house in the middle of this block for a long time.

After lingering by a large oak tree for a few minutes, he methodically worked his way back toward the Walker place. Every few minutes he stopped to look and listen and take mental notes. He absorbed every inch of his surroundings, identified and remembered all the details: landscaping, parked cars—both those used regularly and those under repair, security lights, streetlights, escape routes. Nothing escaped his gaze.

He had already learned all the names of Walker's neighbors. He knew who in the neighborhood still held a job and who was retired and what their hobbies were. He knew their children's names and where they played and which ones were away at school. And he obviously knew he would be very much alone at this hour of the morning. Thor had done his homework well.

A train whistle blew in the distance, somewhere near Interstate 35.

Thor was directly across the street from the Walker house when he glanced at his watch. It was 3 A.M. "Right on time," he whispered. He looked both ways before walking toward the left side of the house.

Once on the grass, he followed the edge of the driveway to the garage, and then disappeared into the tall bushes lining that side, until he reached the side fence. He tested the gate's hinge pin as a foothold, stood on it, and looked over the fence and up and down the alley behind the house, as best he could with the limited view. Dropping deftly back to the ground, Thor stood hidden in the shrubbery for nearly forty-five minutes before setting his watch timer, retracing his exact steps, and disappearing once more into the mist at the end of the street.

CHAPTER TWO

"AHHHHH-CHOOO!" WHITLEY TALMADGE lurched forward on the park bench, muffling her sneeze with one hand while latching onto her wide-brimmed straw hat with the other.

The startled chocolate Labrador retriever that had been lying at her feet jumped up to look at her.

"Bless you," an elderly man remarked, patting the dog's head as he shuffled by.

"Thank you," Whitley answered and tilted her head up and smiled as he passed. Her thick-framed sunglasses had slid down the bridge of her slender nose and were sitting just low enough for her steel-blue eyes to peek between them and the edge of her hat. "Lay down, Bosco," she commanded.

Wiping her watery eyes with her index finger, she reached into her purse and retrieved a travel-sized packet of tissues. She rushed to cover her nose with one as she felt the pressure of another emphatic sneeze building.

"Ahhhhh-choo!"

Dabbing her nose with the tissue, she looked down at the dog and smiled. "I'm sorry, Bosco. I didn't mean to scare you, baby. And I apologize for not running with you today, but these allergies are kicking my butt, sweetie."

It was late September, and the Austin allergy season was in full force. Wind and a lack of rain had made it even worse than usual.

Whitley imagined she could smell the dust. She had repeatedly heard warnings from her friends: "Even if you've never had allergies in your life, live in Austin long enough and you'll get them. If September's mold and ragweed don't pummel your sinuses early on, December's cedar pollen will make you pray that they had."

Having grown up in Dallas just a couple of hundred miles to the north, she couldn't understand how such a short distance could mean such a noticeable difference in the pollen count. The fact is that Dallas is worse than Austin for allergies. It was just that this year, for whatever reason was to be Whitley's rite of passage; the first time after ten years of living in Austin, that the infamous allergies seriously took hold. And they weren't about to let go.

Whitley watched as a group of Frisbee golfers across the creek packed up to go home. She also noticed a pretty young woman not far from them. Sitting alone and uphill from the rocky creek bottom on a grassy slope beneath a large oak tree, the woman was watching some children play nearby.

Grabbing a water bottle from her purse, Whitley felt around in the bottom of her bag trying to locate her emergency pillbox. When she found it, she looked at the dog and said, "I hope I remembered to put a sinus tablet in here, Bosco. I'd hate to keep scaring you all afternoon with my sneezing."

The dog tilted his head and gave her a puzzled look.

"Here it is!" she exclaimed as she held the pill up in the air for him to see.

Bosco jumped up as if about to receive a treat.

"You can't have this, mister! It'll make you sicker than a dog!" she laughed. She popped the pill into her mouth and took a sip of water while reaching back into her purse. "But you can have one of these," she said, waving a dog biscuit in the air.

He immediately sat down, wagging his tail, never taking his eyes off the food.

"Good boy," she said, then threw the biscuit to him.

4

He barely had to move his head to catch it in his mouth. Bosco gobbled it up and sat whining, eagerly awaiting more.

"That's all you get, honey. I don't want to ruin your dinner before I take you back home. Besides, you don't want to get sick to your stomach, do you? You've been running and fetching the tennis ball all afternoon."

The dog stared as if straining to understand what she was saying, then laid his head on her knees.

Whitley rubbed his ears as Bosco licked her forearm, "That's what I need. Some loving!" she exclaimed. "Now if I could just get your daddy to show me this kind of attention, we'd have it made."

The dog jumped into her lap and nearly sent her tumbling off the back of the concrete bench. In the process, he bumped her straw hat, its leather strap caught around her neck, and her sandy brown hair spilled around her face. She laughed and gave him a big hug.

Whitley looked at her watch. They had been at the park for almost three hours. "We'd better get going." Whitley pushed the heavy dog off of her and picked up his leash from the grass.

As she gathered her belongings, she looked back at the woman sitting across the creek. She had every hair in place. Her toenails, lips, and fingernails were a flattering shade of red. She had beautiful olive skin and a lanky frame. Everything about this woman seemed perfect.

"Is she more along the lines of what you want, Steve?" Whitley murmured. She shifted the sunglasses up on her nose and looked down self-consciously at her mistreated nails. She couldn't remember the last time she had doled out any cash for a manicure. Perhaps it was time.

Whitley sighed and sat back down on the bench to slip into her sandals. She wiped her reddened nose once more with a tissue and stuck her left foot in the air, stretching her toes apart as they peeked from behind the leather strap of her sandals. Her toenails, also unpolished, weren't faring much better than her fingernails.

The dark amber tint of her glasses also did little to hide the sun's reflection beaming back from her pale but shapely legs, "programmer tan" as coined by her co-workers in the Western States Insurance Company's Information Systems Department. This was a common trait found in that phylum of the financial services work force that spends weeks, months, or even years tethered to a computer in a secure but often windowless environment.

Her inspection migrated up from her legs, past her shorts to the Luckenbach, Texas tee shirt she was wearing. It too needed attention, dull and faded by too many years' worth of wear. It was one of her favorites and didn't have any holes, so that was reason enough to continue wearing it.

Whitley had never been a slave to fashion, especially since she spent most of her time, free or otherwise, concealed in the claustrophobic basement of her office building, far removed from the majority of her coworkers. Except for the occasional excursion out to the business units, in order to assist the production support team set up an employee's workspace or to fix unexpected system glitches, lunch and quitting time were generally her only reasons she had to exit "The Dungeon."

On her salary alone, she could easily afford nicer clothing, but wearing designer clothes had never been a priority. The company's business-casual environment gave her all the more reason to save on the fashion dollar. Even so, she found herself to be uncharacteristically self-conscious in the presence of this striking woman.

Although her friend Steve Latham had never in the least indicated a desire for a fashion-forward woman or for that matter any type of woman after his divorce, Whitley was feeling desperate. She had begun to wonder if the only way he would ever notice her as anything more than a chum would be if she went through a radical metamorphosis more on par with this lady in the park.

Good friends before his marital problems, Steve and Whitley's bond had grown much stronger afterward. Allowing a reasonable amount of time to pass after the Latham's divorce, Whitley had tried every imaginable subtle clue to get Steve to ask her out on a real date, but clues were as far as she went. Whitley was adamant about not pushing the issue with him. If Steve didn't make the first move someday soon, she would have to resign herself to the fact that they would always remain friends and nothing more.

Except for an infrequent and innocent dinner date, the best she could get out of their current relationship was an occasional request to housesit and feed Bosco when Steve went out of town on business—tasks she always eagerly agreed to.

Steve would be gone for a total of three weeks on this trip. According to astrological charts she had consulted before his departure, Whitley had felt sure he would ask her to go with him this time. All of the mystical signals she received had indicated that he would. Much to her chagrin, the invitation never materialized.

Whitley continued to watch the woman across the creek and determined by the way that she was beaming at the group of children playing in close proximity, that one of them must be hers. Whitley often thought about having a child of her own someday, Steve's child, a desire she could never tell him, at least not yet. No, first things first, she would need an honest-to-goodness date with him. Children would have to come later.

After a few moments and as if on cue, one of the children broke away from the playgroup and stumbled up the slope toward the young woman and hugged her.

"Do you see that Bosco?" She asked the dog. "Perfect looks, perfect child, and she is hanging out in the park because she is probably married to the perfect asshole!"

The dog looked confused.

"Don't worry hon, I don't really mean it."

"Well, enough sulking," she said to herself. "It's Friday afternoon, Miss Talmadge. What do you have to look forward to on this rare day off?"

Bosco tilted his head again and stared as she spoke. "Let's see. Do you have a date with Steve?"

No, he's a thousand miles away, climbing some mountain.

"Any plans for a date before the end of the next millennium?"

Only if Fate intervenes.

"Any other men in your life with potential?"

Uh . . . no solid leads just yet, Whit.

"Well, what the hell are you gonna do tonight, girlfriend?"

Oh, wait a minute, I remember now. I won't be alone after all! Tonight I'll be spending a romantic evening with . . . my mother!

At that instant, Bosco barked at her.

"Bosco, you know I shouldn't feel that way about Winona, don't you?"

The dog barked again.

"I thought so!" she said as she playfully squeezed the dog's nose. "Yeah, she can be a major pain in the butt, but I wish she'd come see us more often. At least this should be a good visit, because both of our horoscopes were good today."

Whitley rarely left the apartment without first consulting the newspaper's horoscope. Aside from exercising Bosco, the only reason she had walked a good distance to Zilker Park in the first place was because her horoscope had told her, *Take a walk in a green field and contemplate your existence as a woman.* The fact that she also balanced her checkbook and made out her grocery list she had written off as her practical side coming to the surface.

The encounter with the beautiful stranger was Fate. She just knew it had to be. Yes, Fate was telling her that drastic measures were necessary in order to resuscitate her pathetic love life. She was glad to have followed the newspaper astrologer's advice this day.

Many aspects of Whitley's daily existence were ruled by her forays into the extrasensory world. She wasn't faithful to any one discipline. She sometimes used I Ching, palmistry, or tarot card readings instead of, or in addition to her daily horoscope or astrological readings, depending on how much time she had before work. The one day that she had failed to take the necessary time to heed the advice of the stars, an incident nearly killed her.

Whitley had been on her way to a concert west of Austin with some friends, when her car was rear-ended by a pickup truck—a big pickup truck. Except for a minor abrasion or two, the friends with her in the car had escaped uninjured.

However, she had not been so fortunate. Her forehead had struck the steering wheel, and she had been knocked out cold. All told, she had suffered a concussion, whiplash, and a few bruises. All she could remember later was a strange dream about her father. In it she was a young girl being disciplined for riding her bike on the busy street in front of their Dallas home.

Her father had passed away a few weeks prior to the wreck, and he had never before come to her in her dreams. Nor had he appeared during Whitley's two attempts to contact him at séances conducted by Madam Vera, a Spanish medium of questionable reputation near campus. Because of this, when Whitley finally came to, she was positive this vision of her father was some sort of warning about the events surrounding the collision.

After three days she checked out of the hospital and found the newspaper that contained the horoscope from the date of the accident. Once she had read its recommendation to stay in and read a good book on that date, Whitley vowed never to miss another daily prediction.

Noticing the time again, she clipped Bosco's leash onto his collar. As Whitley stuffed the water bottle back into her bag, she noticed some writing on a bill sticking out of the top of her wallet. Pulling it out, she found words written around the border on the back of a one-dollar bill: St. Lazarus—anyone who receives this bill will be blessed with a lot of money if you rewrite this on ten other bills.

Whitley thought for a moment and pulled out her wallet. Leafing through the bills, she found four twenties and a ten. She stuck the ten in her left dress pocket and put her wallet back in her handbag.

She then gathered Bosco and her own things and started the two-mile trek back to her car. Glancing at her watch once more, she saw it was 2:30. With some luck, she'd have just enough time to exchange her bill for ten singles, drive Bosco back to Steve's house and feed him, then get home before her mother showed up for dinner.

CHAPTER THREE

WHITLEY HAD BARELY MADE it out of the shower and started dinner before her mother arrived. Forty-five minutes early.

It was 5:15. Always early, Winona Talmadge couldn't understand why her daughter hadn't inherited this valuable characteristic from her.

After a hug and the exchange of a few kind words, Whitley was back in the kitchen working on a salad. Her mother started inspecting the premises.

Whitley eyed her momentarily and said, "Mother, would you please stop doing that."

Mrs. Talmadge had only been there a few minutes and was already busy wiping dust off of and adjusting the figurines and candles that adorned the mantel in her daughter's tiny apartment.

"I'm just trying to help, honey."

"I know, Mom, but this is the first time you've come here to eat in eight months. The last thing I want you to do is my housecleaning and redecorating."

"Well, someone has to do it."

"Mother!"

"All right. All right. I just don't understand why you choose to live in this ridiculously small place, Whitley. At least let me get you a maid."

"Enough, Winona! We've been through this a thousand times," Whitley said, shaking her head back and forth in a disgusted fashion.

"Okay." Mrs. Talmadge hated for her daughter to call her by her first name. "I get the message."

"Good!" Whitley snapped. The sound of the knife blade rapping on the cutting board became more amplified with each forceful slice into the cucumber. Her mother knew just how to push her buttons. Whitley snatched the slices and slung them into a large wooden salad bowl.

Winona Talmadge was staying a few miles away at the Driskill Hotel, a turn-of-the-century beauty on Sixth Street in downtown Austin. The hotel was a popular haunt for visiting politicos and celebrities, and its close proximity to Austin music venues increased its allure. Mrs. Talmadge could care less about the music. She and Mr. Talmadge had always stayed at the Driskill whenever they came to Austin for U.T. football games, something they had done for over thirty years. Both were Texas grads and burnt-orange fans to the core. Even though her husband had passed away three years earlier, Winona had continued the seasonal pilgrimages to Royal-Memorial Stadium with friends to root for the Longhorns.

"I don't suppose you'd be interested in going to the game with us tomorrow, would you?"

"No, Mother, I wouldn't." The University was also Whitley's alma mater, but she didn't care about football.

"Jason is going to be there."

"So?"

"I know that he'd love to see you."

"Well, I don't want to see him. In fact, I don't know why you think I would."

The Scott and Talmadge families were the best of friends. Jason Scott had been Whitley's first love. Sixteen years ago, as a Dallas teenager, she had lost her virginity to him, a miserable experience that was to be her first and last with him.

"Did you know that he's divorced and has set up his new practice in Dallas?"

"No, Mother, I didn't, nor do I care."

"You two were so cute together."

"Christ, don't make me sick, Mother. That was almost twenty years ago."

"He is so handsome now. He finally put some meat on those skinny little bones of his. I wish you would reconsider."

"Yeah? Well, if memory serves me, he needed to put meat on one bone for sure."

"Whitley!"

"Mother, listen. I'm not interested in football, nor am I interested in Jason Scott. End of story. OK?"

"I just want to see you happy, honey."

"I am happy, Mother. Very happy. God! If Frank was still alive, he'd swat your butt."

"Don't disrespect your father, hon."

Whitley clutched a head of Romaine lettuce and began rinsing it off. Plucking a handful of leaves, she added them to the increasingly bulging salad bowl.

"I just thought for sure that you'd have been married by now and have had two or three grandchildren."

"Children, Winona."

"What?"

"Children. You thought that I'd have had two or three children, not grandchildren."

"Oh, you know what I mean."

"You bet I do." Whitley was firm with her mother, but she didn't push too far.

Her parents had always been close, more like giggly teenagers than a couple married for over thirty years. Ever since her father's death, she knew the strain and loneliness her mother had been contending with. Winona had been traveling a great deal over the last couple of years, even during holidays. She told her daughter that the trips were opportunities to meet new people, but Whitley knew it was more likely that her mother was avoiding staying at home alone.

"I'm going to run to the ladies room, baby."

"You want me to fix you something to drink, Mother?"

"Have you any wine?"

"No wine, but I have some beer."

"Beer? Honey, what kind of man do you think you will attract with beer in the fridge? I'm going to call Luis and have him pick out some appropriate groceries for you. He has the most divine deli and wine cellar in Dallas. Oh, and perhaps it's time for you to find a new circle of friends, dear."

"Winona, my men friends are just that. My friends. They aren't pretentious, callous jerks like Jason. They like me just the way I am now, and they will like me when I finish all that beer in the fridge and turn into a fat, belching, beer-guzzling, bar-hopping spinster down on Sixth Street."

"Really, dear. There's no need to snap. I'll just have water, thank you." Winona turned and walked primly down the narrow hallway to the bathroom.

Whitley knew her mother almost as well as her father had. She also knew how badly her parents wanted her to be happily married and producing their grandchildren. Whitley was saddened when her father had passed away so young, disappointed that he would never see her married or get to know his grandchildren. She had done her best to keep her own feelings of loss in check during that rough period and offer as much support as possible to her mother.

Winona had been in the bathroom for ten minutes, on what Whitley suspected was one of her mother's reconnaissance missions. The fact she had started so soon after her arrival came as a bit of a surprise.

Chuckling, Whitley guessed her mother must be ransacking the bathroom drawers and cabinets about now, on a diligent crusade for her daughter's birth control pills. She knew if Winona found any, she would come back into the room, waving them in the air and spewing the negative effects brought about by using them. So Whitley had hidden them, and hidden them well. She felt that at this point in her life, if Winona were so hell-bent on having grandchildren, she wouldn't even bat an eye if her daughter had a child out of wedlock.

Besides, she wanted to teach her mother a lesson about being so nosy, as if it would do any good since they saw each other so infrequently. During a planned trip to the drug store earlier in the week, Whitley had bought seven large boxes of condoms, seven being one of her lucky numbers that day. Before opening them, she had "roughed up" a couple of the boxes, kicking and pounding the containers around the apartment like soccer balls to give them a regularly-accessed appearance.

Now stored in plain sight under the sink, long connected strands of brightly packaged latex protection snaked out of the bruised cardboard boxes. Just to ensure Winona would detect them, Whitley had strewn a few empty condom wrappers about the apartment in strategic spots; even the wastebasket next to the toilet held a few. In the bedroom alone she had planted so much latex color; Winona would soon think she had been on an Easter egg hunt.

When the bathroom door opened, Whitley heard Winona's shuffling feet head toward the bedroom door. She could see the light go on from her vantage point at the kitchen sink. She was starting to cramp from holding back her laughter.

Moments later, her mother's body language told all as she skulked back into the den. She didn't miss a beat before asking, "So. Who have you been seeing lately?" Her voice cracked and had taken on a markedly firmer tone.

Whitley squatted down to get a pot from under the cabinet, biting her tongue to keep from giggling and giving away her little ploy. "Oh, I've been seeing a few different people lately, Mother."

"Really?"

"Yeah."

"Anything . . . serious?"

"No, just playing the field. Mostly legislative types in the downtown area. You know decent salaries, wife and kids out of town. That sort of thing." She stuck her face just inside the cabinet opening to hide her grin.

14

"Whitley, that's dangerous. You'd better not be seeing married men!"

"I use protection, Mother."

"So I see."

"What is that supposed to mean, Mother?" She couldn't contain herself any longer and let out a shriek. "Hah! Been scrounging around in my bathroom cabinets again, haven't you?" Whitley was still holding the salad tongs as she stood up and covered her mouth with the back of her hand. She began laughing in earnest. "You've been set up, Wi-no-na!"

"Whitley!"

"Hey! You wanna borrow a box or two? You might get lucky at the ball game tomorrow."

"You little devil." Winona's face turned a deep shade of scarlet, a sharp contrast to her tall, white hairdo that vaulted skyward like a Pharaoh's headdress. "If I hadn't given birth to you personally, I'd never believe we were related."

Whitley volleyed back in an extremely guttural Texas draw, "Yep, I burnt through a box anna haff last week alone," she said and pretended to wipe her nose with her shirtsleeve. "So damn sore ah cain't hartly set down."

"Whitley! Stop it. You are such a mess." Winona laughed as she walked across the room and hugged her daughter.

"Now that's what I call a perfectly executed plan." Whitley reached for the water glass on the counter and handed it to her mother.

Winona eyed the glass momentarily, sighed, and handed it back to Whitley. "Keep it. I'll take the beer instead."

"Now you're talkin', Winona. Hell, we'll be sharin' a trailer outen the country before long."

"Let's not overdo it, sweetie."

CHAPTER FOUR

THOR INTENDED TO LEAVE for Dallas early Friday afternoon and not return until midday Saturday. He called to put a surveillance team in place outside Saint Anne's Catholic Church where Miller Walker worked as the bookkeeper. "I need a babysitter until tomorrow evening. Same location."

No voice responded, but two beeps signaled that his request would be carried out.

Ten minutes later, Thor left a building at the east end of the church property and headed toward a waiting Suburban. Even disguised, he made sure no one but the driver witnessed his exit. The passenger door swung open, and Thor jumped in. The truck pulled a short distance up the street and idled there until the "sitters" were in place. The driver signaled to the surveillance team by turning on his lights. They responded by turning theirs off. Then, the glossy black truck wheeled down a side street toward Interstate-35. They would be in Dallas in a little over three hours.

Most of the organization's senior members no longer participated in the riskier operations. Many had already paid their dues anyway and were more than happy to pass that torch on.

Lower level associates would occasionally be paired with a partner, but opportunities for revealing the identities of co-workers were always kept to a minimum. Information about another area of the organization could only be passed between associates when one was assigned into a new territory, and this only occurred when the new person was replacing an associate who had been transferred—or removed permanently.

Five out of the twenty associates in the Texas region had been "removed" from their positions in the last year alone. Reasons for the individual disappearances ranged from embezzling cash and botched assignments, to attempting to leave the organization too soon. Those who knew of the removals always believed that Thor was involved. Fear was an extremely powerful management tool, one that Thor utilized with great effectiveness. The right amount of fear created a productive entity, and his reputation for swift retribution was legendary and more than enough of an incentive to keep most everyone in line and silent.

In the minds of the organization associates who knew of him, Thor was a ghost, an entity that could materialize instantly. As long as they followed orders, they had nothing to worry about. No subordinate associate knew his true identity. That privilege was afforded only to a few division heads and Thor's direct superiors. Those in the highest ranks took painstaking measures to help ensure his privacy, probably out of fear for their own lives as much as a means of concealing him for the benefit of the organization.

Division heads were allowed the discretion to deal with problems in their own unique way, often using the same elite team of hired professionals. Thor, however, was different. He felt additional personnel only increased both the propensity for mistakes and the odds of everyone getting caught. A perfectionist and meticulous planner, he felt it best to take care of obstacles as quickly as possible with no outside assistance. He told virtually no one of his intentions, executing his plans quietly, smoothly, and efficiently, willing to let all others wonder what had happened after it was already too late.

The sitters rolled the car windows down and prepared themselves for what would likely be another uneventful Friday night. The occupant in the passenger seat lit up a smoke.

"You ever seen Thor?" the young driver asked.

"Hell, no. No one has. At least they didn't know it if they did or didn't live to talk about it. And I don't want to neither." He took a long drag on his cigarette.

"What's the deal with him? I mean, I hear everybody freaks out when he comes to town."

"How old are you, man?"

"Twenty-nine."

"I'm gonna give you a piece of advice. If you wanna live to be thirty, you'll shut the hell up about Thor right now. Comprende?"

"What?" his partner chuckled. "No, I don't *comprende.* Why has this guy weirded everyone out?"

"How long you been with the group?"

"Two years."

"Two years?" Holding his arm out the window, he tapped nervously on his cigarette and exhaled as he spoke to his new partner. "Two freakin' years! Where were you before you came here?"

"El Paso."

"El Paso? Do you even know why you got this job?" He tapped his cigarette again.

"I was told someone retired."

"And you believed that?" He shook his head before taking another drag on his cigarette.

"Why wouldn't I? I mean, they never lied to me before."

"What a Boy Scout." Tap, tap, tap. "What'd you do in El Paso before you took this gig?"

"Pretty much the same surveillance thing, but I learned to set up a few wires and video while I was there."

"Two years and you're a Cable Guy already, huh?" He shook his head in disbelief. "Okay, listen up, El Paso. I'm gonna tell you this one time and one time only. This is the real deal, so pay attention with your ears only and keep your eyes focused on Walker.

"My last partner was this great-lookin' broad, a blonde about forty-two, forty-three years old. Best damn cable guy you ever seen. She could talk her way in anywhere." He took a long, deliberate puff on his cigarette and stubbed it out in the ashtray.

"Well, she gets this crazy idea when Thor comes to town to find out who he is. I mean, as soon as he comes to town, she starts talkin' crazy like this, and this goes on for at least six or eight months, this crazy talk. Anyway, we were on this assignment, and we get the call to clear outta the area because Thor had a little 'house cleaning' to do at the little office building we're camped in front of. We assume it's for the guy we'd been sittin' on for the last few days, but it ends up bein' one of our own that he's after, only we don't know this at the time. Anyway, this crazy bitch decides she's gonna hang around and see if she can catch the action first-hand.

"You still watchin' for Walker?"

"Yeah, man. Relax."

"Anyway, like I was sayin', this crazy bitch jumps outta the car up the street from this office building. I'm yellin' at her to get her ass back in the car, but she's not listenin' to any of the shit I'm sayin'. 'Oh, I'll be fine,' she says. 'Nobody's gonna know I'm here,' she says.

"I tell the dizzy bitch that I'm havin' no parta this and she's got one more chance to get the hell back in the car. 'I'll be fine,' she says." He paused to grab his pack of cigarettes off the dash board and light another.

"So? What happens?"

"I'm gettin' to it. So I tell her that's it, I'm leavin', and she's gonna have to find her own damn way home. 'Fine,' she says. So I leave her there." Tap, tap, tap.

"So? Did she see him?"

He turned and glared at his partner. "I'm gettin' to it! Keep your pants on. So, I leave her there, and that's the last time I ever see her."

"That's it?"

"How many times I gotta tell your country ass to shut the hell up and listen." He took another drag and exhaled. Tap, tap.

"Jesus! Alright. I'm sorry, man."

"So two or three days go by, and I don't hear nothin' from this broad. Nothin'. No check-in calls. Nothin'. Well, outta the blue I get this call to make a pickup at this drop box. So I go, and there's this package addressed to me. No instructions to take it somewhere else and drop it. No, sir. The sonofabitch was addressed to me."

"No shit?"

He waited to answer, taking a drag on the cigarette, "NO SHIT. So I open this damn thing, and guess what's inside? Just try to guess what's inside this box."

"I don't know. What was it?"

"One of this broad's fingers."

"Get out! Jesus! What happened to her?"

"Thor happened to her, man. And that's not all he did. No, sir." He pointed his cigarette at his partner. "He had a morgue tag, a FREAKIN' MORGUE TAG, tied to her God-damned finger. With a note typed on it."

"Get out!"

"No shit. And I wasn't the only one. I heard rumors that the sick bastard cut every one of her fingers and toes off and mailed them to all of the associates in the area."

"Ho-ly shit!"

"Yeah! Holy shit!"

"What did the note say?"

He paused and stared at the young associate, then reached into his back pocket and pulled out a thick wallet. He unfolded it, carefully pulled the tag out from behind his driver's license, and handed it to his partner. "Here. You tell me what it says."

El Paso took the tag and read aloud, "Try my patience as she did, and you will join her."

"Well?"

Eyes blinking in disbelief, the young man whispered, "Ho-o-ly shit! This is for real?"

"You're damn right it's for real."

"Holy shit. What a psycho. How do you know it was really her finger?"

The older man snatched the tag out of his hand and gave him another disgusted stare. Without saying a word, he turned and looked in the direction of the church. "Cool it. We got movement."

Miller Walker had left the church by a side door and was making his way west toward Guadalupe Street, "The Drag" as it was called, the main thoroughfare running along the west side of the U.T. campus. He trudged uphill, away from his car parked in the lot behind Saint Anne's.

"Stay put until I get to the corner of the street. Then pull up and park there." He pointed to the corner of Thirty-first and Guadalupe Streets. "Get as close as you can, but don't even look like you're freakin' followin' him. And don't look at me either."

The sitter pulled a baseball cap from under the seat and put it on, put on his sunglasses, and hopped out of the car. He lit yet another cigarette and waited until Walker was a block away from Guadalupe before following him from the opposite side of the street. Both men crossed The Drag at the light and turned left, heading south toward the University of Texas campus.

Walker ambled down two blocks more before stopping at a small coffee shop. During the bookkeeper's ten-minute stay inside, the sitter had time to smoke two more cigarettes from his position across and down the street.

Large cup of coffee in one hand and worn briefcase in the other, Walker soon continued south to Twenty-Fourth Street, where he crossed back over The Drag. He made his way from the Main Mall downhill to Twenty-First Street near Speedway, the location of the business school. The evening accounting class he taught would begin at 6:00.

The sitter pulled a small cell phone out of his jacket pocket and called the driver, "Park the car back down the street where we were and get over here to Twenty-first and Speedway. Take your time. He's got the freakin' class again tonight." He hung up and called another number. "Baby's got school. Better get the sitter to the house by 7:00."

"Beep . . . Beep."

Class ended at 7:30, and Walker ambled out of the building, maneuvering the short downhill section of the sidewalk until he reached Speedway and turned north. He wasn't about to pull his 300-plus-pound frame back up Twenty-first Street. He would need the next ten blocks to prepare himself mentally for the 200-yard uphill section on Thirty-First Street that would bring him back to his car.

The sitters hadn't let Walker out of their sight. El Paso wove a path in and out of the buildings to the west of Speedway, appearing and disappearing but staying more than 100 yards in front of his man. The elder sitter stayed a manageable distance behind and across the street from them. It was a much easier task under the dark veil of the night sky.

Walker arrived at his Toyota twenty minutes later. He threw his tattered briefcase into the front seat.

The sitters were already in their vehicle and had started driving away after signaling their replacements.

Squeezing his oversized frame into the small car, Walker drove home, still oblivious to the tail.

The sitters changed places the next morning, again with different vehicles, again with no verbal communication, again remaining just distant enough from each other for any distinguishing features to be indiscernible when signaling.

After another uneventful day the sitters followed as Walker left his home and arrived at the church by 4:00. They all had to navigate through a portion of the nearly 100,000 football fans already converging on the 200-acre U.T. campus. Miller went inside the office and pulled up spreadsheets at the computer, prepping them for an infusion of entries from parish contributors. Saturday evening mass always meant large amounts of money in the collection plates, even with a home football game in progress. It was up to him to record who the largest donors were.

Outside, the older sitter asked, "You pickin' up anything, El Paso?"

"Not a word. He's just using his computer again."

"Listen for anything out of the ordinary."

Both sitters watched the pastor leave his residence and make his way to the church.

"Now there's a line of work for you, El Paso."

"What's that? A priest?"

"Yeah, then a baby-faced prick like you would have a reason for bein' a middle-aged virgin!"

"Screw you."

"Ha-haaaah. Take it easy, El Paso. I'm just jokin' with ya, you know? Givin' you some shit."

"Real funny. You're a regular Rodney Dangerfield, aren't you?"

"Ha-haaaah. Yeah, no respect. That's me alright."

In the church office on this warm September afternoon, Walker was perspiring as he reached into his shirt pocket and retrieved two flash drives. He put one into USB port on the desktop computer and began to copy files onto the computer. Halfway through the process, he removed the first drive and began copying the same information back onto the second flash drive. He slipped the original into his pocket while he waited for the computer to finish.

The priest stuck his head into the office as he was walking by. "Miller." He spoke loudly enough that he startled the bookkeeper.

"Whoa. Sorry, Father Al. I was daydreaming. I didn't hear you come in. You ready for mass?"

"I am. Can we expect you there?"

"No, I'm afraid not. I've got some work to finish up that I didn't get done last night. You know, class and all, but I'll see you bright and early tomorrow morning."

"Looking forward to it. God bless you, Miller." He tapped twice on the doorframe as he left.

"You, too, Father." He listened for a moment as the sound of the priest's footsteps diminished, stopped, then started getting louder as the priest came back toward the office.

"Miller, I almost forgot. I didn't give you the collection envelopes yesterday. I've had some of them since last Tuesday. Could I get you to pick them up before you leave so we can get them entered into the computer? I left them on the kitchen counter in the rectory."

"Sure, Father. I'll go get them right now."

"Do you still have your key?"

"Right here." Miller reached into the desk drawer and pulled out the key to the front door.

"Thank you, Miller."

"My pleasure, Father." Grunting a bit, he stood and waddled past the priest and out the back door as the priest made his way toward the chapel where he would begin the Saturday evening service.

The last of the congregation was filing in; mass would be starting any minute.

Watching Walker pant as he trudged over to the priest's residence, the sitters were surprised by a call on the cell phone. The older one answered without saying a word and waited for the caller ID to display the source from the pre-programmed list of names in the phone. It spelled out "Mr. Norseman."

"Keep me on until I tell you otherwise. Beep me twice when the baby comes back to the main building. I'm alone inside; at least for the moment. The priest will be starting mass soon."

The sitter pushed the mute button on the phone. The color had faded from his face.

"What's the word?" El Paso asked.

"Oh, Christ."

"What?"

"Keep an eye out for Walker coming back. Thor's inside the church."

"What? How do you know it's him?"

He shoved the phone up to El Paso's face so he could read the screen. "Satisfied?"

"My God! It is him!"

"Now, we gotta signal Thor as soon as Walker comes out of the house. I can't believe he's in the damn church already. He said the priest was just starting mass, so keep watching for Walker."

"He's gonna kill him in the church? Why doesn't he do it in the house, away from the church?"

"Shu-ut the hell up. I got him on mute, you asshole! I don't know what the hell he's gonna do! Just keep quiet!" His hands were shaking as they waited for their man to show.

Thor sneaked into the office and sat down at Miller's desk. Keeping the phone to his ear with his left hand, he clicked the mouse to open the flash drive still protruding from the computer's USB port. His face reddened at the information displayed before him. Over the past three years Miller had compiled his own list of locations for all the company money drops as well as a running tally of all dollar amounts sent to each. Thor now had the proof he was looking for.

There is no way this idiot knows what these numbers mean, he thought. Only two Division Heads knew the entire code for the Austin region, and one of those Division Heads was Thor.

Thor's predecessor had blackmailed Miller into taking care of the organization's money distribution problems in Austin. The predecessor believed Miller could be trusted.

Although Miller had done an excellent job in the organization's eyes, soon after meeting him, Thor sensed the accountant was suspect. Of course, Miller had no idea the man he had met was Thor. Instinct also told Thor that Miller would try to get out of the company long before his "usefulness" had expired. Disengaging him at this late stage in the game wasn't going to happen.

Miller's gluttonous eating and drinking habits didn't help Thor's perception of the man, but the fact that the accountant was overweight and unkempt was just part of the problem. To make matters worse, Miller appeared to be suffering from depression in the years since his wife had left him. Thor viewed Miller's past marital instability and lack of self-respect as warning signs.

After taking control of the Austin operations, Thor had monitored Miller constantly, following him to and from the office, even wiring his car and phones. Thor had tracked every aspect of the bookkeeper's daily routine, looking for any evidence of disloyalty to the company. He knew that something wasn't right about Miller, but Thor needed evidence that would indicate or, better yet, confirm his duplicity. Now he had finally found it.

Although the information compiled so far was only a small link in the company chain, Thor couldn't risk Miller getting lucky and stumbling across any other portion of the data. Should he put the information into the wrong hands, the whole operation would be compromised. Miller was indeed a time bomb, so best diffuse him now.

"Did this idiot really think he could get away with this? Shame, shame on you, Miller," Thor muttered.

The older of the sitters was still listening on the other end of the phone. He was frightened by the paradox of this calm conversation that is undoubtedly preceding what will be a violent end to Miller Walker.

Expeditious damage control was paramount, but Thor opted not to act in the church. He desperately needed to retrieve all information Miller may have downloaded and decided to allow Miller to leave the building with the drives. The sitters could keep him under close surveillance until Thor found the optimum time to remove him and retrieve the data.

Thor heard two beeps to warn him Miller was on his way back from the rectory. "Good work," he told the sitter. "Baby is hot. Baby is extremely hot. Keep him covered up, and wait for further instructions."

By the time Miller returned to his desk, he was panting hard and sweating profusely from the short uphill walk. With a crumpled handkerchief he wiped his face and sat down to retrieve the remaining flash drive from the computer. He stuck it in his shirt pocket alongside the original. He stayed at the church for another twenty minutes, before heading home.

For the next five hours, the surveillance team tailed Walker without being spotted. About 10:30, Thor took over the watch from the team, his plan formulated. Now he just needed to wait for the exact moment to execute it.

Crouching between the east side of Walker's house and the overgrown mountain laurels that rose nearly eight feet high, Thor was invisible from the street. Ahead of him on the west side of the neighboring house was a single opening of little consequence—a small bathroom window fitted with diffused glass, impossible for anyone to see out of. At his back was a seven-foot cedar fence that separated the two lots. His position was secure.

In spite of a few errant tree branches, Thor's position next to the breakfast room window provided him an otherwise unobstructed view into Miller Walker's den.

The house was dark except for the glow from the television's 10:00 P.M. newscast. The random flicker illuminated Miller's paunchy silhouette, reclined comfortably in his Lazy Boy. The heel-worn socks on his extra-wide, size-ten feet dangled in space, extending just beyond the chair's footrest. His tie, loosened from his substantial neck, no longer concealed the fact that he couldn't fasten the top button of his frayed polyester dress shirt. He had just finished a colossal ham sandwich and three beers in record time.

Thor had observed Miller's activities for an hour, just as he had done so many times before. Through the kitchen window he had a partial view of the same neglected array of dirty pots, pans, and dishes overflowing the sink and cluttering the counters that had been there for weeks. He was sure that Miller's ex-wife must have found married life with him intolerable.

Thor much preferred for the subordinates to remain unattached, as he was. Significant others often introduced variables that were difficult to control in this line of work. He himself had myriad lovers discreetly spread throughout the world. True to his nature, he had made sure the women he chose lived at least a thousand miles from each other, most in different countries, which virtually eliminated the possibility of any of them ever crossing paths. The fact that few spoke the same language, and none knew him by the same name provided an extra level of security.

His focus shifted from the kitchen to the home's weathered exterior. The paint on the kitchen window casement was old and peeling; caulking around the panes of glass gaped in obvious disrepair. Thor reached down with his left hand and peeled off a large paint chip at the base of the window frame. He examined both sides of the fragment as best he could in such low light, and then cast it aside in disgust.

A small bead of perspiration glistened as it crept from under the edge of his mask, down to his eyebrow, onto the bridge of his nose. He didn't flinch. He simply continued to watch, eyes trained on his target.

"What a pathetic slob," Thor mouthed quietly.

In his hand he clutched a solid steel bar, anodized black to eliminate any possibility of reflecting light. Thor had acquired the unusual implement during one of his trips to Munich, intrigued by its simplicity and effectiveness. It fit perfectly in his gloved hand, the smooth, rounded ends protruding just beyond each side of his fist. He rolled the bar from his palm to his fingertips, then back again. Switching hands, he continued the ritual slowly, methodically, never taking his eyes off Miller Walker. Thor had a job to do—and although he didn't show it outwardly, he was a very angry man.

Gorged and with a slight buzz from the beers, Miller was having difficulty staying awake. This was not surprising since he had lost so much sleep over the past few nights. He was prone to worrying anyway, and he now had genuine reason to fret because of the especially dangerous gamble he had just undertaken. His thick glasses hung low on his nose as his balding head slowly bobbed forward. Miller's bottom lip protruded outward as far as gravity would allow, and his multiple chins limited his head's downward progress.

Thor continued rolling the bar back and forth in his hand as he kept watch.

Miller's eyelids were becoming heavy. Slowly they started to close, flicked opened again when he fought momentarily to stay awake, then finally shut.

It was time.

With catlike agility Thor scaled the fence and sprang across the back patio, still clutching the bar. He slipped through the unlocked back door. In a matter of seconds he had crept up behind Miller and placed the bar against his victim's right temple.

Miller jerked at the touch and immediately awoke. "Wha. . .?"

Thor rapidly placed his free hand on the left side of Miller's head. The short, powerful blow to the right temple fractured the man's skull.

Miller died instantly, cleanly.

Instinctively, the murderer stashed the weapon in his fanny pack, and then found the bookkeeper's bulging briefcase. Rifling through scores of documents, he was frustrated to discover that the flash drives weren't there.

The immensity of the dead man's body perched atop the recliner had concealed Thor's actions from anyone outside the house. Thor had to be sure his next moves also went unnoticed. Working swiftly, he closed the drapes on the window to the right of the rear door. He raced to the dinette area, then into the kitchen, closing the drapes in each of those rooms before he turned on any lights. He could leave nothing to chance, especially since his time inside might now be longer than he had originally planned.

His search for the drives began again.

First, he examined Miller's body. Thor slipped his latex-gloved hand into Miller's shirt pocket. It contained a grocery list, a couple of pens, and one of the flash drives, the same drive that Thor had carefully put a scratch on at the church in order to distinguish it from the second one.

"Bingo... Oh, forgive me, Miller. I'm sorry about that church reference. Let's see about retrieving that other drive now, shall we?"

He checked Miller's front pants pockets, but no luck. Next, he placed his right foot at the bottom edge of the Lazy Boy in order to gain some leverage and reached across the lifeless body. Grabbing the belt, he rolled the body over just enough to gain access to the right rear pocket.

"Work with me, Miller," he whispered sarcastically. He pulled a wallet out, but the drive wasn't in the pocket. He rolled Miller over again in order to put it back. When he released his hold on the belt, the massive body flopped back into place in the chair.

Thor stood up, hands on his hips for a moment before making a sweep through the den. Calmly but hastily, he went through the file cabinet, then the bookshelves. The results were the same. Nothing.

When his search of the garage, kitchen, bedroom, and bathroom yielded no drive, he continued his probe in the main hallway.

He pulled down the attic staircase. Dust and residual fiberglass insulation coating the wooden steps told him that no person had used the ladder in quite some time. He took a couple of steps up the ladder and pulled a small flashlight out of his belt pack. Fanning the light across the space, he looked around for a moment. Still nothing.

He murmured as if the dead man could hear him, "Miller, you lazy bastard, you couldn't have hauled that fat ass of yours up here, could you?" Thor jumped to the floor from his perch. He allowed the staircase springs to pull the unit back up into its niche in the ceiling.

A quick glance at his watch showed him it was 11:15. He had been inside almost fifty minutes. This was taking too long. Thor had searched every drawer, closet, and box in the house and garage. Still no drive.

He thought about the possibility of another person being involved, but Walker had had no chance to give the second drive to anyone else. The only time that could have happened would have been during the short period of thirty to sixty seconds when Thor jogged to the house and the surveillance team left the area. Walker couldn't possibly have passed it off to anyone else.

No, the drive was here. But where?

Thor was out of time. Angry but without hesitation, he knew what he had to do. He walked to the fireplace and with wrathful force grabbed the matches from the hearth. Striking a match on the side of the box, he lit the small candle on the left side of the mantel. He blew out the match and threw it in the fireplace. His grip on the box tightened as he strode toward the kitchen, glaring at the lifeless body of Miller Walker, his eyes bulging, mouth agape, his face still bearing the fear that had consumed his final moment of life.

He threw the matches onto the dinette table and turned off the kitchen lights before he walked back to the recliner. He kicked the footrest down in order to bring Walker to an upright position. Thor knew that if anything was left of Miller for investigators to examine, the higher center of gravity would make it seem plausible that the force of an explosion had toppled him out of the chair and also give the illusion that debris hitting the right side of his body caused his death.

Thor strode back into the eating area. Unzipping his fanny pack, he retrieved a small roll of cellophane tape and half threw it on the small table next to the matches. He reached above the table, unscrewed the light fixture, and removed one of the two bulbs from inside. His gloves did little to prevent the remaining heat in the bulb from scorching his fingertips, but he didn't flinch. He just stared across the room at Miller Walker.

Breaking the tips off two matches, Thor set them aside. He then peeled a one-inch-long piece of tape from the roll and used the small scissors on his Swiss Army knife to cut it into separate pieces. One piece he discarded by sticking it back onto the small roll. The width of tape that he kept was just slightly larger than the length of the broken match heads. Attaching the match heads to the top edge of the tape, Thor carefully wound the adhesive around the glass shank of the light bulb just below the metal threads. He screwed the bulb back into the fixture, replaced the diffuser, and walked over to the sink.

From one of the lower cabinets he retrieved a pot. Setting it in the sink, he turned on the tap to let the pot fill with water. Then he blew out the pilot lights on both sides of the stove. Once the pot had enough water in it, he placed it on the front right burner, backed up an arm's length away, and turned the burner's dial to *High*.

He walked back to the light switch, stared at the fixture, and checked the time on his watch. He knew that it would take several minutes for the gas to concentrate at ceiling level in the drafty old house, so he waited. He also knew that the heat from the light bulb would eventually ignite the match tips and was confident that the gas would explode as a result.

Thor knew very well he would only get one chance to destroy any potential evidence. If the matches didn't ignite the gas, the candle by the fireplace would. If that happened, the tape on the bulb might be discovered.

He mentally retraced his route through the house, making sure he had left nothing out of place in the event the explosion didn't occur. At last, Thor felt that he had allowed enough time for the hissing gas to escape from the burner. Flipping the light switch to the on position, he left.

The murderer slipped out the back door where he had entered and locked it behind him.

Five seconds, and he was at the back fence. After a quick glance in each direction, he was over it and jogging down the alley.

Twenty seconds. He was two short blocks away from his vehicle. The mask and gloves were already off and cushioning the murder weapon in his small black fanny pack.

Forty-five seconds. The backup vehicle was just a half-block away. His key was out and ready in his hand.

Sixty-five seconds. He scanned the neighborhood looking for anyone who might be outside, then unlocked the door, and slid into the car.

Ninety seconds. The car pulled away from the curb as the lights came on, still no one visible in the neighborhood. He turned right onto Duval Street and quickly blended in with traffic.

Two minutes and twelve seconds. The explosion lit up the night sky.

CHAPTER FIVE

THE POWERFUL DETONATION SHATTERED windows and shook foundations and windows for several blocks. Frantic 911 calls bombarded police station switchboards. Since the neighborhood lay directly in the flight path of the airport, many callers mistakenly thought the explosion and tremor were the result of a plane crash. Some even thought it might have been an earthquake. Neighbors in the immediate blast area provided the 911 operators with the correct location, so the proper authorities could be guided to the damaged residences.

The Austin police and fire department units arrived in minutes. Once the fire trucks were in place, officers taped off a wide area of the street in front of the house as well as behind it in the alleyway, protecting the large debris field as best they could.

A small crowd of neighbors, students, and media camera crews was already converging on the area to witness the aftermath.

Blistering flames shot out from under the eaves of the garage roof, which by this time was fully consumed. It wasn't long before the fire fighters were dousing the blaze with their high-pressure hoses and had the fire under control. Several police officers were already mingling among the crowd asking questions. Horrified onlookers heard the eerie sound of the police radios announce that a body had been found in the residence.

Another patrolman's radio sounded from atop his left shoulder. "One-nineteen."

"This is one-nineteen, go ahead," the patrolman responded.

"Have the photographer pan the crowd with the video. Let us know if you guys see any suspicious individuals hanging around. Also, make sure your Q & A of the neighbors and any eyewitnesses is detailed and accurate."

"One-nineteen, confirmed." The young APD patrolman turned to his partner and motioned for him to get the photographer.

The police photographer had just taken still photos of the alleyway and was snapping pictures of the street in front of the Walker residence. He could see that the gaping hole and ensuing fire in the middle of the residence hadn't been completely extinguished, so it would be quite a while before he and his assistant could get any shots inside the house.

"We need you to get some video of the crowd," the patrolman said.

The photographer turned to his assistant. "Video the crowd before the excitement dies down. I still need to get the shots from up the block and a few more of the exterior."

"You got it."

"And try to look for anyone that might be enjoying the view."

"Will do."

Two of the patrolmen stood for a moment staring at the gathering crowd. With the fire at the officers' backs, they watched as the light from the flames performed a surreal dance on the faces of those in attendance.

"Look at 'em. Like moths to a flame. You'd think they were going to a party."

"How many of these have you seen?"

"Too many. Enough of 'em to know that anyone is suspect." The older patrolman radioed his superior, "Captain, this is One-nineteen. Come in."

"Go, One-nineteen."

"The photographer and his assistant are taking shots and video as we speak. He said he'd get back to us, after he's had time to download the photos and prep the videos for review."

"Have him keep taking intermittent shots of the crowd every few minutes or so. As long as they keep showing up, there's a possibility that one of 'em could be our guy."

"One of them is shooting video of the crowd right now, but I'll let them know. Over."

With the help of some of the neighbors, a few police officers checked on the occupants of the surrounding houses to make sure there were no other injured parties. Paramedics stood at the ready to treat any of those in need. Miller's elderly next-door neighbors who lived on the kitchen side of the home, one of the couples who had called 911 from their cell phone, had been hit by flying glass and debris while asleep in their bed. They suffered some minor cuts and bruises, but neither had sustained any life-threatening injuries.

It was 5:30 A.M. before the fire department got the okay from the coroner to remove Miller Walker's remains from the twisted structure that had been his home. Once they had determined there were no other bodies in the house, the fire fighters kept watch vigilantly until daylight for any hotspots that might flare up from the embers.

First light came just after 6:00. The morning sun made it easier to search for any accelerant residue that might suggest evidence of arson. Chuck Watson and Mel Brian who comprised the Cause and Origin team were already at the site, monitoring the fire department's activities, questioning those first on the scene, patiently waiting for permission to duck under the police tape.

The cleanup phase of a fire investigation was a tedious but necessary process because it could prove or disprove arson. Even minute pieces of debris from the explosion were meticulously examined, tagged, and bagged. Determination had to be made as to whether one waterlogged piece of material was more important than another. One miss and the results could be completely different. Even the smallest fragment could help establish the fire's origin.

A specially trained dog was brought in when it was thought that an ignition point had been found. It turned out to be a box containing linseed oil and mineral spirits. A neighbor later explained that he and Miller Walker had used the liquids in years past while refinishing furniture. Although the solvents aided in spreading the damage to the garage, it was determined that they were not the source of the fire.

When the investigators finally removed the debris and exposed the slab in the garage, the Cause and Origin team discovered a conspicuous seam in the floor.

"Mel, come over here and take a look at this."

Mel noticed the puzzled look on Chuck's face and walked from the driveway to the area near the east garage wall.

What Chuck had found was something out of place, something hidden underneath the most substantial of three workbenches. A small, round seam ten inches in diameter was cut into the concrete.

Mel squatted down next to his partner and examined the area below the workbench.

"My, my. What do we have here?"

As he pushed down at one edge of a concrete circle, it moved up about a quarter of an inch on the opposite side. The circle returned to its flush position when Mel took his finger off. "I think it's some kind of a lid. Maybe for a safe?"

"That's my guess. Look at the small chips in the concrete here." Chuck pointed to the edge of the circular form. "They go all the way around its perimeter seam. But it's more prevalent right here." He pointed to a specific region of the circumference. "It looks as though this piece has definitely been pried off before."

"That circular crack sure as hell wasn't caused by the slab settling," Mel said. "Yeah, your best bet is a safe. Let me get the camera for some shots so we can move the table."

"Yeah. Alright." Chuck grabbed the edge of the bench's tabletop and pushed on it. The table moved slightly. The large rollers attached to the legs hadn't been damaged too badly in the fire and once unlocked would allow the table to be moved easily.

While Mel photographed the area and had the massive table

pulled away from the remains of the garage wall, Chuck retrieved a crowbar from his vehicle. Once he got the okay to proceed, he pried up the concrete lid. Below, embedded in the garage foundation, was indeed a small, cylindrical floor safe.

Chuck pulled a small flashlight from his shirt pocket and shined it down the hole. "United Vault, huh? Well, make a note to give them a call." He looked up at Mel.

"Okay."

"But let's not get anyone in here too early. If we have too many people disturbing the area too soon, we just might miss something. Let's wait a couple more hours before we contact them."

CHAPTER SIX

TRENT OSBORNE WAS BLESSED with, but also tortured by a creative mind. Sitting motionlessly at his computer terminal, he stared into space, mindless of his surroundings. Lost in this state for an inordinate amount of time, he finally let out a heavy sigh.

Damn it! Concentrate, you moron! He ordered himself. *Snap out of it already!*

The chair springs squeaked as he leaned back and stretched his arms overhead, inhaling deeply as he yawned. He brought his arms down, rubbing the back of his neck in a circular motion with the palms of his hands just as his feet touched the floor.

The only thing that kept him going each day was the knowledge that he would be spending the next two months in the Special Investigations Unit, or SIU, of the claims fraud department. Fortunately for Trent, a newly instituted, cross-training program had teamed him four months earlier with his mentor, Steve Latham. He seemed to have finally found his niche in the claims side of the company, but he knew that the assignment was temporary. Although his interview for a more permanent underwriting position was just a couple of weeks away, he was having second thoughts about going through with it.

Trent came from Texas roots with wealth on his mother's side, whose lineage connected him directly to the founders of the Texas Revolution. His father had left the two of them just before Trent's fifteenth birthday, right at the time Trent needed him the most. His grandfather Carl Douglas, was the grandson of the town's original namesake and owned the largest cattle ranching operation in Douglas Creek. Because his grandfather had worked so hard in his own youth to make something of himself, he felt it best to avoid nepotism and make Trent do the same. It was decided that Trent would work elsewhere, outside of the family business, to save money and pay his own college tuition.

With the sparse number of employment opportunities in Douglas Creek, shortly after his fifteenth birthday, Trent had gotten a job at the local Dairy Queen, part-time during the school year and full-time during the summers, for three years. Almost overnight, the boy was transformed. From a fun-loving teenager he soon morphed into an extremely serious, levelheaded young man, but also something of a control freak. What most people considered an admirable trait, Trent's unyielding ability to focus on his work, was in fact the result of a sad and lonely internal struggle that stayed with him throughout his adolescence.

With no guarantee of income from his grandfather for his college tuition, Trent was forced to become tight fisted, squirreling away money at every opportunity lest his college dreams fade. His friends in Douglas Creek used to tease him, saying they could easily tell which change had circulated through Trent Osborne's palm because of the resulting stretch marks on the coins, created by him not wanting to release the money from his tight-assed grip. To Trent's benefit, however, by the time he graduated from high school, he had saved a considerable sum to help finance his education.

Shortly after his graduation, his mother remarried and moved to Phoenix. Trent was finally on his own. After attending school in a small town, Austin and the University of Texas offered Trent a new view of life. Prior to his arrival in Austin, the most expensive pair of shoes Trent had owned were a pair of size ten basketball shoes, a

Christmas present from his reclusive father; he didn't play basketball, nor did he wear a size ten. During his early undergraduate years, he became quite the clotheshorse, much to the dismay of his creditors. Before he knew what was happening, the reckless pace of his spending habits swelled and overtook him. The once-conservative, driven boy from Douglas Creek, Texas, had become a financially irresponsible adult.

The phone rang.

"Western States Claims. This is Trent Osborne."

"Trent? Dan Griffin." He spoke in a smooth Texas drawl. "Pullin' Sunday duty, huh?"

"You got it, Dan-O. Need the overtime bucks. What's up?"

"I was gonna try and reach Steve, but I just remembered that Amy told me a couple of weeks ago that he was going on vacation."

"Yeah, man. He's on vacation for another week and a half or so."

"Well, good for him. How the hell did you convince him to go?"

"I can't claim responsibility for that one, Dan-O. Rick Taylor, the V.P. out of Portland, got Steve to meet him in California to do some backpacking."

"Well, he deserves a vacation all right. Listen, I just wanted to see if he would like to ride over to the site of the explosion last night."

"The one near campus? That's one of our insureds who died?"

"Yeah, it is. We got his car and his house, and we got a big life policy on the guy, too. I caught the six o'clock news this morning and ran the guy's name through my laptop, and he checked out. No pun intended. I saw Mel Brian on the same station with an update just a few minutes ago."

"Who's Mel Brian?"

"He's one of the C&O guys we use a lot. I called his office, and they put me through to him at the scene. Apparently they've uncovered something, and he asked if we wanted to come down to take a look. They've also called a couple of detectives back to the site."

"Wow! Sounds interesting."

"Well, since Steve isn't around, I thought you might like to come with me instead. The cops and the fire department usually won't let us onto the scene too early, but I've worked with a lot of these guys over the years, and they've had time to finish most of their investigation, so we should be able to get in, no problem."

"Oh, man, that would be great. I've finished all my files and was looking for something else to do. You leaving right now?"

"Meet ya on the circular drive out front in ten minutes."

"Roger, Dan-O." Trent hung up and dialed an extension while he threw a legal pad and a couple of pens into his cluttered briefcase.

"Western States Operator."

"Jeannie? Trent."

"Hi, Trent. Whatcha doin'?"

"Dan Griffin just called and wants me to go with him to a loss site. I should be back in a couple of hours or so."

"I'll hold down the fort."

"Thanks, Jeannie. I'll see you after while."

"Bye."

Trent gathered his briefcase and sunglasses and headed across the department toward the elevators. "This is the kind of work I want to be doing all the time!" he said aloud since no one was around to hear him.

The thought of going back to work in an uninspiring environment was frustrating for Trent. It was even more frustrating than his love life or, more accurately, his utter lack of one. Just recently his girlfriend had grown tired of his incessant bitching about his employment future, as well as everything else in his life, so she took a hike to greener pastures, 6'4" and 240 pounds' worth of pasture.

He cursed himself for dwelling on his unfortunate situation, for not trying to remedy it sooner. His chronic daydreaming was a constant reminder of what he believed would be one of the worst mistakes he had made, allowing money to influence his better judgment by asking Steve to refer him as a candidate for the recently posted Senior Underwriter job.

Trent knew if he was offered the position after the upcoming interview and decided to accept it; his minuscule world would then consist of underwriting auto and property insurance applications and renewal policies for eight to ten hours per day.

Combine this possible life scenario with an infrequent trip to the cleaners or grocery store when he tired of wrinkled shirts or pizza, and a couple of hours' worth of television each night, and he might as well take a swan dive off an eight-story building.

Trent definitely needed the extra cash. All his credit cards, of which he had many, were maxed out. Add another thirty-thousand dollars in student loans accumulated during graduate school, and he was barely able to stay out of bankruptcy court.

Trent's best friend had just e-mailed him to tell him that he had sold everything and walked away from a lucrative financial analyst position in Houston. He planned to attend a renowned culinary school in Connecticut and open a restaurant after he graduated.

Envy pervaded every ounce of Trent's existence as he thought of the freedom his friend now possessed. His friend had done nothing magical, he thought. He just followed his passion. Trent however, knew he needed a change, but the unenviable financial position he had created for himself made the possibility of strolling into the Insurance Services manager's office and turning in his resignation seem light years away. He needed the underwriting promotion. He *really* needed the promotion.

CHAPTER SEVEN

DAN AND TRENT PARKED well behind the police tape. It roped off the debris field for at least half a block in every direction out from the Walker house.

"Jesus! That must have been one hell of an explosion," Trent said.

"No kiddin'. Natural gas isn't too forgiving when ya put a spark to it."

They walked to the edge of the tape, showed some identification to the patrolman guarding the perimeter, and were reluctantly allowed access after Dan dropped a few names. The young patrolman told them to keep out of everyone's way.

"Rookie asshole," Dan muttered under his breath, pleased to see Trent nod in agreement as they continued toward the house. Dan noticed Detective Kelly already at the scene and quietly walked up behind him.

"Well, look what the cat drug in." Dan patted his friend on the shoulder, and then extended his hand.

Kelly's look of surprise changed into a huge grin. "Hey, ugly. Long time no see. Is this guy one of your clients?"

"Yeah, he is . . . or was."

"I should have known this claim would be one of yours. You always did have a flair for the dramatic. By the way, where were you last night between 10 and 11 P.M.?"

"You know there are laws against harassing innocent citizens. I have a good mind to report you." Dan patted Kelly on the back again. "Kel, meet Trent Osborne. He's soon to be Steve's number one assistant in claims."

"Andy Kelly, Trent. Nice to meet you," he said and shook Trent's hand before he pointed at Dan. "Stay the hell away from this guy. He's nothing but trouble."

Trent didn't miss a beat, popping off, "Funny, he told me the exact same thing about you as we were walking up here."

"Dammit, Griffin, you cloned yourself, didn't you? That's all I need, a successor to you. Jesus! This headache of mine could go on for decades." He winked at Trent, and they all chuckled.

Dan cut in, "Don't listen to him, Trent. He's still pissed that our softball team kicked their ass in the playoffs. Hell, if they'd quit campin' out at the donut shops and breakfast taco stands all mornin', they might be able to keep up with the likes of me!" He rubbed his own considerable belly in a circular motion with both hands.

"Y'all are both scaring me," Trent responded.

"So where's Steve hiding?"

"Backpacking in California for a few weeks," Trent said.

"Shit, I wish we'd get some of that California weather here pretty soon. I'm about sick of this heat."

"What have you found so far, Kel?" Dan asked in a more serious tone.

Kelly looked around and moved the men away from others who might hear him. He whispered, "Just looks like an accidental gas explosion so far. And the C&O guys found this safe a little while ago. They hadn't confirmed the exact ignition point yet. They are ninety-nine percent sure it's the stove, but they still have a lot of debris to examine. You got here just in time. We're about to crack the safe."

The three men stood in the driveway and watched.

The locksmith hurriedly unlocked the small vault, then moved aside and called Detective Kelly over to come investigate the contents.

Kelly reached inside the cylinder with a gloved hand and retrieved a large bundle of cash.

"Holy shit! Look at that," Trent whispered to Dan. "This guy didn't believe in banks, or what?"

"Doesn't look like it, does it?" Dan smiled but never took his eyes off the safe, intently watching to see what else might be retrieved.

Next, Kelly pulled out and opened a manila folder. It contained several stock certificates, a will, and a computer flash drive. These items were cataloged and put into separate evidence bags. The detective walked back to Trent and Dan.

"Anything in there that might concern us?" Dan asked.

"I don't think so."

"Well, if your guys don't mind, Kel, I'll get started on my preliminary assessment of the loss. I can get most of it done from the street, so I'll be out of your way. I'll come back later in the day to get more detailed measurements in the badly damaged areas."

"Sounds good, Dan. I'll have a report done in the next day or so, and I'll copy you on it once our investigation is complete."

"Well, make it legible, dammit. You got worse handwriting than my doctor."

"If you'd quit tightening up when Doc's rubber glovin' you during your physicals, he wouldn't have such bad arthritis today." Kelly laughed at his own joke and shook hands with Trent. "Nice to meet you, Trent."

"You, too."

"Good to see you, Dan." Kelly smiled and shook his hand.

"You, too, amigo. We'll talk soon."

CHAPTER EIGHT

THE SUDDEN BLAST OF the crosswind came without warning, abruptly waking Steve from his daydream. "Son of a bitch!" he yelled at himself.

The wind forced his Porsche into the oncoming lane of traffic. His left hand locked onto the steering wheel as his right hand snapped up from its resting place on the console. He threw the wheel to the right, and the car darted back into the proper lane. Fortunately, no oncoming traffic accompanied him on this desolate expanse of California highway.

"Jesus! Watch what the hell you're doing!" He shouted.

He knew how lucky he was not to have met another vehicle while in the throes of his mental lapse. Steve thanked God, his guardian angel, and any deceased relatives who might have just saved his body from intimate personal contact with an oncoming tractor trailer rig.

Steve Latham managed the Special Investigative Unit in the Claims Fraud Department at Western States Insurance Company, or WESIC as many of the employees jokingly called it. A former Portland, Oregon police officer, Steve had given in to his wife's urging for him to find a safer line of work. One year after landing the more innocuous and much-better-paying job at WESIC's Austin office, he was surprised to discover that his lawyer-wife had filed for divorce. Apparently, she had been having an affair for quite some time with one of their oldest friends in the Portland District Attorney's office. She had moved back to Portland and married the man, shortly after the Latham's divorce was final.

Steve had a tough time getting over the divorce and had literally buried himself in his work. Other than Whitley Talmadge and his friend Rick Taylor in WESIC's Portland office, it was months before anyone else knew of Steve's divorce. He was a serious and focused man at work, and cordial to everyone, but not overtly so. His superiors as well as his co-workers loved him. When word of the divorce spread throughout the office, it wasn't long before the gossip pools started up and friends began intervening on behalf of his love life. He attended a few casual gatherings where co-workers attempted to set him up with potential mates. Not caring to mix business and pleasure, however, he kept the relationships strictly platonic, to the dismay of many would-be suitors.

Roy Whitton, his boss and vice president of the claims division, had almost forcibly shoved Steve out the door to get him to take his first vacation in three years. Now nearly two weeks into it, Steve was finally beginning to relax. The journey had begun with a long drive from Austin to Albuquerque where he stayed at his brother's home, located in a neighborhood at the base of the Sandia Mountains. Besides completing three, long day-hikes in the eleven days he was there, he took it easy in between and visited Santa Fe and Taos with his relatives.

With another ten days off, he had planned a combination climbing-hiking trip in Yosemite National Park and would be meeting Rick Taylor at Yosemite Lodge later in the evening. They would eat dinner and spend the night at the lodge before setting out early tomorrow morning on the 16-mile trek up and down Half Dome.

The rugged scenery of the past few miles had been lost on Steve, victim of a lack of attention brought on by the cool mountain air and the hypnotic drone of his tires on the smooth pavement. The sudden burst of adrenaline had cleared his head momentarily, so he decided to heed Mother Nature's warning and pull over at the next town to refill his thermos with coffee.

On the road for just over eleven hours since leaving Flagstaff earlier that morning, he had made good time. Near the town of Lone Pine he spied a convenience store and turned off the highway into the parking lot. As he downshifted, the finely tuned engine roared deeply. He parked beside the gas pumps and switched off the ignition. Removing his sunglasses, he tilted his head back against the leather headrest, rubbed his tired eyes with his fingertips, then crawled out of the car and stretched. While refilling the gas tank, he stared at the peaks of the Sierras off to his west.

The view was electric; the colors warm, belying the cooler evening air already settling into the valley. With the rapidly setting sun, the lavender alpenglow on the jagged granite crags became more radiant by the minute. The sight reminded him of his last climbing trip in the Tetons with Rick.

Anxious to see his best friend again, Steve relished the fact that he would be out of the rat race for several more days. Finished at the pump, he opened the passenger-side door, grabbed his thermos from the floorboard, and ambled across the pea-gravel parking lot to the store. The attendant was busy ringing up another customer, so Steve left his thermos next to the coffeepot and walked around the corner to the men's room.

Steve returned to find the attendant leaning against a front counter badly in need of resurfacing, looking in his direction expectantly.

"Nice car," the man said.

"Thanks," Steve replied, cautiously examining the man's tattooed fingers while he unscrewed the cap from his thermos. He filled it with the pallid liquid the establishment called coffee, screwed the cap back on, and walked to the counter.

The attendant started ringing up the sale. "Where ya headed?" he inquired in an animated tone.

Steve handed him a twenty for the gas and coffee.

"Up to Yosemite to do some climbing."

"How long ya goin' in for?" he asked, just as exuberantly.

"A few days," said Steve, somewhat irritated by this lively interrogation.

"Well, you're goin' at the right time. Weather forecast says smooooth sailin' all week!"

"That's great. Glad to hear it." Steve took his change from the attendant's thick hands and began backpedaling toward the door.

"But ya gotta watch it. Weather in them mountains kin change onna dime."

"Thanks for the advice. You have a nice evening," Steve said near the exit.

"You, too. Come see us again." The man smiled, exposing a cavernous gap in his teeth.

Steve was no sooner out the door with his back to the attendant when he chuckled about man's gap-toothed grin and muttered, "Likely a 'gift' from a past customer."

He jumped in the Porsche and sped off, traveling up Highway 395 toward Bishop. The sun had just dropped behind the Sierras, causing the expansive hedge of rock to cast a mighty shadow to the east. It was getting noticeably cooler.

About 7:30 he arrived at the park's Tioga Pass entrance and followed Highway 120 across Tuolumne Meadows toward the Valley Road. In the darkness he periodically glimpsed a sparkle of light coming from a secluded mountain cabin. When he passed historic Tuolumne Grove and its giant Sequoias, he knew Yosemite Valley was just a few miles away. Speeding downward into the canyon, he appreciated the smooth buzz of the Porsche's engine that intensified and reverberated in the semi-enclosed tube of the Tioga Flat Tunnel. Steve wished it were still daylight so he could catch a glimpse of El Capitan and Half Dome when he came out of the tunnel.

At the junction with Highway 140, he turned left toward the valley floor. Crossing the Merced River, he looked back to his left. His vision partially obscured by massive pines, he could just make out the monumental silhouette of the valley rim thanks to the glowing moonlight. Several faint lights decorated the towering walls of El Capitan to pinpoint the bivouac locations of teams of climbers making their way up the infamous mile-high block of granite. The lights looked like stars that had literally fallen out of the sky, a pleasing contrast to the dark valley.

Because it was a Sunday night, much of the weekend traffic had disappeared. It seemed as though the ancient valley had taken a deep breath and exhaled, blowing the tourist masses and air pollution out and returning the area to a more natural state, as natural as a wilderness area could be with hotels, gift shops, and gas stations scattered throughout.

Steve had no trouble finding a parking space near the lodge entrance. Three Mule deer were scouring the sparse ground surrounding one of the lodge's cabins, foraging for cast-off French fries or bread, their diets forever changed by uneducated or indifferent tourists.

Stepping out of the car, he stretched as he had done a few hours before. He looked up at the stars, closed his eyes and inhaled slowly, relishing the crisp pine scent that permeated the dry night air. His senses, previously dulled by the day's fourteen-hour road epic, were starting to come back to life. He heard the crickets' chirps echoing across the valley floor, freed from their usual competition against the thunderous flow of water from Yosemite Falls. Reduced to a trickle at this time of year, the falls were just a short walk from the lodge. In the distance he heard the familiar groan of a valley shuttle bus, its noisy gears shifting as it left one of the many stops on its way back to the lodge. It had picked up straggling tourists, climbers, and employees from all across the valley and was depositing them at their respective bivouac sites for the evening.

Once more stretching his stiff body with his arms over his head, he yawned. It was a well-deserved sigh of relief at reaching the end of the drive. As Steve lifted his soft fleece shell from the passenger seat and shrugged into it, he observed that the canopy of stars overhead seemed somehow brighter than normal. He stared up at the sky for a moment longer, then at the silhouetted tops of the pines that swayed in the gentle breeze blowing through the valley.

He turned and walked up the sidewalk toward the inviting glow of the lodge's main entrance, recalling how Rick had described this trip, *No more suit and tie. No more paperwork. Just man and nature. And if we're lucky, we'll meet some lonely women on the trail.*

His old friend had been right so far—he did appreciate the comfortable feel of his well-worn jeans and trail running shoes. He caught himself smiling and shook his head, thinking, *Rick has always had a way with words.*

Steve opened the thick glass door and entered the lobby. His investigative skills weren't going to be greatly challenged in order to ascertain where Rick might be this time of night. He would most likely be waiting in the Mountain Room Bar.

After checking in at the front desk and confirming that Rick had indeed already arrived, he crossed the courtyard to the valley's infamous watering hole.

The last backpacking vacation trip he and Rick had taken together had been three years earlier at Glacier National Park. Steve couldn't help but notice the differences between the two parks' facilities. The Lake MacDonald Lodge had been a cavernous place with massive log beams overhead and rustic elk horn chandeliers dangling between them. The entire place had enough rough-hewn wood and dead animals hanging on every wall to make a taxidermist green with envy. It exuded masculinity more akin to Yosemite's Ahwahnee Hotel situated near Royal Arches, a well-known granite formation just a little farther up the valley. Yosemite Lodge was just as comfortable as Glacier's best, but without all the bells and whistles. As Rick always said, when the lights are out, all rooms look alike.

Steve preferred the company of the gypsy element that more commonly frequented the Mountain Room Bar to the affluent group that often made it a point to sleep in the luxurious confines of the Ahwahnee. The former had a heartier spirit, a tribal quality that Steve felt a kinship with. These "mountain warriors" would rise stealthily before dawn, march to the bases of immense granite walls, and then scale them. Like soldiers returning from war, they would emerge late that evening or perhaps several days later, and gather at the local pub to tell heart-stopping tales about their exploits, explaining how fortunate they were to have cheated death one more time. The volume and level of danger in their stories were always directly proportional to the amount of alcohol consumed up to that point.

An enormous metal fireplace occupied the center of the room near the bar area. Steve was scanning the rows of tables and bar stools when a voice bellowed out, "Laaaaaatham!"

There, in the middle of a worn leather couch near the end of the bar, was his old friend Rick. Not surprisingly, he appeared very content to be in the company of two rather attractive women seated on either side of him. He jumped up and bounded across the floor, nearly tackling Steve when he gave him a powerful embrace and a few well-placed pats on the back.

"How the hell are ya, man?" Rick locked onto Steve's bicep with a mighty grip.

"I'm doing great, Rick. It's good to see you."

"Long time no see. Come on over, man." Rick put his arm around Steve's shoulders and led him back to the sofa. "I've got some friends I'd like you to meet."

At the couch, the introductions commenced.

"Steve Latham, I'd like you to meet Sally Reid and Michelle Grayson. They both work for Western States in Portland."

"Really?" Steve was perplexed. He hadn't expected anyone else to be with Rick, but he kept his cool. "Sally. Michelle. It's a pleasure to meet you both." He shook hands with the women while Rick returned to his spot between them.

When the two men weren't looking, Michelle and Sally winked at one another, silently approving of the newly arrived guest.

Steve took a strategic position in an overstuffed chair across from the trio. His calculating mind began to assess the situation. *What the hell is going on here?* He thought. *Rick wouldn't have invited anyone along without consulting me first. I hope this isn't going to be another matchmaking attempt.*

Before his imagination got the best of him, Steve decided to relent and wait for an explanation before rushing to judge.

"The usual?" Rick asked, as he stood up.

"The usual."

"Coming up." Rick turned to the women. "Can I get either of you ladies a refill on your drinks?"

"No, I think we're okay."

Michelle nodded in agreement with Sally.

"I'll be right back then." Rick ambled over to the bar.

"Steve, how old is Rick?" Sally asked.

"He just turned fifty-seven this year."

"You're kidding. He's in great shape. I've never noticed before, since he's always wearing a suit."

"Yeah, he's been a runner for years. A few years ago, he got into cross-country skiing and rock climbing and got really strong."

"Without the graying hair, I'd think he was barely forty."

"If that were true, it would also mean that he joined the FBI when he was sixteen," Steve added.

"He worked for the FBI?"

"As an agent. Went to work for them right out of college and stayed for twenty-five years. He's only been at WESIC for the past six or seven years."

"And you think you know someone," Sally said. "How did you two meet?"

"I met Rick on a climbing trip up Mt. Shasta in northern California. I was a Portland cop at the time. As we started talking, we found out we had a lot of common interests, both work and play. We started hiking and climbing together, and he eventually gave me my start at WESIC."

Michelle had been quietly examining Steve up to this point. "So, Rick tells us that you work in SIU in Austin."

"That's right. I've been there for about three years now."

Michelle continued, "I've applied for a senior underwriting position in Austin, but I'm not sure I should take it if they offer it to me. I sure hear a lot of good press about Austin."

"How do you like it there?" asked Sally. She scanned Steve's hand, checking for a ring or, worse, a white line where one had been.

"I love it. It's a great city. The people are very friendly, and there are lots of outdoor activities and a great music scene. I do miss the mountains, though. And the summers in Texas can be unbearable." Steve kept a poker face, still wondering why in the hell they were here. "What brings you two to California?"

"We planned this trip about a year ago with our travel agent," said Sally. "We both like to hike, so we decided to go to a place that wasn't too remote. Neither of us had been to Yosemite before, so our agent recommended that we try it."

Steve looked confused. Rick had contacted him only three months ago with plans to come here. Surely he wouldn't have hidden this from him. "How did you guys end up coming with Rick?"

"Oh, we didn't come with Rick. In fact, we had no idea he was coming here." Sally replied. "We had a wedding to attend yesterday, then flew into Fresno and rented a car today. We just got here a couple of hours ago. You can imagine how surprised we were when Rick Taylor came strolling into the lodge right after we arrived."

Rick returned from the bar, beers in hand.

"It was too good a coincidence to pass up," Michelle giggled. "I told him that we had come to Yosemite so that we both could present him with our resignations in person. I think he believed me for about half a second."

"I believed you for more than half a second," Rick chuckled.

Steve looked across the table toward Michelle. His initial tension began to ease. She smiled and ran her fingertips through her hair, pulling the thick brown locks away from her face.

As if right on cue, a young hostess came over to the sofa and announced, "Rick, your table is ready."

"Thanks, Karen."

They all stood up, and the women preceded the men across the courtyard to the Mountain Room Restaurant entrance. While they stood in line momentarily at the hostess station, Steve observed several of the men and women among the wait staff who were obviously climbers. Most were thin and wiry and sported chiseled facial features sculpted by innumerable hours of sun and exercise. Their white dress shirts rolled up to their elbows exposed their exaggerated forearms, the result of their constant and rigorous vertical training.

Karen re-appeared and led them from the hostess station to their table. Sally positioned herself next to Rick as he and Steve pulled out the chairs closest to the window for the ladies.

"Thank you," the women chimed in unison as they sat down.

Steve waited for Karen to walk away from the table before he parroted, "Riiiicck, your table's reaaadddyyy. Christ, you're on a first-name basis with the hostess already? She's sixteen if she's a day!" Steve wadded up the damp napkin that had been cradling his beer and threw it across the table at Rick. "You are a sick man, my friend."

Michelle chimed in. "Hmmm. Sounds like Steve might have a little dirt on you, Rick."

He smiled in spite of his red face. The laughter from the table continued, but Rick soon began tapping on his beer bottle with his salad fork to get everyone's attention. "I have an announcement to make. I hope you guys don't mind, but dinner is on me tonight, and I'll have no arguments to the contrary."

"Actually, I was counting on it," Steve snapped, jokingly.

"You don't have to do that, Rick," Sally said.

"Sally's right. We can go Dutch," Michelle agreed.

"I said NO arguments, ladies. Besides, I'm bigger than you are."

"Let him pay, ladies." Steve saluted his friend with his beer bottle before taking a drink. "It's a control thing that he's been fighting all his life. If I was able to see him more often, I could pay off my mortgage because of gestures like this."

"Don't listen to him. Besides, I'm going to bill this to the company as an offsite meeting." Rick winked at the women and looked at Steve. He then picked up the knife and pretended to conceal it in his jacket. "That'll cost you, you asshole!"

Michelle and Sally glanced at each other and laughed, then Michelle said, "Thank you, Rick. It really is a nice gesture."

"Yes, thank you," Sally chimed in.

"The pleasure is mine, ladies. Steve, I believe it's your turn to pick the wine."

"You got it." He scoured the typical four-bottle National Park wine list, chose a California Cabernet, and ordered it from the waiter who appeared shortly thereafter.

"So what are you guys going to do tomorrow?" Sally asked.

"We're going to hike up to Half Dome and go up the cable route," Rick responded.

"What's the cable route?"

Steve began gesturing with his hands as he started to speak. "On the shoulder of Half Dome there are galvanized posts stuck into the granite with aircraft cable running through them. They run all the way up the forty-five-degree left side of the dome so that non-climbers can use them to access the top of the dome. Climbers use them to walk off the top after a climb."

"Sounds exciting," Michelle added. "What else do you guys have planned, Rick?"

"We'll do some climbing on Tuesday. Wednesday we left wide open, and the rest of the week we'll be backpacking and camping in the Tuolumne area. How 'bout you two?"

"We're going to hike around and get familiar with the valley for a couple of days. And I think we might visit the Mariposa Grove of Sequoias later in the week."

"Is climbing difficult?" Michelle asked Steve.

"It depends. Some climbs are really difficult; some are really easy."

"How do you know ahead of time which one you are on?"

"Well, the first person or team to climb a route will give it a numerical rating from 5.1 to 5.14 in order to designate its difficulty. The higher the number, the harder the climb."

"How can they tell a 5.1 from a 5.14?"

"It's all pretty subjective. Subsequent parties that climb the same route confirm whether or not the rating is accurate. Most climbing spots have guidebooks that show all or most of the routes in an area along with their difficulty ratings. This allows climbers to pick and choose routes within their ability levels. So if you're a beginning climber, you may want to stay on routes rated, say a 5.6 or less, at least until you feel more confident. As your skill level improves, you can move up to more difficult climbs."

"Interesting."

The waiter brought the wine to the table and showed it to Steve, then cut and removed the outer wrapping and uncorked the bottle.

"A fine vintage. Excellent choice, Steven," Rick exclaimed with an exaggerated elitist air.

The waiter continued with the protocol, handing Steve the cork. He didn't bother smelling it and placed it on the table.

"Go ahead and pour the glasses for the ladies. We'll let it breath a bit."

"Yes, sir."

Michelle reached in front of Steve, picking up the cork and examining it. "You know, the first time I ever had a decent bottle of wine, other than screw top or box varietals that is, I was with a girlfriend of mine at a nice restaurant," she began. "We were about nineteen years old. I don't have a clue what we ordered, but I know it was a nice bottle. When the waiter opened the wine and handed me the cork, I didn't have any idea what to do with it," she paused, looking at each of the other three, "so I licked it."

"You . . . licked it?" Rick barely got the words out before he bellowed with laughter.

Even the waiter, joined in. Sally used her napkin to muffle her shrieks.

"Funny," Michelle said with a deadpan stare when she could talk above their laughter. "That's the same reaction I got when I did it."

The waiter chuckled once more, then excused himself to attend to his other customers.

"That is one tough act to follow, Michelle." Rick raised his glass. "To friends, old and new, welcome to Yosemite. Here's to all of us sharing a wonderful outdoor vacation."

"Cheers." They all touched glasses and took a drink.

Michelle looked up from her glass, raising an eyebrow and

smiling at Steve, then looking at Rick, before focusing back on the contents of her wine glass.

Steve smiled back, feeling a little awkward.

Rick reached into his small camera bag and pulled out some photographs from their last outing in Glacier National Park. "I saved these until you got here, Steve." He handed one envelope full of prints to the ladies and a thumb drive to Steve. "These are your copies, bud."

"Hey! The Glacier photos! Thanks, Rick."

"This is the spot that Steve and I traveled to on our last outing, a little over three years ago."

"It's only taken him that same length of time to get the photos to me."

"Hey, it's the thought that counts, right?"

Sally leaned over and admired the photographs. "Oooh, Michelle, look at the lake," she whispered in a hushed, almost reverent tone.

"It's beautiful."

"Yeah, that's Lake MacDonald. We stayed at the lodge right on the lake."

"Start making plans for next year, Michelle," Sally said.

"God, these look like postcards."

"No kidding," Michelle agreed. "You're quite the photographer, Rick."

"It's hard to take bad pictures when a place looks like that. This place is no different. You'll see. In fact, if it wasn't dark outside, we would see Yosemite Falls right out there." Rick pointed to the wall of windows at the back of the restaurant. "Well, at least you could see location of the falls. No more water until the springtime."

"I can't wait to see this place in the daylight," Michelle said. "It was pretty dark when we got here earlier."

"You won't believe it. Words can't describe the beauty of this valley," Rick said

The main course soon arrived, and they all enjoyed a hearty dinner and another bottle of wine. Conversation progressed until they were one of three parties left in the restaurant. They made plans to rendezvous mid-week for a day hike.

The grind of the drive and the affect of the alcohol soon got the best of Steve. "Guys, I hate to be a party pooper, but this boy is pooped. I've got to get some sleep, or I'll be completely worthless in the morning."

Michelle looked at her watch. It was nearly 11:30, and the restaurant was now devoid of customers. "God, your right. I'm sure these people want to get home, and you two are getting up early."

"Yeah, 6:00 A.M.," Rick exclaimed.

"We're going to hold you two to your promise about hiking with us in a couple of days." Sally smiled.

"Count on it," Rick replied as he signed the dinner check. "We'll meet Wednesday morning at the Awahnee. Say between 7:00 and 7:30 for coffee?"

Steve nodded his head in acknowledgment.

Michelle and Sally stood up from the table and hugged Rick, then Steve.

Michelle waived her finger at Steve. "You be careful now. We don't want to have a couple of lame guides to have to drag around on Wednesday."

"Yes, ma'am," he replied with a hint of sarcasm and winked at her.

The men walked the ladies up to their second-floor room and bid them a hushed goodbye. From there, Rick followed Steve to the Porsche to help him gather his rucksack and small suitcase. Their accommodations for the evening would be a cabin at the edge of the riverbank, directly across the road from the main lodge.

Rick led the way to Cabin 12. Once inside, Steve deposited his gear on the floor, and Rick headed to the bathroom to brush his teeth. Steve followed suit, then stripped to his boxer shorts and fell into bed. He was soon lulled into a deep sleep by the slow gurgling sound of the Merced River flowing just outside the cabin window.

CHAPTER NINE

THE NEXT THING STEVE realized, Rick was vigorously shaking him. "Steve! Wake up! It's 6:00! Time to hit the trail."

He sat up in bed and rubbed his eyes. "Man that felt good!" Steve exclaimed after a big yawn.

"What? You want me to grab you again, Sugar Pants?" Rick queried in an effeminate tone, and then let out a bellow.

"No, you wise ass. The sleep."

Rick had been up since 5:30 getting his daypack together. Steve hastily followed suit.

"So are you ready for a short trot to Half Dome?" Rick asked sardonically, knowing full well the nearly sixteen mile length of the upcoming hike.

"Piece of cake," Steve chimed.

After running down a quick checklist of all of the essentials, they stuffed and cinched their small daypacks close to capacity. Still sporting a pair of patterned boxers, Steve removed them and stepped into a pair of briefs from his suitcase, then into his hiking shorts and boots. His thermal top and jacket came next, and he was ready to go. It was 6:30.

Rick was across the room, looking in the mirror and testing the weight of his backpack. "This feels great!" he said. "Come on, dude! We're burnin' daylight."

"Right behind you, chief." Steve threw his backpack over one shoulder and followed Rick out of the comfort of the warm cabin into the crisp morning air. Every few steps and with each exhale of their warm breath, white plumes trailed into the air and spiraled upward around them.

They followed the dusty trail from the cabins to a sidewalk that ran alongside the park road and on out across the valley floor. There were few cars in the parking lot when they arrived at Curry Village. Both knew that wouldn't last long. Two coyotes were scavenging the area underneath the bus stop benches for scraps left behind by inconsiderate visitors. The two men marveled at the animals' antics, enjoying the absence of the usual throngs of prodding camera-toting tourists that often got too close to the animals.

The sun was just emerging from behind the east side of the mountain range.

Rick put on his Sherpa hat, an ornate, twenty-year-old wool relic he had acquired during a trip to Nepal in the Seventies. Steve put on his fingerless fleece gloves and a ski cap, then hurriedly blew into his cupped hands and rubbed them together to keep them warm.

"Damn, I didn't expect it to be this cold already."

Rick didn't seem to hear him. "Did you bring your bear spray?" he asked.

"What?"

"Your bear spray. Did you bring any?"

Figuring that Rick was trying to pull a fast one on him, Steve decided to play along. "All right. What in the hell is bear spray?"

"Bear repellant spray. That stuff park rangers use."

"Right!" Steve barked in a sarcastic tone. "Don't feed me that line of shit."

"Seriously, man. No joke. Check it out." Rick reached into one of the side pockets of his daypack, pulled out an aerosol can of bear repellant and tossed it to Steve.

Steve caught it and examined the canister. Reading the ingredient list, he noticed that one of the ingredients was skunk urine. "Skunk piss? Where in the hell did you get this?"

"At the backpacking store in Portland. It's some kind of pepper spray."

"Does it work?"

"I hope we don't have to find out, but I bet it beats the hell out of wearing or carrying those stupid fucking bells on the end of a walking stick. Dinner bells. That's what those things'll do for ya. They just tell the Goddamn bears to come and get it. There's probably some ancient, silver-backed grizzly up in Montana that sounds like Santa Claus coming down the damn trail because of all the bell-wearing tourists he's eaten so far," Rick bellowed. "I figured that I could use the stuff on the ground around our campsite and the bear boxes later in the week. It was tested on grizzlies, but I assume it'll keep the black bears away as well."

Steve could always tell when Rick was at ease. He cussed like a sailor but only around those who knew him really well. The man was a social chameleon, spinning from the boardroom to the gutter in an instant, depending on the social strata of the guests.

"Can you imagine who the Rhodes Scholar was that they got to field test this crap?" Steve mimicked a stern faced chemist, "That's right, Mr. Smith. Your initial duties as a research associate with our company include getting your scrawny ass into that pen with a two-thousand-pound grizzly bear, a beast that runs at speeds over 35 miles per hour, and as he is charging and salivating in your general direction, you will have nothing more than a 16-ounce aluminum canister of skunk piss for protection, and you will proceed to fend him off." Laughing, Steve pitched the can back to Rick.

Rick roared as he put the spray back into the side pocket of his pack and wrestled his arms through the shoulder straps.

"What other surprises do you have for us?"

Rick unclipped a small pouch from his shoulder strap and pulled out a hand held GPS unit, "I have this."

"A GPS? Man, you're such a gear-head," Steve said. "Let me guess. Waterproof, more reliable than using the GPS on a smart phone?"

"Yep. Plus the cell service sucks in the mountains. We'll never get lost with this."

"Right, unless the batteries die."

"It's got an internal lithium battery. It'll keep all of the stored waypoint info for ten years. Plus I have extra batteries."

"Of course you do. But do ya really think we'll need it with this superhighway of a trail we're on?" Steve chuckled loudly as he wrapped his hand around the back of his friend's neck and drug him in the direction of the trailhead. "I'm kidding. You'll have to show me how to use that thing later on."

"Let's go, amigo!" Rick shouted, invigorated by the coolness of the morning.

They made their way from the asphalt parking lot along dusty paths through the tent cabins to the Happy Isles Trail Center, where they found the John Muir Trail marker. They would be traveling up to the Mist Trail beside Vernal and Nevada Falls, a steady ascent into the back country. They hadn't gotten far from Curry Village when they spied a pay phone right next to the trail.

"Check this out, Rick."

"When the hell did they put that in?"

"Years ago, probably."

"No way. I'd have remembered that."

"Well, you are getting older, Steve." Rick winked.

"Who should we call?"

They looked at each other and simultaneously replied, "Whitley!"

Steve dialed her office number. The phone rang twice before her voice mail picked up. "Voice mail," he announced to Rick, then held the phone so they both could talk into the receiver.

"Hey, Whit. It's Steve and Rick. How's everything in Austin? How's Bosco?"

Rick chimed in. "Sorry we missed you, Whitley. You're not going to believe it, but we are calling you from the trailhead on our way up to Half Dome today. See you soon. Bye."

Steve added, "Cell phone service sucks out here, but since they are bastardizing the wilderness with pay phones nowadays, we couldn't pass up the opportunity to say hi. I'll call you later in the week, Whit. Take care, kid." Steve hung up, and the men crossed the bridge over Happy Isles, which was nearly dry, and picked up the trail on the other side.

"Whitley's a great lady," Rick said.

"She really is."

"I know you don't want to talk about it, but I always thought you guys would be perfect together, even while you were married to Connie."

Steve smirked, but remained silent, so Rick said nothing more.

Their moderate pace soon quickened, even with the uphill grade of the trail. The hard rubber soles of their hiking boots clomped as they pounded the combination of asphalt, granite, and sand that covered this artery into the wilderness. The alternating thuds of their footsteps at last gave way to a synchronized cadence. Their minds drifted as they settled into their steady pace. They talked little on the trail unless taking a water or photo break.

Steve watched as small clouds of dust floated up around Rick's ankles with each step of his boots. He always followed Rick, never ceasing to be amazed at the stamina of this man who was his elder and mentor.

Near Vernal Falls, which was as dry this time of year as many of the smaller creeks, they crossed the wooden bridge spanning the rocky spillway and marched up the stone staircase leading to the top of the falls. The chain-link barrier along the last few steps near the top surely must have prevented many a hiker from falling from the precipice. Moving into Little Yosemite they added a few pieces of trash left by hikers to the plastic bag Rick kept in his pack, and then started up the back side of the granite shoulder that would eventually bring them near the top of the valley.

Even after their many visits to Yosemite, even after the hundreds of miles logged up this same trail, Steve and Rick were continually amazed at the immense forces that had created the granite marvel that was Half Dome. Nearly halfway through the hike, the men climbed the last few steps atop the shoulder, stopping to catch their breath and to absorb the enormity of their surroundings.

A slight haze hung in the valley to the south, air pollution that filtered into the San Joaquin Valley from western cities and traveled southward until captured within the steep valley walls. The light wind rapidly dried the small beads of perspiration on their foreheads.

"I can't wait until winter comes and blows this smog out of here," Rick said with disgust. He spoke clearly and calmly, without a hint of the exertion the climb had required.

"It is a shame, isn't it? But you're right. It won't be long."

Steve looked up. "God, it's Monday. I thought we'd have this place to ourselves for a few minutes at least." They had passed no one on the trail, but there were a dozen or so people already queued up at the bottom of the cable route.

"They must have camped in Little Yosemite last night," Steve said.

"Yeah. Probably the same assholes that left the trash." Rick placed his right hand over his eyes to shield them from the glare of the morning sun and squinted toward Half Dome's summit. Several people were visible cresting the top of the cables. "I see some people milling around near the top."

"Either some climbers just summited, or the Breakfast Club got up really early to catch the sunrise on top."

They strolled from their viewpoint among the last of the pine trees down to the small saddle connected to the upward thrust of granite that was the left shoulder of Half Dome proper. Without saying a word they both removed their packs and fumbled in their respective front zipper pouches, retrieving two pieces of nylon webbing and two carabiners.

Rick untied one piece of webbing and retied it snugly around his waist. He clipped one carabiner onto the brightly colored web belt and pushed a bite from the second loop of webbing through the same carabiner gate. He spun the locking mechanism tight, securing the webbing to his body, and clipped one more 'biner to the dangling web loop. Throwing his pack on, he walked to the cables and snapped the carabiner to the right cable. Simultaneously, Steve completed a similar anchor setup and clipped in behind Rick.

A couple of dusty hikers had their backsides anchored to a large boulder as they shared gulps from a plastic bottle full of Gatorade. They watched curiously as Rick and Steve began their ascent up the forty-five-degree slab.

Every few feet they came to a galvanized fence post stuck in a hole that had been drilled into the granite. They unclipped their 'biners from behind the post and reclipped them to the cable in front of it. This procedure continued as they methodically, but quickly ascended the steep angle until finally they reached more forgiving ground near the top of the dome. At this level the angle was reduced significantly, curving gently from the cables all the way to the summit.

The duo summited Half Dome at 9:30 A.M. They both quietly sat down and admired the majestic view. Rick reached into his fanny pack and pulled out a small, dog-eared journal. He thought for a few minutes and began to write, "MG/SL—step 1/Complete."

Steve couldn't see what Rick was writing, but watched him for a moment, then stared southward into the massive chasm of the valley.

Rick finished writing a few more notes, then closed his journal and looked at Steve, who was sitting cross-legged, facing the sun, eyes closed as if in a meditative state. Rick smiled and silently nodded his approval. He truly valued his friendship with this man, and he had sorely missed spending time with him over the last three years.

Steve dug into his pack to retrieve two Power Bars. "Hey, man. You want a bar?"

"Sure." Rick caught the energy bar tossed his way and hungrily tore open the foil wrapper. The bar disappeared in a hurry. He washed it down with several large gulps of water from one of the bottles in his pack, and then stuffed the wrapper in his trash bag.

"You ready to head back?"

Steve was still chewing. "Yeah. Let's go."

Retracing their steps took a fraction of the time they had spent on the ascent. They were already two miles down the trail, when someone behind them shouted, "ON YOUR LEFT!"

Steve and Rick shuttled to the right to allow two trail-runners to pass them.

They soon got into a rhythm again as they followed the joggers toward the valley floor. The runners soon outpaced them and disappeared behind the thick pine foliage that lined the circuitous trail.

"Man, I forgot to ask if you were seein' anyone," Rick said.

His body now warmed from the exertion, Steve removed his long-sleeved shirt. "Nope. How 'bout you?"

"Yeah, I'm dating, but nothing serious."

"Like you've ever been in a serious relationship! When was the last one? 1940?"

"Actually, I joined one of those dating services about three months ago."

"Really? I thought all of those places were rip-offs."

"Yeah, I did, too, but I have a friend at the gym who turned me on to it. It's a real professional outfit. I've met a few real nice ladies there."

"A few? How many is a few?"

"I've been on a couple of dates a month since I started."

"Wow! How much did that set you back to join?"

"A thousand bucks a year."

Steve whistled. "That's a lotta dinners."

"Yeah, but all the knotty lumber is culled out ahead of time. You go in, look at a few videos, and select the ladies that interest you. If they also select you, the service notifies you and you make a date."

"Seems like a sterile way to meet people."

"Hey, pal, this is the new millennium. Romeo and Juliet died a long time ago."

"I guess so."

"Hey! What about Michelle?"

"What about her?"

"If she moves to Texas, you two should hook up."

"Why is that?"

"So that your friends can stand to be around you, Einstein. You gotta take advantage of situations like these, oh sexless one."

"I don't know, man. First, Whitley. Now, Michelle. We'll just see."

"Okay. Be a fuckin' monk the rest of your life, you Dali Lama sonofabitch!" The tone of Rick's voice made Steve glance at him, but Rick was grinning.

"It's just that I hate the whole dating scene. You ever tried to have a lucid discussion with a twenty-something Millennial?"

"If I was you right now, I'd be thinkin' about something a helluva lot more important than a lucid discussion. And who said anything about a Millennial? Just because you look too young for your own good and attract pre-pubescent jailbait doesn't mean you have to date two decades out of your age group. Michelle would be good for you. She's a good woman and a hell of an underwriter. Hell, she could be running the Austin department with a little more experience."

Steve remained silent.

In less than half the time it took for the ascent, they arrived at the edge of the Curry Village parking lot. An attractive woman was stepping into a pricey, late model SUV. Rick jabbed a finger into Steve's ribs to get his attention.

With a raised eyebrow and a wide grin he pointed to her and exclaimed, "There's another possibility for you!"

Steve gave her the once over. "Cool it, Don Juan. Our wallets combined couldn't keep her in cell phone minutes!"

"I bet you're right."

"It's still early. You want to check out the Mountain Shop and see if they have any gear we can't live without?"

"Sure."

They continued across the parking lot toward the Yosemite Mountain Shop. It was home to the Yosemite Mountaineering School and offered every item one would need to scale the surrounding rock faces, except courage and the genetic grip of an orangutan. The shop was also an occasional gathering place for climbers queuing up for the short trip around the building to the Curry Village Patio for beer and pizza.

Rick looked at the sky. "It's gonna be a cold one tonight, as clear as it is."

"Yeah, it will," Steve acknowledged as they walked into the shop.

They milled around for about thirty minutes examining the latest shoe designs, porta-ledges, and camming devices. Rick picked up a couple of rolls of climbing tape and walked to the register. Steve walked up from the T-shirt rack to stand beside him.

"I think Michelle will take the Austin position if everything's packaged right. I don't think it's possible that she won't be offered the job," Rick said.

"Trent's up for the same job."

"Really? How's the kid doing?" Rick asked.

"Great. If his drive was as strong as his work ethic, he could also be on the fast track someday. I don't know if his heart is into the underwriter job, though."

"He's still young."

"Yeah."

"Anyone else you know of that would be more qualified than Michelle?"

"Not on our end."

"Sounds like our Miss Grayson will be a Texan soon!" Rick winked as he said it.

"You know my rule," Steve said.

"Rule! What rule?"

"Don't date anyone. . ."

Rick finished the sentence, "you work with. Who gives a shit? And Michelle's not working with you yet. You need to get into the game. It'll do you some good. If not with her, just promise me you'll get off your ass and get back in the game soon."

"We'll see." Steve paused for a moment, looked around the shop, then stared oddly at Rick, and whispered in his ear, "You know . . . I've always thought you were kinda good looking!"

"Back off, asshole." Rick shoved him away jokingly. "You couldn't afford me either." After paying for the tape, Rick shoved the paper bag emblazoned with the Yosemite Park logo into his pack and asked, "How 'bout some grub?"

"What were you thinking about? Curry Village Patio?"

"You get the pizza, and I'll get the beer," Rick said.

"You got it."

The two made the short walk to the large patio next to the Curry dining hall. Feeling a blister developing on his heel, Steve walked gingerly across the wooden deck and took his place at the end of the line. It was full of hungry campers flowing toward the pizza counter. In no time at all, Rick secured an ice-cold pitcher of beer and a table. Steve gave his name with their order to the cashier. Rick looked on while his friend hobbled back to the table and plopped his tired body into a chair.

"Walkin' like you got a cob up your ass, amigo." Rick poured him a beer.

"My ass is the only thing I can feel at the moment."

"Three or four of these twelve-ounce doses, and the doctor will have you back to normal in no time." He slid a full mug in front of Steve.

"Man, this is gonna taste good!"

"You sit there and admire it all you want. I'm gonna be two beers ahead of ya by the time you get through gawking at that damn mug." Rick saluted Steve and took a huge gulp. "Ahhhhhhhh. The only reason I exercise."

An extra large mushroom and olive pizza was no contest for the two hungry hikers. The men soon had devoured nearly all of it and started on a second pitcher of beer. Both were helping to abate their residual aches and pains.

"So, how's everything in Portland?"

Rick had a deadpan look on his face. "Same ol', same ol'. If it was fun, they wouldn't call it work, right?"

"Yeah, yeah. Get new material. Seriously."

"All kidding aside, we had a great year this year. How 'bout you? How's it been, working with Roeder?"

"He's a pretty good guy, a heart attack waiting to happen, but a pretty good guy nonetheless. I have to admit that the Austin operation is a lot smoother than I thought it would be. When the hell are you moving down there to take over for him?"

Rick stared at Steve as if surprised, while biting into the last slice of pizza. "Whenever the summertime temperature averages 72 degrees," he mumbled. "Actually, there's a good possibility I may be there within the next year. But keep that under your hat."

"What? Are you kidding?"

"Nope. Roeder's going to hang it up next summer and retire. They've really been pushing for me to come down there."

"Man, that's great."

"It is. But again, don't tell anyone. It's going to piss off a few other candidates if they find out the decision has already been made."

"My lips are sealed," Steve said, as he noticed a piece of cheese hanging precariously from the corner of Rick's mouth. "I can't say the same for you, though. I think you're full, man. There's crap spilling out of your mouth onto your clothes. You'd better stop eating."

Rick couldn't have appeared less concerned as he barely looked down and flicked the food off with his middle finger. "Whatta ya say we knock back another pitcher and hit the lodge? I mean, they are small pitchers..."

"Yeah, I guess I can handle splitting one more, even with the early call in the morning." Rick walked to the counter, and Steve gulped the remaining contents of his mug and set it on the mesh patio table. He found himself drifting back to last night's dinner with Michelle.

CHAPTER TEN

WHITLEY SAT IN THE old oak rocking chair she had moved out onto the balcony of her apartment, the same chair in which Winona had rocked her to sleep as an infant. The rug she kept out there warmed her feet on cooler nights while she gazed at the night sky.

Whitley lived in the upstairs left unit of a fourplex on Thirty-first Street, a location she believed was imperative for her well-being; she had read somewhere that if bad neighbors lived above her, their negative auras could "rain" down upon her space and greatly affect her mood. She wasn't quite sure she believed it, but if being aware of it did nothing more than keep her thinking in a positive way, that was fine with her. Closing her eyes, she began rocking slowly, breathing in the elegant scent of flowers, flowers that she cultivated in a quirky assortment of vessels that formed a miniature jungle along the railing around her patio.

Her habit was especially comforting tonight. She hadn't slept well the past few nights, ever since the explosion at the Walker residence had caused her to rocket out of bed. Even though the blast had gone off more than twenty blocks away, it had been so loud, it had sounded like it was just down the street from her apartment.

As she was about to drift off, an angry shout interrupted the evening calm.

Whitley stopped rocking and listened. She was surprised to hear an argument so late on a Tuesday night. She thought it was coming from the parking lot of Saint Anne's Catholic Church across the street.

Silent most of the time, the lot was one of the darker spots in the neighborhood and thus much better for viewing the sky than her balcony; she regularly lugged her telescope over there for stargazing—with the permission of the resident priest, Father Alonso Ochoa, who lived in the rectory at the east end of the church. On cooler nights when the skies were clearer, Father Alonso would often bring out hot tea to warm her.

Whitley, along with Saint Anne's regular parishioners, adored Father Alonso. She wasn't Catholic. Whitley had been raised Methodist but considered herself "multi-non-denominational," a genre that she had coined. She made it a point to attend houses of worship for all religions in the Austin area, hoping to extract the best traits from each and use them as she could in her daily life.

The argument drew her attention again. One man was very composed, speaking quietly enough that Whitley couldn't understand him. The other, the bigger and louder of the two, was animated, throwing his arms about wildly, pointing at the other while he shouted.

Quietly, Whitley reached beside the chair, picked up a bottle of water, and unscrewed the cap. She squinted before taking a drink, hoping to get a better view of the two men, but in the darkness it was impossible to make out their identities. Somewhat alarmed by their behavior, she capped her water bottle and listened. *Where,* she wondered, *is Father Al?*

A large tree along the street obstructed her view of the calmer individual. Slowly, she set the bottle down and eased out of the rocker toward the railing, taking care to conceal herself behind the jungle of leafy plants that occupied most of her balcony space. She opened a cloth bag and pulled out the mini-binoculars she often used for birding at various parks around town. The foliage before her, however, was just too thick to give her a clear view of the men.

"What are you trying to do?" the loud one questioned. "Do you want to blow fifteen years of hard work?"

"For the last time, keep your voice down."

Whitley heard him clearly this time and identified a thick French accent over his English. Try as she could, they were just too far away for her to hear both sides of the conversation.

More curious now than afraid, she inched her way along the railing. Binoculars glued to her eyes, she hoped to get a clear view of the participants. The lenses protruded outward approximately five inches from her eyes, just far enough to clip the edge of a small clay flowerpot. It tumbled off of the railing and crashed onto the sidewalk below.

The unexpected noise abruptly ended the men's dialogue.

The outspoken man walked a short way across the parking lot toward Thirty-First Street. He stopped just at the edge of the light cast by the street lamp. He looked both ways down the tree-lined avenue, and then peered sternly across the street toward Whitley's apartment building.

Still crouched behind the tangled strands of vines and stems, Whitley could just make him out through the now-vacant spot on her balcony railing.

He was a huge man with a thick mane of long, black hair. The darkness exaggerated his facial figures. Shadows carved deep, well-defined canals into his face accentuating an already threatening demeanor. The cut of his tight black shirt, worn tail out over dark gray slacks, gave him the appearance of an East Coast hood and re-affirmed her earlier fear. Slowly, deliberately, he took a drag off his cigarette and flicked it into the street in the direction of Whitley's apartment. For a moment longer he stood, staring at her building.

Whitley felt a chill not from the balmy night air but from her feelings of helplessness and was thankful all her lights were turned off. She remained perfectly still, but wondered if her pounding heart might jump through her chest.

As the man exhaled, the smoke lingered in front of his face, hanging like an unnatural shroud in the still air of the night. At last he turned away and walked back into the shadows of the church parking lot. It wasn't long before a dark-colored Suburban squealed out of the parking lot and drove away from her apartment toward the opposite end of Thirty-First Street.

Whitley felt some very negative vibes about this man and remained motionless. She tried to recall anything in today's horoscope that might have warned her about encounters with strangers.

The other man stepped from the shadows of the parking lot and picked up the loud man's cigarette butt from the middle of the street.

She didn't see him because she was hurriedly crawling back in through the open, sliding glass door to the darkness of her apartment. Once inside, she closed and locked the door, drew the draperies, and ran to the land-line phone on the counter, since her cell wasn't close by. With shaking hands, she punched in the speed dial number for the church rectory.

"Pick up, Father Al! Hurry!"

The phone rang seven times before the church's answering machine picked up. She hung up without leaving a message. She ran to her bedroom and picked up her cell phone from the nightstand. She quickly located Trent's number from her contact list and pressed the screen to dial it. Breathlessly, she waited for him to answer.

"Hello."

"Trent," she whispered unnecessarily.

"Yeah, who is this?"

"Whitley."

"Whitley?" He was stunned to get her call. Seven years her junior, Trent still adored her. "Are you okay?"

"Yeah, I think I might have seen something. Since Steve is out of town, I thought I'd call you."

"Whatta you mean? What'd you see exactly?"

"I was sitting out on my porch in my rocking chair, and I heard some people arguing down the street. I tried to get a better view of them with my binoculars and accidentally knocked one of my plants off the railing. Then, there was this real creepy guy staring at my complex, trying to figure out where the noise came from."

"Did he see you?"

"No. I don't know. I mean, I don't think so, but God," Whitley shivered, "he looked so mean."

"What was he doin' while you were watching him?"

"Like I said, the big creepy one was arguing with some guy. I think the other guy was French, but it was hard to hear them. He was probably some drug dealer selling to a foreign exchange student."

"Yeah, it could be. Whitley, you gotta be careful if you're gonna spy on people."

"I wasn't spying on them. Well, at least, not at first. Besides, they were the ones doing the yelling."

"Are you okay now? Would you like me to come over and get you? You could stay over here at my place." Trent would have rented a limo if it would have made her accept his offer.

Whitley paused. She could only imagine what his place must look like. Neon beer signs and posters of Victoria's Secret models came immediately to mind, in addition to the stacks of dirty laundry piled high enough to rival Mount Everest, not to mention the leftover food in his refrigerator that would probably require a forensic pathologist to identify. No, she had to force herself to keep from playing the helpless girl routine too heavily, lest it get back to Steve, the only man she really cared for. And she wasn't about to play that game with an uncontrollable hormone that manifested itself as Trent Osborne.

"Oh. I'll be alright."

"Okay, but if you need me, call me."

"Thanks, I will."

"Alright, I'll call you in the morning to check on you."

"That won't be necessary, but thanks anyway. Good night."

"Bye." Trent hung up.

Whitley couldn't help but wonder if she had just created a monster. She decided it would be best to go to Steve's house for the night in case the stranger or, worse, Trent decided to pay her an unexpected visit.

She peeked out her sliding-glass door toward the church parking lot and saw that the coast was clear. She threw on a baggy T-shirt and a pair of sweat pants and walked out of her apartment, locking the door behind her. Putting one key between each finger, she made a fist around the key chain and remaining keys, a move she had learned years earlier in a self-defense class, then bounded down the stairs. She hugged the apartment building as she ran around the west side to the back parking lot that harbored her ample vehicle.

Whitley drove a '77 Cadillac, a huge chocolate-brown, two-door El Dorado with an interior as big as Texas. It was a car tailor-made for the nouveau riche oilmen of the late seventies when it was built; the kind of men who sported ostrich-skin boots, buckskin jackets, and ostentatious gold nugget rings. The inside had more than enough headroom to embrace the big-haired Texas women of that decade. Despite Winona's repeated attempts to replace the Caddy with a new, more compact and fuel-efficient car, Whitley had declined all her mother's offers. She felt much safer surrounded by the ample steel of her "Molé Grande," as she called it. Besides, she saved a fortune on insurance costs by carrying only liability coverage on the ancient car.

Firing up the powerful engine, Whitley slipped out the back exit of the parking lot and headed toward Steve's Westlake bungalow. She arrived at 11:15. After a week of regular visits, Bosco had become accustomed to the sound of her car's engine. His barking began before she could get out of the car.

"Hi, Bosco," she called out.

The Lab yelped with excitement from behind the cedar fence at the left corner of the house.

"Are you ready for a late-night treat?"

Bosco bolted from the side of the house to the back and squeezed through the dog door into the garage. By the time Whitley was inside, had the alarm disabled, and made it to the utility room, Bosco was barking and scratching at the door in earnest. Had it not been for the plastic shield that Steve had installed on the lower half of the door, Bosco would have surely clawed right through it.

"Hello, baaaaby." She squatted down and scratched his face as he licked hers excitedly in response. "What a good boy you are. You'll protect me, won't you?"

He rolled onto his back and allowed Whitley to scratch his stomach.

"Come on, boy. We've got to inspect the premises." Together, they walked through the house. She examined the windows and every other possible point of entry to make sure nothing was out of order. She knew every inch of that house as if it were her own. Once she was convinced that nobody had miraculously entered the house, disabled the alarm, and politely re-set it before she arrived, she relaxed a bit.

Bosco followed her into the living room and jumped onto the couch. Grabbing the remote control from the coffee table, she plopped down beside him and turned on the television set in order to catch the late news.

The news anchor's dialogue soon became an indiscernible hum as her mind drifted to another place. Bosco had already adjusted his position so that his head fell into her lap where she could stroke his head. Anxiously awaiting Steve's return, all she wanted to imagine at that moment was living there full-time, in that house, with that dog, in a full blown relationship with Steve.

Whitley awoke early the next morning after another restless night. She rolled over and pushed Bosco's bulky body to the edge of the bed so that he would jump off. He had eagerly joined her in the bed around 3:00 A.M., an act his master never allowed. He oozed off the edge of the bed as if to savor every last second of this rare treat and reluctantly walked over to his usual accommodations on the pad in the corner of the bedroom.

Exhaling, she sat up in bed and looked lovingly down at the dog. "Sorry, big fella."

Other than the big brown eyes looking up at her, his tail was the only portion of his body that moved. It sounded a thump, thump, thump on the wooden floor with a regular cadence.

Checking the bed for any stray dog hairs, Whitley made it up and led Bosco to the garage, where he could access the dog door into the back yard. She filled his dog bowl with a scoop of dry food. Wearing nothing but one of Steve's T-shirts, she walked through the den and peered through the narrow window beside the front door, making sure the coast was clear. She scampered outside to retrieve the newspaper and shuddered as the cool and humid air rushing up under the T-shirt gave her a chill. Back inside she turned on the coffee pot and sat down at the kitchen table to check her horoscope. Her eyes widened and a chill of a different nature shook her as she read the short blurb: "The month will prove to be revealing, and you should take precautions when dealing with strangers. A previous action on your part may have placed you in a position that will require you to make quick decisions. A new point of view brings a mini-revelation and a change in your course of action. Pressure from the past is alleviated with understanding and help from friends."

Most people would have read the lines and chalked them up as another incongruous horoscope. Whitley was different. She put a considerable amount of stock in the written words. The events of the previous night made the text even more believable.

It was too dark last night. There was no way he could see me from that distance, especially with a street light between us, she thought.

She sat for several minutes, drinking her coffee, thinking about last night, and contemplating what she had just read. After a time she felt better, but a voice in her head told her to exercise caution.

Whitley folded the paper and walked to the counter to top off her cup. She poured the rest in the sink and rinsed out the pot. After turning off the coffee maker, she dressed back into her sweats, locked up the house, went back through the list in her mind, and headed back across town to her apartment.

Arriving back at her complex, Whitley anchored Molé Grande back in its slip behind her building. Once again she used extreme caution approaching the apartment, imagining that someone could be waiting for her inside. Scurrying past the broken flowerpot that still remained on the sidewalk, Whitley crept up the stairs, quietly inserted the key into the deadbolt, and unlocked the door. The coast was clear. She set down her things, grabbed a broom and a dustpan from the utility room, and went downstairs to clean up the mess on the sidewalk.

While she was sweeping, Whitley peered back across the street toward the church parking lot. She noticed that Father Al's porch light at the rectory was turned off, a sure sign that he was up. Throwing the pottery shards into a plastic bag that she had brought with her, she salvaged the potting soil by spreading it beneath one of the nearby shrubs. Running back upstairs, she put away the broom and walked to her answering machine. The light indicated she had one message. She pressed play.

"Hey! Whitley, Trent. Just thought I'd call back and check on you. You know, make sure you're safe and all. Uh, don't hesitate to call me back if you need anything. Bye."

Whitley knew better than to call back. She erased the message, grabbed some cash out of the opaque Tupperware container kept in the back of the freezer, and stuffed it into the rear zippered pocket on her sweat pants. Locking the door on her way out, she ran down the stairs and across Thirty-First Street.

Whitley marched the quarter mile to the bagel shop on Guadalupe Street where she purchased a dozen bagels of different varieties, small containers of plain and sun-dried tomato cream cheese, and two cups of coffee. Juggling the two bags, she retraced her route until she strolled down the sidewalk adjacent to Saint Anne's and the church parking lot. At the front door of the church rectory where Father Alonso lived, Whitley set her bags down on the small landing and opened the screen door. She rapped loudly, and then rang the doorbell.

"Whitley!" Father Alonso greeted her warmly in his thick Spanish accent. "What brings you by? It's been a while."

"I know. I've been neglecting you, but I've brought some breakfast if you're interested."

"Fantastico! Come inside." Father Al held both doors open for Whitley until she made it inside the rectory. "I was just finishing with the paper. Would you like to read it?"

"Sure. I've glanced at it already, but I really haven't had time to finish it." Whitley made her way into the kitchen as if she lived there and plopped the bags down on the table. She fumbled inside one bag and retrieved two cups of Café Mocha. Father Al would never splurge on designer coffee, but he never turned it down when Whitley brought it by.

"Café Mocha, extra large, sir!" Whitley exclaimed and handed him the coffee.

"Thank you so much," he said, as he took the beverage and gave her a hug. "Now tell me something." Father Al had a stern look on his face as he crossed his arms and looked down his nose at her. "Why haven't we seen you at mass, Miss Talmadge? Have you been visiting some of our competitors again? And remember, you go to the same place for lying as you do for stealing!"

"No, it's not that. I know it's no excuse, but I've been busy chasing after a man that doesn't even know I'm interested in him, among other reasons, but that's not why I came by. Did you hear those guys arguing in the parking lot last night?"

"No. I was visiting Mrs. Stewart at the hospital last night. What happened?"

"Well, I was making a sad attempt to stargaze with my mini-binoculars when I heard this foreign guy and some loudmouth going at it in earnest in the lot."

"What were they arguing about?"

"I don't know. I couldn't make out much of it. Probably some drug deal gone bad or something." Whitley took a big gulp of coffee and started spreading cream cheese on two bagel halves. She handed one to Father Alonso, never missing a beat with her story. "But anyway, here I was, watching in the dark from my balcony, and you know how clumsy I can be. I accidentally knocked one of my plants off of the rail, and he heard me."

"Who heard you?"

"The loud guy. Well, both of them, I guess. Then I hid on the balcony, and the loud man walked under the street lamp, and I saw him. He was this huge, creepy-looking guy."

"Did you call the police?"

"No, he didn't see me."

"What did he do next?"

"He just stared at my fourplex for a while, and then left in a big truck."

Father Alonso listened intently, alternating between bites of the bagel and sips of coffee. "Well, I wish I had been here last night. I hope they weren't vandalizing any church property. I'll have to look around."

"I don't think these guys were vandals, Father. They were, or at least the one guy was, very well dressed, at least in a greasy Italian mafia kinda way." Whitley caught her faux pas. "Sorry…No offense to the Pope, and I didn't see the foreign guy at all."

Father Al tilted his head back and laughed. He enjoyed Whitley's visits. "It sounds as though it was much more exciting here than at Mrs. Stewart's bedside last night."

Whitley took a mouthful of bagel and a smear of cream cheese stuck to the corner of her lips as she spoke. "She was in for gall bladder surgery, wasn't she?"

"Yes, and she's doing much, much better. Did you know that she's eighty-two years old? They should be releasing her within the week."

"Good for her."

"So how have you been? It's been at least two months since I saw you last."

"I've been pretty well for the most part. Mom came by for dinner Friday night."

"Ah, in town for the game on Saturday?"

"Yep. And she was trying to reunite me with my old, or rather my first, real boyfriend."

"By real, you mean. . ."

"You got it! The real first. Mom's hell bent on having grandchildren again. 'Tis the season, you know. As soon as she hears about any of the other boosters' grandkids and gets the 'How many grandchildren do you have?' knife stuck in her, football season becomes my four-month personal hell week."

Chuckling, Father Al said, "I'm sure she's just lonely. I'd be happy to talk to her if you'd like."

"Thanks, but no thanks."

"Well, you know where to find me if either of you change your mind."

"Hey, maybe I should try to set her up with someone for a change. You know, give her a little of her own medicine."

"Games won't help, Whitley. Just tell her the truth about how you feel."

"I do. It's like she doesn't hear me, though."

"Or refuses to?"

"Exactly."

"Well, I'll say some prayers for you both. And it wouldn't hurt if you would show up in that big room on the other side of the yard once in a while." Father Al pointed in the air toward the Church. "You know the one. It has a lot of wooden benches and tall ceilings!"

"I will. I promise." She smiled.

"This Sunday? On the front row?"

"It's a done deal." She walked over to him and gave him a hug. "Thank you so much for the way you are. I always feel so much better when we talk."

"You'd feel even better if you'd talk with someone other than your newspaper astrologers more regularly."

"Okay, you got me two weeks in a row, but that's all a militant Methodist girl can promise at this point."

"God takes whatever we are willing to give, Whitley." He saluted her with his coffee cup and grinned.

CHAPTER ELEVEN

STEVE GOT OUT OF bed around seven on Wednesday morning. The soreness in his body was tangible evidence that the previous day's climbing workout had been an overwhelming success. Even though he was in great shape, climbing a few long routes in Yosemite could reduce almost anyone to Jell-o.

Rick was still asleep. Mercifully, the small air conditioner had made enough noise through the night to soften the foundation-rattling snores emanating from him.

Returning to the Sierras was exhilarating, and though he wouldn't admit it to Rick, the expectation of seeing Michelle again was certainly a bonus. Doubts still plagued him about whether Rick might have set the whole thing up, but the more he thought about it, the more he realized that he didn't really care.

Rick extricated himself from the comfort of the bed and looked at Steve. "Whatta ya wanna do today?"

"Doesn't matter at all."

"You want to take the girls bouldering?"

"Yeah. Why don't we do the boulders from Swan Slabs down to El Cap? If afterward we think they're up for it, we can do a few shorter protected routes this afternoon. We can do Washington's Column or another route tomorrow after our stint with the ladies."

"Oh, so are you now telling me you're changing your mind about Michelle?" Rick said with a slightly acerbic tone.

"We made plans, remember?" Steve said, remaining expressionless as he searched through bags for a variety of gear.

Rick just smiled, knowing he was starting to get under his friend's skin. "Don't bother packing all of your gear, amigo. We'll use mine, and you can carry more of the munchies and water. I've got plenty of cams and wedges. You might want to bring ten or fifteen 'biners though, just in case."

"Sounds like a deal to me," Steve replied. He figured that negotiation netted Rick an additional twelve pounds of weight and wasn't about to argue. If he wanted to play macho by grabbing more of the load, more power to him.

By the time both men had showered and dressed, they were running a little late. They jogged along the now familiar path from the lodge to the Awahnee, where Michelle and Sally were already waiting.

Michelle shouted as they neared, "Good morning, guys! How was your climb?" Steve noticed immediately how her black running tights accentuated her muscular legs. She wore a dark green fleece jacket and a black fleece headband that sheltered her ears from the chill of the morning.

Steve finally diverted his gaze from her lower half, but noticed the delay in his response was almost too long. "It was terrific!" He finally said. "Looks like it rained last night. I must have slept right through it."

"Yeah. Everything's kinda damp." Michelle patted him on the back twice and casually rubbed the same spot, as if they had known each other for years.

Steve needed coffee. "Have you two been in the dining room already?"

"Nah, just a cup of coffee in the lobby," Sally said. "We're not much on breakfast."

"That's cool. I'll grab a cup for each of us, Rick. We can munch power bars as we hike."

"That'll work," Rick said.

Michelle took a closer look at the men. "Rough night, huh?"

"Why do you say that?" Rick asked.

Sally responded, "You're both sporting beer goggles this morning, aren't you?" referring to the obvious circles under the men's eyes.

"Actually, it's dehydration. Ten hours on these walls can suck it out of you in no time."

Michelle took charge, "I guess we'd better take it easy on you two shrinking violets until you get plenty of water and some coffee in you. I don't want you to have any excuses for wimping out too early on our training today."

Steve started to say something clever, but stopped. "I'd better get the coffee," he smiled at her and walked into the lobby.

A couple of minutes later, Steve returned with two cups of black coffee and handed one to Rick.

"Thanks."

"So where do you guys want to start?" Michelle asked.

"Let's go down to Swan Slabs. It's a short hike from here, and we can start with some easy bouldering and perhaps move to some top-rope climbs later," Steve suggested.

Rick and Sally agreed, and the four of them marched south from the Awahnee.

The trail wove through towering pines, across a bridge, and then hugged the west side of the cliff just past Yosemite Falls. The first boulder that came into view was a five-foot-high overhanging chunk of granite.

"That one is about the right height," Sally said.

Rick smiled. "That boulder is called The Sloth. It's a helluva lot harder than it looks."

"We'll let you ladies attempt that one after you've gotten your feet wet on some easier rocks." Steve led the way to an unnamed slab of rock just beyond The Sloth and threw his daypack against a nearby tree. "We'll start on this one," he announced.

The women pulled rented climbing shoes from their packs and began lacing them tightly around their feet.

"God, these shoes feel almost as bad as ballet slippers," Michelle exclaimed.

"No kidding," Sally confirmed.

"Are you two dancers?" Steve asked.

"Were," Michelle replied. "Fifteen years of pure hell on my feet."

Steve watched as Michelle's well-painted toenails disappeared into the climbing shoe. That explains the lithe physique, he thought.

Rick already had his shoes on and was helping Sally get into hers.

"Show 'em how it's done, Rick," Steve said.

Rick hopped up, dusted the dirt from his backside, and grabbed his chalk bag.

"We didn't rent one of those," Sally proclaimed. "Should we have, Rick?"

"It isn't necessary. You can use ours." Rick chalked up and tossed Sally the small pouch of gymnastic chalk.

"What does it do?"

"Helps keep your hands dry," Steve responded. "It's the same stuff the gymnasts use to keep their hands from slipping off of the different bars and rings they fly around on."

In just a matter of seconds, Rick had climbed the 5.6 lie back route and was preparing for the 5.8 under cling.

"Wow, check him out," Sally said. "I'm impressed, Rick."

"You'll both be doing this in no time," Rick replied.

"I can't wait to try!" Michelle was staring at a 5.4 face climb, the easiest route on the boulder.

"Before you two get started, let me show you how to spot your partner in case of a slip. Michelle, step up onto the boulder right here." Steve pointed to an easy ledge about two feet off the ground. Once she was in place, he commanded, "Now jump off."

Michelle jumped to the ground and when she did so, her upper body bent toward the rock to absorb the fall. She put her hands against the rock to prevent herself from scraping against it. Sally watched intently.

"Did you see how her upper body fell forward when her feet hit the ground? The higher you are when you jump off of a boulder, the more pronounced that motion will be, so you want your spotter to prevent that from happening. Climb up there and jump off one more time for me, Michelle."

She complied, only this time Steve caught her under the arms and used her momentum to pull her away from the rock. Michelle took advantage of the situation and leaned back against Steve's chest.

"Oh, I see what you're doing. You want to keep the climber from falling forward onto the rock and possibly hitting their head or something."

"Exactly. Okay, Sally. You try this and then trade places with Michelle."

After a few more practice falls, Michelle was ready to give the boulder a try.

Steve remained quiet, watching to see what she would do.

Placing her hands on the polished granite, she deftly placed her left foot on a small knob and stood up. She gracefully made her way to the top of the boulder after a few more moves.

Steve traced the length of her body with his eyes, following her sinewy muscles as they flexed with each nimble step. "You make it look easy," Steve complimented her.

"Way to go, girl!" Sally exclaimed, and let out a hoot.

"Thanks! This is great."

"See if you can come down the same way you came up," Steve said.

Michelle turned around and walked down the rock as if she were descending a ladder. Near the bottom of the boulder she hopped to the ground, and Sally caught her correctly, just as they had practiced.

Sally ticked off the 5.4 almost as easily.

"Woo-hoo! Way to go, Sally!" Michelle applauded.

Sally was beaming as she hopped off of the boulder.

"Atta girl!" Rick shouted.

Steve was lacing up his shoes. "You ladies are naturals. That dancing really helps with your form."

"Michelle's the real dancer," Sally said. She could have attended Juilliard if she wanted to."

"Juilliard? That's impressive."

"After fifteen years, I just wasn't into doing it anymore. It wasn't fun. I'm really happy now with the career I've chosen."

"Good for you," Rick replied.

"The pay is definitely better," Sally added.

"No doubt about that," Michelle agreed.

"Tell you what guys. Since you seem to have this in hand Steve, I'm going to work on a couple of problems down the way on another boulder."

"We'll catch up with you in a few." Steve continued to watch the women work out the varying routes on the boulders, taking turns spotting one another.

"What's great is that neither of you try to muscle your way up the rock. That's a common mistake we guys make. You both have excellent form. Keep practicing, and we will work you up to something a bit more gymnastic on some shorter boulders."

"Sounds great," they said enthusiastically.

"I can see where this sport can take its toll on your fingertips," Michelle said. "Mine are already stinging."

"Just don't overdo it. It takes a long time to get your fingertips callused enough to not feel the pain."

"Hmmm, leathery fingertips. Those will look very pretty with a manicure," Sally replied sarcastically.

"I'm afraid long fingernails and climbing don't mix," Steve said, as he stood up and took his shirt off, tossing it on top of his pack.

Descending from another trip up the boulder, Sally elbowed Michelle to get her to look.

Oh my God, Michelle mouthed silently to her friend.

"I think I'll let him catch me now," Sally whispered. "It's only fair. You had your turn."

The women giggled and sat down to watch Steve make seemingly impossible moves look easy.

Sally whispered, "Would you look at that stomach? Jesus Christ! I wonder what that feels like."

"Amen to that," Michelle said, as she watched Steve's forearms explode with strand after strand of muscle fibers as he worked over every inch of the granite.

"If you don't hook up with this guy, you're nuts. At least for one night."

"Will you please stop?" Michelle responded.

"I can tell he's interested. He may not know it yet, but he is."

Michelle smiled and bit her lower lip. "What about Rick?"

"What about him?"

"You're already trying to get me to jump into bed with Steve. What about you. Rick's only about ten years older than you are. Why don't you two hook up?"

"I'm not sure Rick's my type. He's definitely cute, though."

"Hey, it's only one night, right? After tonight, they'll be backpacking in the mountains somewhere," Michelle prodded.

Sally gave her a dry glance, cocking her head to the side. "So you *are* interested in Steve. Good girl. You had me worried there for a second."

"I'm not rushing into anything."

"Who said anything about long-term? Just let me know what that stomach feels like pressed on top of you, will you?"

Michelle swatted Sally's thigh.

An hour had passed, and the couples had separated by a short distance. Steve joined Michelle atop the Sloth Boulder to have some water while Rick was guiding Sally through a maze of boulders to the south.

"Tell me more about Austin."

"You've never been there before?" Steve asked.

"No. It looks like a great place, though. I've seen all the Chamber of Commerce stuff."

"It really is a great city."

"Everyone tells me I'll love it there."

"Well, it's not anything like Portland. And it's definitely not Yosemite, but yes, it is a great town."

"I'd heard stories about how hot and humid it gets in the summer, even before you mentioned it at dinner."

"It can be that," Steve acknowledged, then launched into a short litany of 'must see, must do' things. "It's a college town. Vibrant. A lot of high-tech companies. It's the state's capitol, and while it does get hot, it's not nearly as humid as Houston and other cities nearer the Gulf of Mexico."

Michelle hung on every word, unsure whether to focus on the description being given or the person giving it.

Steve could tell she was a good listener.

"Well, when I get there, you'll have to show me around."

"I'd be happy to be your tour guide, but do you cook?"

"Do I cook? What the hell is that supposed to mean?"

"Well, I just want to know if I am going to get dinner out of this deal when you come to Texas?"

"Forget if *I* cook. Do *you* cook? Wait, let me rephrase that. Do you cook well?"

Steve stammered intentionally. "Yuh -yes. Yes, I do."

"Good, it's a date. Dinner at your house when I get to Texas. That is, if I get the job."

"From what I understand, the odds are pretty good. You have a very good reputation in the underwriting circles of both offices."

"Really?" She acted surprised. The news made her smile, not because of the compliment, but because Steve's words confirmed the fact that he had been talking about her with Rick, and that she had a good shot at getting the job. *Maybe he is interested,* she thought.

Michelle unscrewed the top of her water bottle and took a drink before continuing, "When I first heard of the opening, I wasn't too sure I'd even put my hat into the ring. After HR told me the move would allow me to move up in WESIC and that I would get a decent increase in pay, I decided to go for it." She paused. "Then I heard from Rick that the great Steve Latham was down there! I mean, how on earth could I pass up such an opportunity?" she giggled.

"Yeah, right," he said.

"You think you guys would be up for a hike after lunch?" Michelle asked.

"Definitely. What did you have in mind?"

"I'm up for pretty much anything. Hey, here comes Rick and Sally. Let's see what they're up for."

"Hey, you guys! Where did you disappear to?"

"We did some great boulders," Sally replied," and you should have seen these other guys on this huge boulder called Midnight Lightning. It was amazing how gymnastic they were. Absolutely incredible."

"Steve and I were thinking about doing a hike this afternoon. You guys up for it?"

"I think we might pass. I'm still a bit sore, and Sally wants to check out the Sequoias at Mariposa Grove."

Sally nodded.

"What were you thinking about doing?" Rick asked.

"Not sure," Steve replied.

"Why don't you two hike up the Four Mile Trail to Glacier Point? Sally and I will play botanists for the afternoon, and we can hook up later at the Awahnee for dinner. Say eight o'clock?"

When Michelle saw Sally winking at her, she said, "What do you think, Steve?"

"Fine with me, but do you have bad knees?"

"No. Why?"

"The uphill hike won't be too bad, but the descent is four miles of knee-pounding switchbacks."

"I'm game if you don't think it's too tough for me."

"You won't have any problem," Rick said. "It gets a little warm starting out in the middle of the day like this, but the trail moves into a gully that is pretty shaded. And the views on this trail are some of the best."

Sally chimed in, knowing that this would be the best chance for her friend to spend some alone time with Steve before they left, "It's a done deal. You do a hike with Steve, I'll go with Rick to the trees, then you and I can play tour guide to each other later in the week for these two spots while these mountain men look for bears in Too-la-mee or Taw-la-mee or however-the-hell-you-pronounce-it."

Steve shrugged his shoulders. "I guess it's just us, Michelle. Let's grab a couple of sandwiches from the lodge store to take with us. I'll get a pack and a couple of things from my car, since it's right across the street. Do you have a change of clothes in your daypack?" he asked.

"Raincoat, shorts, T-shirt, socks."

"Perfect. This isn't a long hike, but the weather can change in a minute. We don't want to have to haul ass in order to get back in time for dinner."

Rick put in his suggestions. "Sally, what do you say we grab some lunch at the lodge? Afterward, we can make reservations at the Awahnee and head over to the Grove."

"Okay." She looked at Steve and Michelle, "You two have fun, and we'll see you tonight."

"Eight o'clock sharp," Michelle replied.

They strolled together from the slabs and parted ways in the lodge parking lot. Steve picked up a pair of sunglasses, his camera, and a baseball cap from the Porsche. In his room he switched to his larger daypack and filled four quart-sized water bottles from the faucet. They would be glad to have the water to offset the effects of the warmer temperatures in the valley where there would be no wind to speak of.

Walking with Michelle from the cabin to the lodge store, Steve asked, "What kind of sandwich would you like?"

"As long as it isn't vegetarian, I'll eat anything."

Steve picked out a couple of turkey sandwiches from the cooler along with a couple of small bottles of water as backups to the gallon of water in his pack. He paid the attendant and led Michelle to one of the concrete benches in front of the lodge.

"We can catch the shuttle here and get off near the trailhead, unless you'd rather walk."

"I'm sure the hike will give us more than our share of exercise for the afternoon."

"No argument there."

A few minutes later the shuttle pulled up, and they got on.

The young driver cautioned everyone as they boarded the bus to watch their step. He was obviously exercising his authority as a means of showing off for the group of teenage girls seated on both sides of the aisle just behind him. Steve and Michelle took seats together on the right side, three rows behind the giggling teens.

As the driver pulled the door closed, in true train-conductor style he announced, "Next stop, Yosemite Village!"

The young girls seemed to hang on every word.

Michelle glanced at Steve, wide eyed and with just a trace of a smile as if to say, "Wow, we are in the presence of real authority!"

Steve mimicked the driver by giving her a crisp salute with two fingers just above his right eyebrow.

They both chuckled.

After exiting the shuttle, Steve once again imitated the driver with over-exaggerated hand motions and sense of importance, "This part of our journey will take us over the Swinging Bridge to Southside Drive. The trailhead is one quarter mile west. Please take advantage of the facilities as there are none on the trail."

Michelle laughed as he finished the announcement.

"This is going to be so much fun! And the scenery is just breathtaking. I'll bet it's absolutely gorgeous here in winter."

"It is. Traveling around here in the winter can be treacherous, though," Steve added.

Steve pointed to a group of outcroppings opposite Sentinel Rock and said, "Those are Cathedral Rocks. On the other side is Bridalveil Falls." Looking up from the base to the summit, he nodded, "And that's Sentinel Rock. Glacier Point is beyond that. Wait 'til you take in the view from up there."

"Are you sure we'll have enough time to get there and back?" Michelle had a concerned look on her face.

Steve glanced at his watch. "It's eleven-ten now. Average time to get there is three or four hours. And the descent will be much faster. It could start getting dark on us near the end of the descent. Do you have a flashlight?"

"Actually, I do."

"Good, I think I have a headlamp and an extra small flashlight as a backup." Steve used a tree to support himself as he stretched his legs. He alternated pulling his right leg up and behind his back, then his left, giving his thigh muscles a good stretch.

"You look like you're warming up to go for a run. Should I be worried?"

"Just workin' out the kinks from yesterday. You wouldn't know just yet how it feels to be getting old."

"Oooh, you do know how to compliment a girl, don't you? Very smooth, Mr. Latham."

The Four Mile Trail led them by Sentinel Rock and then on to Glacier Point. They made it past Union Point in less than two hours. Michelle kept up with ease, but Steve could tell she wasn't used to the rapid gain in altitude. They decided to stop for lunch and a brief rest.

"Let's eat! I'm starved!"

"Me, too." Michelle had already slipped out of her backpack.

"How are your legs holding up?"

"So far, so good. We'll see how much energy I have left when we get to the top. I may have to call a cab."

"Actually, they do have a bus pickup near the point."

"I'm fine." Michelle took a bite out of her sandwich. "Mmm. Now that tastes good. Why is it that everything tastes so much better outdoors?"

"Because most of the time when you're outdoors, you're also having fun."

"Touché."

Michelle took a sip of Gatorade from a bottle she had pulled out of her pack

"So, if you do get the job in Austin, when would you start?"

"As soon as they want me to."

"Sounds like you've got to make your decision pretty quickly."

"Yeah, but as I said earlier, they've got to offer me the job before I can make plans to move. Jesus, those HR people wait until the very last minute before deciding or implementing anything it seems. I found out the day before we left that I had another web-based interview. I had to reschedule it for when I get back. I can get everything packed and moved, no problem, but I didn't want them to feel they would be rushing me and use that as an excuse to give the job to someone else."

"That shouldn't be a problem. After all, they're a 100-year old company that moves like one, so I wouldn't worry about them making any snap judgments."

"Good point."

"Will they include a relocation package if you get the job?"

"Yeah, definitely, or I wouldn't even consider moving. It would cost me over ten grand to move."

"If you do get the job, let me know if there is anything I can do for you when I get back."

"I just might take you up on that." Michelle winked at him and smiled.

Steve had polished off about a third of his bottle of water but noticed that Michelle hadn't even drunk a quarter of her Gatorade. "I think we overdid it yesterday. I'm dehydrated a bit."

"How long did you guys climb?"

"We were at it most of the day. I can sure feel it. It's been a while since I climbed anything of length outside of Austin."

"You look like you can handle it." She squeezed his bicep and smiled. There was a pause in the conversation before Michelle continued. "So tell me about you. All we've been talking about up to this point is my situation. What about you? Ever married? Kids? Girlfriend back home?"

"Married once; divorced a while back. No kids. No girlfriend at the moment. How 'bout you? Ever married?"

"No, I broke up about six months ago with the man I thought I would marry. It only took five years for me to figure that one out."

"What happened? That is, if you don't mind me asking?"

"Not at all. We had lived together for the last three years. He worked as an engineer for a high-tech company and made a lot of money, so we didn't have any financial problems. We just got comfortable and lazy in the relationship, to the point where we had a better time apart than we did together, so I broke up with him. We were opposites in many ways. But here I go again about me. How did your relationship break up?"

"My wife was having an affair."

"You're kidding!"

"I think she had some issues to work through. I thought that she was missing her family when we moved from Portland to Texas, but instead it was a Portland attorney that she missed."

"Bitch!"

Steve smiled, surprised by the abruptness of her comment.

"I'm sorry. I don't even know her. . ."

"No, you hit the nail on the head. I couldn't have said it better myself."

"So, why aren't you seeing anyone now?"

"The four letter word. Work."

"Now that's a cop-out, don't you think?"

"I've been practically living at work for the past three years. I suppose I could date more. I've gone on a few dates, but most of the people I have the opportunity to meet, work in my area which can be inconvenient, especially if you want something casual and they want something more."

"I see what you mean." Michelle took another gulp of Gatorade and stuffed the sandwich wrapper and bottle back into her pack. "Well, are you ready to make the top?" She motioned at the trail.

"Yes, ma'am." Steve replied.

They kept a leisurely pace, continuing to converse, getting to know more about each other, and arrived at Glacier Point within an hour.

"Look at this view!" Michelle exclaimed. "It's spectacular."

"I thought you'd like this." Steve pointed out the notable formations from their towering vantage point—the Awahnee Hotel, Half Dome, El Capitan, Yosemite Falls—as Michelle clicked away with her camera.

"God, this is so beautiful," she said reverently.

As they wandered around the summit of Glacier Point, it wasn't long before time began slipping away from them. Steve looked at his watch. "Wow, it's almost 4:00. We'd better start down soon so we can get back before dark and have time to clean up for dinner."

"Let me get a picture of you, first." She had Steve stand atop a boulder with Half Dome in the background.

"Now it's your turn," he said and duplicated the shot. "You'll want this as proof for any nonbelievers."

"Let's get one of both of us. Stand back up here until I can get this camera set up."

Jumping from the boulder, she trotted to another rock where she found a perch for the camera, set the timer, and then ran to get in place beside Steve. When he put his arm around her waist, she moved closer to his side, putting her arm around him, and leaned her head snugly against him. They smiled like Cheshire cats until the camera finally clicked.

Steve paused momentarily, not releasing his grip from her waist. She turned to him as a gust of wind blew a few strands of hair into her face. He softly brushed them away with his fingertips. Michelle reached up with her right hand and gently pulled his head down, bringing his lips to hers for a long, deep, wet kiss.

CHAPTER TWELVE

BY THURSDAY, DETECTIVE KELLY hadn't garnered much new information about Miller Walker, other than the fact that he was a quiet man who not surprisingly kept to himself. Known well by only a few of his neighbors, Kelly was able to locate two families who did know, like, and respect the bookkeeper. One was the Dennis family, an elderly couple who lived next door, on the garage side of Miller's home. According to Mr. Dennis, he and Miller used to refinish furniture together regularly in his garage, a hobby that they had practiced much less frequently over the last three years.

Kelly did confirm that Miller Walker had lived in the small, modest home in an older part of Austin within walking distance of the University, for most of his life. Tax records showed that after the death of his parents, Walker inherited the unassuming residence when he was in his early twenties. Shortly after completing his university education, he had married his high-school sweetheart Natalie. The timing of the inheritance proved fortunate, giving the newlyweds a home that was paid for.

The house had remained much the same as it had been when Miller's parents had lived there, a small but comfortable home in the middle of Forty-fifth Street. The majority of the homes around it were older and smaller, but it was a prime location and many homes in the area had already been remodeled. This part of town had experienced a Renaissance in recent years, and its close proximity to The University had made the area somewhat recession proof. To the delight of local real estate agents, many houses were snatched up within days of being put on the market because of the influx of people moving to Austin for jobs in the booming high-tech industry. The homes on Forty-Fifth Street were especially in demand because they sat on large lots. Also, the street was one of only a few in the area that had an alley.

Kelly had dug up some interesting facts about Walker's youth. He had been a great high-school football player until he had torn a ligament in his knee early during his senior year. As a tight end, he was a bit short at 5' 10" but was still being actively scouted by several schools in the South prior to his injury. No longer able to fulfill his dream of playing college ball, he focused his energy on scholastics and earned an academic scholarship to Texas.

Kelly couldn't believe the college yearbook photos were of the same portly man he had seen in the morgue just a few days earlier. Even though the body was badly burned, it still seemed as though these were two completely different individuals.

One thing Kelly was able to determine was that since divorcing Natalie, Miller had become more reclusive. According to some colleagues, it seemed that being around anyone for more than a few minutes, perhaps a class period at best, was painful to him. It was around this same time that he had really begun to let himself go physically, gaining an extreme amount of weight.

One characteristic that acquaintances brought up was Miller's Spartan approach to dressing. Kelly confirmed this while examining Walker's closets. Damaged more by smoke and water than by the explosion, the closet in his master bedroom held only three suits, all of the same inexpensive brand and same cut. The only differentiating feature was their color. One was navy; one was black with a charcoal pinstripe; one was dark gray with an ash-gray pinstripe. Kelly also found only three pairs of slacks—navy, black, charcoal gray. Three sport coats coordinated with the slacks.

The ties were all dark and plain with little or no pattern. Several pairs of black socks and several pairs of navy blue had been neatly hung next to the slacks. On the closet floor were two pairs of dress shoes, one black and one dark brown. Finally, there was one pair of tennis shoes, still in the box, as though they had never been worn.

Kelly was determined to keep pushing on this case because he knew something wasn't right. With Walker's athletic background and all that money in the garage, why wasn't he able to pull himself up by the bootstraps or at least pay someone to help him?

The funeral service was held Saturday morning at 10:00. Detective Baumgartner attended with Kelly. Both were surprised by the number of guests in attendance.

"I thought this guy didn't have any friends?"

"You wouldn't think so by the responses we got from his neighbors for the police reports. You didn't tell anyone that over a quarter mill was found in the guy's safe, did you?" Kelly chuckled.

"Yeah, right."

"Well, you know how it is. Old friends and relatives come out of the woodwork when someone dies. Whether guilt or the possibility of an inheritance, either way there's enough motivation to bring the leeches out. Then you have the freaks, the professional funeral-goers that don't have a clue who the deceased person is. Those bastards give me the creeps."

"Me, too."

"And on the rare occasion when we do get lucky, the obvious psycho will show up and give himself away."

"I don't know, man. If this was a homicide, it was so well covered that I couldn't imagine someone capable of this sort of job risking it by showing up."

"You never know."

Baumgartner noticed a green Toyota Camry parked on the other side of the cemetery. He pulled a pair of binoculars from under the seat and focused them. Inside the car was a woman who was visibly upset. He handed the binoculars to Kelly. "Check out the emotional gal in the green Camry."

"Well, well. You'll never guess who that is."

"Who?"

"That's his ex-wife."

"Natalie Walker?"

"Natalie Carlson, now." Kelly played with the knobs to bring her into a tighter focus. "She's a looker, isn't she?" He handed the glasses back to Baumgartner.

"She is pretty. Doesn't seem like Walker would be her type, though."

"I thought it was strange until I saw pictures of him as a kid. He was a stud."

"No kidding?" Baumgartner said. "Another strange thing is that she seems a little too upset for an ex-wife, doesn't she? Maybe those are tears of monetary joy."

"She acted the same way when I interviewed her last week. Man, there are some strange things surrounding this case."

"What do ya think? She have anything to do with it?"

"Hard to say. She is the beneficiary of a half-a-million-dollar insurance policy. And if no surprise next-of-kin shows up to contest the will, she'll get the proceeds from the homeowner's policy and the $250K and stocks that were in the safe. I think we need to have Western States hold off paying her as long as possible and see if she gives herself away, gets antsy, or something."

"Will they do that?"

"Hell yes. Wouldn't you if it could save you five-hundred grand plus? Besides, I know a guy who works there and he may be able to help us out. He's outta town right now, but I'll call the adjuster and tell him not to contact the ex until I have a chance to talk to my friend. We need to squeeze her until the last possible minute."

A long line of mourners took turns placing flowers on the casket. Father Alonso presided over the graveside service. The detectives stayed far enough away to observe without being a distraction.

"That priest looks awfully young."

"He's a great guy," Kelly said. "I go to St. Anne's also. At least, my wife does."

"Now, the truth comes out." Baumgartner smiled.

"Ochoa's his name. He ID'd the body for us. He also gave me the lowdown on Walker's duties at St. Anne's. All of the church's financial records seemed fine to him, and he even let us examine them in case he missed something. Everything was clean."

"You know the chief isn't gonna let us sit on this case much longer if we can't come up with a smoking gun of some kind. Hell, there may not even be one."

"I know, but those numbers have got to mean something big. I just feel it. Why else would he have them and all that cash hidden in his safe?"

"I think you're right. There sure seems to be too many coincidences going on here."

"You know, the toxicology report showed that there wasn't any evidence of gas in his lungs. That isn't necessarily a guarantee that he was dead before the explosion. It could just mean that the ignition occurred before the gas reached the den, but I have a strange feeling. . ."

"Yeah, anything could have ignited the gas. I've read somewhere that even the tiny spark from a telephone ringing could set it off."

"That's true. But for the gas to sit in the house for the length of time it would take to concentrate at that level, Walker would have to have inhaled a considerable amount. You know, I think I'm gonna get my buddy at Western States to help us out in another way. He's the one I was telling you about, the former cop. I'm gonna have him go back and interview Ms. Carlson and act like it's part of the claim settlement protocol. You know, just in case we missed something. He could hand-deliver her check to her instead of turning that job over to some flunky."

"That's a great idea."

"She was definitely holding back during our interview. Either she killed her husband or knows something about who did. I can feel it."

CHAPTER THIRTEEN

MONDAY MORNING AT 5:30 Steve's alarm clock put a sudden end to a glorious few hours of sleep. He opened his left eye, glared at the glowing red numbers on the radio, and tapped the snooze button. Steve repeated the ritual twice more before finally throwing the sheets aside and sitting up. He rubbed his left calf and noticed both legs were still a bit sore from the trip.

Reaching over to his nightstand, he turned on the lamp and stared at the clock. He was anxious to get back to work, but it was all he could do to get his mind off Michelle. It figures—the first woman to hold his interest in two years lives 1,500 miles away. He hoped she would nail the interview and get the underwriting job in Austin, but tried not to dwell too much on that either.

Steve stood up, yawning and scratching as he lumbered into the bathroom. Switching on the light, he groped for his toothbrush in the ceramic holder below the medicine cabinet. Grabbing the toothpaste, he squeezed out a generous amount and furiously scrubbed his teeth. He caught sight of the foaming lather that poured from the sides of his mouth and laughed, nearly choking on the toothpaste. With his medusa-like hair and the froth spewing from his mouth, Steve spoke to his reflection, "You look exactly like a WESIC client whose claim has been denied!"

Steve could faintly hear the coffee pot starting to brew its elixir in the kitchen as he turned on the cold water and stepped into the shower. He had begun taking cold showers after coming to Texas, feeling that the cold-water ritual was a consistent daily reminder of his beloved Pacific Northwest as well as a damn good way to light a fire under his ass when he was feeling a little sluggish, like he was today. He gasped, and his entire body tensed up until he acclimated to the icy contact. He lathered up his washcloth and speculated what surprises might be queued up on his desk awaiting his attention. That speculation and continued thoughts of Michelle followed him to the office.

The Austin branch of Western States Insurance Company was housed in two eight-story, glass-and-steel buildings that held nearly 1,500 employees. Cut into a hillside off the Capitol of Texas Highway, the buildings sported impressive views of the surrounding area.

Steve braked to a stop at the parking garage entrance and swiped his badge through the card reader. Driving in out of the glare of the morning sun, he was swallowed by the shadowy mass of steel and concrete. On the third parking level, he found a parking space, got out, grabbed his briefcase and a small plastic bag from the passenger seat, and headed down to the WESIC campus. He could still feel a slight sting in his calf and thigh muscles while descending the staircase. Once inside the building he took the elevator to the fourth floor. Heading down the rows of cubicles toward his office at the southeast corner, he met his clerk Amy, approaching with an armful of case files.

"Well hello, stranger. Welcome back."

"Thanks, Amy."

She gave him a friendly pat on the shoulder on her way to the copy machine.

Several adjusters, phones or headsets glued to their ears, waved or gave a thumbs-up to acknowledge his return. The floor was buzzing like a big honeycomb, the sounds of keystrokes and muffled voices rising from each cubicle.

Steve had almost reached his office when he noticed Trent, sitting motionless in a cubicle, located on the left outside his office door. The young man seemed to be staring at the wall in front of him.

Steve slowed his gait and watched momentarily, then spoke, "What the hell are you . . .?"

Trent quickly put his left hand up, signaling for Steve to stop talking.

Steve smiled and stood still to see what his young protégé was up to. He had found Trent to be a fantastic worker, prone to an occasional immature bent, but otherwise incredibly productive. Just out of a master's program in business from UT, he was also vastly overqualified for his entry-level adjuster position. However, at 24 he didn't seem sure just yet what career direction he wanted to pursue.

Steve had been coaching Trent on his interviews for the senior underwriting position. Prior to going on vacation, he had mixed emotions about doing so because he knew that this kid would be nearly impossible to replace. Now that he was back and knew Michelle was in the running for the same job, he was even more reticent about giving up Trent. He was just glad the final decision was not his to make.

Trent kept his upper body as still as possible while keeping his eyes trained on the irritating fly that had been dive-bombing him for the last ten minutes. It finally touched down on the wall approximately fifteen feet from him, sitting there, taunting him, daring him to react.

Trent fumbled in the dark recesses of the drawer, located a medium-sized rubber band, and untangled it from a cluster of paper clips. Keeping both hands hidden under the desk, he hooked the elastic band under the fingernail of the index finger on his right hand. With his left hand, Trent pulled the band taught, then fully extended his right arm. He zeroed in on the fly, which hadn't budged from its original spot on the wall.

The missile flew across the room.

The fly fell limply to the floor.

"Impressive," Steve commented in a sarcastic tone. "Good to see you're still working hard."

"Hey, dude! Welcome back!" Trent spun around in his chair and stood up in order to shake Steve's hand. "Sorry about that. That damn fly has been screwing with me since last week. I couldn't take it anymore. It figures he finally decides to sit still when you show up."

"Don't worry about it. You continue to amaze me with these previously undisclosed talents."

"It appears that you made it back in one piece."

"Yeah, it was nice. The weather was incredible. We did some really great routes."

"Did ya take any photos?"

"Rick took a few."

"Cool, I can't wait to see 'em." Trent had been taking climbing lessons with a local guide service, hoping to go on a climb with Steve sometime in the near future.

"Anything blow up while I was gone?"

"Funny you should use that expression."

"What do you mean?"

"Something, or rather someone, did blow up while you were gone. Literally."

"Really?"

"Yeah, one of our insureds apparently left the gas on for one of the burners on his stove top and accidentally blew himself up. Bad pilot light or something."

"Bummer."

"Way bummer. Dan Griffin called to take you to the site. Since you were out, he took me instead."

"That's great! Should have been a good experience for you."

Trent stood up and leaned toward Steve's ear. He talked quietly, so no one else could hear, "Dude, it was awesome. They uncovered a butt load of cash and a bunch of papers out of a floor safe hidden in the guy's garage."

"No kidding?"

"Yeah, man. It was like something you'd see in a movie. I got to meet the C&O guys and everything. God, this is so much better than underwriting."

Steve chuckled. "When did the loss occur?"

"About a week and a half ago."

"Anything suspicious?"

"A couple of things. The first thing is that we've got a half-million in life insurance on this guy, and the beneficiary is his ex-wife."

"Is she alive?"

"Yeah. Pretty strange, isn't it?"

"That's not necessarily unusual. Sometimes they forget to change beneficiaries after a divorce."

"Yeah, but we have it in our files that one of our agents called to advise him about it for its renewal each of the last two years, and he still wanted to leave her on as primary beneficiary. And. It's in our files that he didn't want to let her know about it."

"Maybe he didn't want the divorce."

"Dan said that he was the one that filed for it."

"Stranger things have happened. Is she a suspect?"

"I dunno, dude. You're getting over my head on that. You'll have to call Dan and find out if he's heard anything from the cops."

"What's the second thing you were talking about?"

"I don't know if it's anything, but it must be important if the guy had it in his safe."

"What's that?"

Trent looked around once more to make sure nobody could hear him. "Dan told me not to tell anyone but you. Apparently, there was a weird list of numbers on sheets of paper inside an envelope, along with a thumb drive that contained the same info. I haven't seen 'em myself. Dan got the info from Detective Kelly."

"You met Andy? How's that rat-bastard doing?"

"He was really cool."

"Don't believe a word he says," Steve joked. "I'm kidding. He's a great contact in the department for us, as well as a damn good friend to a lot of us here in the office. "

"I think Dan may already have a copy of the numbers for you. I put the file on your desk."

"Claims already referred it to us?"

"Yeah."

"I'd be surprised if Dan has any of the police info in the file already, unless Kel needs our help on something. The cops rarely give out that kind of info until the case is closed."

"Dan wanted you to call him as soon as you got back. I don't think that they found anything unusual with the fire, but because of the value of the loss and the unusual stuff in the safe. . ."

"It does sound a little odd."

"It gets better."

"How's that?"

"I reviewed all the info we had on Walker's ex-wife. That's the insured's name, Miller Walker. And I found out she lives in Douglas Creek!"

"Douglas Creek? Texas?"

"Yeah, can you believe it? And it gets better still."

"How?"

"Get this. She bought my grandparents' old home from the people my parents sold it to."

"Really? Small world, huh?"

"I swear I couldn't believe it either. She actually bought the old house a couple of years ago, right after she got divorced, and turned it into a bed and breakfast."

"Tell you what, let me go through my mail and get caught up, and I'll give Dan a call."

"Gotcha, boss. Good to have ya back."

Steve turned and opened the door to his office, switching the lights on as he went in. There was a big welcome-back banner draped against the back wall; Amy had been decorating again. Steve usually didn't care for the attention, but with the way his vacation had gone, the damn thing could stay up permanently for all he cared.

Setting the bag and his briefcase down on the computer table beside his desk, he looked up at the wall, staring at the picture hanging alongside his college diplomas. He and Rick were encased in puffy down jackets and Gore-Tex atop Mount Shasta. Both had enormous grins on their hooded faces. He flashed back momentarily to that time before sitting down to look over the accumulated work on his desk.

Steve punched in the code on his telephone to update his voice mail and retrieve any direct messages that Amy hadn't screened. He looked at the framed picture on his desk while waiting for his messages. It contained a real estate ad that he had cut out of a magazine. He had always wanted to own an isolated place of his own, and this Hill Country ranch, or one like it, was something he had been saving for. Although it would likely sell long before he could afford it, Steve called the agent every three months or so to confirm it was still available. Six hundred acres, a small cabin, and three stock ponds—what it lacked in amenities, it made up for in beauty and solitude. This was the motivation Steve needed to come to work every day. One more year, maybe two and he would be able to afford this ranch, or one very much like it.

"Hi, Steve. It's Whitley. Welcome baaaack. You'd better call me the second you get in, Mister Three-weeks-vacation! Bosco and I missed you terribly. We've had a wonderful time since you were away. I'm ready to claim him as my dog now because I'm sure he won't recognize you. Talk to you soon. Bye."

Steve smiled and thought, *I am really lucky to have that woman as a friend.*

He grabbed the plastic bag containing the T-shirt he had purchased for her in Yosemite and placed it on the filing cabinet beside his desk.

Glancing at his bookshelves, he caught sight of the picture of Whitley, himself, and Bosco taken at the company picnic the year before. When she had found out he didn't have any pictures of his "only child" at the office, she had framed it for him. Of course, Whitley thought the idea of having her picture in front of him every day might also have some positive ramifications.

Steve lifted the legal-sized envelope from his In-box, his interest piqued by Trent's debriefing about his first outing with Dan and the Cause and Origin team. He couldn't remember the last time a residential gas explosion like this had occurred. Pulling a sheaf of papers from the envelope, Steve saw that Dan had noted the particulars of the case in a handwritten letter.

"Welcome back!

"This should help you get right back into the swing of things! In your absence, I took Trent with me to the scene. (He's quite the go-getter!)

"It appears that the insured, Miller Walker, evidently left the gas to his stove on. He must have had a faulty pilot light. It appears to me from the initial reports that the cause was accidental. The dwelling is a complete loss as the damage from the explosion was extensive, not to mention the smoke damage to the contents. Several structures around the dwelling sustained damage as well.

"The insured had replacement cost coverage on the dwelling at a limit of $235,000. Contents were covered up to $80,000. He had a liability limit of $300,000 with $5,000 medical payments coverage limit. He also had a $500,000 term policy. I estimate that the total value of this loss could reach $900,000 or more—including the cost of collateral damage to neighboring structures. There were some minor injuries suffered by his next-door neighbors, but in my first discussion with them I found them to be very cooperative. I feel that we can settle their claim under the medical payments limit of $5,000. The damage to their home was the most extensive of all the neighboring structures. My estimate would be in the neighborhood of $27,000.

"The C&O team found a floor safe during their investigation. The contents were turned over to the police."

Dan had placed a large yellow post-it note next to this sentence. Steve knew it was done this way so that the information mentioned on it wouldn't become a permanent part of the claims file. It read, "According to Det. Kelly (and this is confidential info), the safe contained $250,000 in cash—all in $100 bills, some stock certificates worth about $37,000, a computer flash drive, three pages of numbers, a will listing his ex-wife as the only beneficiary, and a couple of old rings (possibly family heirlooms). The discovery of such a large sum of money will likely require an IRS investigation. As you know company policy dictates that we must establish that the proximate cause of death wasn't due to any illegal activity before settling the claim. That, in and of itself, could negate any death proceeds from the life insurance policy."

Steve stuck the note in his desk drawer and continued reading the formal report.

"As I mentioned earlier, we haven't found anything that would lead us to think that it was anything other than an accident, at least not to date. Further, company policy mandates that settlements of this size must be investigated, and concurrence of the findings must involve at least two departments. I will definitely need your help on this one to push it through within the 90-day maximum. (You know how slow the government can be!)

"Please contact me with any questions, and keep me abreast of your investigation into this loss if you decide to pursue it.

"Good luck,

"Dan"

Steve was struck by the contents of the floor safe, especially the cash. He wondered why someone would have that much cash lying around, even if it was in a floor safe. It seemed peculiar that an accountant, of all people, would have a mistrust of banks, so he made a note to check out Walker's bank accounts and financials. *Maybe this guy was involved in some kind of extortion plot,* he thought.

The pages of numbers really didn't draw his interest nor did the remainder of the contents. He reached over and entered Dan's extension.

"Dan Griffin."

"Mr. Dan!"

"Hey, guy! Welcome back! I guess you're calling about the envelope?"

"Yeah, as a matter of fact, I am."

"First things first—How was your trip?"

"It was great!"

"I take it you got a lot of rest and relaxation."

"Yeah, I did, and I squeezed in some backpacking with Rick. As much as I hate to admit it, I really needed to get away."

"I'm not gonna say I told you so."

"I know. I know. I should have listened to you a year ago. But now I'm back, and my batteries are recharged."

"Welcome back to the real world. You've reviewed the package, obviously."

"Yeah."

"In the past week, we haven't found anything remarkable, at least nothing concrete that would definitely indicate foul play," Dan hesitated.

"Well, I'll need a complete rundown from C&O when you get the report from them."

"I've got it on my desk."

"Any new items to add to the floor safe list?"

Nothing. I'll get you a copy within the hour."

"Good by me. What's your gut reaction?"

"Gut reaction?" Dan paused. "I think the dumb sonofabitch didn't completely turn off the gas, so he blew himself up. That's what I think. But, you know, you gotta come up with that on your own."

"What's your spin on the cash?"

"I deal with what caused whatever it was that happened. How should I know about what somebody was thinking or who might have had a bone to pick with him. That's your bailiwick. Besides, what the hell are you asking me for? That's why they pay you the BIG bucks!" Dan roared with laughter.

"Lowly, my ass." There was no doubt in Steve's mind that Dan Griffin was the best adjuster on staff of any company he'd ever worked with.

"Seriously though, Steve, I honestly feel that there's some connection between those numbers and all that cash. I don't know if this guy was small time and had just been skimmin' money from his clients for the past twenty years, or whether he got himself up to his eyeballs in some serious shit he couldn't handle. Call it a gut feeling, intuition, whatever. I just have a feeling in my heart of hearts that they're connected."

"Any thoughts on what the numbers mean?"

"I couldn't say for sure. Maybe he listed his clients in some sort of code or something. Crazy lookin' things aren't they."

"Yeah, maybe they reference bank accounts or something. That would explain the dollar amounts beside them."

"I don't know, but there is definitely a piece of that puzzle yet to be found. If you come up with any bright ideas, let me know if I can do any legwork for ya. I'd be happy to help out."

"I appreciate it. How soon do you think we'll be ready to call a meeting?"

"I'll be ready tomorrow, but how about if I give you another week or two to get everything caught up from your trip and review the case thoroughly?"

"Okay, I'll get Amy to set it up in the next couple of weeks."

"I guess with the size of this loss, it means we'll have to invite Rafter Head?"

"Afraid so."

"Goddammit, doesn't that sonofabitch have to play golf on that day?"

"I don't know if he will even be in town, but I'll have Amy call everyone. Any particular time that would be better for you?"

"Any time is fine, but afternoon is better. If I'm gonna take a nap, I'd rather do it then, after all the mornin' chores are done. Know what I mean?"

"I gotcha. I promise you this won't be a repeat of Tracy's last underwriting meeting. I'll keep this one on track."

"Jesus, when is that pot-licker gonna retire? He's as worthless as tits on a boar hog."

"I don't know." Even though Steve agreed with Dan's assessment of Underwriting Manager Bill Tracy, he held his tongue. "I'll have Amy call and e-mail everyone with a confirmation, and I'll look for that C&O report later on today."

"You betcha! Talk to you soon."

After hanging up with Dan, Steve began to put his list to paper.

1. Check Walker's bank account(s) and financials—with Andy Kelly if necessary
2. Did he owe a lot of money? any money?
3. Could he be involved in any illegal activity?—skimming, extortion, etc. and if so, why?

4. Check out C&O report
5. Review items found in safe—numbers, etc.
6. Why was Natalie Carlson still his primary beneficiary?
7. Check for any complaints with CPA associations

He figured this would be a good list with which to start.

Steve thought about his earlier conversation with Trent and the fact that Natalie Carlson was still the primary beneficiary. He needed to try to ascertain why this was so, especially since Mr. Walker had initiated the divorce. The divorce was another item to add to his list, as was the fact that Ms. Carlson had purchased Trent's boyhood home in Douglas Creek.

An outside call came directly to his private second line. The caller ID system showed the number, but it wasn't one that Steve recognized. Probably a wrong number.

"Hello."

A man's raspy voice came on the line. "Hello. Mr. Latham."

"Yes."

"Mr. Steve Latham."

"Yes, it is."

"World-class mountaineer and super insurance sleuth?" Laughter. It was Andy Kelly.

"Hey, how did you know I was back?"

"I called 'Lieutenant Dan,' and he told me where I could find you, Forrest!"

"Boy, I'm sure glad the City of Austin has guys like you at the helm. We'll all sleep better at night knowing you're on the streets protecting us." They both laughed. "How are ya, bud?"

"I'm doing fine. How was your trip?"

"Had a great time, but as usual too short."

"Hell, you were gone for a month, weren't you?"

"Just about. So what's up?"

"We don't have much right now. I've interviewed quite of few of the neighbors, a few distant relatives, and his ex-wife, but nothing earth-shattering has come out of it."

"Really?"

115

"Yeah, and that's partially why I called. You guys have ninety days to pay on the life insurance policy. Right?"

"Yeah. Why?"

"I had an idea."

"That's a first. Should I notify the media?"

Andy chuckled. "I don't know that it warrants media coverage just yet, you smart ass, but I do know one thing. Natalie Carlson, your insured's ex-wife, has been acting really strange. When I interviewed her right after his death, she was really evasive with her answers, and I'm at a loss as to why. She came across as a very smart lady, but I have a feeling she was playing us."

"You think she's smart enough to have something to do with the explosion?"

"Possibly. We verified the fact that she graduated from the university with a psychology degree. Whether or not she was putting that education to use, only time will tell. Another strange thing was that we spotted her at the cemetery during Walker's funeral."

"That's not necessarily odd."

"No, except that she didn't attend the funeral. She wasn't at the church ceremony, nor was she up front graveside. She sat in her car at a pretty good distance from all the festivities, crying her eyes out. Call me paranoid, but she was way too upset for an ex-wife. Aside from the grief, it really looked like she was feeling guilt or something close to it."

"That makes sense."

"That's why I wanted to ask you a favor."

"Shoot."

"There is a good possibility this case will grind to a halt if we can't find any supporting evidence that the explosion was anything more than accidental. You guys haven't already notified her that she's getting a check have you?"

"No, we haven't."

"Good! Here's what I was thinking. Because of your background with interrogating suspects, I thought you and Dan could do a double whammy. Why don't both of you deliver the insurance check to her in person. It might give you another opportunity to pull something out of her."

"That's a great idea. What else do you have so far?"

"You get the copy of the coroner's report I sent to Dan?" Kelly asked.

"Yeah," Steve replied. "I'm reading it as we speak. Death was ruled accidental."

"So he says. By the way, keep that sucker hidden. If the chief finds out I've sent you any more of these, he'll have my ass."

"Dan sent the report to me in a confidential, inter-office envelope. Nobody else saw it."

"Did you see the part about the blunt force trauma to the right side of his head?"

"Not yet, but I'm getting to it." Steve flipped through the pages until he found the head profile diagram. "Yeah, here it is. 'A perfectly symmetrical fracture to the right side of the skull. Only his right pupil was dilated.' Hmm, lucky for us there wasn't more damage to his body from the explosion and fire, or we wouldn't have been able to review anything but ash."

"No kidding."

"Did you guys or C&O find anything in the debris that could have caused this?"

"Absolutely nothing."

"You think there's a chance someone could have killed him first?"

"As good a chance of catching something you wouldn't want from a drug-using Haitian prostitute."

"I take it that's a yes?"

"You insurance guys are a smart bunch, aren't you! Seriously though, you can see the coroner's diagram on the report, but you should have seen the x-rays of his skull. It looked like someone used a ball-peen hammer and gave him a perfectly placed thump on the cranium. There was a small, round depression right on his temple with radial fractures emanating directly and evenly from the center. Just like ya dropped a rock into a pool of water."

"Really?"

"Yeah, I mean, look at it this way. First, you've got a fat guy in a recliner. But he wasn't reclined in the chair. He was sitting upright, okay? If he supposedly fell asleep in his chair, why wasn't he reclined in it? When I interviewed his ex, she said that when they were married, he always fell asleep in that chair, but he was always reclined. And he only fell asleep after he watched the ten o'clock news. Ten years of marriage, always the same routine. Now, flash forward to that night a couple of years after they divorce. According to the coroner, he drinks a few beers, chows a ham sandwich that could feed a small nation and suddenly decides he wants to boil some water on the stove? For what, hot tea or something? Bullshit!

"Second, he has no trace evidence of gas in his lungs. Granted, the natural gas is gonna collect at ceiling level for the most part. But unless the explosion was instantaneous, he's gotta be breathing in some of it right?"

"Right."

"So he's gotta be dead since he didn't breathe any of this in."

"One would think so."

"I know so. Third, the cause of death was ruled to be accidental from blunt force trauma to the right side of the head with a small but perfectly spherical object that is nowhere to be found."

"And you'd think with the force generated by the explosion, any object that could make this kind of impression would have imbedded itself completely in his skull or at least show up somewhere in the vicinity of the body."

"Exactly. It had to be small, a round or curved object. Christ, it would have blown right through his head! No way this death could have been caused by a piece of wood. But I tell ya, I'd like to take a piece of wood to our coroner and beat some sense into him. Accidental death my ass."

"Could it have been a softer object that caused the damage? Something that might have been destroyed or disintegrated? Maybe burned up in the ensuing fire?"

"I guess that's a possibility, but what are the odds? And what would the object be? Something like a marble?"

"What about a chard of something? Maybe a golf ball?"

"A golf ball is too big to have caused the fracture, not to mention that Walker was entirely too big to have any reason to be within a hundred miles of a golf course. The odds of a guy that overweight making it through even nine holes are about as good as me gettin' a blow job from my ex-wife. Impossible!"

"Well said, officer."

"And last but not least, you've got no sign of forced entry. None! The back door was locked, the front door was locked, and the garage was locked. Why? Because, whoever did this, either had a key, or the door in fact was open to allow them entry in the first place, and was locked on the way out. After the murder."

"Makes sense to me. You may have something with this one. You know, I was thinking. . .I actually may have a better way to deliver this policy."

"How's that?"

"I'll take my assistant Trent instead of Dan."

"The kid?"

"Yeah. Did you hear how he ties in with Walker's ex?"

"No."

"She owns a bed and breakfast in Douglas Creek. She converted it from the home that Trent's grandparents used to own. I was thinking that he would be an ideal person to bring. His history in the area might lighten the conversation, you know, put her a little more at ease. Get her talking about the house's history or something while we plant $750K in her lap for the life insurance and the coverage for her newly inherited, albeit destroyed, Austin residence. Maybe she'll slip up and divulge something."

"That's a good idea. You think the kid would be up to it?"

"The next Elliott Ness? Hell yes, he'd be up for it."

"Whatever you think is best. You know I trust your instincts."

"Listen, I was just making a list of things to check out on my end. Have you gotten anything on Walker's financials."

"Yeah, he's clean. Paid all his bills on time. No back taxes due. Nothing."

Steve lined through that entry on his list. "Can you copy me on what you found? I want to indoctrinate Trent into our group and see if he comes up with anything different than we do. You know, new eyes and all."

"I'll courier it over to you today."

"Thanks. What about all the cash in the safe?"

"That's a good question. He definitely made enough money over the years to put that much away. I thought perhaps he didn't want a bank record for some reason, such as drugs or paying off someone. But nothing came up."

"Any deposits being made to his ex-wife's accounts?"

"None, we even checked her relatives' accounts. Nothing. Another theory I had was that Walker was skimming the money from somewhere. He is, or rather was, the bookkeeper at my church. I thought he could have been taking some of the collection plate every Sunday. But I checked it out with our priest, and everything balanced out. I think I even may have met Miller years ago at a church function. If he's the one I remember, he was definitely thinner and a really nice guy. If he was involved in something illegal, he would be the last guy I'd expect. But what else is new?"

"You mentioned interviewing his distant relatives earlier. No possibilities that they could be involved?"

"Aside from his ex-wife, he had no blood relatives within a thousand miles. She is the only beneficiary—on his will and on your policy. As far as we could tell from years' worth of phone records, he's never even called any of them."

Steve lined through the next two items on his list. "Well, you're saving me a lot of legwork on this so far. I appreciate it."

"We aim to please."

"Did you check his background with the licensing agencies for accountants?"

"Yes, and he came out smelling like a rose. Squeaky-clean. I'll copy you on all this that I can."

"It seems all roads point to the ex-Mrs. Walker, so far," Steve said.

"So what do you think about staying on this thing for me until we can get a few more questions answered?"

"Whatta ya mean for you? With nearly a million-dollar payday from our end and knowing those piranhas in Actuary will be chewing on my ass about it, you don't have to twist my arm!"

"I'm going to get you as much additional info as I can from our files."

"I'll do what I can on my end."

"With you buying us the extra time by doing a little more investigation, I think that we'll get to the bottom of this thing. I'll also get with Miller's lawyer and see if I can hold off telling her about the safe's cash, and the house until we get a bit more info. Since you guys are at the mercy of the insurance regulators, you can pay her whatever you see fit from a company perspective. I'd just like to do a bit more digging to see if I can track this money source."

"Sounds good. I'll keep you posted as often as I can."

"Thanks, Steve. Bye now."

"Later."

Steve tapped his pencil eraser on the documents and thought about what he had just been told. The phone interrupted him. He could see on the readout on his phone that it was Trent. "Hey, Trent! I was just going to call you. Could you come to my office?"

"Sure. What's up?"

"We can discuss that when you get here."

"Uh. . .okay. I was just calling to see if you wanted to get some lunch later today, so I could hear a little more about your trip."

"Lunch? We've got a helluva lot more important things to do today than stuff our faces in the cafeteria. I'm sorry to be so blunt, but we need to get your investigative instruction started pronto. So, if you're not too busy playing John Wayne shooting flies off the wall, I'd like you to trundle your ass into my office as soon as you can."

Trent was completely taken aback and remained silent at his end of the connection. Never before had Steve talked this way to him.

Steve paused, waiting for any reaction from Trent, waiting until he felt the silence had lasted long enough. He knew he had him and began to laugh, "Gotcha!"

Trent felt an overwhelming sense of relief. "Damn! They should give me hazardous duty pay to work for you! I'll be right there."

Not long after Steve had hung up, Trent entered his office still blushing.

Steve greeted him, still chuckling. "Sorry about that. I just couldn't resist."

"Damn! You must be rested. That's the first practical joke you've ever played on me."

"Well, this is no joke, my friend. How long has it been since you saw Douglas Creek?"

"The epicenter of all things chicken-fried? It's been a while. Why?"

"We're going to deliver a death claim check to Walker's ex-wife."

"We? Cool! When?"

"I haven't decided, but I want to take our time. I've got to wait until I get the report from C&O and the final okay from the committee. Dan doesn't seem to think there's anything to prevent WESIC from paying the claim. Depending on everyone's schedule in the next couple of weeks, I'm gonna have Amy set up a committee meeting so we can discuss the case. You should sit in on it since you were at the site."

"Sure thing. But if I know you, you didn't call me here just to tell me about the meeting and the fact that we're going to Douglas Creek. You've got something else you want me to do, right?" Trent's face reddened slightly, as if he thought he had overstepped his bounds.

Steve picked up on it right away and smiled. "No, go on. I'm impressed. What would be your first step in this investigation?"

"Well, uh, uh. . .Walker had $250,000 in cash in a floor safe. I'd like to know why. I think I'd want to see everything that was in the safe, to see if one piece might give a clue about another. . ." Trent's voice trailed off. "We should check into his financial statements to see if we can find anything strange."

"That's a good point. I like the way you're thinking. Just remember this one piece of advice when beginning any investigation. Everything is significant until you rule it out."

Trent was absorbing every word. The young man respected his mentor and appreciated his willingness to indoctrinate him into a world about which he still had a great deal to learn.

"I just got off the phone with Detective Kelly," Steve continued. "I want you to look over this claim file from Dan and compile a list of everything we need from APD. I'll compare your list with the info Kelly is couriering over to us and see if you come up with anything he may have missed. I can't stress to you the importance of keeping this privileged info from APD top-secret. Kelly's doing us a favor, and he's agreed to bring you into the loop with Dan and me at my suggestion."

"Thanks," Trent said proudly.

"They should have looked into all of his financials for major debts or recurring payments. I don't mean charge card debts. I mean debts that look suspicious, that sort of thing. Look over everything. If you are not certain about something, bring it to me."

Trent had taken almost a page of notes. There was no doubt in Steve's mind that Trent would do a thorough job in the research task he had just been assigned. Steve held back the fact that Kelly had already checked out virtually every angle because of the items recovered from the safe and looked forward to comparing Trent's natural research instincts with the APD information.

CHAPTER FOURTEEN

MICHELLE SLID HER ACCESS card through the slot located on the doorjamb to gain entry into the Portland office's main conference room. This was to be her final interview for the Senior Underwriter position in Austin. Drawing a deep breath to dispense with the butterflies that had occupied her stomach for the past two hours, she glanced at her wristwatch, which showed she had fifteen minutes more to prepare before the web-based interview would be initiated from Austin.

Taking one of the high-backed chairs across from a large flat-screen monitor, she placed the portfolio containing her interview notes on the conference table directly in front of her. She had taken great pains to record questions she wanted to ask and additional items about notable cases on which she had worked during her tenure in the Portland office. Making a great impression was uppermost in her mind. After reviewing the notes, she waited anxiously.

Ordinarily calm in these situations, Michelle found herself in unfamiliar territory with this bout of anxiety. But she had acquired a new variable that made her desire to move to Austin all the more compelling, a variable quite frankly that she hadn't expected. That variable was Steve Latham.

First to enter the teleconference room was Bill Tracy, in the Austin office. Jan Mitchell, his boss and the underwriting director, entered shortly after him.

"Good afternoon, Bill," she acknowledged as she sat to Bill's right.

"I'm glad we're down to the last interview. I can't wait to get this position filled."

"I agree. It appears Michelle will fit nicely if she is as good in person as she is on paper," she responded as she thumbed through some documents she had printed from Michelle's employee file.

"You sound like you've made up your mind."

"It's up to Michelle to make it or break it on this one, Bill. No other candidate comes close to her."

"Well, you're right. This interview will tell the tale."

Unseen by Bill, a cynical look crept across Jan's face. She had had the unfortunate privilege of attending too many meetings held by Bill and found them to be uncompromisingly dull and tedious because of his monotonous delivery style and unoriginal approach to most topics. She hoped that with George chairing the interview, Bill would be relegated to providing only minor input.

Jan looked at her watch and noticed that it was nearly time to start the meeting. "Is George on his way?"

"He was on a call when I left my office. Should be here soon."

"Okay. Why don't you start us off, Bill, and I'll chime in as necessary."

They sat in front of an elongated semi-circular conference table. The opposite wall held a very large monitor that faced them. Above the monitor sat a camera that sent their images to the conference room in Portland where Michelle sat waiting.

Michelle glanced from her watch up to the monitor as it simultaneously came to life, displaying the images of Bill Tracy and Jan Mitchell seated at their conference room table.

"Good afternoon, Ms. Grayson." Bill's normally monotone voice sounded vaguely human for a change.

Nodding his head toward Jan, he began, "This is Jan Mitchell, Director of Underwriting. Jan is my supervisor."

"It's nice to finally put a face with a name, Michelle," Jan greeted her cheerfully.

"Likewise!" Michelle responded with a smile. "I feel like I already know you."

'Mr. Monotone' continued, "I am Bill Tracy, Manager of Underwriting. George O'Grady is, as you know, the AVP of Underwriting and will be joining us shortly. He's on a call. Since we only have set aside an hour, I think we should go forward." He paused as he leafed through his pages. "I see you have been with WESIC for a period of nine years. You moved from policy-owner services to underwriting three years ago. I also see you have applied for other postings. . .um. . .three postings in the last two years."

"That's correct, Mr. Tracy."

". . .one in claims and. . .one in marketing, and now this one?"

"Yes, sir."

"And I also see that you were offered those first two positions and turned them down."

"That's correct."

"Why?" he asked.

"My primary reason for applying was at the advice of my supervisor, Gwen Waltz."

"Great lady," Jan observed.

"She is indeed. Gwen likes to have her staff prepared for advancement opportunities when they arise. She suggested that I request informational interview status for each of those positions, so that I could go in and learn about the jobs but not be considered a candidate. It was a way for me to get an idea about what other areas of the company were like, as is suggested in our employee manual."

"Right you are," Jan said.

"Neither of us expected that I would be offered a position after an informational interview, much less that it would happen a second time."

"I think that speaks volumes about your reputation in this company."

"Thank you, Jan."

Bill continued his questioning. "Michelle, where do you see yourself in. . .say. . .the next five years?"

"I'd like to be at least an Underwriting Director as a business goal and complete my MBA for my personal goal."

126

"I see you have worked on several, high-profile cases," Bill continued. "We've had some pretty big cases here, too."

"Yes, I've heard," Michelle replied.

"As a senior underwriter, supervision of certain staff members is inherent. To what degree have you worked in a supervisory role?"

Her anxiety had dissipated, and Michelle was becoming much more relaxed. "I am in charge of the Employee Wellness Program, where I have supervised up to 1,200 fellow employees and guests at large events, such as the company picnics and Christmas parties. I have had the pleasure of supervising and training six junior underwriters and up to twelve individuals in special underwriting task forces."

"What have the task forces involved?" Bill continued.

"Taking the initial look into suspected fraud files, insurance-to-value task forces for homeowners' policies, and training seminars for new agents. I especially enjoy being in a supervisory role. In fact, I welcome the opportunity to do it on a more regular basis. I believe that I possess a lot of experience I can pass on to other employees."

"What do you think. . ." Bill was interrupted by the familiar click of the door in response to the swipe of a pass card.

George came through the door and took a seat next to Jan, who sighed with relief, knowing that the interview would move more smoothly now with George at the helm.

Bill continued, "Ms. Grayson, this is George O'Grady."

"Hi, Michelle! Sorry I'm late." He glanced to Jan, then Bill. "I hope these guys haven't been grilling you too intensely."

"Oh, no. . .not at all," Michelle replied with a smile. She looked great on camera, and everyone seemed to notice.

"So, the position requires someone who can work independently and proactively. I've reviewed your employment file and see that you have had excellent reviews. I'm impressed with your tenure. You have exceeded the average of most underwriters."

He turned to Jan. "Have you discussed the relocation package?"

"No, that's next," Jan responded.

"Do you have any more questions, Bill?"

"Yes."

In his typical get-it-done fashion, George ignored Bill's answer and asked, "Michelle, if you were offered the position today, how soon could you be here?"

Michelle was surprised by the question. "As soon as you need me, but I would like to have at least thirty days to tie up loose ends here at the office. I would need to clear out my caseload, set up logistics with movers, pack and drive my car to Texas."

"Okay," George agreed and smiled approvingly. "Bill? Questions?"

Bill picked up where he left off. "I see you have taken the proficiency exams and have scored well. In addition to the exams, what else have you done to increase your knowledge of underwriting in the past year."

"I completed my CPCU designation."

"Congratulations! Good for you!" Jan and George praised her.

Bill continued his questioning. "What do you know about the differences in underwriting policies in the states handled at this office?"

"There aren't any major differences in underwriting a case in any of our states. There are some minor differences among state mandates. . .minimum auto coverage amounts, insurance-to-value requirements, that sort of thing. I was told that this position would be primarily involved with Texas policies. I have thoroughly studied Texas requirements," Michelle caught George smiling reassuringly at Jan, "and have a good understanding of virtually all Texas regulations."

Bill's facial expression never changed. "Do you think you would have any problems working within these regulations?"

"None, sir."

"Have you familiarized yourself with our applications?"

"Yes. Completely."

"I see your underwriting has mostly been P&C. Property and Casualty is markedly different than. . ."

George interrupted, "I'm sorry, Bill, but I think we are all more than aware of and equally impressed with Michelle's credentials. Frankly, a lot of people could meet the requirements of the job on paper. What I'd like you to do, Michelle, is to tell me a little about yourself, your life. Anything you'd like to tell us that we couldn't find on a resume."

"I'd be glad to. Why don't I start at the beginning? I grew up here in Portland. I spent most of my spare time in my youth studying ballet. By the time I was ready for college, I had the opportunity to study dance at Juilliard but opted to get my business degree instead."

"Why did you opt not to continue your dance career?" Bill asked.

George inconspicuously scribbled a note and discreetly passed it under the table for Jan to give to Bill. It simply stated, "NO more questions."

Bill eased back in his chair, content to hand the reins over to George.

Michelle continued, "I was burned out on the dancing. I had participated in the same routine for fifteen years. While all of my friends were dating, going to the beach, going to summer camp, going on vacations, I was dancing. All I could envision was this same lifestyle perpetuating itself for another decade. In my heart I knew I was ready for some new experiences. So I found a small campus in the Blue Ridge Mountains, Roanoke College, where I earned a degree in business. That was, absolutely, the best decision I had made in my life to that point. It opened up a whole new world to me.

"I came back to Portland, applied at Western States, and have been here ever since. When this opportunity came up, it sounded like another chance to gain job as well as life experience by starting a new position in a new city.

"I love it in Portland, and all of my friends are here. But I am definitely ready for a life change, and it's my understanding that the opportunities with WESIC are in Austin, Texas."

"Well said, Michelle. I'm going to need to break away from the meeting. But before I go, I'd like to thank you for your time and for your candid conversation."

"Thank you, Mr. O'Grady."

"You're welcome. And it's George. If you don't mind, I'd like to mute this conversation for about sixty seconds. Sit tight for just a minute."

"Certainly."

George turned off the audio and called Jan and Bill to the side of the room where they couldn't be seen on the monitor.

"Very quickly, Bill, Jan. I think she's answered all of the questions we need to ask. She probably knows more than we do about our policies. I know she's got me sold. Jan, any other candidates that have her qualifications?"

"None even close. In fact, Rick Taylor gave her a very high recommendation."

"Good. Follow through with the interviews of the other candidates as a courtesy to keep Home Office happy, but don't tell them we've picked Michelle until you're through." George looked at his watch. "We have twenty minutes left in this conference room. Offer her the job and tell her to keep her mouth shut about it also, until it's formally announced. Don't want to create an HR issue with the other candidates. Give her whatever bump in salary it takes, as long as it's in the range for her grade level. Explain the relocation package, but give her sixty days to get here instead of thirty. Get a commitment from her today, and throw in an extra week of vacation for her troubles. No way she can tie up everything for a cross country move in a month. Let's also get the moving and relo office to have a rep call her right away."

"Consider it done," Jan said.

"Bill, you come with me. Let's leave this in Jan's hands to close the deal."

"Yes, sir." Bill gathered his notepad from the table.

"Thanks, George. I'll take care of it."

After the men had left, Jan turned on the audio, "Michelle, it appears it's just you and me for the remaining fifteen minutes of our meeting time. Let's talk."

CHAPTER FIFTEEN

AMY HAD SCHEDULED STEVE'S meeting in the senior staff conference room for one o'clock on a Tuesday afternoon, and she had emailed copies of all files to be discussed to the committee members the day before.

Trent was the first to arrive. Other attendees would include Dan Griffin from Claims, Steve Latham from SIU, in-house counsel Jim Vincent, Underwriting Manager Bill Tracy, and Underwriting Director Jan Mitchell.

Because of the size of the loss in the Walker claim, Vice President of Claims Roy Whitton, Vice President of Actuary Milt O'Brien, and Senior Vice President Walter Roeder would also be attending. Well-liked but notoriously late for meetings, Roeder was affectionately known as "Rafter Head" because of the perfectly symmetrical and rectangular bald spot that ran across the top of his head.

A huge, oval, mahogany table occupied the center of the large, rectangular room. The table was surrounded by plush burgundy leather chairs. The mahogany walls and ceiling matched the table. Pictures of past company presidents lined one wall; community awards lined another.

Trent placed his notepad on the table and sat down in one of the chairs. He rubbed his hands across the tightly upholstered armrests and closed his eyes, imagining that one day he would be an executive with perks and a paycheck to match.

Steve walked in and sat next to Trent.

"I could get used to this," Trent said softly.

"You keep bustin' your tail, and it'll be sooner than you think," Steve winked.

The others filtered in one at a time, and Steve introduced Trent to each of them. After everyone except Roeder had arrived and gotten their coffee, the meeting began. Amy was present to take minutes. In Roeder's absence, Roy Whitton assumed the lead position as meeting coordinator. "Okay, let's begin. Dan, what have you got for us?"

"Well, as all of you know by now, our insured, Miller Walker, died last month in total fire loss to a residence located at 4518 Forty-fifth Street here in Austin. You all have copies of the Cause and Origin report in front of you. It appears that Mr. Walker died as a result of injuries sustained during a natural gas explosion due to a faulty pilot light.

"To get everybody up to speed, the short report is that in addition to his residence, which is a total loss, some of his neighbors sustained property damage, and one of his neighbors has some minor bodily injury. There does not appear to be any chance of a lawsuit after discussions with the neighbor. Apparently, they were friends with the deceased and aren't looking to gain from Mr. Walker's demise. We have however, set aside $100,000 in reserve as a precaution. Just in case their minor cuts and bruises get, shall we say, infected."

Everyone in the room chuckled at Dan's joke as he continued.

"We don't have a hard amount yet, but with the life policy of $500,000, it's safe to say that the total loss for this claim will be in the ballpark of $900,000. Any questions so far?"

Roy responded, "I have one, Dan. Have we gotten all of the reports—Medical Examiner, Police, Cause and Origin?"

"Yes. I believe all of them are in your meeting folders and in the file." Dan looked toward Amy who nodded to confirm that she had indeed taken care of this.

"I e-mailed copies to all of you yesterday afternoon," she said quietly, "and hard copies are also in the folders in front of each of you." She went back to taking notes on her laptop.

Steve drew a tolerant breath, unnoticed by anyone, and expanded on Roy's question. "For those of you that haven't read the files, the Medical Examiner and Police reports don't indicate any foul play. C&O found nothing out of the ordinary, that is, if a violent explosion and death are ordinary. I'd recommend that all of you look through your copies of the files and get with Dan and me by the end of the week with any additional recommendations."

Bill Tracy began to shuffle through the folder and said, "I should be able to finish by the end of the week."

"Good, Bill," Steve replied and rolled his eyes inconspicuously at Trent.

Jan Mitchell, Bill's supervisor, gave him a disgusted stare as she answered, "Both of us will have our recommendations to you by the end of the week, Steve."

Jim Vincent cleared his throat, and everyone prepared for an inevitable and lengthy legal discourse. Jim began with his thick Texas drawl. "I haven't completely reviewed the reports, but I can be finished by this afternoon."

"Terrific, Jim."

Walter Roeder opened the conference room door and waddled inside, taking his chair at the head of the large table. His bald spot gleamed from the recessed can lights overhead. In a mock Texas drawl he asked, "You can be finished with what by this afternoon, Tex?"

Polite laughter reverberated in the closed room.

Roeder could be difficult at times, but he was well respected by everyone, and he made every attempt to personalize his interactions. Once Roeder had taken over the Austin regional office of WESIC, it immediately began to whir like a finely tuned engine. Productivity and efficiency jumped to all-time highs.

In Roy's typically thorough manner, he gave Walter a quick overview of the past twenty minutes of the meeting, an overview that took more than ten minutes. Trent watched the group during Roy's long-winded speech as they bobbed back in forth in their chairs, fiddled with their notepads, or stared off into space.

"Thanks, Roy," Walter looked at Steve and smirked as if they were both thinking the same thing. "Three weeks off and the whole place goes to hell, huh Steve?"

"I told you I shouldn't take that much time off, but you wouldn't listen."

"How's Taylor doing? I haven't talked to him in a couple of months."

"He's fine. Same ol' Rick. He sends his regards."

Steve knew that Roeder must have an early afternoon tee time at his club by the fact that the V.P. was wearing a pullover, short-sleeved golf shirt, so he decided to give him some detail that Roy couldn't provide in order to push the meeting along. "As a heads up to the team, I want to discuss some things that should be off the record. Will you excuse us for a moment, Amy?"

"Certainly," she said and stepped outside the conference room.

"There were some items found inside a safe at the insured's residence that give an indication that there may be something more to this case than the reports show. Without saying how I know this, it is possible that the ex-Mrs. Walker, Natalie Carlson was somehow involved in Miller Walker's death. I want you to know we are going to meet with Ms. Carlson very soon to deliver the life insurance payment in person and see if we can clarify a few things. I don't want any of this information included in her claim file, but if we can prove that she was involved, it will void her claim to the $500,000 in life insurance proceeds."

Walter leaned back in his chair and folded his arms over his protruding midsection. "Steve, I appreciate your ambiguity on this, but what do you think? Is she involved? I don't want to generate a lawsuit over this."

Steve looked Walter square in the eyes, "Quite frankly, I'm not sure. And I can understand your concern about a lawsuit and her being paid what she is owed if she is entitled to it. But I don't think she has a clue that she's a beneficiary of anything or she would have contacted us by now. Besides, we're well within the state-mandated time period for payment. That's why I'm going to sit on this for a couple of weeks and see what APD can stir up."

"I want you to be extremely careful on this one. Make sure everyone in this room is on the same page at all times. I'll need a report by Friday afternoon every week until we settle this. If anything unexpected comes up, let me know immediately. Interrupt me if you have to."

Walter turned to Roy, who had yielded the floor. "I want you and Jim to provide Steve with anything he needs."

"I'll e-mail you our preliminary overview by the end of the day, Walt," Steve offered.

"Good." He unfolded and raised his arms, clasping his hands behind his head. Everyone was quiet. "Well? Are we through?"

Everyone was quiet.

Roeder looked at both sides of the boardroom table then said, "Thank you, everyone."

The group began gathering their belongings to leave.

CHAPTER SIXTEEN

"WHERE DO YOU WANT to be in the next five years, Mr. Osborne?" Bill Tracy asked

"Well, my goal is to be at a management level position and to have completed my CPCU designation within that time frame, sir."

"Mmm-hmmm. I see."

It was all Trent could do to muster enough energy to stay awake during the interview. *What a complete asshole,* he thought. Trent had been grilled for nearly 45 minutes now and still hadn't answered anything substantive. He felt like jabbing his pen right into his own thigh. It would be a hell of a lot less painful than this monotonous interview.

Trent was on automatic pilot, volleying his well-rehearsed responses against the weak but constant barrage of Mr. Tracy's unimaginative questions. "I have already passed three courses toward my designation, and I am planning on taking some management courses offered by the company starting later this year."

"Mmmm-hmmm," Mr. Tracy reiterated. He seldom looked at Trent. His furrowed brow was pointed downward, alternating between Trent's resume and the dog-eared legal tablet that contained his outdated interview questions.

Even though he was given the mid-level manager position overseeing the underwriting department, Bill Tracy was no people-person. Labeled "Mr. Bill," he was the butt of more than his share of office jokes, not only among his immediate staff but in most other departments as well.

As an incentive to get experienced people to staff the Austin office when it opened, WESIC offered promotions to people who ordinarily would not have earned them. Bill Tracy was the poster boy for this poorly advised campaign. It was common knowledge that Bill was coasting toward retirement. With only a year and a half to go, he was adamant about not rocking his boat. The executive officers had tolerated him because of his willingness to move to Austin, but most agreed that his output didn't nearly match the needs of his position.

Following his agonizing interview, Trent burst into Steve's office exclaiming, "Just kill me now."

"What?"

Trent reached under his jacket and into his shirt pocket, retrieving his Mont Blanc pen. He took the cap off it and held it on Steve's desk with the tip pointing skyward.

"Hold this for me."

Steve obliged, reaching across the desk to keep the pen in its upright position. Trent placed his hands on each side of the desk and lunged downward in a mock attempt to impale himself on the writing instrument.

Steve chuckled at the melodrama playing out before him. "What the hell is wrong with you?"

"I just got out of Mr. Bill's office, for. . .for the senior underwriting job. Man, I can't go to work for that guy. Jesus, he's got the personality of a freakin' doorknob."

"What happened?" Steve asked, still very amused.

"The interview went fine, but I knew every question that moron was going to ask. I think, or rather I know, that he took the Human Resources Manual and asked the interview questions verbatim from it. I wanted to jump across the desk and stick his letter opener into his jugular."

"Didn't impress you, huh?"

"Jesus, I hope he doesn't offer me the job."

"Don't give him the chance. If you don't want to work there, just call HR and have them remove your name from the list of applicants." Steve knew if Trent was out of the running, Michelle would have absolutely no competition for the job.

"No, man, I don't want to let you down. Not after you went to the effort to make a recommendation for me to the Underwriting Department and all."

"So what? I'd do it again, but you've got to do what's best for your career. If you don't like what you saw, obviously the best thing to do would be to withdraw your name."

"Yeah, you're right, but I really need the cash. I am so damn tired of living paycheck to paycheck."

"I may be able to come up with something more for you to do here in claims."

"Really?"

"Tell you what. Let's take your mind off of this life-altering decision for a while. C'mon. I'll take you to lunch at Chez Cafeteria—My treat."

"Sounds great!"

Steve punched a button on his speaker phone.

"Hi, Steve," Amy responded.

"Trent and I are going to lunch."

"Okay. Have a good one."

Steve followed Trent out of the office, turning the light off and closing the door behind them. As an executive, Steve had the privilege of eating in the executive dining room, a mahogany-paneled suite complete with wait staff and bussed tables. He found this to be ironic, especially when the company had resolved to "flip" the company flow chart and have employees at the top filtering their ideas to the execs at the bottom. Yes, the flow of information came from those in the trenches was fed to the executives at the bottom of the chart, but those bottom feeders dined on trout almandine and filet mignon for lunch, while "those in the know" feasted on bad spaghetti and chicken-fried steak.

Unless he was summoned to mahogany row for a lunch meeting, Steve opted for the main cafeteria on the few occasions he would even take a lunch break. The people were much more interesting. The last thing he wanted to do was to listen to actuaries gloating amid the mahogany about how good the company loss ratio was or how well one of the executives shot on the golf course over the weekend.

He grabbed a plastic tray from the rack at the start of the lunch line and leaned into the chilled box containing the salad plates.

"Well, I heard it was down to three people for the underwriting job—Me, one of Jan Mitchell's staff underwriters, and an underwriter from the Portland office. Rumor has it that the woman from Portland, Michelle something-or-other, is the one to beat."

Steve kept a poker face. "I've heard she's good."

"How did you hear about her?"

"Senior staff meeting. We do talk about other things besides claims there."

"You think I have any chance against her?"

"Maybe I'm in a giving mood, but I'm going to break my own code of silence on this one."

"What do you mean?"

"Her name is Michelle Grayson. I met her in Yosemite with Rick."

Trent gave a confused look, "She was with Rick?"

"No, but I initially thought she was. Her travel agent suggested she check out Yosemite, so she and a co-worker came down from Portland. It was just a big coincidence that we all showed up there at the same time."

"So what did you think of her?"

Steve paused, "She's smart, attractive, and apparently very well-liked in the organization."

"That does it. I'm screwed."

"Easy now. You just said earlier, you hoped you wouldn't be given the job."

"I know. I just need to make some headway on the financial front."

"Don't let the money influence you. If it's not a good fit, you won't be helping yourself, and you won't be doing the company any favors either."

"You're right."

"Besides, I told you I'd try to come up with something in claims if you're really interested in hanging around for awhile."

"Are you kidding? That would be awesome!"

"We're coming up on the budget meetings for next year. I'll see if I can't get something in the works for a little bump in status for you. But it may take a few weeks to get it pushed through. Can you wait that long?"

"Absolutely."

"Good. Let's talk about something else. I had another interesting discussion with Andy Kelly."

"What did he say?" Trent asked.

"Not much. Just that he still has some suspicions about Walker's death."

"Really?"

"Yeah. How's your investigation coming along?"

"I'll have all of my recommendations in the system on the case folder."

"Good. That will give me something to read for the trip."

"Trip?" Trent asked.

"We are going to visit your family's old homestead sooner than I thought."

"Already? What's the plan?"

"Unless you've come to an epiphany in your research, we're going to deliver a big fat check after we conduct a little interview with Miller Walker's ex-wife. The rest of the plan will have to be formulated once we get there."

"What kind of interview did you have in mind?"

"A probing one. To see if we can get her to slip up on something."

"You mean to see if she murdered him?"

"Something like that. You up to the task?"

"Hell yes, I'm up to it. Do you want me to set the appointment?"

"No, we're not going to make an appointment for this delivery. I don't want her to be prepared," Steve said thoughtfully. "I think we'll do a little cold calling on this trip."

CHAPTER SEVENTEEN

STEVE HAD RESERVED ONE of WESIC's inconspicuous company cars for the trip south. He was seated quietly in the passenger side of the white Ford Taurus, as Trent sped across the coastal plains toward Douglas Creek. Much flatter than the rocky landscape of Austin and the Texas Hill Country, the plains looked like one enormous front yard, reaching for miles in every direction, only occasionally broken by stands of mesquite or dwarf cedar. This area of Texas had suffered through the ill effects of a drought for over a year, and the prairie had long since turned a dirty yellow from dust that had been accumulating over the entire region.

"Pretty flat and dry terrain around here," Steve said, breaking the silence.

"Yep. Not a whole lot of topography in this part of the state," Trent replied. "The drought has been kicking ass in these parts," he looked into his rearview mirror, "but it may not last much longer. Check out the weather coming in behind us."

Steve turned to see an ominous dark wall looming in the sky behind them. As cool northern air slammed into the warmer air being sucked in from the nearby Gulf of Mexico, angry clouds jutted thousands of feet into the air.

"That doesn't look too promising."

"November in Texas always means a change in wind direction. I bet the hicks in Douglas Creek will be buzzing about this. The rain from this cold front will make front page news in the land of all things Bubba."

Steve laughed, "Aren't you one of those hicks?"

"Yeah, but don't tell anyone while we're here. Wouldn't want them to think I'm an uppity college boy coming back to gloat. Nothing's worse than 'uppity' in a small town."

"Don't worry. It's our secret."

The menacing squall line continued to curl up behind the men like a wide row of clenched fists. Gathering dust on its leading edge, the storm promised to put a welcome but forceful end to the area's parched and cracked earth.

The two were silent as they passed the city limit sign, anchored across the street from the Catholic cemetery where many of Trent's ancestors lay. Trent slowed as they passed under a span of regal oak trees that arched sturdily across Main Street and extended into the stately, landscaped yards of some of Douglas Creek's earliest settlers.

"Pretty town," Steve said.

"Yeah, it looks good on the outside, but I bet it's just as backwoods now as it was when I was a kid."

The scenery definitely was that of a small town. Absent were the lunchtime fashion contests of the big city, where well-kempt men and women sported designer clothes and nibbled designer cuisine while jockeying for positions at the best tables in gourmet restaurants. Meat and potatoes still topped the menus of the establishments in this formerly rough-and-tumble town of the early-1800s. Douglas Creek boasted a Dairy Queen, a hole-in-the-wall Mexican restaurant called Sid's, and Jett's Steak House, the "fancy place" in town.

Twenty years ago, for any special occasion, Jett's Steak House and Bar had been the destination of choice within a fifty-mile radius of Douglas Creek. These days, it was the weekend haunt where patrons from all over the area donned their stiffest pairs of

Wranglers and loudest western shirts and prepared for a night or two of overindulgence.

Trent drove the next half-mile to the town square, and it became readily apparent that the downtown area had grown. Even so, the shops he saw now and the ones he remembered from his childhood were a far cry from the opulent stores and salons of larger metropolitan areas in the state.

Warped, knotty planks lay along the storefront walkways like piano keys, fronting the old mom-and-pop operations that wrapped completely around the courthouse square. The aged timbers creaked and echoed with the timbre of a different era, orchestrated by the hurried steps of storekeepers rushing their displayed wares inside before the cold rain arrived. Hand-painted signs bolted to walkway awnings swayed in rhythm to the wind gusts that were forcefully making their way southward down Main Street.

Trent turned left onto Market Street and noticed a group of domino enthusiasts crowded around a patio table in front of Reinhardt's Tavern. The south-facing enterprise provided some shelter from the north wind. This local watering hole, passed down through three generations, was strategically located directly across the street from the main entrance of the county courthouse.

After half-a-block, an unusual shop called Buddy's on the corner of Market Street and First caught Steve's attention. There were several tie-died T-shirts proudly displayed in the store's window along with an eclectic mix of folk art and pottery. This looked like a place that any Grateful Dead fan would be proud to visit, more indigenous to a place like Austin than some backwater Texas town between nothing and nowhere.

Steve looked at his watch. "We're a little early. Pull in here." He pointed to an open parking spot in front of the store.

"Check this out. A head shop in Douglas Creek! God, this place is actually progressing," Trent said as he guided the car into an empty parking space in front of Buddy's. He was careful not to hit the unusually high concrete curb in front of the store.

Steve surmised that the building must have been erected around the turn of the century because of the ornate stonework that decorated the facade. Looking upward toward the second story, he noticed the year 1907 was carved into the block of limestone that capped the center of the building's pediment. He also noticed a pair of rusted iron rings, once used to tie up horses, embedded at the edge of the concrete walkway. "What a great building."

"Yeah. It was a bank years ago."

Trent pressed down on the latch with his thumb and opened the large front door. It creaked as it swung to the right. He held it open for Steve to follow him inside.

A large bearded man with a braided ponytail greeted them as they entered. "How's it goin', guys?" He wore a tie-dyed Ben & Jerry's Ice Cream T-shirt.

"Great," Steve said.

Then Trent answered, "Fine. How about you?"

"Can't complain. Anything in particular I can help you guys find?" He looked up and down at their suits. "I've got some clothes here that would be a helluva lot more comfortable than those suits."

They chuckled, then Steve responded, "No, we're just killing some time."

"Well, let me know if you find something you can't live without."

"Will do."

The men milled around in the store for about twenty minutes longer. Trent eyed Steve picking up some tie-dyed shirts and asked, "Did you find something?"

"Yeah, I'm going to pick up a couple of these to work out in," Steve said.

Trent, as usual, had no disposable income whatsoever. He just watched in envy as Steve made his purchases, then followed him back outside to the car.

They looked toward the square before getting back into the car. The vehicle of choice for the area was obvious to them both. Pickups surrounded the courthouse. Fords, Chevys, and GMCs working their way around the square bore competing bumper stickers from The University of Texas and Texas A&M. Trent saw a bumper sticker on one of the pickups that read, "My boy can whip your honor student's ass."

"Dude, check out that bumper sticker."

Steve read it and chuckled. "Noble, huh?"

They got in the car.

"Ignorant sons of bitches. This place is still a hell-hole."

"It's not bad, Trent."

"Right," he responded sarcastically, looking at the gas gauge. "We'd better fill up while I still have feeling in my hands. It's going to be cold as a well-digger's ass when this thing finally hits."

Driving less than a mile, he found a gas station and stopped to fill up the car.

Steve handed him the company credit card. "Use this so we don't have to expense it. I'm going to grab something to drink. Can I get you something?"

"Yeah, I'll take a Coke."

Steve walked through the door toward the coolers in back of the store. He grabbed a soda for Trent and an iced coffee for himself. Working his way down the line of doors, he grabbed a sandwich out of another cooler and walked to the counter to pay.

Trent came through the door and handed the gas card back to Steve.

"Is half of this ham sandwich okay with you?" he asked Trent.

"Yeah, sure—Sounds good." Trent looked out the door of the establishment and across the street at a man standing in front of the high school entrance. He was gesturing wildly in the direction of the store. "What the hell does that guy want?"

The clerk looked outside to see what Trent was talking about and started to laugh.

Trent and Steve stood quietly, confused by his reaction.

The man explained, "Oh, that's Buster, saying hello." He waved at the man. "Crazy son of a bitch. He's harmless. . .A bit slow, but harmless. He works over there at the school."

Trent felt guilty about pointing the guy out. "I'm sorry... I didn't. . ."

"Funny thing about Buster. He likes to brag about the fact that 'cause he's the maintenance man for the local high school, he gets free tickets to all of the school's football games. Only problem is, he works every afternoon and evenin', includin' Fridays, from two until eleven at night. The school's games are always on Friday night. Poor bastard. He has yet to see more than a quarter of any ballgame in person, and he's been workin' there goin' on 22 years. But, boy, he sure brags about those tickets." The clerk chuckled, shaking his head as he rang up the drinks and sandwich.

Steve paid for the food, and they walked back to the Ford. After a brief sightseeing tour around Douglas Creek, it was time to make their way to Natalie Carlson's bed and breakfast. By the time they arrived and parked in front of her home, it was nearly two. The temperature had dropped considerably.

Steve cautioned him, "Let's keep in mind the reason we're here today, okay? I need you to be extremely careful in any conversation you have with this woman. We want her to think our only purpose for being here is to present her the claim check. We can't tip her off to anything else. If we're lucky, we might get a little more info out of her that we can give to Sergeant Kelly."

"So, I shouldn't let Ms. Carlson know that we think she blew up her fat-assed husband?" Trent teased.

"Ex-fat-assed husband." Steve smiled briefly before giving him a firm glance, letting him know this was no time for bullshit. "If she did have anything to do with the death, our actions will prove to be the most critical part of this investigation. So, watch carefully. I'm going to try and steer the conversation to where she will give up something we can use against her. That is, assuming she has anything to give up. The art of this whole thing is getting the information we need without her realizing it or before she realizes that she's given it to us."

As they got out of the car, Steve noticed the drapery in the front room move ever so slightly.

Steve leaned back into the car and whispered to Trent. "Don't look up. Just keep facing me."

"What's up?"

"We have an observer looking out the front left window."

"Gotcha."

They casually strolled to the front door where Steve rapped three times, avoiding the large brass knocker that hung at about chest level. With the rapid temperature drop from the cold front, the tapping with his knuckles sent needle-like shocks up his forearm. "Ouch! Damn! That stung," he muttered quietly and winked at Trent.

They heard the bark of a small dog and the sound of its claws scratching and tapping on a wooden floor as it rapidly approached the front door.

"Here we go," he whispered.

The barking continued and was soon followed by the sound of footsteps shuffling toward the door. Steve listened carefully as two deadbolts were unlocked and a chain unlatched from inside. The door was opened slightly, its chain kept in place.

"Ms. Carlson?" Steve asked.

"Yes. How can I help you?" She sounded agitated.

"My name is Steve Latham, and this is my associate, Trent Osborne."

Ms. Carlson eyed them cautiously. "I'm not interested in buying anything nor donating anything. As you can see here, I don't allow solicitors on the premises." She pointed to a small brass plate near the doorbell that read NO SOLICITORS.

"I can appreciate that, ma'am, but we're not selling anything. We're here to talk to you about your ex-husband's passing."

She bristled at his statement. "I've already talked to the police. I see no need to talk to anyone else about it. I'll take it kindly if you would leave my property now. Please."

Steve knew he had struck a nerve. "Ma'am, I'm sorry, but I'm afraid I haven't made myself clear. . ."

She cut him off mid-sentence, "No, you've made yourself perfectly clear. Now both of you get off of my property, or I'll call the police!" and she slammed the door.

Steve immediately knocked on the door and spoke loudly as he heard the deadbolts being locked. "No, no, Ms. Carlson, you don't understand. We're from Western States Insurance Company, and we have a check to deliver to you."

There was a pause, then the door slowly opened until the chain caught. Through the narrow opening Steve handed her his generic business card that said Claims Manager, the card devoid of any reference to the claims fraud unit.

"A check?" She acted surprised. "There must be some kind of mistake."

"No mistake, ma'am. May we speak with you for a few minutes?" he asked politely.

She hesitated. "A check for what?"

"Ma'am, your ex-husband listed you as the primary beneficiary of his life insurance policy." The wind was whipping in earnest through the neighborhood by now. "May we please come in?"

She examined his business card and appeared to get choked up. "I'm sorry. Yes, please, come in." She shut the door, unhooked the chain, and ushered the men inside.

Natalie Carlson was not the woman Steve had envisioned. She was well dressed and very attractive.

"Ms. Carlson, how do you do? I'm Steve Latham." He extended his hand and she took it.

"Yes, hello, Steve."

"And this is my associate, Trent Osborne."

"Ma'am."

"Hello, Trent. Won't you please come into the living room. I'm sorry, it's just that I get so many salesmen here."

"Believe me, I understand."

The Yorkshire Terrier's barks quickly gave way to its excitement at having visitors in the house. The dog began jumping up on Steve's leg.

"Stay down, Murphy," Natalie commanded. "I apologize. We don't get many visitors this time of year—Small town and all. I'm afraid he gets a little attention-starved."

"That's OK. I have a chocolate Lab that behaves in much the same way."

The old home was comfortably warm, considering the age of the structure. Steve and Trent followed Ms. Carlson as she guided them into the living room. They sat side by side on the couch across from her.

Murphy sprung from the floor onto Trent's lap.

"Murphy, you get down from there!"

"I don't mind. Really. I love dogs. Especially other people's." Trent scratched behind the dog's ears.

"You surely won't be able to get rid of him now."

Trent grinned and scanned the interior of the familiar old house, surprised at how much smaller the place looked to him now.

Ms. Carlson was polite but seemed nervously reserved. "May I get you both some coffee?"

Steve declined. "No, thank you very much."

"None for me either, thanks." Trent followed Steve's lead. Since this was going to be his first investigation, he didn't want any distractions, but he knew that a cup of coffee would have helped to warm him up. He inconspicuously rubbed them together when she wasn't looking or cupped them around Murphy.

"What's this all about?" she asked.

"As I said, we're here to present you with a check, a check in the amount of five-hundred-thousand dollars."

"Five-hundred-thousand dollars! Oh my God, Miller!" She broke down, grabbing a tissue from the box on the end table near her.

Upon hearing "Miller," Murphy jumped off Trent's lap and ran whining over to Ms. Carlson. His front legs pawed at her, trying to get her to let him up in her lap.

Steve and Trent looked at each other as Miller's ex-wife wiped tears away, unsure whether to believe this reaction was genuine.

While Ms. Carlson dabbed at her eyes with a tissue and shushed Murphy, who finally laid down beside her chair, Steve discretely put his finger to his lips to tell Trent to keep quiet. "Ms. Carlson, did you know that you were still listed as a beneficiary on your ex-husband's life insurance policy?"

"No. . .I didn't. . .I. . .didn't even know he had an insurance policy. We never talked much after the divorce."

"Actually, it has been in force for over eight years."

"Eight years?" she blinked in disbelief. "No, I had no idea."

"Ms. Carlson, I have a few questions to ask and a couple of documents for you to sign. First of all, here's your check."

Natalie Carlson took the check out of the envelope and looked at it. Her hands were trembling. "Oh, Miller. What have you done?" She covered her mouth and tears welled up in her eyes again as she looked at the check.

Steve could see that she was fighting to maintain her composure. "I'm sorry that it's under these unpleasant circumstances that we have to meet."

"Yes, I understand." She put the check back into the envelope and placed it on the coffee table between them.

"These meetings allow us to get to know each other a little better and show you how we can continue to serve you even after a claim such as this has been settled. Some people aren't used to receiving this amount of money in one lump sum."

"I can assure you that I am not," she said through a watery smile.

Steve continued, "Often, beneficiaries are confused as to how to handle and protect these large amounts. We are here just to give you a brief overview of your options. Now understand, just because we give you this money, doesn't mean you should feel any obligation toward us. This is a shock for you, I know. I want nothing more than to explain what your options are and leave it at that. I'm going to leave you some brochures to look over." He reached into his briefcase, pulled out a folder of material, and laid it on the coffee table.

"Look over this material. If you have any questions at all, however insignificant you may feel they are, call this toll-free number. We have a group of professionals that can handle every imaginable situation. If you are interested, our company can also provide investment counseling and help you decide the best way to get the most out of your money.

"But the first thing you want to do is get this deposited. Now, I know getting to the bank today is out of the question, but you can call first thing in the morning, and our representatives will have you void this check. . ."

"Void it?"

"I'm sorry. I didn't mean to startle you. What I'm trying to say is that they can wire the entire five-hundred thousand directly into your account so that you don't have to make a special trip to the bank. You can call and give them your routing number and account information, and they will have you void the check after the transfer is complete."

"They can do that over the phone?"

"They sure can. In fact, I'd recommend it, especially if you have any nosy, small-town neighbors that might overhear your transaction with the bank teller." Steve smiled and winked.

"We definitely have our share of those," she joked. "That's so convenient. I'll be sure to call them first thing." Natalie wiped her nose with the tissue.

"You won't be disappointed." Steve was a master at diplomacy.

"I appreciate that."

Steve went through the short WESIC questionnaire and had her sign a couple of forms.

Ms. Carlson was more at ease now. She looked at Trent and asked, "You're awfully quiet, Trent. Just what do you do, besides spoil Murphy?"

Trent was caught off guard, "I'm sorry, ma'am. I'm new with the company. I'm what you would call an adjuster in training."

Ms. Carlson halfway smiled and turned to Steve, "He looks nice. I'm sure he'll do just fine. Excuse me for a moment. As chilly as it is, I'm going to make a pot of coffee. Are you sure you both wouldn't like something to drink?"

Steve agreed to a cup, even though he really didn't want any. Ms. Carlson got up and headed to the kitchen, followed by Murphy. "Last chance, Trent. You sure you don't want to join us?"

"You talked me into it."

"Fine. I'll be right out."

Steve looked at Trent when she was out of the room and gave him a thumbs up. Trent just shrugged his shoulders as if to say he didn't know what to think of her. Steve extended his arms and

151

pressed his palms downward in the air a couple of times, mouthing the word "relax."

Trent nodded, and mouthed back, "She's hot!"

Steve smirked.

Five minutes later Natalie came back into the room. "Here are some snacks for you two until I can get that coffee brewed."

"Thank you, but that wasn't necessary."

She placed a small tray of cookies, fruit, and nuts in front of them and walked back into the kitchen. When she saw Murphy eyeing the tray, she told him to lie down.

Trent was about to dive in, then remembered he should play it cool. He turned to look at Steve and got the signal to go ahead. Grabbing a handful of peanuts he tossed them one at a time into his mouth. He grinned at Murphy who was watching him intently, waiting for Trent to miss.

Steve picked up a cookie, broke it in half, and placed one of the halves in his mouth. He leaned back and began in earnest to scour the contents of the room, just in case there was anything he had overlooked on the first pass.

After ten minutes Natalie carried in a coffee tray and rejoined the men. "Now, Murphy, you go lie down," she said before she dutifully poured three cups and doctored the men's cups for them.

The wind outside was howling, and parts of the old house creaked with the rapid change in temperature.

They had been with Natalie Carlson for about half an hour and had not garnered any new information. They needed to look around the place if at all possible.

It was Trent's turn to talk. Steve glanced at him and winked. They had agreed that this would be the signal for Trent to tell Natalie Carlson about his family ties to the home.

"You know, Ms. Carlson, I used to visit here every summer when I was young," Trent interjected.

"You're still young!" Ms. Carlson teased him. "You were in Douglas Creek?"

"Here in this very same house."

"Really?"

"Yes, ma'am. My grandparents were the Douglas's who owned the home for years. My parents sold it to the Wilsons after both of my grandparents passed away in the '80s."

"Oh, for heaven's sake. What a small world."

"I've gotta say, the place has never looked better."

As their conversation continued, Steve inconspicuously scanned the areas of the room he had missed beforehand, still looking for anything that seemed out of the ordinary. Leaning forward on the sofa, he began eyeing the bookshelves that ran slightly behind him and along the side wall and spotted a thin paperback that had been out of his field of vision earlier. In bold type on the binding he read "Ham Radio."

Trent continued, "My bedroom was on the top floor in the back corner. Is it still intact?"

Trent was soliciting an offer to have Ms. Carlson show them around the stately home. Steve was impressed.

"Your old room is now one of the more popular rooms I rent to visitors. Would you like to see it?"

Right on, Trent! Steve thought.

"I'd love to see all of the changes you've made. It was getting so run-down when I last saw it. You've really restored it to its original grandeur. But I wouldn't want to impose." Trent politely offered a little resistance and turned to wink at Steve when she wasn't looking.

This kid is smooth, Steve thought.

"It's no imposition at all! Let's go!" With that, Ms. Carlson got up and led the way.

Steve followed Trent, who followed Ms. Carlson and Murphy. This would allow him to hang back and spend more time getting a better look at everything they passed.

She took them through the ground floor first. It contained a kitchen, the living room, a dining room, two bathrooms, and the master suite.

Nothing after the ham radio book caught Steve's attention.

As they climbed the stairs to the second floor, Trent tried to remember how the house had looked when his grandparents had lived there. He ran his hand along the banister, recalling how he often had gotten into trouble with his grandmother by sliding down it. He complimented Ms. Carlson on the way she had remodeled the second floor into five cozy rooms, each with its own bath. When the tour took them past a door that obviously led to the attic, she made no mention of what lay behind it.

"Where are all your guests?" Trent asked innocently.

Ms. Carlson put her hands on her hips and said, "Well, it's almost winter, and most of my business is spring through fall when it's a little more bearable to be outside. I close up over the winter and try to take little vacations to warmer climes."

After looking at Trent's old room, the tour ended at the top of the stairs on the third floor. Steve and Trent had been with Ms. Carlson for about two hours.

Steve commented, "I visited an old bed and breakfast in Colorado Springs once. It was nice, but nothing like this. I really like what you've done with the place!"

"Thank you. I like my bed and breakfast, too." She noted, "Now, thanks to that cold front, there's quite a chill in the air. I'd better check the forecast."

"I wouldn't mind getting it myself," Steve replied. "I'd hate to get stuck in an ice storm on the way back to Austin."

"For sure," Trent added.

"You may very well be facing that with this front. Let's see what they say."

Steve and Trent followed Ms. Carlson and Murphy back to the living room where she tuned the set to the Weather Channel, announcing, "Weather on the eights." Steve was impressed by her body language. She was acting so natural. She wasn't giving up anything at this point.

The ham radio guide was the only clue that she might not have been forthright in her interview with the police. It intrigued him. Was she in on something with Miller, perhaps contacting him via the radio? Or maybe she had gotten greedy and wanted the cash he had kept in the safe. Except the police interview showed that when they asked her about it, she claimed to know nothing about the safe. That would explain why he could have been killed and the contents of the safe would have remained intact. If this were true, what could they have been involved in that would generate that kind of cash? And why were they trying to hide it unless it was illegal? Steve knew he would have to spend a great deal more time with her in order to find out.

Trent sat on the couch and waited for the forecast. "I hope it's not too bad this evening. We've got to make it back to Austin soon."

They didn't have to wait long for the local forecast to scroll across the bottom of the screen.

Trent read aloud, "Rain and freezing rain is occurring in Austin and the Hill Country in advance of the season's first arctic blast. Temperatures are expected to be well below normal and will continue to drop with the movement of the front. Colder temperatures are expected. Possible snow mixed with sleet and freezing rain is expected this afternoon with accumulations of up to one inch overnight. Dangerous accumulations of ice are expected on overpasses and bridges. Extreme caution is advised. Do not travel unless absolutely necessary."

"Well, gentlemen, it looks as though you two won't get very far in this storm," Ms. Carlson cautioned.

Trent interjected, "Just a little ice. . .No problem."

"We're not in a four-wheel drive. I think we'd better get a room and wait 'til morning," Steve advised.

Trent could tell that Steve had an ulterior motive.

Ms. Carlson eyed their exchange.

Steve watched her closely when he asked, "Can you tell us of a decent hotel nearby? We need to get going so we won't be stuck on the road somewhere tonight."

"You've got to remember, Steve, you're in a small town. You could walk to the motel from here. But you're both in luck. You can stay here for the night and be safe. It would be inhospitable of me to allow you to go off into the night with all the bad weather coming in. I won't charge much for two rooms and a meal." Then Ms. Carlson grinned slightly. "I'm kidding you, of course. Everything's on the house. Thanks to Miller, I think I can surely afford to comp you two for one night." Her bottom lip trembled, and tears once again welled up in her eyes.

They both thanked her for her gracious invitation, but Steve interjected, "We appreciate the generous offer, but company protocol dictates that we must pay. Besides, it's easier to generate an expense report than having to report complimentary lodging on the company gift log."

"If you say so," she replied.

Even with the good fortune of being able to stay in the house, Steve still couldn't gauge whether she was being genuinely sincere. *What is she up to?* he thought.

"Can I have my old room on the third floor?" Trent blurted out.

She laughed before offering, "You can have any room you want!"

Steve thought she appeared to be excited about the prospect of having company. He wasn't ready to trust her just yet. They would take advantage of this opportunity and hopefully spend more time with her. Maybe, just maybe, they could get some answers to at least a few of the nagging peculiarities surrounding Miller Walker's death.

"Did you bring any bags with you?" Ms. Carlson asked.

"Since our trip to Douglas Creek was supposed to be nothing more than a day trip, neither of us packed any essentials. We hadn't intended to stay over," Steve responded. You, know Trent, we may have a CAT team bag in the trunk. If so, there could be some Company issue sweats we could get by with.

"What is a CAT team?" Natalie asked.

"Short for catastrophe team."

"Oh," she said.

"I'll check," Trent said. "And you have the T-shirts you bought."

"True," Steve said.

"And I have a couple of our guest robes that you both can use," she offered.

They could hear the anniversary clock chiming the hour of five. Ms. Carlson was the consummate hostess. "Dinner will be at six-thirty. Coats and ties are optional!" She grinned.

Trent ran outside to check the trunk of the Taurus. He found the gym bag full of sweat pants and WESIC giveaway shirts, then smiled and gave Steve, who was standing at the front door, a big thumbs up. Trent grabbed Steve's t-shirts from the back seat and ran back to the house.

He was already shivering and his cheeks were bright red. "Boy! It's getting cold out there!"

"Come along. I'll get you guys into your rooms and lay out the robes for you."

"Thanks, but I can find mine okay!" Trent chimed and bounced upstairs followed closely by Murphy.

Calling the dog to come back, Ms. Carlson showed Steve to his room, then went to the kitchen to prepare the meal.

After changing into sweats and a WESIC golf shirt, Trent made his way to Steve's room. He tossed a pair of the sweat pants to Steve. "Here you go."

"Thanks." Steve slipped out of his slacks and put the sweats on. He slipped his feet back into his loafers.

"Can you believe the luck?" He whispered.

"I know. We really need to make the most of this. I doubt we'll get another opportunity."

"What do you think about her?"

"She's definitely hiding something. I saw a ham radio book on the shelf downstairs. Since you know this place so well, I'm gonna need you to snoop around tonight and see if you can find one in any of the rooms."

"A ham radio? You think she was communicating with her ex?"

"It's possible, but I need you to confirm it. Are you up to it?"

"Hell yes, I'm up to it."

"You'll need to check all the closets of the upstairs rooms we visited today and the attic. And somehow you've got to get into the damn master bedroom downstairs before she goes to sleep. If I can distract her before dinner, you need to haul ass in there and check it out."

Trent swallowed hard, recognizing a seriousness to Steve's voice that he had never experienced. "I'll do my best."

"Then I have no doubt you'll pull it off. Well, let's go down and see if we can help Ms. Carlson with dinner."

At the bottom of the staircase, they could hear the howl of the north wind whipping unabated across the coastal prairie. They agreed that staying the night was a wise choice.

Ms. Carlson looked up as they walked into the kitchen. She was preparing salad in a large bowl. She handed a paring knife to Trent and said, "Trent, would you please peel this cucumber; and when you've finished that, you can dice these carrots."

Trent took the knife and said, "I'd be happy to."

"What can I do, Ms. Carlson?" Steve asked, not to be left out.

"First thing both of you can do is start calling me Natalie. Second, how good are you at building a fire?" She motioned to the large stack of seasoned oak in the backyard.

"I've built my share over the years," he proudly announced.

Trent looked up from the cucumber.

Steve avoided him, realizing he had to go out into the biting north wind to get the wood.

Natalie said, "Don't worry. I'm going to help you. I've got a wheelbarrow in the shed that we can load up. Might as well get a bunch in case we're stuck inside for the rest of the night."

"Are you sure I can't help?" Trent asked.

Steve almost bit his tongue off at his request, but knew Trent was just being polite when he winked at him before Natalie turned around.

"You already have a job. But don't worry. You'll get your chance if we run out of wood tonight. I'll make sure of it!" Natalie pulled an old overcoat from a hook hanging beside the back door. Steve opened the door and let her lead the way out. He looked back at Trent who gave him another thumbs up.

The moment the door closed, Trent bolted out of the kitchen into the dining room. He flew through the living room into the small hallway that led to the master bedroom. Once there, he rummaged through dresser drawers and looked under the bed and into the closets before running into the bathroom. There was a small closet over the bathtub that could be reached by standing on the toilet. He dropped the lid down over the seat and jumped on top of it. He leaned across and opened the cabinet doors.

Wires! Had he found the clue they needed? His heart raced. He pulled at them only to find that they were connected to a long strand of Christmas lights. No ham radio. The rest of the boxes contained holiday decorations. He was closing the doors as he heard Steve and Natalie coming up the back steps. Jumping off the toilet he raced into the dining room. As he reached the living room he panicked. He had forgotten to put the toilet lid back up! He ran back into the bathroom, tossed the lid up, then ran back outside as he heard Natalie coming in.

She noticed that Trent hadn't finished with the vegetables. "Trent?" She seemed nervous to Steve as she rushed out of the kitchen and into the living room. "Trent? I hope I didn't run you off?"

Steve thought anxiously, *Come on, man. Get out of there. Get out of there.*

Natalie was just entering the hallway from the living room when she heard a toilet flush to her left.

The door to a small bathroom opened, and Trent walked out. He jumped when he saw Natalie in front of him. "Whoa!" he said. "I'm sorry, but I had to use the restroom. I remembered this one was here. I hope you don't mind that I used it instead of going upstairs."

"Not at all, Trent."

His response seemed to have quelled her suspicions. He followed her back into the kitchen where he resumed his cutting duty, winking at Steve as he passed him in the dining room.

Steve sensed that the mood needed changing. "So, what's the main course this evening, Natalie?"

"What do you want?" she asked. "You two are my guests."

"Whatever you want is fine with us," Trent said.

Steve walked outside to put another load of wood in the wheelbarrow. Natalie opened the huge side-by-side commercial refrigerator-freezer and took out three steaks. Trent wondered how she felt living alone and providing room and board to strangers in her home.

"I don't eat red meat that often. This is an occasion for me to cull my freezer! And since it's off-season, this is a good time to eat steak."

The knob on the back door turned, and Steve entered with a

bright red face and an armload of cold oak. Natalie and Trent looked at him. She laughed. Trent followed suit.

Steve mustered a whimpered "Heh, heh!"

Natalie and Trent erupted with another round of laughter. She helped Steve carry the oak into the front room. While Trent continued to dice the carrots, Natalie came back to the kitchen, handed him three potatoes and a small plastic brush, and said, "Scrub these, but not too vigorously. The skin has all the nutrients."

Steve pulled the flue open. He could hear the wind buffeting the house even harder and that sleet had started rattling on the roof. With the fire lit, he returned to the kitchen. Rubbing his hands, he said, "No wonder Murphy stayed with you. It's still warmer in here than in there. I did get a fire going and will keep an eye on it. With the wind blowing like that, I wouldn't want embers on your rug."

"Good idea," Natalie agreed.

"Is there anything else I can do. . .inside!?" Steve asked.

As Natalie took the freezer wrapping off the steaks, she remarked, "Just watch the fire, and keep us company."

"The potatoes are cleaned. Do you want to bake them in the oven or the fireplace?" Trent asked.

"Let's do them in the oven. It will take half an hour or so to thaw these steaks." Natalie threw the freezer wrap into the trash can, then placed the meat into a gallon sized zip-loc bag and submerged it in hot water in one half of the commercial grade sink.

After the rest of the meal was prepped, Natalie checked on the steaks. "The steaks are ready. Trent, would you mind helping me to set the table?" Natalie motioned to the cupboard where the plates were. "How do ya'll want your steaks?"

"Cook mine medium rare, please," Steve responded.

"Same with me," Trent replied, as he stacked three salad plates atop three dinner plates from the cupboard.

"This won't take long. Maybe twenty minutes," Natalie announced.

Trent had completed setting the table by the time Natalie came into the dining room carrying a bowl of salad. She began to rearrange the silverware, placing the utensils in their proper places.

Natalie returned to the kitchen and brought back a pitcher of iced tea. "Please sit, and we can get started."

Trent poured dressing on his salad as Steve nudged him under the table. It was apparent that Natalie was a religious person and was prepared to say grace. She asked if Steve would say the prayer and he obliged.

"Dig in!" she said. "The steaks will be ready shortly."

The fire from the front room crackled against the ruckus of the howling blue norther. Steve was still chilled after his earlier foray outside. Natalie went to the kitchen and returned shortly with the steaks steaming from a large serving platter.

"See if these are to your liking."

Steve and Trent each cut into theirs and agreed they were cooked a perfect medium-rare. With that, Natalie sat and began on hers. It was evident to Steve that she was used to entertaining strangers. He surmised that she must repeat this scenario many times during the year, that it must be a satisfying lifestyle to do something one really enjoyed.

"Do you guys drink?" she asked.

They grinned after looking at one another, then Steve replied, "Yes, we do."

"Good. After dinner we can enjoy a glass of wine by the fire. I have a great bottle of Port if you like sweet or Cabernet and Chardonnay if you prefer something dryer. I think you'll find any of them to your liking."

"That'll be great!" Steve acknowledged.

Trent didn't have a clue about wine. He was much more preoccupied with the finest meal he had enjoyed in months. He devoured the meal and finished well before the others.

Natalie felt his impatience, "Would you like something else to eat, Trent? I don't want to you to go away hungry."

"No, ma'am, I'm full—Couldn't eat another bite." He patted his palms on his protruding stomach.

"After such a good meal, the least we can do is clean the dishes," Steve offered.

"I won't hear of it. Besides, you're paying guests. You've already done too much. And working for an insurance company, if you were to cut your hand or something, you might sue!" She grinned.

After the dinner dishes were cleared and the kitchen was closed, the three sat in front of the fire in the living room sharing a bottle of Cabernet. Murphy lay in a small wicker basket lined with a red pillow. Steve observed Natalie as she stared into the well-fueled fire. It was obvious that she was somewhere else entirely. He felt it a good time to probe for information.

"I know it's been just a few hours, but have you put any thought into what you're going to do with the money?" he asked.

Natalie came out of her trance and smiled. "Well, it couldn't have happened at a better time. I'll probably finish the last bit of remodeling here and perhaps take a couple of months off until spring. Probably invest the rest. I mean, it was so unexpected."

Steve sensed she was relaxing and decided to take a chance, "Natalie, I don't want to be rude, and I know that this is a lot to handle in one day, but may I ask you a question or two about Miller?" Steve watched her body language for any sign of tension but saw none.

She took a sip of wine. "I suppose so."

He was deliberate in his questioning. "Well, first of all, did Miller ever cook?"

"Are you kidding? Not at all. He could barely boil water. That is, unless he took it up after we split. That's a pretty strange question, Steve. Why do you ask?"

Trent followed their dialogue intently, careful not to interrupt.

"Well, it appears that at the time of the accident, he was cooking. The explosion occurred in the kitchen and breakfast area, but the source was the kitchen stove."

"How do you know that?"

"Natural gas will rise from its source until it hits an obstruction, such as a ceiling, and then spread at that level within a building. For example, in a house as large and open as your home here, it would take a long time for any significant amount of gas to collect in the kitchen. There are just too many areas where the gas could escape. But in your old home, the one you shared with Miller, it was confined to a much smaller area. Once the gas ignited, the explosion blew apart the top of the outside wall causing the ceiling to collapse."

Steve saw her wince slightly, as if she was imagining the force of the explosion.

"He never cooked," she muttered, letting out a deep breath and staring off into space as if the two men weren't even there. A tear rolled down one side of her face.

Steve pretended not to notice her wiping it off, but he had no doubt that she felt uncomfortable answering the last question. He knew he'd have to be careful. "Natalie, I apologize if I'm out of line."

"No, no. It's okay. I'm just a bit emotional about the fact he wanted to do this for me. The insurance, I mean."

"I understand. If I may ask one more question? Did he have any enemies? Or do you know of anyone who would have a reason to hurt him?"

"No. None at all." She answered curtly, then took another sip.

He had hit a nerve and he knew it. Her body language now said it all. Natalie's answer was polite but not helpful. She was shutting down. Curling up in the chair, she stared intently at the fire. It was time to back off.

Steve gave a hand signal to Trent. Pointing upstairs, he motioned that it was time for them to get to bed. "Natalie?" Steve said.

"Yes."

"We won't take up any more of your time and hospitality. It's bedtime."

"Well, there are extra blankets in the armoires in each of your rooms. I bet you'll need them tonight."

"No doubt," Trent said.

"I'll be sure to keep the heat at a comfortable level for you tonight."

"Thank you so much, Natalie. I wish this trip could have been made under much better circumstances." Steve shook her hand.

"Me, too. But I have to admit, it's flattering to know my ex-husband still cared enough to do such a thing for me." She was getting choked up again. "Well, good night, gentlemen."

"Good night, Natalie."

Trent was already heading up the stairs. "Thank you for the wonderful meal, Natalie."

"You helped! But you're welcome, Trent. I'm glad you both enjoyed it."

The dog bolted from his bed and chased Trent up the stairs. "Murphy, you get back to bed!" Natalie commanded. The Yorkie hung his head and crept back to his basket.

The men climbed the stairs to their respective rooms. Trent waited for the lights to go off downstairs before walking down the hall to Steve's room. He tapped on the door before he pushed it open. Steve was on the bed making notes on his legal pad. He motioned for Trent to come inside.

"Whatta ya think?" Trent whispered.

"I think if we're going to find anything in here, it's going to be in the attic."

"You think she's got a radio up there?"

"I think there's a good possibility. While I was out back getting the wood, I noticed a coaxial cable running out of the wood siding from the upstairs level of the house."

Trent looked confused.

Steve clarified his statement. "The cable could have been attached to an antenna."

"There wasn't one?"

"No, the cable looked as though it had been cut. It also didn't look like it had been there very long."

"How do you know?"

"It wasn't painted. Some of the conduit that was running down the back wall was painted, but the cable was still black. Plus, it was coming out of the wall from the left side of the third story. This would mean whatever it is or was connected to would have to be and might still be stored in the attic."

"Damn! It's like I work for Sherlock Holmes."

"Well then, Watson, I suppose the next phase of this investigation will be up to you."

Trent smiled.

"After we're sure Natalie is asleep, you're going into that attic.

We'll get up at 3:00. That should give her plenty of time to fall asleep. You've got to get in and out of there fast. And be as quiet as you possibly can. I won't be able to cover for you if she catches you."

"I'll do my best."

CHAPTER EIGHTEEN

STEVE WOKE UP MOMENTS before the 3:00 A.M. alarm on his watch was set to go off. Avoiding any errant squeaks, he crept across the huge area rug that covered the majority of the room's wooden floor and pulled the door open. He walked to the railing overlooking the front room and listened for any activity downstairs.

All was quiet.

The raised-panel door to Trent's room slowly swung open, and he peered around it toward Steve's room.

Without saying a word, Steve pointed down the hallway beyond Trent in the direction of the attic and gave him a thumbs up.

Trent nodded and in sock feet proceeded down the hall, away from Steve to the small attic corridor.

Like the attic door to which it was attached, the ornate, almond-shaped doorknob was small. A decorative hole designed for a skeleton key was situated directly below one of the knob's tapered ends. Taking a deep breath, Trent closed his eyes and twisted. The beaded-board door wasn't locked. As he pulled it open, the tarnished hinges groaned loudly, too loudly as far as he was concerned. He turned abruptly, only to see Steve placing his index finger over his lips. He waited until Steve signaled for him to continue.

A familiar musty aroma emanated from the attic, as though it hadn't been opened in a while. It smelled just as it had when he last visited the house in the days after his grandmother died. Trent's thoughts flashed back to that time.

His parents had just met with the family attorney downstairs. They had to go through his grandmother's personal effects and prepare the house for sale.

A young Trent Osborne had clutched the handrail on the old staircase and pulled himself up the steep and narrow corridor that led to the attic. He was short and overweight for his eight-and-one-half years, and the three-story journey was taking its toll on him. Breathing heavily and perspiring, he finally arrived at the landing in front of the attic door. Most adults had to stoop on the landing in order to insert the rustic skeleton key into the lock, but Trent fit into the space perfectly. He angled his tired and pudgy body forward until just his head touched the door, panting as he jabbed his stubby fingers into the pocket of his loose-fitting shorts and retrieved the key.

He had relished his time at this house when he was younger. He had spent most of his summers here with his grandparents, occupying much of his time going through the rich collection of items stored in the attic.

Trent came back to reality and ducked through the unlocked door. He stepped into the attic and closed the door behind him. Once inside, he turned on his mini-flashlight and scoured his surroundings. It was neater now. The beaded-board paneling that covered the walls looked the same, cured dark and hard from the constantly changing humidity levels of the attic.

A veneer of dust covered the boxes and objects that occupied the space. The boxes were of a size that could easily hide a lot of radio equipment. Some of the lighter kitchen supplies, such as paper towels and soaps, were stored against the right wall. To the left were boxes marked as Christmas decorations.

Directly in front of him was a partially obscured opening he remembered well, a small door into a separate storage area where years earlier he had often hidden and played, a door into the area where from the outside of the house Steve had noticed the coaxial cable running in. A cluster of boxes was stacked in front of the opening. If Trent was going to find any clues, he suspected they would likely be in that room. As he moved toward the door, small dust particles cascaded across the beam of his flashlight, like small restless bugs agitated with the intruder invading their space.

The faint sound of footsteps in the hallway startled Trent. He twisted around suddenly and listened. His heart was pounding. He heard the steps again, quick tapping steps. They were getting closer, but he relaxed. They were too light for a person. "Murphy," he whispered. Steve would be proud of his observation.

Steve was still in the hall keeping watch. The dog had walked right past him and laid down in front of Trent's door to keep watch when a light went on downstairs.

Someone was in the kitchen. There was whispering. One of the voices was definitely Natalie's. The other voice belonged to a man.

Trent, stay put. Please don't come down, he thought. There wasn't any way for Steve to warn him. He slid back away from the railing, feeling with his hands as he backed toward his room.

Trent hadn't heard anything except Murphy. He gently moved the boxes and took a step toward the door.

The old floor squeaked again.

"Shit," he mouthed quietly. He opened the door and at about the halfway point, the bottom edge scraped the uneven floor. He pulled up on the doorknob to eliminate any further noise.

Footsteps were moving toward the direction of the landing at the bottom of the stairs.

Steve eased back inside his room and left a slight crack through which to peer.

The silhouette of a man wearing a bulky coat and ball cap came up a couple of steps and stopped.

Steve knew there was no way the man could see him. It was too dark.

Making little noise, the man continued up the stairs.

Trent pointed his flashlight toward a small table at the back of the room. A tiny wooden chair was slid underneath it. Wires ran down the backside of the table; a sheet was draped over the objects on top.

Just as he walked toward the table, the click of a light switch made him turn around. He could see light shining through the crack at the bottom of the attic door. The hall light was on!

His heart began to race. He stepped toward the table and lifted the sheet. It was a ham radio! Trent didn't know whether to scream or hide. He hurried back to the door and pulled up on the doorknob. The door would only close so far. As he stepped back, the floor squeaked. He cringed and ducked behind some small boxes near the radio table.

Just then the attic door opened, and the light came on. A beam from the exposed bulb overhead shone through the gap in the door and landed on the wall right in front of him.

Oh God, please let me get through this, he thought.

There was silence.

Was it Natalie? he wondered.

Eventually, the light went off, and Trent heard the sound of footsteps moving away from him. They were too heavy to be Natalie's.

Steve saw the silhouette pass his door once more, this time going the opposite direction.

The man walked down the stairs and back into the kitchen.

Trent was shaking as he waited in his hiding place for at least thirty minutes. He looked at his watch. It was 4:00. He needed to get out of there. Retracing his steps, he successfully maneuvered out of the attic and back to Steve's room.

Steve stood in the darkness of his room waiting and hoping Trent was industrious enough to avoid detection. Fighting the urge to leave his room to find Trent, he decided he'd go downstairs under the pretense of getting a drink of water. As he was about to open the door, he heard three light taps. He slowly opened his door. Seeing that it was Trent, he pulled him inside. "What happened?"

"Man that was a close one!" Trent whispered. His adrenaline level was peaking.

Steve held his forefinger to his lips cautioning him to lower his voice.

"Whoever it was, I know he didn't see me. There's definitely ham radio equipment in there."

"I knew that's how they kept in touch. That explains a lot."

"Explains what. . .exactly?" Trent asked.

Steve again held his forefinger to his lips. "We'll talk when we go back to Austin. Go on back to your room. Natalie will have breakfast for us at six. Be ready to go, and we'll get outta here right after we eat."

Trent slipped out and went to his room.

Steve closed his door without a sound and went to bed. He raised his left arm and pressed the button on his watch to illuminate the dial. It was 4:30 a.m. on Tuesday morning. Knowing Natalie began serving breakfast at 6:00, he set the alarm on his watch for 5:15. He knew he wouldn't sleep.

Steve was surprised that he dozed off for an hour before the alarm beeped. He hopped out of bed and dressed. More out of habit than necessity, Steve made one last pass around the room to make sure he hadn't left anything behind. Closing the door, he met Trent in the hall and walked downstairs with him.

A deep voice echoed from the kitchen. As they neared the entrance, they also heard Natalie. Steve led the way through the doorway and saw an elderly gentleman seated at one of the chairs around the small kitchen table. He was conversing with Natalie while she was scrambling an egg mixture on the stove top.

Murphy barked and jumped up and down, going between the two men.

"Mornin', sleepyheads!" She turned from the stove to smile at them, then ordered, "Murphy! Down! Bad dog!"

"Hey, Murphy! He's okay, Natalie." Steve smiled back at her and looked at his watch. "Sleepyheads? Heck, the roosters haven't budged yet." He walked toward the seated gentleman and extended his hand. "Steve Latham, sir."

"Oscar Carlson," the older man said, shaking Steve's hand.

"And this is Trent Osborne."

"Trent."

"Nice to meet you, sir."

"I'm Natalie's father."

Steve recognized him as the man in the hallway last night. "Well, you have a wonderful daughter, sir. She has gone overboard for us with this ice storm and all."

Natalie announced, "I have a nice breakfast for you. Please sit. There's coffee on the table. Would you like juice?"

"Coffee's fine," Steve acknowledged.

Mr. Carlson's eyes examined Steve.

"Fine by me, too, Natalie." Trent took a seat at the table.

"Did you sleep okay?" Mr. Carlson asked and tilted his head inquisitively.

"Like a log," Steve replied.

"I thought we had a coon in the attic last night. I tried to be as quiet as I could as I snuck up the stairs, but I thought I might have awakened somebody. It was actually that fool dog, Murphy. He was plopped down in the hallway looking for someone to play with."

At the sound of his name, the dog's ears perked up, and he jumped up on Trent, begging for attention.

"Didn't hear a thing."

Trent was scratching Murphy's ears while he nodded in agreement, then replied, "You probably heard me snoring."

Mr. Carlson laughed. "If you snore like that and you're married, I feel sorry for your wife!"

"No, sir. Fortunately for the eardrums of the gentler sex, it's just me."

"Well, I can't say I'm surprised that you didn't wake up. Most of you city boys are probably used to gunfire and such, not some ornery coon."

"Alright, Daddy. That's enough."

"Hee, hee," Mr. Carlson cackled. "I guess I'd better set a trap up there tonight. I suppose it could've also been a possum poking around up there as cold as it was."

"Daddy, Trent's grandparents were the original owners this house."

"Well now, I recall that Mr. and Mrs. Douglas were quite the fine couple."

"Are you from here, Mr. Carlson?"

171

"Born and raised. And call me Oscar. I'm too old to worry about formality."

"I hope you two are hungry. I'm making migas for breakfast."

"They smell delicious." Trent was salivating at the aroma.

Natalie soon arrived at the table with a platter of migas and a plate full of biscuits and bacon. She set them on the table. "Please help yourselves. Murphy, sit!"

Trent dove in like there was no tomorrow. Oscar and Steve chatted as they ate and watched in amazement as Trent finished off a large plate of eggs, six to eight pieces of bacon, and four biscuits. There was plenty for all, but the two men combined ate less than Trent.

"You must not pay that boy enough!" Oscar exclaimed.

"Why's that?" Steve asked.

Oscar winked. "Hell, he just ate all my leftovers for the next two days! You obviously don't pay him enough to afford decent groceries. I mean, look how skinny he is." He reached over and pinched some skin from Trent's waist.

"Daddy, stop!"

"That check you gave my daughter came as quite a surprise to us."

"They say that good things come out of bad situations. I just hope Natalie can put it to good use. Obviously, Miller still cared a great deal for her."

Tears started to well up in Natalie's eyes. "Okay, you two. Stop before I start crying again."

Steve wiped the edge of his mouth with the cloth napkin and folded it neatly on the table. "Natalie. Oscar. It has been a pleasure. We can't thank you enough for the hospitality."

"Hell, I didn't do nothin'. Natalie's been the worker bee."

"Even though the ice didn't make it here, you know you won't be able to get all the way to Austin until it melts. You sure you two don't want to stay one more night?"

"No thanks," Steve said. "We need to get back. If we have to stop along the way until the roads open up, we'll just find a place to take a long lunch."

"Well, I hope you two can come back to visit soon. Perhaps in the spring."

"We'd like that."

Natalie looked at Trent. "Trent, a cat must have gotten your tongue."

"No, ma'am. I was just about to cry at the thought of going back to my typical breakfast routine when we get back to Austin. You think I could move back here into one of your spare bedrooms?" he said with a twinkle in his eye.

Natalie swatted him playfully with her dishtowel. "You wouldn't want to move back. Daddy would wear you out with all the chores he'd have you doing."

"It would be worth it," Trent replied.

"Now don't you have some cute girl in Austin that can cook for you."

"I have one that I'm interested in."

Steve flashed his assistant a surprised look.

"Well, I'm sure it'll work out," Natalie said. "You're way too handsome to be single for any length of time."

"Thank you very much. And thank you for breakfast. This was so delicious."

"You're quite welcome."

"Excuse me for just a moment. I left the CAT team bag upstairs."

Trent jogged out of the kitchen and upstairs to his room, followed by Murphy, as Steve made his way to the foyer to wait for him with Oscar and Natalie. Trent reappeared a few moments later with his bag. The men expressed their thanks once more, said their good byes and petted Murphy, and left.

Natalie closed the door behind them, locked it, then paused and looked at her father. "Do you think they suspect anything?"

"I'm not sure. But you'd better get that money in the bank as soon as you can."

They both watched as Trent started the car. Steve used a credit card to scrape some of the ice from the windshield as the Taurus heated up. He got in and they drove away.

They had barely reached the end of the street before Trent started in, "I knew I'd find something up there."

"Okay, Watson. Fill me in."

"There's a small room at the back of the attic. That's the area where you saw the cable coming into the house. She has a whole ham radio setup in there. It was covered up, and there was a lot of dust over everything, so it was obvious she hasn't used it in a while."

"Not necessarily. If that place is drafty, it wouldn't take too long for a layer of dust to build up. I mean, look at the wind that hit here yesterday."

"That's true. But man was I scared when I heard the dog, then Oscar snooping around up there. I thought it was Natalie!"

"Yeah, I saw him walk down the hall. I had my door cracked open. I barely got out of the hall myself before he came by."

"God, it was like some B-movie watching the flashlight come through the cracks in the attic wall. I thought my ass was nailed for sure. But at least I knew what I'd say if I got caught."

"Oh, really?"

Yeah, I'd tell him I used to sneak in the attic late at night when I was a kid. I was feeling a little nostalgic and since I wasn't sleeping, I thought I'd check it out."

"Oh yeah, that might have worked. Right up until the time he shot your ass, thinking you were the biggest raccoon he had ever seen," Steve chuckled. "But in all fairness, you were on the right track. Planning for those types of situations is crucial."

"Thanks. . .I think."

"And what's this about the mystery lady you're interested in? I haven't heard about this before, have I?"

"No. Promise me you'll keep this between us."

"Sure."

Trent chewed on his bottom lip before speaking, "It's Whitley."

"Whitley? I would have thought she was too old for your taste."

"I don't know. There's just something about her."

"Do you think she's interested in you?"

"I was hoping you could tell me. But if you ask me, I think she's interested in you," Trent said.

"Why would you say that?"

"Haven't you ever noticed the way she looks at you."

"Trent, we've been friends for a long time. Besides, she's never mentioned anything to me. I think you may be reading way too much into your observations in that area."

"Well then, do you know if she's seeing anyone right now?"

"No, not that I'm aware of. Why don't you call her and ask her out?"

"I don't think she'd go. In fact, she called me while you were out of town."

"Really?"

"Yeah. She had heard something one night while you were on your trip, and it really scared her."

"What did she hear?"

"She said she overheard some strange people arguing. She was sitting in the dark out on her balcony. It scared her a bit."

"So she called the young, virile Sir Lancelot to come and rescue her?"

"Not exactly. She wasn't too receptive to my coming over. I think she blew me off, then spent the night at your house."

"Oh? Well, she was taking care of Bosco for me. I gave her a key to the house before I left so she could get my mail and feed him." Steve didn't think it was any of Trent's business that Whitley had her own key to his house, even if it was completely innocent.

"Maybe I'll ask her to lunch one day."

"Yeah, just keep it innocent at first. You know, test the water a bit. But hell, who am I to give advice. I haven't dated in months."

"But you could if you wanted to. Don't feed me that line of crap. What about that Michelle in California? What did she look like?"

"Very attractive." Steve paused then looked out the passenger-side window, his thoughts drifting back to his recent encounter with Michelle. He hadn't broached the subject with anyone other than Trent upon his return, and he hadn't heard from her during the two months since the Yosemite trip. All he knew was that he wanted to see her again.

CHAPTER NINETEEN

BACK IN THE OFFICE on Wednesday, Steve found himself thinking once again about Michelle. He had suppressed his desire to check with Human Resources and find out whether she had gotten the underwriting job, since he had no business reason to do so.

In the days that had followed his return to work, Steve had found himself thinking about her constantly and their brief encounter in Yosemite, imagining how he should approach perpetuating the relationship, if at all. Assuming she got the Austin job, Michelle had told him she would call when she arrived in town. For that reason, he had made it a point not to initiate any contact. He didn't care for the possibility that he could be dating a co-worker; but the fact was, he thought he may justify it in her case. If she took the job, she would be working in another building and would have little to no contact with his department. This likelihood made the situation easier for him to rationalize.

Michelle was the first woman who had interested him, or rather the first he had allowed himself to be interested in, since his divorce. Getting away from the office did indeed have the curative effect that everyone had predicted. He had been so sure that burying himself in his job and his home restoration projects would help his mental state, when in fact all it did was delay his mental healing and regaining peace of mind. Whether it was the mountain air, his chance encounter with Michelle, reuniting with Rick, or a combination of all three, a true rejuvenation process had begun.

He picked up the phone and dialed Andy Kelly's number.

"Detective Kelly."

"Kel."

"Steve! How'd the meeting go?"

"Nothing earth-shattering, but it went okay, I guess. We got stuck in Douglas Creek during the ice-storm and got to know our Mrs., let me correct that, Ms. Carlson a bit better."

"What did you find out?"

"I'd say it's a pretty safe bet that she was in contact with Miller via ham radio at some point in the past. Trent was snooping around in her attic and found a complete ham set up. But I don't have anything hard to give you."

"I'm not even going to ask how you got into the attic. But hey, that's a start, huh? I bet the old cop juices were flowing in earnest."

"Yeah, they were, and I think you were right about being suspicious. I got to look outside the house a bit and noticed that the coax cable going into the attic, where the radio equipment was, had been cut. I'm assuming it happened whenever the antenna was taken down, but I never saw an antenna and wasn't able to get into the garage to see what might have been stored there."

"Well, what do you think?"

"It's all pretty circumstantial. Without something more concrete, I don't think there is anything else we can do. And as nice as she was to us, I don't think she'll be volunteering anything more. Barring some miracle, we may just be looking at a permanent accidental death ruling for Miller Walker."

"Damn it. I was hoping she'd give us something."

"Yeah. Me, too."

"Ya know, Steve, we may still have one more opportunity."

"How so?"

"I asked Miller's lawyer to hold off paying Natalie the cash from the safe and the proceeds your guys sent him for the house until I give him the go ahead."

"How'd you get him to agree to that?"

"He is the secondary beneficiary on Miller's estate."

"That snake."

"Yeah, a real tough sell. Once I told him about the investigation we were conducting on Natalie, I swear I saw him salivating. He'll definitely hold out as long as we ask him to."

"Based on her reaction when we gave her the life insurance check, I assume Natalie knows nothing about being the primary beneficiary in his will either."

"What was her reaction?"

"Total surprise. Cried like a baby."

"Did you believe her?"

"Yeah, I did. If she was acting, it was the best performance I've ever seen."

"That's the same way she was at the funeral. Hmmm."

"I can hear those wheels spinning, Kel. Where do we go from here?"

"Maybe we've been taking the wrong approach here."

"How so?"

"If Natalie Carlson had something to do with Miller's death, wouldn't she show up at the funeral to pay her respects?"

"Yeah, you'd think so."

"Okay, then why else might she show up at the funeral and stay in her car?"

"Because she was too upset to be around all those people? She was really teary when we mentioned Miller in our conversations with her."

"Sure, it's possible. But what else could drive a person to act that way?"

"Fear."

"Ex-act-ly. I think that's the key. She's afraid of something. . .or someone. I bet if we can figure out what or who it is, we can trace a path directly to the explosion at Miller's house."

"You don't have your sights on the lawyer, do you?"

"No, he's greedy as hell, but he's also clean. I checked him out very early on."

"Call me if you come up with any suggestions on how I can help. If I think of anything, I'll let you know."

"Thanks. Have a good one."

"You, too."

Steve hung up and began to peruse the Walker files on his desk. He had to formulate a way to get back in front of Natalie.

Before he could get too deep into thought, his phone buzzed. "Steve?" Amy's voice came over the speaker-phone.

"Yes."

"There's a call for you on line two."

"Who is it?"

"She wouldn't say, but I think it's an insured."

"Uh, see if you can take a message. I'm in the middle of something."

"I've already tried. She won't have anything to do with it and is demanding to speak with you."

Steve rubbed his temples and let out a deep breath. "Okay, put her through."

"OK. Sorry. Here she comes." Amy released the caller.

"Steve Latham," he answered.

"Mr. Latham. I'd like to file a complaint with your organization."

Steve didn't recognize the voice. "What type of complaint, ma'am?"

"A formal complaint, Mr. Latham." Her voice was firm, articulate, professional.

"I'm sorry, but if you don't mind, could you clarify your request for me. What type of formal complaint do you want to file, ma'am?"

"A formal complaint about the fact that I got the underwriting job, I've been in town three days, and you have yet to call and invite me to dinner!"

"Michelle?"

"Yes. Hi, Steve," she giggled.

"Damn, what a relief. I thought you were some psychotic claimant we'd pissed off. It's great to hear your voice. How are you?"

"I'm terrific."

"So you got the job! And you've been here for three days already? Congratulations."

"Yes. Thank you, and where have you been?"

"I went out of town on a case and got stuck in the damn freak ice storm. You should have left me a message."

"I called on Monday morning, and your assistant told me you were out of town. Besides, I knew where to find you. I wanted to surprise you, but I think I'm the one who was surprised. My God, is this the mild Texas winter that I can expect every year?"

"Just an anomaly, my dear."

"Jesus, I hope so. The first day I got here it was perfect. Eighty degrees. At least the movers got my stuff into my condo before it all hit."

"You've already found a place to live?"

"Yeah, I got this great little rental near Sixth and Lamar on the first day. The service I used promised me that I would be in a prime location."

"You are."

"Good. I haven't been able to see anything of the city yet, but the weather is supposed to warm up into the 70s by the weekend. In November! Jesus, doesn't this state have seasons?"

"I'm afraid not."

"Beats Minnesota winters, I guess."

"Definitely. . .Well, congrats again on your promotion. So when do you start work? Or have you started already?"

"Thanks. No, I haven't started yet. My first day is next Monday. I wanted to take a few days to relax and get oriented with the city a bit. You know, figure out where the closest bar is in relation to the office, that sort of thing."

"Sure, and you're right. I do still owe you dinner. How about Friday night at my place?"

"You really are going to cook?"

"That was the deal, wasn't it?"

"A man of his word. Hard to believe. Friday night sounds great. That will give me a couple more days to unpack."

"Do you need any help?"

"No, the movers got all of the big stuff in place already. Just a matter of going through the boxes and organizing everything. But

I appreciate the offer. This way I figure you'll have tomorrow and all day Friday to work out any kinks in your recipe. I wouldn't want to be the guinea pig that ends up with food poisoning. Heavens, that could scar you and your culinary dreams for life!" she chuckled.

"Such little faith."

"I'm teasing. . .As a matter of fact, I'm looking forward to dinner. . .and seeing you again."

"I can assure you the feeling is mutual."

"Well, I'll let you get back to work. I know how busy you must be. I need to get some of these boxes cleared out of here anyway before I become a mass of paper cuts. Plus I'm having to use my cell phone for all-things-technical right now, until I can get my internet access set up. The cable company is behind because of the storm, but they're supposed to have me hooked up by tomorrow. I'll call you Friday morning for directions."

"Sounds good. I'll talk to you Friday."

"Bye."

Steve started thinking about recipes as soon as they hung up. He wanted to make a good impression this weekend. It will be fun having a real date for a change, he thought.

CHAPTER TWENTY

MICHELLE CRANED HER NECK, trying to see address numbers on the widely spaced mailboxes staggered up and down the hills of Lake Street. Besides being new to the city, dusk and the lack of streetlights in this West Austin neighborhood combined to make her task even more difficult. Steve had told her that his house was not easy to see from the road. After getting lost twice and surviving a few near misses with the whitetail deer population, she was thinking "invisible" would have been a better description. Compounding her situation was the condition of her car; the "check engine" light had come on a couple of miles into her drive.

She finally stumbled upon 6819 and headed into the driveway.

Its sharp grade dropping from street level caught her by surprise. Her headlights moved from the oaks atop the hill, through the sharp angles of the driveway, to house at the bottom. Outside lights illuminated a large sailboat anchored on the right side of the driveway with a large Ford F-250 pickup parked in front of it. She pulled in beside the boat and parked, quite ready for a drink.

Michelle swung her car door open and stepped out, throwing the brown leather strap of her purse over her tanned shoulder. The heels of her sandals clicked on the concrete as she walked around the backside of her car, and between the boat and the truck. She crossed the nicely manicured yard, steered by a landscaped arc of oak and cedar trees that led to Steve's front door. She noticed that the faint twinkle of light behind the trees to the right of the house gave the only clue that a neighbor's home was nearby. Michelle found the privacy very appealing, quite a contrast to the bustle of traffic passing below her cramped but comfortable Sixth Street condo.

At the door, she took a moment to inspect one of the many plants along the lengthy porch. She leaned down to touch a large fern, examining its delicate fronds, impressed at the healthy condition of the plant. *This guy is too good to be true. He must have a yard-man,* she thought, while ringing the doorbell.

The wind had picked up, and a slight creak emanated from a branch on one of the oak trees. Michelle looked up at the few clouds beginning to mask the night sky. With the warm weather, she had forgotten her sweater and umbrella in spite of hearing the five o'clock news mention the possibility of rain ahead of another cold front later in the evening.

Steve answered the door dressed in a baggy pair of tan shorts, a pair of black flip-flop sandals, and a threadbare Hawaiian print shirt. He wore a faded red apron containing enough stains to rival a work by Jackson Pollock. It read, "Don't mess with the kook."

"Don't we look comfortable?" Michelle jibed as she raised her eyebrows. "You've got quite a few stains there," she added, tilting her head down and pointing at Steve's messy apron. "Are you going to strain it and make soup for us this evening?"

Steve smiled and gave a quick response. "Watch it, lady. I can still put anything into your dinner that I damn well please." Steve bowed jokingly and beckoned to Michelle with an exaggerated sweep of his right arm, "Won't you come in." He was already feeling the effects of his first glass of wine.

"It's good to see you again," Michelle hugged him after he stood upright from his bow and kissed him on the cheek.

He held her tightly. "You, too."

"What an incredible location you have."

"Thanks. It feels good to finally have everything done and in the right place."

Steve took Michelle's hand and led her over to the couch. "Have a seat right here, and I'll get you a glass of wine."

"That sounds great." She tossed her purse aside and sat down on the sofa.

Billy Holiday crooned "Blue Moon" from the stereo, and candles glowed invitingly as Michelle looked around the well-decorated room. The aromatic smell of garlic and basil radiated from the kitchen, reminding her how hungry she was.

"You'll have to take me on a tour of your place after dinner." She spoke loudly, so that Steve could hear her over the bustle in the kitchen.

"I'd be happy to." Steve returned with a glass of Cabernet for her.

"Thank you," she said while cupping the bowl of the glass with both hands.

Steve stood over her. From his vantage point he couldn't help but notice that Michelle's sleeveless white blouse had the top three buttons undone, surely for his benefit. He did his best not to get caught staring at the lace adorning the top edge of her bra and sat down on the couch next to her.

"I'll have you know that you and Rick spoiled Sally and me with the wine we had in California. I hope that this vintage lives up to National Park wine standards." She nailed him again with an infectious smile.

"I think you'll like this just a tad more than that," he said, giving her a wry look. "I've got the cork in the kitchen, if you'd like to lick it."

She laughed and playfully slapped him on the shoulder.

"So how is Sally?"

"She's fine. . .I miss her already, though."

"I'm sure she'll visit you soon."

"She will."

"Tell me, did you have any trouble finding this place?"

"Other than my car's engine light coming on and nearly adding venison to this evening's menu, I have no comment." Michelle joked.

She brought the wine glass to her mouth and savored her first sip. "Mmmm. This is exactly what I needed."

"Happy to oblige. Is there anything I can do to help you with your car?"

"No. I think it may just be a short. It's been running fine. I'll have it checked out next week just to be sure."

"Let me know if I can help."

"Thank you."

Steve patted her on the thigh and excused himself in order to check on the sauce he was creating in the kitchen.

"The question is, can I help you with anything?" Michelle asked.

"No, ma'am. You sit right there and reee-lax," he said in his best Texas accent.

"It smells wonderful."

"Thanks."

Michelle slipped off her sandals, slid back on the couch, and crossed her legs. The smooth leather was cool and felt good against her bare skin. She took another lingering taste from her wine glass and surveyed her candle-lit surroundings.

She couldn't help but admire the masculine style of Steve's small, nicely remodeled bungalow. Remembering their conversations at Yosemite, Michelle knew he and his ex-wife had begun the restoration together, but he had completed the project by himself, stealing whatever time he could when he pulled himself away from the office. She could understand why it had evolved into a therapeutic process after the divorce.

Wandering around the living room, examining and admiring Steve's eclectic mix of art and furniture, Michelle said, "I love your things."

The varied objects reflected Steve's habit of purchasing unusual items as pleasant reminders of his travels. A pair of tall rusted-iron candlesticks from Santa Fe. Contemporary and classical paintings from galleries in Colorado and Washington. Tables from Mexico. Crosses from Europe. Michelle picked up a small bronze sculpture from an end table, surprised by the weight of the object.

She suddenly had an odd sensation that she was being watched and thought she saw some movement outside. Slowly, she turned her head and looked toward the bay window. She was startled to find that her instinct was correct. She was being watched—by a large, chocolate Labrador Retriever.

His head was down, parallel to the window. He looked sheepishly inside at Michelle with his enormous brown eyes.

"Looks like we have a visitor."

"What's that?" Steve peered into the den from the kitchen.

Michelle cupped her wine glass in her left hand and pointed toward the window. "I said, it looks like we have a visitor."

The dog continued to stare at her.

"He's beautiful."

"That's Bosco."

"Aren't you afraid he'll run away?"

"No, I have one of those invisible fences in the yard. I rarely have it on any more because he never leaves the yard without a leash. I let him out at night for a few minutes. Once he's sniffed around and gets a nose full of all of the deer that have been in the front yard, he's content to come back inside. I'm surprised you didn't see him when you came in."

"I didn't. Can I let him in?" Michelle asked.

"Sure, but I'll take no responsibility for his actions."

She walked toward the window, talking to the dog. "Hi, fella. Whatcha doin? You wanna come inside, Bosco?"

The dog barked, spinning around in obvious anticipation as Michelle walked toward him. She set her wine glass on an end table and unlocked the door.

Bosco ran inside, his momentum vaulting him past Michelle. He slowed himself as best he could on the hardwood floor, then spun around and rushed back to greet his new visitor. From the tail-wagging and licking of her shins, it was obvious that he readily approved.

Michelle squatted down to scratch Bosco's stomach, which by this time was pointing skyward. He bellowed out a low groan of approval, the timbre vibrating with each stroke of Michelle's arm.

Steve looked in on the two of them from the kitchen again while drying off a pan. *She likes dogs. That's good,* he thought.

"Do you have a dog?" he asked.

"No, not since I moved out of my parents' house to go to college. What a goooood boy you are," she said, increasing the vigor with which she scratched the dog. "Your daddy has spoiled you rotten."

"I'll have you know he is a fully trained, professional lapdog. It took me years to get him to that level, so don't you screw him up and teach him any good manners."

"Yeah, right. Like anything I do is going to change him." Michelle rubbed him under the chin one last time before retrieving her wine and returning to the couch.

Bosco made his way into the kitchen to greet Steve.

Once she was settled on the sofa again, Michelle could see into the hallway. She spied the flashing red light of the answering machine that sat on the small table beside the telephone. "You check your messages lately?"

"No, why? Did you call earlier when you got lost?"

"No, smart ass, your answer machine light is flashing."

Steve walked into the hallway. "It sure is." He pushed the play button.

"Hi, Stevie." It was Whitley, speaking in a very sexy, breathless voice. Michelle listened intently.

"I know it's short notice, but I wanted to see if you'd like to join me for dinner tonight. I'm making your favorite. Chineeeeeeese." Her voice began to return to its normal state. "I guess you must be working late again. What else is new? Call me. I'll be up late so feel free to call or drop by. Squeezes!"

Steve chuckled.

Michelle found herself somewhat ruffled even though she knew she had no right to be. "It sounds as if I may have disrupted someone's dinner plans," she said.

"Oh, no, not at all," Steve said. "Whitley is one of my best friends. We look out for each other, kinda like the lonely hearts club. She'll stay here and take care of Bosco when I go out of town.

She works for WESIC, too, in the IT department. Smart lady. I'll introduce you."

Michelle felt her pangs of jealousy start to dissipate.

"I'd better call her. Excuse me for just a moment."

"Sure, by all means," Michelle replied, acting nonchalant now that her confidence was restored.

Steve rang Whitley.

"Hello."

"Hey, you."

"Stevie! Where are you? Can you make it for dinner?"

"I'm sorry, kiddo. I've been in and out all evening and didn't even notice the answering machine. I've already made dinner plans for tonight."

"Shoot! I've hardly seen you the past couple of months you've been back."

"I know, kid. As usual, I've been swamped with a couple of big cases."

"I know you're busy. I just miss seeing ya, " Whitley said with an exaggerated pouting tone. "So what do you mean by dinner plans?" She added, "Have we got companeeee? Possibleee feeemale companeeee?"

"Yes, we do."

Whitley's heart sank at the news, but she fought to keep her composure. After a short pause she replied in her usual voice, "Really? And what might her name be?"

"Her name is Michelle. We met in California. But keep this between us."

"In California? You dog! That was fast."

"She just came to work for us."

"For WESIC?"

"Yes, in the underwriting department."

"Is her last name Grayson?"

"Yes. How did you know that?"

"I just got a work order to set up her cubicle late today. As usual, I'm helping out the Production Support group, so I'm going in early Monday to take care of it."

"That's her." Steve looked at Michelle and could see that she was confused by the conversation.

"Well, I'll just have to check her out, won't I? Is it serious?" Whitley did her best to hide her envy of the woman and, most of all, her obvious frustration.

"No, it isn't."

"Kinda difficult to talk, huh? Well, I won't keep you any longer. I'll save the stir-fry for one night later in the week if you're interested."

"Count on it."

"Before I go, I'll give you a quick synopsis of how lucky you'll be tonight. I saw your horoscope in the paper here somewhere."

Steve could hear her shuffling through the newspaper. "Okay," he chuckled.

"Your love level is about a six tonight, so don't go overboard."

"Thanks, Whitley."

"Your communication level is at nine, so this would be a good night for talking only. Don't try to rush anything." Of course, Whitley was making it all up as she went along, hoping Steve would abide by her manufactured suggestions.

"Thanks, Whitley."

"I'll look forward to meeting this mystery lady on Monday."

"I'm sure she'll enjoy meeting you too, Whitley. Okay, hon, I'd better run. I'll call you tomorrow." Steve cut her off while he had the chance and hung up.

"You're not going to tell me that she knows me, are you?" Michelle asked.

"No," Steve replied. "She saw your name on a work request form. Whitley will be setting up the computer in your work area Monday."

"Really? I look forward to meeting her."

"Well, let me check on the sauce. How are you doing on your wine? Need a refill?" Steve asked.

"I'm okay for now."

Steve stirred the sauce, tasted it one more time, and tapped the wooden spoon on the edge of the pot. "I declare this sauce ready."

"Fantastic! Let's eat."

"You have a seat right over here, and I'll serve us both." Steve pulled her chair away from the table so she could sit down.

"Thank you. I've forgotten what good manners are like."

Dinner and conversation lasted two hours before Steve cleared the table, rinsed the dishes, and loaded the dishwasher. "Can I get you a refill?" He pointed to her glass.

"If I didn't know better, I'd think you were trying to get me drunk."

"Guilty as charged, your honor."

"I don't know. I mean, I wouldn't want to give you the upper hand that easily. I think I should play hard to get and refuse."

"Oh, are you saying I have to earn it fair and square?"

"Absolutely!"

She grinned, then turned around, peering out the living room window toward the driveway. "I love your boat."

"Thanks. I haven't gotten to use it much at all lately."

Steve stood up and walked into the kitchen to retrieve a bottle of Moet from the fridge.

"Well, maybe you'll make time and take me out on it soon."

"Count on it," Steve yelled as he removed the cork with a loud pop. When he returned he carried the bottle, along with two glasses.

Michelle looked over her shoulder with a devilish expression, stood up, and slowly walked toward Steve. "Champagne? You *are* trying to get me drunk. Don't you understand that 'no' means 'no'?"

"I'm sorry, miss. I don't understand a word you're saying."

"You keep this up, and I'm not going to be able to drive home."

Steve looked up at the ceiling. "Hmmm. . .I suppose we'll just have to work through that. I could always call you a cab."

"Don't you dare!" Wrapping her arms around his waist, she smiled and gave him a long, deep kiss. "I've been waiting entirely too long to do that again," she said.

He set the bottle and the glasses on the coffee table. "I hope it was worth the wait."

"Umm, I haven't decided yet." She leaned into him, and they kissed again. Her back tingled as he reached behind her and ran his fingers up her shoulders to the nape of her neck, pulling, pressing her body more closely against his. She was getting extremely aroused by the feel of his muscular back where it curved powerfully to his waist.

They stopped for a moment, and Michelle looked passionately into Steve's eyes. "Thank you for a wonderful dinner." Michelle stood on her tiptoes and kissed him once more.

Delaying their mutual desire to continue, she pulled away from Steve's embrace slowly, seductively, until she reached the front door.

Steve was puzzled as he watched her retreat.

"I have always had this fantasy about making love on a boat," she said, staring at Steve and carefully unbuttoning her blouse to reveal the sheer lace bra that had intrigued him earlier in the evening. She removed her top and gently tossed it over the chair that sat in front of the bay window. "We may not have an ocean, but at least we have a boat."

She reached between her breasts with her right hand and released the hook of her bra. She opened the door with her left hand and spun around turning her back toward Steve, allowing the bra to slide down her arms as if she were removing a vest. Deftly throwing it on top of her blouse, Michelle cast an inviting look back at him one more time, before she ran across the lawn toward the boat.

Steve stood there, his senses reeling. He hesitated, as he thought about Whitley's recommendation to play it cool tonight.

No, we don't have the ocean, Steve thought for a moment. He was glad that he hadn't sold the boat yet. He was planning to do so, to make up any savings shortfall he would need to buy his ranch. He walked back into the kitchen, through the utility room door, and into the garage. He stopped to set the timer and headed back through the house, picked up the champagne and glasses, and continued toward the front door. Holding the doorknob, Steve briefly looked at his watch. Even if it doesn't rain, the sprinklers will go off in about twenty minutes, he thought. No water, huh? He smiled as he unbuttoned the top two buttons of his shirt and casually strolled toward the boat.

CHAPTER TWENTY-ONE

THE NEXT MORNING STEVE found himself in bed lying beside Michelle's naked body. The second cold front in less than a week had chased them off the boat. Steve closed his eyes and thought back to how they had rushed inside, continuing their lovemaking well into the night. The storm had rumbled through the city and he recalled the streaks of lightning splashing their bodies with sudden bursts of blue-gray light that intensified the atmosphere as well as the vigor with which they explored one another. Even though he was feeling the effects of slightly too much alcohol, it had been a glorious night.

Steve sat up in bed. In stark contrast to the evening's stormy passion, the broken morning sunlight sifting through the shutters created intermittent bands of shadows and light that traced gently across the sheets and over the impeccable form of Michelle's backside. Steve reached over and pulled the comforter up to her waist. She was still sleeping.

Bosco had been asleep on his pad underneath the bedroom window. He popped his head up when he saw Steve rustling out of bed. Steve led him quietly out of the bedroom, down the hall, and into the backyard.

The sounds and aromas from the kitchen would soon bring Michelle out of her slumber. For the first time in months and for the second time in a matter of twelve hours, Steve was cooking for a woman who interested him greatly. This comfortable feeling had been nothing more than a fading memory for too long. He was finally ready for a relationship.

CHAPTER TWENTY-TWO

WHITLEY AWOKE MONDAY MORNING much earlier than normal, and with good reason. After the third sleepless night in a row, it was time to meet her demons head on. In this case, the demon known as Michelle Grayson would be her first confrontation.

Only a few hours after talking with Steve on Friday, the impulse was so strong that she had given up on will power and driven to his house at four o'clock on a chilly Saturday morning to see if anyone was parked in his driveway. Because she couldn't chance the possibility of being seen if he and Michelle were still there, and because she certainly didn't want Bosco to bark if he happened to be wandering around in the back yard and recognized her, she had parked her car down the road. Given that she could not see the house from the street, she had jogged part of the way down Steve's driveway to check out the situation.

Much to her dismay, Whitley saw parked in the driveway a car with Oregon plates that had to be Michelle's. No lights were on anywhere except the front porch.

Dejectedly, she realized Steve hadn't heeded her advice after all. She drove to an all-night café and drank coffee until the sun came up. Her mind raced, wondering how long Michelle had stayed at Steve's house and what they had done. She couldn't bear the thought of him being with another woman, especially one she had never met. Worse, she was furious with herself for allowing these negative thoughts to fill her head. The rest of the weekend she had spent in a mildly depressed state, watching videos alone in her apartment.

As she stood applying more makeup than normal to hide the deep circles under her eyes, Whitley became more and more anxious about the impending meeting with Michelle. Jealous twinges continued to creep into her mind. Had he known her for longer than he was letting on? Had he lied? Was he on vacation with her from the start? She wanted to see the woman Steve Latham was seeing, because if Whitley Talmadge wasn't his type, she wanted to know who the hell was.

"Damn it, Steve! I can't believe you did this!" she screamed and threw her hairbrush into the bathtub.

Fighting back tears which were now more a result of fatigue, she pulled on a pair of form-fitting black slacks, a white pinpoint cotton blouse, and a pair of black dress shoes retrieved from the farthest recesses of her closet. Even though she had banked a total of ten hours of sleep since Friday, she looked great. She just had to stop crying.

Whitley greatly outranked Michelle in the WESIC salary-grade hierarchy, but some individuals didn't give the Information Systems employees much respect. Even though Whitley was going to be setting up this woman's workstation, she was going to look good doing it, and she wasn't about to allow a lower-level employee to treat her as if she were a personal laborer.

After a six-mile commute, her run-away emotions were in check by the time she reached the WESIC complex. It was 6:30, and most of her co-workers wouldn't arrive for another thirty minutes at best. She swiped her access card through The Dungeon's reader and walked inside to her office. Her department was harbored in an ultra-clean environment with the highest level of security in the building—one way in, one way out—and its own elaborate defense system.

Within ten minutes she had Michelle's telephone and computer access codes entered into the system. Whitley reviewed the job order again to verify that she had given Michelle the proper access, all of the system hardware and software specified by Jan Mitchell, and the correct type of telephone for her position. The only chore remaining was to finish the manual connections at Michelle's cubicle.

Michelle pulled into the WESIC parking lot at 7:30. Drawing a deep breath and looking like someone out of CEO Magazine, she felt a rush of excitement as she walked to the main entrance. She was looking forward to the increased responsibility as well as the increased pay of a senior underwriter.

After taking this step toward a senior staff position within WESIC, she now needed just one more promotion to reach a director's position. Once she achieved this, she would have reached her first major business goal. She smiled as she approached the receptionist.

"Yes, ma'am. May I help you?" the receptionist asked in a cheerful Texas twang.

"Yes. I'm Michelle Grayson. I've. . ."

"Hi, Michelle! I'm Sandy," she interrupted and extended her hand. "Welcome to Austin. We've been expecting you! Jan Mitchell has asked that you wait in your cube on the third floor. She'll meet you there at 8:30. That's a beautiful suit you're wearing, by the way."

"Thank you."

Sandy handed Michelle a stack of papers. "If you'll take this paperwork down the hall to Security, two doors down on the right, they'll get you fixed up with a new ID card. Joe's already there, so he can make one up right away. If you need anything else, I'm kinda known as the WESIC concierge, so don't hesitate to ask me for anything."

"Thank you so much for your help, Sandy."

"You're welcome. See you around, Michelle."

"See you." Michelle turned and walked down the hallway. Her heels clicking on the granite floor echoed down the quiet hallway.

Michelle had no trouble finding the security office, located directly across from the elevators. Once she had her photo taken, her card was assembled and tested. Joe Alvarez clipped it to a nylon cardholder that she could wear around her neck.

"You're ready for business, Ms. Grayson. Take the elevator behind you to the third floor, and Michelle Grayson headquarters is located right here." Joe had circled a cubicle on the piece of paper mapping out the third floor. "Would you like an escort?"

"No, thanks, Joe. I'm a little early, so I thought I'd snoop around a bit if you don't mind."

"Hmmm. You don't look like a corporate spy. I guess I'll have to allow it, but remember, the walls have eyes!" He pointed two fingers toward his eyes then turned them toward Michelle.

"I should be okay as long as you don't sell anything to the tabloids," she cracked.

Joe was still laughing when Michelle glided out to the elevators and pushed the third-floor button. As the elevator door closed, she could see her reflection in its brass-plate trim. She straightened her suit, making sure everything was in place for her first meeting. She wore a well-tailored, dark-blue pinstripe suit with a white taffeta blouse open at the neck. The heel clicks of her navy shoes were muffled by the carpet as she exited the third-floor elevator and walked across the vestibule to the Underwriting Department.

Rounding the corner to her cubicle, the sight of two legs protruding from under her desk startled her to an abrupt stop. She surmised it must be Whitley. Michelle said nothing and watched, all the while taking stock of the sparse furnishings in her work space. Behind the desk facing her, a wall of glass revealed the parking lot and a view of the outside lunch patio. Two double-drawer lateral file cabinets flanked her desk. The walls of the cube were bare except for a company calendar hanging unevenly to the left of the computer. Looking forward to applying her own appointments, she looked back at the legs under her desk and said, "Nice shoes."

"What?" Whitley jumped. "God, you scared me." She looked through the space between the keyboard tray and the desk. "Michelle?"

"Yes. Are you Whitley? I'm sorry. I didn't mean to scare you."

"I am," she said and pulled herself out from under the desk, "and thank you. About the shoes, I mean. Nice to meet you." She smiled and shook hands with Michelle, all the while thinking, *God, she's stunning, and she's nice. I hate her already.*

"Steve has told me nothing but great things about you."

"I hope he didn't tell you everything."

"I bet as smart as he said you are, you haven't told him everything either, now have you?" She smiled. "We've got to show the opposite sex who's boss, right?"

"Amen to that."

She clapped her hands together, "Am I ready to start work?"

Whitley couldn't believe with all her preparation this morning, she was still out-dressed. "A couple more connections, and you'll be up and running."

"Take your time. I'll check out the rest of the floor."

Whitley slid back under the desk to finish her installation, as Michelle wandered around checking out the artwork on the walls. Ten minutes later, she stood up from the desk and saw Michelle returning. Whitley retrieved her clipboard from the desk and began checking off the completed tasks.

"Okay. You're ready to go. Have a seat and power up." She handed Michelle a post-it note with two six-digit alphanumeric numbers. "I'm sure you already know all of what I'm about to tell you, but we're required to treat everyone as if they just came in off the street. The top number is your ID. The middle one is your password. The number at the bottom is my extension. You should change the password right away since it's the same one we give all new installations." She cautioned Michelle about WESIC security procedures regarding passwords, advised her not to use certain words, then summed up, "In any case, the password must have at least one numeral and one special character. After you've had a chance to look over the software, let me know if there's anything else you might need."

"Got it. Hey, while we're talking computers here, I was thinking about taking some night courses for some different software programs. Do you have any suggestions?"

"Sure. If you are looking for higher-level courses, try Austin Community College or University of Texas extension courses. Between the two of them you should be able to find exactly what you want."

"Thanks, I'll check them out."

"You're welcome. And one other thing. . .This place can be a rumor mill. I'd keep the fact that you and Steve are seeing other down to a minimum, at least for a while. It'll help prevent either one of you from having to explain your way out of an uncomfortable situation. I'll give you a run-down on who to look out for."

"Thanks, Whitley. I appreciate the heads up." Michelle noticed that Whitley looked tired. "Forgive me for my boldness, but you are a beautiful woman, Whitley."

Surprised by the compliment, she responded, "Thank you, but I look like hell today. I think I'm a little under the weather with allergies."

"If this is a bad day, you should have been a model."

"Well, thanks." Whitley had a good feeling about Michelle. At least the woman seemed sincere.

Whitley and Michelle turned to see Jan Mitchell striding down the aisle.

"Hi, Whitley! Is she all set?"

"All done!" Whitley replied.

Jan patted Whitley on the shoulder, "Whitley is our resident lifesaver, Michelle. How many top-end software developers do you know who will also jump in to help set up our folks' workstations?" Jan extended her hand to Michelle. "Welcome to Austin! How was your trip?"

"It was nice. And I'm already moved in. I was getting pretty tired of living out of a suitcase."

Whitley hurried to collect her things to leave. "Excuse me. Michelle, I've got two more connections for new employees to finish. Let me know if you need anything else. And call me if you don't have lunch plans. I'll show you around."

"No lunch plans. I'll call you. Thanks, Whitley," Michelle responded.

Disappointed or not, I can't help but like that lady, Whitley thought. *It appears that Steve may have found a good one after all.*

Pushing her dolly toward the elevators, she scarcely noticed the conversation between Jan and Michelle growing fainter as tears welled up again and threatened to spill over.

CHAPTER TWENTY-THREE

CONSIDERING THE INFORMATION HE had read the latter part of the weekend in pouring over Detective Kelly's notes and the police reports, Steve had decided to backtrack and re-interview some of those surrounding the case, in the event the police might have missed something.

He attempted to turn from Twenty-fourth Street onto Guadalupe Street in the midst of a morning swarm of college students. Tapping the steering wheel to the beat of a Stevie Ray Vaughn CD cranked up on the Porsche's formidable sound system, he caught more than his share of second looks from a cluster of young girls. However, it appeared that his presence on the scene wasn't going over quite as well with a few of their testosterone-laden boyfriends following just behind.

Glancing at his watch, he noted that it was 7:30 and realized Michelle was probably at the office. He wanted to call her, but business had to come first.

Steve turned left on Guadalupe Street after the horde finally crossed the road. He worked his way through a series of aggravating traffic signals until he reached Thirty-first Street.

There he turned right and drove about half a block to his first stop, Saint Anne's Catholic Church where Miller Walker had been the bookkeeper.

Although Steve had seen the beautiful 1920s Gothic structure several times from Whitley's balcony, he had never been inside. The church's group of buildings was positioned between the northernmost part of the U.T. campus and Whitley's apartment complex. The church was nestled beneath a cluster of oak trees, some of the oldest and largest in the area. Their root systems had seized much of the sidewalk in front of the church, splitting, cracking, and elevating the concrete slabs in such a fashion that the walkway had become a series of angled planes leaning in all directions. Wooden stakes placed in the ground and connected by a length of orange ribbon gave notice that the sidewalk would soon be under repair. Steve unfolded a piece of paper, upon which he had scribbled a list of questions before leaving the office.

"Father Alonso Ochoa," he read, and he tried to recall the bits of information about her favorite priest that Whitley had shared during the past months.

Father Alonso had moved to Austin from Venezuela four years ago as assistant to the aging Father Matthew Flaherty. The young priest had soon become popular among his parishioners. Father Matthew's untimely passing came a little over two years after the new priest arrived. It had been no surprise to anyone that Father Alonso was the parish's unanimous choice as a replacement.

The Archdiocese had summoned a representative to assist the new leader of St. Anne's and to help the parish with the transitional period and their grief over the loss of Father Matthew. The representative had remarked to his superiors that this was the easiest change in church leadership with which he had ever been involved. Usually a number of parishioners would voice some opposition to a candidate or request that other prospective candidates be brought in for the transitional period. However, there had been no such requests. In fact, Father Alonso had single-handedly lifted the spirits of the entire congregation after Father Matthew's death.

Only the age of the young priest belied his scope of knowledge, which was well beyond his 38 years. Intelligent, fluent in four languages, and sickeningly handsome, the joke around the diocese was that the female parishioners would sin just for the opportunity to spend time with Father Alonso during confession.

For what appeared to be a relatively small church from the outside, the interior of St. Anne's was breathtaking. The carved limestone entrance gave way to Corinthian columns lining the sanctuary. The pillars formed solid anchors beneath a soaring rib-vaulted ceiling, which drew the eye up toward stained glass images decorating the clerestory windows. A massive wooden crucifix loomed behind the altar with a carved wooden sculpture of a frail Jesus nailed to it. The darkness of the upper regions of the church hid the cables and gave the illusion that the crucifix was floating in space. Steve took a moment to absorb the beauty of his surroundings. He found the church to be quite awe inspiring.

"Wow! This place is unbelievable," he whispered aloud.

"Indeed it is," a man replied in a Spanish accent.

Steve jumped, surprised by the unexpected comment from a corner pew.

"I am sorry to startle you, my friend," he said. "I too love the view from back here." A priest stood up and walked toward Steve.

"It's easy to understand why, Father."

"I try to spend at least one hour of every weekday meditating in this spot. I find it so peaceful and uplifting when I can enjoy my quiet time."

"I am very sorry, Father. I didn't mean to intrude during your prayer time."

"Nonsense, you didn't interrupt me at all. I am glad to have a visitor today."

The priest shook hands with Steve and said, "I am Father Alonso Ochoa, but my friends call me Father Al. I hope you will do the same."

Steve observed the priest carefully, caught off-guard by his kind disposition. Even more surprising was his striking appearance. *This guy could have been a movie star,* Steve thought. *For someone who looks to be in his late-30s or early-40s, he must have had one hell of a good reason to join the priesthood and live a life of celibacy.*

"I'm Steve Latham from Western States Insurance Company, Father."

"Western States? Do you know my friend, Whitley Talmadge?"

"Yes, I do. She's one of my closest friends."

Father Al paused a moment, realizing the man before him was the very source of Whitley's unrequited love, then said, "Then you are a friend of mine. Welcome, Steve Latham. What brings you and your company to St. Anne's today?"

"Well, Father, I came to talk to you about one of your former parishioners. Miller Walker."

"Ah, yes. Poor Miller. What a tragedy."

"What can you tell me about him, Father?"

"He was such a dear friend of the church. However, Miller had become a bit reclusive. He wasn't what you would call a conversationalist."

"What exactly did he do for Saint Anne's?"

"He was our treasurer. He kept up with our banking and did our taxes. He did a wonderful job, by the way. He will be sorely missed around here, sorely missed indeed. But, Steve, I've already talked to the police about Miller. You're questions are quite similar."

"I used to be a policeman several years ago. I guess old habits are hard to break," Steve smiled.

"Is there a problem with his insurance?" Alonso asked.

"No, Father. His house was a total loss, and I'm just trying to get as much detail as possible before we close out all of our files and pay his claims. What can you tell me about his personal life, Father?"

"His personal life?"

"I'm sorry, Father. In other words, did he and his wife get along? Did he have any personal or emotional problems that you might know about? Those sorts of things."

"I see. Well, unfortunately, he divorced his wife soon after I arrived at St. Anne's. I only met her once. She was a pleasant woman but like Miller, not very talkative. I offered to have them come in for counseling on one or two occasions after Miller had mentioned divorce, but he declined. He stated that their differences were irreconcilable, and he had to let her go. Regrettably, I pushed the issue no further. That is really all that I know of his life away from the church. Just as his wife, he was a rather quiet and introspective individual, but he did a wonderful job with our books."

"I see," Steve replied. "Did he ever speak of his ex-wife after the divorce? Whether or not they might have kept in touch, for example?"

"Well, he did mention the fact that she moved out of town, but he didn't elaborate beyond that point." Father Alonso looked at Steve inquisitively. "Steve, let me ask something, if you don't mind."

"Not at all, Father."

"Excuse my ignorance, but why might your company be interested in his ex-wife?"

Ordinarily, Steve wouldn't have divulged any information about a client, but he felt that the priest might be able to help him. "Mr. Walker had taken out a life insurance policy with our company and listed his ex-wife as the beneficiary."

"Oh, I see. Is that commonly done?"

"It isn't that unusual to have an ex-spouse listed. Sometimes, people forget to change the beneficiary after a divorce, especially with coverage under health plans from their employers or just the fact that the policy had been in force for a number of years. Others just leave the ex-spouse listed so that they can bestow one final gesture of love upon them, especially if they were against the divorce in the first place."

"I hope that the latter is true in this case, Steve."

"Me, too, Father. Well, I won't take up any more of your time. It's been a real pleasure meeting you."

"And you, Steve. I do hope that you will come back for a more personal visit one Sunday very soon, and bring Whitley with you. She owes me a couple of visits, and I miss so much seeing her."

"You can count on it, Father. You have a beautiful church."

"Thank you." Father Alonso walked Steve through the church entrance onto the stair landing that led down to the sidewalk below.

"Go with God." Father Alonso used both hands to clasp Steve's with a firm grip.

"Thank you again, Father."

Steve made his way down the short flight of stairs and navigated the sidewalk construction beside the church to his car. Father Alonso watched him and waved goodbye as he drove away.

Steve waved and looked back through his rearview mirror, catching a final glimpse of Father Alonso walking back into the church. As he drove toward his next appointment where he would interview a couple of Miller's neighbors, he wondered again why this man had ever decided to became a priest.

CHAPTER TWENTY-FOUR

"SO, TELL ME. HOW have your first few hours at WESIC Austin been going?" Whitley was determined not to let her emotions get in the way of building a friendship with this new woman in Steve's life.

"So far, so good. Everyone is really nice in this city. I guess that's what they mean by Southern hospitality. It's so much better than I expected," Michelle said.

"I'm glad you like it. I think Austin's the best place to live in Texas, if not the whole country. But forget about stuff I already know. Tell me about how you and Steve hooked up. That man is like a closed book when it comes to his personal life." Whitley took a bite of her sandwich and listened intently.

"I'm sorry. I really shouldn't kiss and tell right away," Michelle looked up at the ceiling momentarily, then at her watch. "Okay, I suppose that's been long enough."

They both chuckled.

"It was totally unexpected, Whitley. I had finally gotten out of a bad, long-term relationship and had some free time. My friend Sally who works, or rather worked, with me in Portland had been trying to get me to go on vacation with her for a while. We met with a travel agent and decided on a healthy vacation destination with lots of hiking. Yosemite sounded like the perfect spot. So we flew to Fresno, rented a car, and drove to the park.

"After we showed up at our hotel, we threw our suitcases into our room and immediately began our quest for health by making a mad dash to the bar! And who is the first person we see? None other than our fearless leader from Portland, Rick Taylor."

"I know Rick. You've got to be kidding me!"

"I'm not. I mean, you try to leave work behind by traveling hundreds of miles from home only to run into one of the head honchos of the company."

"What are the odds?"

"I know. So there we were, having a couple of drinks with Rick. After we made sure he didn't follow us down there, he told us that he was waiting on a good friend that used to work with him in Portland."

"You didn't know Steve when he was working in Portland?"

"No, I didn't. Anyway, Sally and I are sitting there with Rick when this hot-looking guy comes walking in. Sally saw him first and told Rick she hoped that was his friend Steve. And it just so happened that it was."

"Lucky you."

"I'll say."

"What happened next?"

"We went our separate ways for the first couple of days, then later in the week we all hiked around the valley. The guys taught us how to climb a bit."

"Forget about the exercise recap. Give me the good stuff."

Michelle chuckled, "Steve and I talked a long time as we hiked alone up to a place called Glacier Point, and that's where he kissed me."

"How was it? It sounds so romantic," Whitley said, doing her best to sound nonchalant as her foot tapped out a drum solo on the floor that would make John Bonham proud.

"It was nice. And other than a good-bye kiss later in the week, there wasn't much more to tell, until I got to Austin."

"You mean you two didn't. . .?" Whitley gestured by poking her right index finger into the circle she made with her left hand.

"Nope, not until after I moved here."

"Well, I hope it lasts." Whitley actually hoped that she didn't notice the clenched fists and the reddening of her skin color.

"I'm not going to worry about it. I just got out of a long-term relationship, and I'm just going to let this run its course." Michelle took a sip of water. Still sucking on her straw, she looked up at Whitley, sensing there was something more to this inquiry than her lunch companion was letting on. "So. Who's the man in your life?"

"That would be my mother," Whitley responded, not missing a beat.

Michelle laughed. "Do I detect some family issues?"

"You got it! Ever since my father died, my mother Winona has taken it upon herself to burden her life with the additional responsibility of fathering me. In her eyes I can't make a good decision to save my ass." On the fingers of one hand Whitley ticked off her mother's criticisms. "My car is too old. My food choices suck. My personal life is non-existent. I'm going to hell because I follow the occasional horoscope instead of the word of the Lord. You know, the usual complaints."

"Does she live in Austin?" Michelle asked.

"Nope. She lives in Dallas."

"How far away is Dallas?"

"Not far enough. Three or four hours."

"That's got to be comparable to a distance of two or three states away anywhere else in the country. At least that lessens the chance of her showing up on your doorstep unannounced."

"I love that woman more than you can know, but I don't understand why her sole purpose in life now is to make my life a living hell. She never used to concern herself with these things when my dad was around."

"Sounds like she loves you."

"Yeah. In a lot of ways I'm very lucky to have her. I just wish she would focus more on herself and less on me."

"I hear you. But the day she's gone will be the day you wish she was still bothering you."

"I'm sure."

"But enough about her. Let's get back to my question. Who's the man in your life?"

"I don't have one right now."

"I can't believe that. Whitley, you're gorgeous."

"I don't feel gorgeous. I've been thinking lately about a makeover of some sort."

"I'd be happy to help you if you'd like. I'm no expert, but I've helped a couple of my friends with their wardrobes."

"That would be wonderful. I saw this woman at a local park a few weeks ago. She had this great hairstyle I liked. It was similar to yours, but a bit longer. As a matter of fact, I saw her around the same time you and Steve were likely giving each other mouth-to-mouth in Yosemite," she winked at Michelle and smiled.

"If you're free, let's make plans to meet this coming weekend," Michelle said.

"Okay. This weekend it is."

"We'll go through some magazines and pick out a whole new look for you. One of my favorite things to do is spend other people's money."

"I may have to take out a loan for this project."

"Faith, Whitley," Michelle replied. "Faith."

As the women continued their conversation, Trent rounded the corner from the cashier and saw them both. Whitley motioned for him to come over. He locked onto the women like a fighter jet on a stationary target, covering the distance between them in what seemed like a single, fluid movement. Whitley barely had enough time to warn Michelle about Trent's need for female companionship.

"Come join us, Trent. I've got someone I'd like you to meet."

"Hi, Whitley. I'm afraid I can't stay long. I'm meeting Amy here in a few minutes."

"This won't take long. Michelle Grayson, meet Trent Osborne."

Trent set his tray down between the two women, "Ah, you're our new senior underwriter. Welcome. It's so nice to meet you,"

Trent couldn't take his eyes off of either of them. His head was bouncing back and forth like a spectator at a tennis match.

"Nice to meet you, Trent," Michelle answered, giving him a firm handshake and looking him right in the eye.

"Trent works in our SIU department. He works for a great guy over there named Steve Latham. You'll have to meet him sometime," Whitley bulged her eyes at Michelle in an exaggerated fashion when Trent wasn't looking, not realizing that Trent already knew about Michelle's involvement with Steve.

"Really? So what exactly do you do in SIU, Trent? Working on any top-secret cases you can share with us?"

"Well, I could tell you about the one I'm working on now, but I'd have to kill you."

"Oh, that's original," Whitley said.

"I'm kidding. We've got a death claim we're checking into. But that's all I can say about it."

"Sounds interesting," Michelle said.

"It is. I enjoy working there. Maybe I shouldn't tell you this, but I was your competition for the underwriting job. Although, competition may not be the best choice of words."

"You were? What a coincidence."

"From what I hear, they gave the position to the right person. In case you didn't know it, you have a reputation that precedes you, and it's a very good one."

"That's very sweet of you to say. Thank you."

"You're welcome. Oops, I see Amy. I better get going," Trent extended his hand. "It was very nice to meet you, Michelle."

"You, too, Trent."

Trent nodded at Whitley, "Miss Talmadge, always a pleasure."

"Bye, Trent," Whitley responded with a disinterested tone.

After he was gone, Michelle looked toward Whitley, "He's cute."

"Oh yeah, real cute. You gonna mop his drool off of the table, or should I?"

"Whitley! He was very nice."

"Give it a little more time with the T-bone, girl, and you'll see what I mean."

CHAPTER TWENTY-FIVE

WHEN WHITLEY'S PHONE RANG on Friday morning, she recognized Michelle's extension on the readout. "Hey, you! How goes it?"

"I'm having a day," Michelle exhaled as she spoke.

"That doesn't sound too good for your first week at the office."

"I had car trouble this morning. The shop sent a guy over to check it out, but he ended up having to tow it to the garage. I have no idea what's wrong with it. I'm not at all mechanically minded. For all I know, they could tell me I need a new engine, and I'd believe them!"

"Oh, I hope it's nothing serious."

"Me, too. And of course I have my community college class tonight."

"You can use my car if you'd like."

"Thanks, but I'm going to rent one."

"You don't have to do that. If you don't have a problem driving a land yacht, you're welcome to it."

"It's not that at all. I just don't want to put you out. Besides, I was planning on running on Town Lake over by Zilker Park before my class."

"Use my car tonight. Tomorrow I can go with you to get a rental if you find out from the shop that you will need one for any length of time. I can catch a ride home with my friend Linda. She lives near me. Hey! It's Friday, and it sounds like you could use the exercise to get rid of some of that stress."

"I'll say. But it's such short notice, Whitley. Are you sure I'm not putting you out?"

"I insist. You can come by the apartment tomorrow morning, and I'll take you back home or to the shop if your car is ready. Besides, we still need to plan my makeover metamorphosis for tomorrow evening."

"Okay, but tonight I'll ride with you to your place and take the car from there. Won't that be on my way to Town Lake anyway?"

"Sure is."

"And I'll bring your car home tonight after class."

"Not necessary. I'm not doing anything tonight and will probably be in bed by 9:00 with this kick-ass social life of mine."

"You party animal."

"That's me, alright."

"I will only agree to this if I can take you to breakfast in the morning before we create the new you."

"Deal. I'll pick the place. I know of a great little hole-in-the-wall you'll like."

"Terrific. Call me when you're ready to leave this afternoon."

"Will do. Bye."

That afternoon Whitley met Michelle in the WESIC lobby and led her to "Molé Grande's" spot on the parking garage roof. The area was sparsely filled with a few larger SUVs and pickups.

"You trying to give me a warm-up workout before I get to Town Lake?"

"I told you, we could have taken the elevator."

"I'm kidding."

"I park up here to have more room since I drive a pretty big Cadillac. When I parked on the lower levels, I was always afraid I'd ding the shit out of the other cars. You'll see what I mean."

They rounded the stairwell exit, and the car came into view.

"Pretty big, did you say?"

"Say hello to 'Molé Grande'."

"My God, do you need a special license to operate something this big?" Michelle joked.

"Wait 'til you drive her. Smooth as silk."

They got into the car and spiraled down to the garage exit.

"Well, tell me. Did your day get any better?" Whitley asked, trying to keep the conversation light.

"Much. And thanks again for letting me use your car tonight."

"You're welcome to it any time."

"I appreciate that. Whitley, I'm no psychic, and I don't want to pry. . ." Michelle paused.

"There's always a 'but' in that kind of observation. Go on. Spit it out! We're friends now."

"Okay. I know you've told me that you and Steve are just friends, but I'm not so sure."

Whitley was caught off-guard by her comment. "I. . .well. . ."

Michelle had never seen Whitley at a loss for words during their short friendship. Michelle lowered her voice. "Look, I like Steve. He's a great guy with a lot going on, but we are in the early stages of our relationship. I don't want to get in the middle of something that may have been going on between you two."

"Michelle, we are just friends. Honest. We have never even kissed before. At least not romantically."

"Do you want to?"

Whitley held her poker face and grinned. "He likes you Michelle and he's happy, and that makes me happy. Don't you think that if I wanted a relationship with Steve, I would have attempted something by now?"

"I guess so." She stared into Whitley's eyes for any hint that she might be masking her feelings. "I didn't mean to..."

Whitley interrupted before she had a chance to finish, "You haven't at all, Michelle."

"I guess. . .I just feel that I shouldn't play games any more at my age, that maybe I'm. . .maturing!"

They laughed.

"You two are going to live happily ever after. I just know it." Whitley didn't reveal anything to Michelle about the card reading she had held a few nights before. It foretold of something ominous surrounding Michelle and Steve, but she couldn't figure out exactly what it meant. After Michelle had car trouble, she was relieved and surmised that was the predicted event.

They arrived at Whitley's apartment in 25 minutes. Whitley parked in her spot behind the building and kept the motor running.

"Wait here a minute," Whitley said. "I have to get the extra car key out of the apartment."

"No problem. I'll check to see if I've gotten any messages," Michelle said and reached into her purse for her cell phone.

A black Suburban pulled over down the street just before Whitley came around to the front of the building.

The occupant tossed his short cigarette butt out the window as soon as he saw the woman running up the stairs. He was about 150 yards away. He paused and was just about to get out of the car when he saw her coming back down. Stepping out, he jogged to the alley that ran between a row of several houses and Whitley's building and looked down it.

"I'll fill it up before I bring it back," Michelle offered. "Why don't you take your free time tonight to rifle through some magazines for makeover ideas. We can look at them together tomorrow."

"Okay, I will."

"Thanks again, sweetie!" Michelle hugged Whitley and fastened her seat belt. As Michelle turned the key, the engine purred with low rumble. She noticed that she had about half a tank of gas as she pulled the ample car out into light traffic.

The man saw the rear end of the brown Cadillac drawing away from the parking area. He jogged back to his truck, jumped in, and raced up the street to keep the Caddy in sight. In doing so, he was already past the apartment building and missed seeing Whitley come back around from the parking area to the front and walk upstairs.

Michelle had an hour and a half for a quick run around Town Lake and a shower before her evening computer lab began at 7:30. The class was at the downtown community college campus near her condo. She made the block and turned left onto Guadalupe Street. Still acquainting herself with the mammoth car, she adjusted the rearview mirror. She checked the view out of the Cadillac's side mirrors, thinking nothing of the dark Suburban to her right and one car length back.

"Molé Grande" rolled effortlessly along.

Driving westward from the downtown area she headed toward Austin High School, one of several parking areas around Town Lake. Nearing the school, she noticed a couple of open spots on the road beside the school. She quickly pulled alongside the curb and parallel parked into one of them.

The Suburban pulled into the school parking lot and the driver watched as Michelle got out of the car.

After completing her stretching routine and a few warm-up drills, Michelle began her run. Starting slowly at first, she picked up her pace after a quarter mile under a sun that was still relatively warm and bright. Her route took her east, under Lamar Boulevard to the Congress Avenue Bridge. She crossed over Town Lake to the south shore of Lake Austin and headed west back towards Lamar. She was unaware that the Suburban had crossed the bridge above her. She passed under the Lamar bridge and continued west into Zilker Park.

The driver had seen Michelle cross Lamar and knew she would likely go all the way to the MOPAC bridge before crossing back over the lake to complete her loop. He sped to Zilker Park and parked on a nearby road where the trail ran alongside one of the park's open fields. Hopping out of the truck, he casually strolled into the dense foliage along the path.

Friday evenings were about the only time the number of runners thinned out, but even then there were too many as far as the driver was concerned. Michelle was enjoying her run. Once she was across the footbridge spanning the tributary that led to Barton Springs Pool, Michelle picked up the pace to get her heart rate up to peak level.

Her running shoes fell lightly on the cinder track, even after she hit her stride. The thick vegetation along the footpath provided protection from the sun, but it also caused an unwelcome chill on this south side of the lake.

The track made a gradual turn to the right.

Rounding the bend, she noticed two runners approximately three hundred yards ahead and decided to catch them before the MOPAC overpass. At her current pace she would win this cat-and-mouse game, no problem.

Coming out of the curve, Michelle felt a sudden thud. Within seconds, an odd sensation instantly consumed her. An incredibly sharp pain knifed into her head. She gasped once, then felt as if her body was beginning to float, gently at first, starting from her feet. The feeling gained momentum and rushed upward through her body. The surge reached her chest, a numbing sensation consumed her entire being. Then nothing.

She was dead before she hit the ground.

The bullet from the driver's suppressed .22 caliber pistol barrel had slammed into her right temple. The force had knocked her off her feet and down the steep embankment toward the water.

The driver calmly but quickly walked to the edge of the brush line. He could see that she was obscured not only by the thick brush but also by the fact she had fallen into a narrow ravine. Listening for the sound of any oncoming foot traffic, he quietly walked back uphill to the edge of the foliage. From behind a tree he peered down the trail in both directions before he hopped from the cover of the woods. Brushing a few stray leaves from his trousers, he pulled a pack of cigarettes from his pocket. He fired one up and calmly walked back up the trail to his vehicle. In a matter of a few minutes he had distanced himself from the crime scene.

CHAPTER TWENTY-SIX

SATURDAY MORNING WAS GLORIOUS. Whitley had already been up for an hour. Her mental alarm clock woke her up at 5:00 a.m., and she was thankful that her prediction about an uneventful Friday evening had proven true after going to bed at 8:30. She went to her door and peered out of the peephole. No newspaper yet. She walked back into the kitchen, poured herself a big mug of coffee, and walked out on the balcony.

It was still dark. Whitley looked toward the church parking lot where the arguing men had been standing. An uneasy feeling instantly came over her. She took another drink from her mug, walked back inside, and locked the patio door.

CHAPTER TWENTY-SEVEN

AT 6:30 A.M., IT was still early enough that not too many joggers filled the hike-and-bike trail. A young father was pushing his child in an ultra-light, three-wheeled jogging stroller. Near the end of his run, he was approaching Zilker Park. At the cutoff for the parking lot, he heard something scurry off into the shrubbery on his right. His curiosity piqued, he slowed to a stop, careful not to wake his son in the cart.

Another bustling sound from the dense wall of undergrowth between the jogging path and the south side of Town Lake lured him to the edge of the brush. He moved some branches aside with his hand and forearm to get a better look. He still couldn't see what he was following, so he ducked under a branch and took a step closer.

He sprung backward in fear when he realized he was looking at a body. The young woman's dark hair was in tangles and covered in blood.

APD dispatched a patrol car that arrived within minutes of receiving the report. An ambulance arrived soon after. Police closed off the portion of the trail where the body had been discovered and cordoned off the area.

Patrolman John Garrett could see that the crime scene needed more security than he and his partner could give. "Al, call in and get a couple more cruisers here. ASAP!"

Rookie Al Ortiz radioed for more uniforms, adding, "and patch me through to Homicide."

"Homicide. This is Detective Wallace."

"This is Officer Ortiz. We got what appears to be a murder at the south side of Town Lake, near the jogging path. The location is in Zilker, south and east across Town Lake from Austin High School."

"You got a perimeter up?"

"Yes, sir."

"I'll notify Forensics. We're on the way."

"Ten-four. Out."

Three patrol cars converged at the same time from different directions, all hopping the curb and driving across Zilker's freshly mown meadow. The plastic yellow police line fluttered in the light, early morning breeze coming off the lake.

Garrett, who stood with the man who had discovered the body, would be the ranking officer on the scene until detectives arrived. He placed patrolmen at crucial points to maintain the integrity of the crime scene.

"John, Homicide is on the way."

"Good. Al, make sure you keep everyone away from the body," Garrett said.

"What about EMS?"

"The lady's cold. They gotta wait for Homicide. They know the drill."

Al blushed with embarrassment. "I knew that."

Garrett knew this was Al's first homicide. In a hushed tone he said, "What do you think?"

"Kind of eerie, isn't it?" Al asked.

"As much as I hate to say it, you get used to it. It isn't always easy, but after a while you learn to distance yourself."

"I can see that you'd have to."

"I have to babysit the man who found her, so stay on top of this."

"Got it under control," Al assured him.

Twenty minutes had passed since the jogger had discovered the body, but already the crowd had grown considerably, many wondering what all the commotion was about.

Garrett started questioning the jogger.

"Can I see your ID, please."

The man unzipped a pouch on the stroller, pulled out his wallet, and attempted to hand it to Garrett.

"Please, take your license out."

The man did so clumsily, still noticeably shaken by his discovery.

"Is this your current address?"

"Yes, officer."

Garrett began to record the man's information from his license. "I'll need both your home number and your work number."

"I. . .uh. . .work at home."

"Can I have the number, please."

"Sure. 512-555-6471."

"What kind of work do you do?"

"I'm a web-developer. What does this have. . ."

"Are you Garrett?" a well-dressed man asked. Homicide had arrived.

"Yes. John Garrett."

"I'm Detective Wallace. This is Detective Soto."

"This gentleman is Mr. Bingham." Garret pointed at the jogger. "He found the body."

"Mr. Bingham, we'll have to ask you to come to headquarters so we can get your statement."

"What about my child?"

"Do you have anyone who can tend to your child? We shouldn't have to take a lot of your time."

"I'll call my wife." Mr. Bingham pulled out his cell phone and placed the call.

Wallace asked Garrett, "Where's the body?"

"Through that small opening. About ten yards."

The child in the three-wheeler awoke and began to whimper. It was obvious the toddler needed changing.

"My wife will be here in a few minutes."

Soto turned to Garrett. "Where's your partner?"

Garrett motioned to Ortiz.

"Have him look after the child while we take Mr. Bingham down to the scene."

"Al, stay with Mr. Bingham's son until we get back," Garrett instructed.

The opening in the shrubbery was essentially a well-camouflaged shortcut fishermen used to get to the water's edge.

"Please lead the way, Mr. Bingham."

When they arrived at the trail, Wallace asked the jogger, "Did you touch the body?"

"No."

"Now, I want you to tell us how you came upon the woman."

"Well, I was pushing Jimmy, my son, and as we came around this small turn, I heard a sound in the bushes. It was a rustling kinda sound. Over there." Bingham pointed in the direction of the body. "I thought it might be a squirrel or something like that."

"Then, what did you do?"

"The sound stopped, and then in a few seconds it rustled again."

"How did you come to see the body since it is clearly not in plain sight?"

Bingham was upset and his voice began to break. "I. . .There was. . .the sound."

Wallace put his hand on the man's shoulder to calm him. "Mr. Bingham, I'm sorry, I know this is tough on you, but we really need your help. Anything you can tell us could be very important. So please take your time and be as clear as you can. We need to get an accurate picture of how you came upon the body. . .that's all. Please, take a deep breath and continue."

"OK. As I said, I heard the rustling again and looked in the direction of the sound, and I saw something that looked like some cloth. I pulled back those branches. . .and. . .and there she was."

"Mr. Bingham, I want you to go downtown with Detective Soto as soon as your wife gets here and give him as much detail in your statement as possible. OK?"

"OK."

"Thank you for your help."

Bingham nodded.

Wallace waited until Bingham and Soto were out of earshot. "Garrett, what do you think?"

"I think he just came upon the dead girl, and that's it."

"Let's have a look. Have the photographer and Forensics come down here."

Garrett turned his head to the left and relayed the request on his two-way.

Standing on the jogging trail, barely ten feet from the body, the brush was dense enough to conceal anything, especially a person. Wallace watched as the forensic investigator inspected the small branches, careful not to disturb any potential evidence. He pulled aside branches as the photographer snapped photos from behind until they got within six feet of Michelle.

Her body was lying face down, her head in an awkward position facing away from the jogging trail.

"No obvious signs of sexual assault. She doesn't seem to be missing any clothes. The only visible wound appears to be the gunshot, possibly from a smaller caliber handgun. Do we know who she is?" he asked Garrett.

"Not yet," Garrett said.

The obvious outline of a set of keys was protruding against the material of her shorts. Michelle had put Whitley's car key onto a key-ring with her extra house key for safe keeping.

"She's got a couple of keys here. I would assume that she drove here, but let me take a look at what she has." The investigator pulled them out of her shorts pocket and looked at them.

"We have a Cadillac car key and a Kwik-Set house key. The Cadillac key looks like an older model. Let me bag them and have one of my guys dust them," Soto offered. "If she doesn't have any form of picture ID on her, you can get a make on the car from the key serial number, then start searching the parking lots to see if she has a car somewhere nearby. Let's hope she's not a distance runner. You guys could be here for days."

A few hours later, Soto radioed the data about the keys to the officers at the crime scene. Ortiz rode with another officer to check the most popular parking lots for users of the hike-and-bike trail. Garrett remained at the crime scene with Detective Wallace. Two hours later they discovered the car.

"Come in, John," Al radioed on the two-way.

"Yeah, Al."

"I think we found something in the Austin High parking lot."

"What do you have?"

"An older model brown Cadillac at the school looks to be vandalized. Nothing in the car. No registration."

"Have you had a chance to run the plates?"

"Yes. The car is registered to a Whitley Talmadge."

"You think she's our Jane Doe?"

"It's hard to say. The driver's license photo we pulled up doesn't look like her; she has lighter hair. But she could have dyed her hair a darker color."

"How was the car vandalized?"

"The driver's window was broken inward. Whoever did it likely has a nasty cut. There's blood on the driver's side armrest and the front seat. It doesn't appear anyone was pulled from the car because there's still too much glass on the seat."

"What about the trunk?"

"Nothing."

"Okay, Al. Forensics is on the way to dust the car. Keep at it."

"Roger."

"After it's been dusted and the blood sample is taken, tell Forensics to have Impound come and get it."

Garrett rubbed his chin pensively and looked at Wallace. "I have a feeling this is our runner's car."

"I think you're right."

"Al, you guys have a couple of things to run down: where this Whitley Talmadge lives and let's try to find out who the blood belongs to."

CHAPTER TWENTY-EIGHT

THE KNOCK ON THE door startled Whitley. She cupped her hands around the peephole and slid the small cover to the right, so as not to give away the fact that she was at home. Two uniformed Austin Police officers stood on the either side of the door; obviously impatient. Neither officer was in full view.

"Who is it?" she asked through the door. She continued to peer through the eyepiece.

The two officers bristled to defensive postures, and each placed their hands near their handguns. It was obvious they hadn't expected anyone to answer them.

Whitley's heart jumped to her throat.

"Austin Police Department, Miss. Could you please open the door?" One of the men held his credentials up to the lens. "We'd like to ask you some questions."

Whitley continued to watch through the little hole. "What's this about?"

"A police matter, Miss. Please open the door." His voice was uncompromising now.

"Just a moment." Whitley ran to the sliding glass door and looked out to the street. A police cruiser was parked right out front. She ran back to the door, unlatched the chain, and fumbled with the other two locks. She peered around the slightly opened door.

"Hello, ma'am. I'm Detective Wallace. This is Detective Soto. And you are. . .?"

"Uh. . .Whitley. . .Whitley Talmadge."

The detectives gave each other a surprised look. "May we come in?"

"Of course, but," Whitley said and opened the door, "what's going on?" She motioned for the men to have a seat on the couch. The detectives took places next to each other and across from her.

"What kind of car do you own, ma'am?"

"It's a. . .uh. . .brown Cadillac. I. . .I loaned it to a friend! Is it okay? Is she alright? What's happened?" Whitley covered her mouth with trembling hands. She was feeling light-headed and had a sudden premonition that bad news was coming.

"Ma'am, may I see your driver's license, please?" Wallace was very calm and could see that Whitley was quite nervous. Soto sat calmly and took notes of the conversation.

"Where's Michelle?" Whitley began to tear up as she reached for her purse. Her hand trembled as she handed her license to Garrett.

"Al, get her some water." Wallace motioned to the kitchen.

Soto found a glass in a kitchen cabinet, filled it, then returned to hand it to Whitley. "We found your car vandalized in the Austin High parking lot. Who's Michelle, Miss Talmadge?"

"A friend. Please. Tell me she's okay! She borrowed my car. . .She was going to class last night." Whitley sat on the edge of the ottoman. "Something terrible has happened, hasn't it?" Tears streamed down her cheeks.

Wallace kneeled next to Whitley. He patted her on the back, attempting to console her. She took a sip from the glass, and Soto offered her his kerchief.

"What's your friend's last name?" Wallace asked.

Between sobs, she said, "Grayson. . .Michelle Grayson. . .She just moved here. . .I work with her."

"Have you heard from Michelle today?"

"No, but she should have come by here this morning."

Wallace looked up at Soto, "Call it in."

"Excuse me just a moment, Miss Talmadge." Detective Soto stood up and walked outside so he could radio in to the dispatcher. "Run an ID check on a Michelle Grayson as the possible Jane Doe we recovered from Town Lake this morning."

"Miss Talmadge, we found the body of a young woman on the running trail this morning."

"Oh, my God."

"We are trying to identify her, and we need to determine whether this woman could possibly be your friend."

Upon hearing this Whitley collapsed, bending over with her face buried in her hands.

Wallace continued his futile attempts at consolation. "Miss Talmadge. We have a few more questions. I know this is difficult. We need to. . ."

Soto came back after his call and gave Wallace a thumbs-up signal to indicate he had gotten through.

After a few uneasy moments, Whitley regained her composure.

Wallace continued his questioning. "Could you give us a description of Michelle?"

Sniffling, she answered, "She's about my height and weight. Medium length dark hair. Blue eyes. Mid to late thirties, maybe. I'm not sure. We just started working together a week ago."

Wallace glanced past Whitley to Soto. They knew Michelle was their Jane Doe.

Whitley's eyes were swollen, and her cheeks were now a bright shade of red.

"Miss Talmadge, we found a deceased young woman matching your friend's description near the jogging trail on Town Lake. I'm sorry, but I think this woman could be Michelle."

Whitley began sobbing again. "What happened? She was supposed. . .to call me today. . .to take her to get her car. We were going shopping."

"Does Michelle have any family nearby that you know of?"

"No, I don't think so. . .She just moved here. . .from Portland. . .Steve would be the one to call."

"Who is Steve?" Wallace asked.

"Steve Latham...Another friend from work," Whitley continued to sob. "He was dating Michelle."

"Were they having any problems that you would know about?"

"Oh no! Not at all! He's my dearest friend. He's also a friend of Detective Kelly."

"From APD?"

"Yes. Steve used to be a police officer, too. I need to call him."

The men looked at each other.

"You want to send a car for him?" Soto asked.

Wallace thought for a moment, "I don't think that will be necessary just yet."

Soto turned to Whitley, "Please give me Mr. Latham's number. I'll call him for you."

The officer took down the number as Whitley spoke.

Wallace took Whitley's hand, "Whitley, we are going to need you to come to APD headquarters to give us a report, but we'll wait until Mr. Latham gets here."

"Okay," she said.

Soto rang the number.

A recording came on: "Hello, you have reached Steve Latham. I can't take your call at this time. Please leave a message at the tone, and I'll return your call as soon as possible."

Soto handed the phone to Whitley. She composed herself and in a low tone, between sobs, left an urgent message for him to call as soon as he could.

Garrett said, "By the way. . .You said Michelle also worked with you."

"Yes, at Western States on Loop 360," Whitley whimpered.

"The insurance company?"

"Yeah."

"Miss Talmadge?" Whitley looked up at Wallace, and he could see the pain in her swollen, bloodshot eyes. He hesitated before asking the next question.

"Yes?"

"If we can't locate Mr. Latham right away, could you help us identify the body?"

"I don't know if I could handle that right now."

"Miss Talmadge, the sooner we can determine that this was indeed your friend, the closer we will be to finding out what happened. I know this is not a good time. Here's my card. Please call me as soon as you can."

Wallace reminded her that he needed to get her statement. "Oh, as soon as we have finished with your car, we'll call you. We had it impounded."

She ushered the two detectives to the door and closed it behind them. She waited for a moment, thinking, then opened the door.

"Detectives?" she asked.

Wallace turned to her. He hadn't yet made it all the way down the stairs. "Yes, Miss Talmadge?"

"I'll go with you. Just let me get a couple of things."

"Thank you. We'll do our best to make this as easy on you as possible."

She went back inside and closed the door.

Wallace turned to Soto, "I'm pretty sure we can eliminate her as a suspect. I didn't notice any scratches on her arms or hands, so I don't think the blood on the car is hers. But make sure when she comes down to give her statement, we ask about getting a sample so we can confirm her blood type. We'll continue to try contact this Latham guy, but let's send a car to go by his house to check him out, just in case."

"I'll contact Victim's Services when we get back to the station. I have a feeling that lady's gonna need help with this. . ." Soto's voice trailed off.

A few hours later Whitley had identified Michelle's body at the morgue. She had been relieved to only have to see her friend's face from a monitor in another room. As difficult as it was to confirm that the body was indeed Michelle's, not having to experience the smells associated with the morgue that she had anticipated during the ride to the station had been a godsend.

The Cadillac had been returned to her on Wednesday, new window in place and blood washed away. It had given Whitley the creeps to drive it for the next few days, even though Michelle hadn't died in the car. For the first time since she had owned it, she actually thought that selling it was a viable option.

Steve and Whitley had both decided to take a few days off after the murder. Steve flew with Michelle's body to Portland and to meet the family for the funeral service. The body was cremated according to the instructions found among her papers; her ashes were kept by the family. Steve had flown back to Austin the following day.

That same day, Whitley decided to go for a drive around town, having no particular destination in mind. It wasn't long after she left the apartment that she noticed a black Suburban parked in a convenience store parking lot. It looked similar to the one she had seen on the night she had knocked the pot off the balcony railing.

"Everyone in Austin with a black truck has tinted windows, Whitley," she said aloud. Even so, her heart began to race a bit when she drove past the vehicle and its lights came on.

She pulled up to the stoplight at Shoal Creek and adjusted her rearview mirror. The Suburban was three cars back, but she paid it no attention.

The traffic light turned green, and she accelerated slowly through the intersection. The two vehicles behind her turned right onto Shoal Creek. The Suburban crossed the intersection following Whitley's same route, heading west on Hancock Drive.

The distance between the vehicles quickly diminished. No other cars were around and before Whitley knew what had happened, she felt a violent impact from the truck's grill guard as it slammed hard into the back of the Cadillac. Her head snapped back against the headrest, and "Molé Grande" yawed to the left.

"Ohhh!" Whitley whimpered momentarily. Then her reflexes took over and she sped up. "No, no, no," she moaned fearfully. "You son of a bitch! What do you want?"

A second thud, just as hard as the first made her lurch forward in the seat once again.

"Stop it you, asshole!" she was screaming now.

The vehicles careened up Hancock, and the Suburban swerved to the left pulling up beside her.

She wouldn't look at it. She couldn't look at it. She had to focus.

The road narrowed into one lane on each side, as they made their way up the elevated overpass atop the MOPAC expressway, but the Suburban held fast in the oncoming lane of traffic, since there were no other cars.

Whitley floored it. The Caddy's powerful engine whined as it gained momentum and sped past the Suburban. She reached Balcones Drive and jerked the wheel to the right, screeching all the way through the turn. Just half a block up there was a Fire Station. She had to get there. She HAD to get there. Careening into its parking lot and slammed on the brakes. The big car slid across the smooth concrete of the driveway laying down two long, distinct skid-marks, before finally coming to a halt in front of one of the open garage bays.

A fireman servicing the water truck looked up abruptly.

Whitley flew out of the car and ran up to him screaming, "Help me! Please! Help!"

"What's wrong?" he asked, wiping his hands with the greasy rag he pulled out of his back pocket.

"You've got to help me! I'm being chased! Someone's trying to kill me! He's right behind me! Please help me!" she cried breathlessly. She turned and pointed in the direction from which she came. No one was there.

"Why don't you come inside the station with me?" He put his arm around her and led her into the bay where the fire truck was parked, then into a side room.

Two firemen raced out to the front of the station as Whitley stayed inside, shaking in terror.

One of the firemen came back. "Lady, are you OK? There's nobody out there!"

"Oh my god. Where did it go?" Her voice was shaking.

"Where did what go?" one of the firemen asked.

Whitley cupped her face in her hands and sobbed heavily. "A big truck. A big black truck," she whimpered, her face still in her hands. "He's gotta be out there!" She got up and ran out to the front of the station.

She looked up and down the street. No one was there. There was no truck in sight.

Everything looked normal—except the substantial damage to the back end of her car.

She had to find Steve.

CHAPTER TWENTY-NINE

WHITLEY WOKE UP ABOUT 9:00 on Sunday morning, one week and a day after the visit to the morgue and two days after the car chase. Although not continuous, it had been her first decent night of sleep during that span of time. She listened to the faint chirps of sparrows as they gathered in the trees outside her bedroom window. Inside the apartment the temperature was very cool. The thick comforter on the queen-size, wrought-iron bed enveloped her in a cocoon of warmth. She was reluctant to leave it.

Clad in an expensive silk teddy her mother had brought her from Paris, Whitley walked quickly across the bedroom to the chair cradling her favorite white terrycloth robe. Shivering slightly she slipped her arms into the oversized garment in an attempt to warm up.

She knew Winona would have a coronary if she saw what Whitley was wearing, especially if she knew that the $600 matching silk robe for the teddy was still on its same perfumed hanger in the closet. Although the teddy was presented as a gift, Whitley knew it was also another of Winona's ploys to get her noticed and subsequently married to whomever she was dating at the time.

To date no one else had seen the garment. Her plan had always been to save it for Steve.

Carefully opening the bedroom door, she peered into the living room where Steve was quietly snoring on the couch. Whitley loved it when he stayed over, even if he always insisted on sleeping on the sofa. She was also glad that she had finally been able to get some sleep. Even under the best of circumstances, even with Whitley's persistent attempts to have him sleep in her bed while she took the sofa, at no time had Steve made an attempt to compromise their platonic relationship.

Not that she would have minded. But as weak-kneed as she got when he was just visiting, she couldn't imagine her reaction should he actually make a pass at her. She was sticking to her guns and would not be the one to instigate a more serious relationship, especially with the events of the past week.

Steve had offered to stay over for a couple of nights, hoping that he might be able to catch whoever had been chasing Whitley should that person also happen to know and show up where she lived. His gun was nearby, as was an unmarked patrol car that had been on the street all night, thanks to Detective Kelly. Since there was only one way into the apartment, the patrol car had radioed around 3:00 A.M. for Steve to catch some sleep.

Whitley had checked on him twice during the night. Her uneasiness about the possibility of someone coming to her door or to her balcony had kept her from sleeping straight through. It had also prompted a desire to confirm that Steve was still there to protect her should the need arise.

She knew that she wasn't the only one that needed to get through the events of the past week. Even though Steve had known Michelle for only a short time, Whitley was sure that there was significant pain in the grief he was experiencing. The loss of a future together, the questions about what could have been, she knew Steve well enough to know that these things surely gnawed at him.

Slipping past him into the kitchen, she turned on the coffee pot that held the beans she had ground last night before they went to bed. Quietly, she opened the pantry door and grabbed a few jars of herbs and seasonings, some of which she had ground up several days earlier. Setting them next to the stove, she retrieved an egg carton out of the refrigerator, then pulled out a skillet, set it on the large burner on the stove, and turned the dial to high. She heard a few clicks before the blue gas flame appeared. She poured a little oil into the pan and beat several eggs before she peeked into the living room at Steve. He was beginning to rustle a bit, likely because the smell of French Roast coffee was wafting into the living room.

"Good morning, you," his gentle voice emanated from the couch, a tone or two deeper than normal.

"Hey, sleepyhead." She cringed at the lack of originality in her response. She hated the way he made her feel so juvenile, so giddy. "You want some coffee?"

"I would love some." Steve reached over to the coffee table and retrieved the radio to call the patrol car. "Let's call it a night, guys. Thanks."

"Our pleasure. We're out."

He turned the television on to one of the 24-hour cable news stations as Whitley rounded the corner from the kitchen. She nearly dropped the coffee as she saw a shirtless and boxer-clad Steve climb out from under the covers. Whitley picked up her pace crossing the room in order to hand him the cup and keep him from rushing to get dressed right away.

"Here you go."

"Thanks, girl."

"Omelet on the way."

"Aren't you sweet."

"It's the least I could do for the show you're giving me." Whitley smiled as she pointed to his wide-open fly and walked back into the kitchen to tend to the skillet.

Steve looked down. "Hello! Sorry about that, Whit." He fumbled for his jeans and hopped into them. "You're not going to turn me in for sexual harassment now, are you?"

"Oh, I think I'll just store this moment in my memory banks for later use." *Good response!* she thought.

"That's fair...I guess." Grabbing his shirt and coffee, he headed for the bathroom.

Whitley had the table set by the time he had dressed and returned.

"I really want to thank you for coming over the past couple of nights. I don't want you to think I'm some flighty paranoid jerk."

"You know I'd do anything for you, Whit. Don't even mention it."

Her heart felt as though it would jump right out of her chest. She wanted him to pick up on her feelings, but it was just too soon and she knew it.

Steve finished his omelet and wiped his mouth with the cloth napkin. "That was great, Whit. Thanks."

"You're welcome. Can I get you anything else?"

"I think that will do it for me."

"Well, after my past week, I'm going to start this day off right—with a toddy."

"On second thought. . ." Steve said, chuckling.

"You're so damned easy. Any preference? I'm having a Bloody Mary."

"That sounds perfect."

"Two Bloody Marys coming right up."

Steve got up, opened the sliding glass door, and walked out onto the deck. After a short time, he yelled back inside to her, "What's going on at the church?"

"Oh, I'd almost forgotten. It's the mother of all bake sales. One hell of a good-cookin' time at St. Anne's."

There was a grand tent striped with wide bands of yellow and white in the parking lot behind the church, the same lot where Whitley had heard the argument a few weeks earlier.

"Then whatta ya say we move this party outside to the balcony?"

"Sure, let's do it. Why don't you grab the thrones?"

Steve trotted back inside and hauled the rocking chair out of the den for Whitley. He positioned it atop the mildew-stained oval rug that was becoming permanently adhered to the patio. Next, he located a folding chair just inside the sliding door and took his usual place beside her. Soon, she arrived with the cocktails and made herself comfortable in the rocker.

Steve sipped on one of the cauldron-sized Bloody Marys that Whitley had concocted. The tangy blend of Worcestershire sauce, tomato juice, and fajita seasoning assaulted his taste buds with a fury.

"Whoa! Holy Mother of God!" he exclaimed. His eyes watered, as did his sinuses. "This could wake the dead. Damn, you make these well!"

"Thanks, sugar, but hold it down. We wouldn't want Father Al hearing you talk that way." She leaned over, slapped Steve on the thigh, and said, "Yeah, I like to keep all of my men liquored up and happy."

Right now she had only one man on her mind.

Whitley watched Steve in silent comfort, secure in the fact that her protector was there, on her balcony. They sipped on their drinks and watched the numbers grow across the street. The last few decorations were being added to the outside of the church.

"You wanna go over there?" she said.

"Maybe after awhile. I think I may have to have another one of these Bloody Marys before we go. If you don't mind."

"Well, OK, I'll join you for another. It'd be cheaper than buying one of those $5 beers across the street. Although the money would be going toward a much better cause."

"What better cause could there be than me?" he asked playfully.

Whitley just looked at him silently and smiled, drawing her knees up to her chest and resting her feet on the edge of the rocking chair seat. She began to teeter back and forth in the rocker while balancing the contents of the cocktail in rhythm with the chair.

They both turned their attention back toward St. Anne's and the dessert-laden parishioners who were arriving. The long rows of folding tables positioned around the perimeter of the tent were filling up with countless confections that many a blue-haired senior carted in. The proximity of St. Anne's to U.T. as well as the prestige of the majority of the congregation helped to make the annual bake sale fund-raiser one of the church's most popular social events of the year. Father Alonso had taken the reins, so to speak, after the loss of Father Matthew and had brought the event to an even greater level of popularity and prosperity for the church. Not only did the older members of the congregation continue to volunteer for the annual outing, but the younger members, a group sorely lacking in representation in previous years, came by the hundreds. It could be said that the attendance by this younger contingent was influenced in great part by the enticements of numerous raffles and copious amounts of cold beer.

Steve noticed Father Alonso standing among a group of schoolchildren. He was dressed in black shoes, black pants, and a black, short-sleeved shirt that sported his clerical collar. The group seemed to be enjoying themselves as they busily erected the beanbag toss area, setting up a huge piece of plywood with a clown face painted on it. It contained a multitude of holes, each varying in diameter with a corresponding score painted above.

"How well do you know Father Ochoa, Whitley?"

"Very well. We've been friends for a year or two. I'll go to church there on occasion, and we'll have breakfast once in a blue moon. Why do you ask?"

"No reason in particular. But doesn't it make you wonder why a guy who looks like that is a priest?"

"Not really. I mean, if you knew him, you'd know what I mean. He came from a really small village in Venezuela. I don't know that they even had electricity. See, if you've lived a sheltered life, you don't realize all the things you're missing. You know, it wouldn't be any different than going to a small Texas town and finding some beautiful girl that's a soda jerk and wondering why she wasn't modeling somewhere. Some people have stronger wills or a stronger faith than others. I think Father Alonso is one of those special people."

"I guess you're right."

"I think so."

"Maybe he's gay."

"No, he's not. Bite your tongue. Besides, you should be thankful he's a priest."

"Why's that?"

"Because, that way there's just one less man on the street that can compete for my affections!" Whitley couldn't believe what she just said. She promptly buried her face in her Bloody Mary and took a mighty gulp. She could feel her face reddening from alcohol and the embarrassment of her bold slip of the tongue.

Steve didn't seem to mind her comment at all. In fact, he looked at Whitley admiringly, as if truly contemplating what she had just said.

She was too embarrassed to notice.

"Whatta ya say we get cleaned up and take a trip to our local Catholic fiesta?"

Whitley breathed a sigh of relief. "I get the shower first. You can freeze your ass off with the cold water!" With that she rocked forward in the chair and uncurled out of it in one smooth motion. She walked by Steve and mussed his hair with her left hand as she passed.

Steve tilted his glass, eagerly gulping the last bit of the thick, sharp liquid. The ice rattled as he finished the drink and stood up. He turned in time to see Whitley stride down the hall, towel in hand.

Whitley walked into the bathroom and closed both the hallway door and the bedroom door behind her. She leaned into the tub and turned the water on. She put the toilet seat lid down and took off her robe, laying it across the seat. She slipped off the silk teddy and stood in front of the large vanity mirror, examining her body.

She had a beautiful figure, especially for someone who spent most of her time indoors and very far away from exercise equipment. Not many would know it because of the less-than-flattering clothing she often wore. She stared at her breasts momentarily. They were small but impeccably shaped. She looked at her right profile, then her left. Her bottom was a little fleshy, but by no means did she need to lose weight.

"Why did this have to happen now? Why couldn't you have sensed my feelings before, Steve?" she whispered.

Whitley walked back over to the tub, fine-tuning with the large, clear-plastic knobs and checking the water with the back of her hand until the temperature was sufficiently hot. She stepped inside and drew the shower curtain closed. Pulling the loofa from the shower rack, she began to apply soap to it. Her eyes were closed; she let her thoughts drift and began scrubbing her face with the sponge.

All she could think about was the fact that Steve was in the other room, just a few feet away from her wet, naked body. She fantasized about the door bursting open, and Steve ripping the shower curtain to the side and taking her right there. In the tub. On the floor. On the countertop. Whitley didn't trouble herself with where it would happen, just when. She just knew if she visualized this fantasy scene long and hard enough, Steve would somehow receive this "transmission" of hers and respond.

Whitley walked out of the shower wrapped in a small towel. "You go ahead and shower. I'll finish up in my room."

Steve noticed how striking Whitley looked with her wet hair slicked back out of her face. "Sounds like a plan," he agreed.

Steve took his turn in the shower and dressed. Within a short time they were walking across the street to the bazaar. Steve paid the admission fee of two dollars apiece, and they walked past the ticket table.

Neither one noticed the large man who had been inconspicuously watching them from the perimeter of the crowd.

"Hey, look. They're raffling off a fishing kayak this year. You want to give it a go?"

"I already have a boat, but I'll get you a couple of extra tickets."

"It says here that it comes with a life jacket, carbon fiber paddle, rod-holders, depth finder, and a GPS monitor. Cool."

"Sounds like a nice one. I've been thinking about getting a portable GPS unit. Rick had one he was using in Yosemite that was pretty nice." His sentence seemed to trail off as though his thoughts were elsewhere.

"Are you okay?" Whitley asked, assuming he might be down if he was thinking of Michelle.

"I'm fine."

"Just checking."

Steve thought for a moment. "You know, I think I will go over to the REI store later today and buy one."

"Why don't you go after we've checked out this party scene."

"Would you like to go, so you won't be home alone?" Steve asked.

"No. I'll be fine. If I didn't have a visitor in the past two days, I can't imagine one will show up tonight."

"Only if you're sure."

"Positive."

The man continued to watch them both as they worked their way around to the different booths, made a few small purchases, then hugged and went their separate ways.

CHAPTER THIRTY

STEVE DROVE ACROSS TOWN to the REI store closest to his home. Wandering through the hiking section, he checked out its enormous inventory of high-tech outdoor gadgets and clothing. He had mixed emotions about the major improvements made in some of the newer gear. He felt as though the industry was trying to bring too many creature comforts to the outdoors, but at the same time, those comforts sure made his trips a hell of a lot more pleasant.

"What can I help you with today?" A cute young associate complete with a stainless-steel nose stud, a lip ring, and a sleeve of tattoos down each arm offered her assistance.

"Oh, I'm just looking around. Thanks. But I will want to look at a GPS unit in a while." Steve was meandering about in the climbing section of the store, viewing some of the newly designed, ultra-light carabiners on display in one of several glass cases.

"Well, let me know if I can help. They are right over here in this cabinet I'll be working in." She pointed to another wooden and glass case nearby.

"Thanks, I will."

She grinned widely and walked to a counter full of sunglasses atop the case.

Steve next camped in front of the climbing shoe display, where he inspected a few of the latest styles. From there he ambled across the carpeted floor to the counter where the associate was busy restocking the sunglass display shelves. Inside the cabinets that surrounded her were not only sunglasses, but also knives, watches, and a couple of hand-held GPS units similar to the one that Rick had used in Yosemite.

"You going on a trip?" she asked.

"Just got back."

"Really? Like, where did you go?" She seemed way too interested.

"Yosemite." Steve's attention was primarily focused on the gear before him.

"God, that sounds great. Like, I've never been there before, but I hear it's like, beautiful."

Steve looked up at the young girl. "It really is. Pictures just don't do it justice." He smiled.

"Can I show you one of the GPS's in here?" Her speech revealed another stainless stud protruding from her tongue.

Steve did his best to keep from staring. "Yeah. A friend of mine has a hand held GPS unit, and I was thinking about getting one. How does this one work exactly?" He pointed at one of the larger devices.

She slid open a door in back of the cabinet and reached inside, pulling out the unit. The edge of yet another tattoo peeked out from underneath her T-shirt collar. "This one has everything. A 2-way radio, altimeter, a compass, and a weather radio. Basically, you just, like, turn the power on and wait a minute. It'll send a signal out that makes contact with satellites that are like, orbiting overhead, ya know? Once at least three of the satellites are contacted, the system kinda pinpoints your exact location on earth. At least, ya know, within a small margin of error. If you've got a minute let's go outside, and I'll show you."

"Sure," Steve said, then followed her through the automatic doors to the front sidewalk. Steve watched intently as she turned on the unit and it started locating satellites.

In a few seconds it displayed the coordinates of the store location. 30.98' N 20.35' W

His jaw dropped when the display was complete, he squinted at the readout. "Could it be?" he mumbled.

"Cool, huh?"

Steve was somewhere else completely. He reached for his wallet and pulled out a piece of scrap paper, upon which he had scribbled some of the numbers from the list found in Walker's safe. He stared at it without expression.

"Is something wrong?"

"Not at all. How much is it?"

"Four hundred and fifty dollars."

"Fine, I'll take one."

"Great! Let's go back inside, and I'll get one in a box for you."

After a few minutes, she returned from a back room with a boxed unit and handed it to Steve.

"Thanks," Steve said as he took the unit from her and hurried toward the register, fumbling through his wallet in search of his credit card.

"Sure," she called after him. "What's your name?"

"Steve. Steve Latham. And yours?"

"Deborah Wallace." She used her full name, as it sounded more mature than her actual years.

"Nice to meet you, Deborah. Thanks again," he shouted.

"My pleasure." She watched as he walked away. "S-t-e-v-e L-a-t-h-a-m." She scribbled his name on a piece of scratch paper. She murmured, "Well, Steve Latham, come back real soon!" Her eyes followed him, watching as he grabbed batteries from a display at the register, paid, then ran from the counter out to his car.

As soon as Steve jumped in, he ripped open the box, located the operating instructions, and unfolded them. He scanned the text. There were German, French, and Spanish translations on the document as well as the English portion he finally spotted. He skimmed the contents, then grabbed his laptop and plugged the GPS's USB cable into it. Turning on the hand-held unit. He waited eagerly as the instrument locked on to the satellites and started spitting out his coordinates.

Steve compared the GPS readout with the mysterious entries on the number list in his briefcase. Although not exactly a match in their content, there were striking similarities between the two, especially if the entries on the numbers list were read backwards. "This could be it!" he shouted as he dialed Whitley's number.

"Whit!"

"Hey, did you get your GPS?"

"Yeah, but listen. I think I may have made a break in the Walker case."

"Really?"

"Yes, so if you're okay with it, I'm going to the office to work for a while. If you need anything, try me there first or on my cell."

"Okay. No problem. I'll be fine. And Steve. . ."

"Yeah?"

"Thanks for everything. I appreciate you staying with me and getting the police involved."

"My pleasure. Don't hesitate to call or come by if you're worried about being alone tonight. You have the key, and the extra bed is always there for you."

"Thank you. But I think I'll get back to my routine and do some stargazing tonight."

"Just be careful. And take your phone with you."

"I will. Bye."

"Sleep well, Whit."

Whitley held onto the receiver a moment longer before she hung up, noticing that since Michelle's death Steve had drawn a bit closer to her. Perhaps it was the lingering melancholy he was experiencing that caused it. She felt some guilt for enjoying the change but cherished it all the same. They had both lost someone in this ordeal. She recalled her last conversation with Michelle and got teary-eyed. It wouldn't be necessary to tell Steve what Michelle had said. On top of that, Steve had a lot of other things on his mind and didn't need additional baggage. At this point, whatever she could do to help him through this, she was willing to try.

CHAPTER THIRTY-ONE

STEVE SAT IN HIS office and stared at the list. The building was empty except for the security guards.

He found his mind wandering back and forth between the list contents and Michelle. He was surprised that he hadn't been more emotional about the loss of his new friend. Perhaps it was his years on the Portland police force that hardened him, or perhaps she simply wasn't the woman he was destined to be with long-term. Steve did find it odd that Rick appeared more upset about Michelle's death than he was. Rick had become downright angry when Steve called him in Portland to tell him about the murder. His reaction at the funeral service wasn't much different.

Steve yelled at himself, "Concentrate! The list! What are these damn numbers all about?

"Let's go over what we have. Each line of numbers has six numbers. The middle two numbers have decimal points before and after them. The first line of numbers has an asterisk before the line of numbers and a pound sign after it. The lines of numbers alternate down the page like that. Look for the common aspects.

"Each line has six digits, sets of two numbers separated by decimals, asterisk on the front and pound sign on the end of each set of numbers, alternating with each row. They can't be bank account numbers and can't be check numbers. They've got to be destinations."

Steve turned to his monitor and pulled up a Waypoint registry website for Global Positioning Systems. Clicking on the state of Texas, Steve watched as a page appeared that allowed input of a city name or waypoint. He took a group of five numbers and began writing down different possible number combinations.

Next, he entered Austin/Texas/USA. The monitor displayed 30.18.21N 97.45.01W.

"The first row of numbers is latitude; the second row is longitude," he mumbled.

Steve held up the list and looked for a similar number in any pattern within the strings of numbers. To his surprise, he found one imbedded in one string reading from right to left. Using the same pattern for another string he entered the coordinates into the Waypoint registry. "Fort Stockton, Texas," he read.

He entered another one, "Gonzales, Texas."

And another, "Corpus Christi, Texas. Dammit, this is it!"

He pulled up a spreadsheet and began entering the information onto a worksheet. The remaining numbers in each string hadn't yet been deciphered, but this would be a huge start.

He would call Detective Kelly and email him the info as soon as he finished.

CHAPTER THIRTY-TWO

IN THE PARKING LOT just behind Saint Anne's modest rectory, Whitley was stooped over, gazing through her telescope adjusting the focus knob. As a child, she used to think the stars represented all the people who had gone to heaven. It was a nice thought, one she felt was even more appropriate now with Michelle's untimely passing.

Such a strong young woman, she thought. *Michelle is likely to be one of the brighter stars out tonight.*

Whitley pivoted the telescope on its base to aim it toward the moon. Slowly, she turned the focus knob on the side of the viewing lens. One of the many craters came into view.

She lifted her head from the telescope and looked up. Something about full moons always gave her an uneasy feeling. Tonight was no different.

She lowered her head and looked through the viewing lens again, gradually scanning the lunar surface.

A slight breeze blew across the nape of her neck and sent a chill down to her toes.

She stood up and looked around the lot. She was once again getting that same uneasy feeling. Other than a couple of joggers running uphill on the sidewalk toward Guadalupe Street, the place was vacant. Whitley noticed the light on in the rectory. Knowing Father Al was at home calmed her.

She went back to viewing the sky.

Behind her, around the corner, a car door shut. Even with a northerly breeze carrying the sound in her direction, it wasn't loud enough to grab her attention. The footsteps were silent. The sound of his pant fabric brushing back and forth on his thighs blended perfectly with the wind blowing through the trees lining the street.

Whitley looked up again, then suddenly her head was snapped back, violently. Before she could react, she found herself being lifted off the ground.

The large man had crept up behind Whitley and caught her completely off guard. His massive left arm locked around her slender body, pinning her arms at her sides and crushing her midsection like a powerful snake.

She twisted side-to-side to try and free her head, to open her mouth, to bite him, to scream.

He was too big, too strong. His huge hand covered most of her face and her mouth and clamped her jaw shut.

She was finding it difficult to breath but could smell the stench of his perspiration and the stale cigarette smoke on her assailant's hands. She kicked wildly and pounded her fists against him, but this proved more irritating to him than effective. She was able to get out one loud scream before his monstrous hands shifted from her mouth to her neck.

He responded by squeezing and shaking her like a rag doll until she stopped.

She was close to losing consciousness. Starry specks of light rained down before her eyes, clouding her field of vision. Everything faded to black, and she hung limp in his arms.

Father Alonso had heard the commotion outside his home and peered out at the parking lot from his second-story bedroom window. When he saw Whitley was in trouble, he bounded down the stairs in an instant.

He jerked open a hall closet, rifled through an equipment bag belonging to the church camp girls softball team, and grabbed an aluminum bat. No sooner had he barreled out the back door than he immediately came face to face with the enormous intruder.

"What are you doing? Let her go!" Father Alonso yelled firmly at the man, then tried to maneuver closer to him.

"Back off, Padre, or you're next." The man eyed Father Alonso, turning his body so that Whitley stayed between them, using her as a shield.

"So help me God, let her go!"

The man just laughed at the priest. "You've got to be joking."

Father Alonso knew that he would have to act quickly or Whitley would die, that was if she wasn't dead already.

"I said let her go!" Father Alonso was screaming by this time. "I won't tell you again!"

Once more the man laughed, his head tilted back ever so slightly.

An opportunity.

Father Alonso saw his opening and lunged at him. In one smooth motion he jumped off the ground while simultaneously swinging the bat. The metal cylinder made a dull thud as it connected with the man's right ear.

The intruder still kept his horrible grip on Whitley's throat, but the blow caused him to double over.

That was just enough for Father Alonso to connect one more time with the back of the attacker's head.

The force of Father Alonso's second blow caused the man to release his hold on Whitley. He staggered backwards, off-balance, disoriented.

Whitley slumped to ground in a lifeless mass.

Amazingly, this colossus of a man was still standing. He gave Alonso a brief, almost quizzical stare before abruptly charging and burying a shoulder in the priest's solar plexus; lifting him off the ground and carrying him backwards in one fluid motion.

Together, they crashed violently through the rectory's screen door and barreled inside. The attacker stumbled as he crossed over the threshold, spilling Father Alonso into the long hallway leading to the kitchen.

The priest sprang to his feet, blood seeping out of a jagged deep gash in his forehead. He turned to look at the man.

His assailant's survival instinct was strong, for he was still able to support himself on his hands and knees. His sweaty mane hung to the wooden floor and left small, circular streaks of perspiration as he wobbled, head pounding from the effects of the two blows.

Unaccustomed to the sense of rage he now felt, Alonso fearlessly marched back toward the intruder.

The man was a frightful sight, and he was still having trouble righting himself. He lifted his head just enough to see Father Alonso's feet. Vein-like trails of blood and sweat left a viscous road map across his face and neck. His dark eyes were glazing over, but he still had enough strength in reserve to push himself upright, then get to his feet with his hands on his knees, before falling back to the ground on all fours. His thick hands and arms quivered as he fought once more to support the weight of his injured frame.

He raised a trembling right arm and pointed in the air at Father Ochoa. "You're a dead man. Do ya fuckin' hear me?" The volume of his garbled speech was increasing. "Fuckin'. . .dead. . .man." He looked menacingly at the priest.

"You won't be killing anyone," Father Alonso responded, "ever again." He then whipped his powerful right leg up and around. It swung in an arc it until it landed solidly on his adversary's left temple.

The slain man crumpled in a heap to the floor.

Father Alonso stumbled out the door to check on Whitley. Touching two fingers to her neck, then to her wrist, he could tell that she was barely breathing but still alive. He picked up the baseball bat, hurried back inside the rectory to the kitchen telephone, and dialed 911. Trying to staunch his own bleeding, he grabbed a dish towel from the counter and pressed it against his forehead.

"911. What is the nature of your emergency?"

Breathlessly he replied, "Yes, this is Father Alonso Ochoa calling from St. Anne's Catholic Church. I need an ambulance sent right away. And please call the police. A man attacked a woman outside of my residence. She is in dire need of help, please hurry!"

"Is the assailant still on the premises?"

"Yes, he is, but I am afraid that I may have killed him."

"Where is he now?"

"He is lying in my hallway at the moment. Please hurry!"

"Okay, Father."

The priest could hear the dispatcher placing the call to a patrol unit.

"Father, please remain on the phone with me until the police arrive."

"I can't. I must go outside and check on her."

"Do you have a portable phone."

"Yes, but it may not reach all the way to the parking lot."

"Alright, but keep me on the line. Just set the phone down so you can come back and let me know when they have arrived."

"Thank you. I will."

Father Alonso grabbed a blanket and ran out to check on Whitley. The wail of sirens from emergency vehicles already filled the night air.

Kneeling beside her, he gently cradled her head in his hands. Her breathing was shallow, and her pulse seemed weaker. Father Alonso was about to perform mouth to mouth when the ambulance pulled into the parking lot. He began to silently mouth a prayer over Whitley as the EMTs ran to his side.

"Thank you, Father. We'll take over now. Did you see what happened to her?"

"Yes. A man attacked her here in the parking lot. He was choking her."

The female technician checked her vital signs and started giving her oxygen. "What happened to the man that did this to her?"

"He's over there." Father Alonso pointed to his door. "I think he's dead. I hit him with a bat, and I think I've killed him. Lord, forgive me," he said on the verge of tears.

"I'll go check on him," the other technician said, then noticed the gash on the priest's head. "Father, are you okay?"

"I'm fine, just a cut. I have 911 on the phone in the rectory. I need to tell them you're here now."

"Sure, Father, let's go. But I'm still gonna want to check out your cut."

They hurried back inside.

The pool of urine beside the man and the growing pool of blood around his head were tell-tale signs that he hadn't fared well in the struggle.

The technician checked for any vitals while the priest talked to the operator and hung up the phone. Both sprinted back outside to check on Whitley.

"The man inside is dead."

"My God, what have I done?" Father Alonso was getting upset.

"It sounds as if you saved a woman's life, Father."

"Will she be alright?"

"She's in shock right now, but she's got a strong pulse. Thanks to you, she has a chance. We'll do our best, Father." With that they loaded her onto a stretcher and into the waiting ambulance. "Why don't you let Jim take a look at that cut of yours before we leave?"

"I'll be fine. Just take care of her, please."

The police arrived within minutes of the ambulance's departure.

Father Alonso appeared distraught as he sat on the steps in front of his mangled screen door. His head was enveloped by the bloody towel that he held in his hands. The police stepped out of their patrol car and walked up on either side of him.

"Are you okay, Father?" they asked.

"As well as can be expected." Father Alonso shook his head, his face still hidden in the towel.

One of the officers noticed the hulking body resting behind Father Ochoa and carefully walked through the twisted aluminum frame that once held the screen door. He pulled a latex glove from his shirt pocket and slipped it on. He bent over and touched the man's eyeball and next checked for a pulse, confirming once again that the attacker was dead.

The officers led Father Alonso away from the body and questioned him until the detectives arrived. Once they were on the scene, the officers backed out and taped off the crime scene. A patrol sergeant and another ambulance soon arrived on the scene.

The detectives questioned Father Alonso and had one of the emergency medical technicians clean up and butterfly tape the cut on his forehead. Once he had calmed down, they drove him downtown to complete their interrogation and report.

CHAPTER THIRTY-THREE

IT WAS WELL into the early hours of the morning, well after the police had finished with the crime scene, well after the reporters and the onlookers had gone home, before it was safe enough for Thor to look for the Suburban.

He was furious that his colleague, Sal had taken it upon himself to make another attempt on Whitley's life. That lack of vision had already caused the death of one innocent woman, and he had nearly been successful with another. Had he possessed the fortitude to see that Whitley was in no way a threat to the organization, none of this would have generated publicity that was currently spiraling out of control.

The fact that he was dead would allow Thor to close up many loose ends. But it would also mean much of the Texas operation might have to be shut down temporarily and moved. This little blunder would cost the organization millions.

Thor had to assume that someone could have stumbled across the numbers list, so he put a copy in a folder. It wouldn't matter if anyone saw them now. The millions of dollars once associated to those locations had already been safely transferred to untraceable offshore accounts. He used the rectory equipment to copy a few other documents and manufacture several new ones, documents containing just enough information to lead investigators down a false trail to solutions for the demise of Miller Walker, as well as expose the money exchange operation that was happening at Saint Anne's.

The papers Thor put into the folder didn't contain obvious clues, just manipulative nudges that would make the simple-minded detectives investigating the case believe that they had pieced together a drug-money laundering operation on their own. The businesses listed as coordinates on the numbers list would appear to be mere contact points for Sal from which he would pick up the money, return to Austin, funnel the cash through the Saint Anne's collection plates to Miller Walker. From that point the trail would disappear.

Hopping on a mountain bike, Thor pedaled down Twenty-Sixth Street. Turning left on Speedway he wove his way through car-filled streets until he found the Suburban parked under a large oak tree. He was relieved Sal had at least had the sense to legally park the vehicle.

He checked the surroundings and saw no campus police in the area. He laid the bike on its side behind the tree. He shook the pack from his shoulders and unzipped the front pocket, pulling out a pair of latex gloves and the spare set of keys he had gotten from Sal. After disengaging the alarm, he opened the back door and tossed his bike inside.

It was 5:45 A.M. and still very dark.

Running around to the passenger-side door, he jumped inside. He was thankful for the tinted windows, so dark he could hardly see out and thus even less likely that anyone could see in.

With a master key Thor unlocked the aluminum briefcase stashed under the passenger seat. Quickly, he placed the damaging folder inside and removed all other important documents from the case, stuffing them inside his backpack. Closing the case, he slid it back under the seat.

He turned on the vehicle's GPS unit and examined the stored coordinates. He made sure the only ones left on the unit were those that matched the hotel locations on the numbers list, so Miller Walker would be implicated. Thor also removed all coordinates not pertinent to the completion of his staged finale.

His head was pounding, throbbing with pain.

Scouring the inside of the truck to make sure nothing else escaped his gaze, he mentally retraced his steps. Once his return plan was formulated, he slid across the console into the driver's seat and fired up the powerful engine.

He drove to Speedway and crossed Twenty-Sixth Street, then turned left into a covered parking structure just before reaching a small kiosk used by the campus guards. Thor had decided it would be best to hide the vehicle on campus in one of the larger covered parking area between. By leaving the truck there, it wouldn't be noticed until later that evening. He saw signs warning that vehicles would be towed after 10:00 if left in the garage. Thor knew that any attempt to tow this one would bring a crowd.

Hopping out, he quietly shut the front door, walked to the back, and removed the bicycle. He looked around again and closed the rear door.

The horn chirped when he turned on the alarm.

He pedaled the bicycle to the top of the ramp on the opposite side from where he had entered the parking garage. Again he made sure the area was clear, then left.

It was 6:15 A.M., and the early-rising exercise regulars were starting their laps around the campus. Thor blended right in to the university scene, looking like a weary grad-student who had pulled an all-nighter and was finally heading home.

CHAPTER THIRTY-FOUR

WINONA TALMADGE HAD TAKEN the redeye from Dallas immediately after she received word from Steve and the police about her daughter's attack. She set a record pace as she grabbed her bulging carry-on bag from the overhead compartment and exited the plane. She flew past the baggage claim area and hailed a taxi. Relentlessly, she prodded the taxi driver to speed up during the twenty-minute ride to the medical center. Upon their arrival she commanded him to sit and wait with her bags in the hospital parking lot and not budge until she returned, regardless of the cost.

Slinging her large purse strap over her shoulder, she rushed inside the emergency room entrance, asked for directions to Whitley's room, then found her way to the elevator. Winona rode to the fourth floor and stepped out. She moved briskly along the corridor toward her daughter's room.

It was 8:30 A.M. when Steve noticed a woman peeking in through the small vertical pane of glass framed in the hospital room's door. The snow-white hair told him it must be Winona.

Whitley was obscured by the curtain that ran alongside the bed.

Steve motioned for the lady to enter as he stood up and walked toward the door.

"Steve?" she asked breathlessly.

"Yes, ma'am. You must be Mrs. Talmadge. Please come in. Whitley's doing fine."

"Thank God. I was so worried." She hugged him. "Thank you for being with her."

"It's my pleasure. I just wish this meeting could have occurred under more pleasant circumstances."

Whitley raised her head from the bed and waved then smiled at her mother.

Winona threw her purse into the guest chair and leaned over to hug her daughter. She began to cry when she saw the bruising around Whitley's neck.

"I'm sorry we had to meet under these circumstances, too, Steve. And please, call me Winona."

"At least we have some good news. Whitley's going to be fine. That is, if we can keep her quiet. I haven't had much luck this morning. Maybe you will."

"That'll be a first," she said quietly with a hint of sarcasm.

Whitley slapped her mother's forearm playfully.

"What in the world did you get yourself into, sweetie?" she asked as she stroked the hair away from her daughter's forehead.

Whitley gestured for her mother to get the answer from Steve. The pressure from her assailant's hands had temporarily damaged Whitley's vocal chords, but the doctors insisted that she would recover completely.

Winona's expression of motherly concern changed to one of breathless horror as Steve related the entire tale; from the night Whitley overheard the conversation between two likely drug-dealers to the attack by one of them in the St. Anne's parking lot. Winona pulled a tissue from the box on the nightstand next to the bed and dabbed her eyes before wiping her nose. The severity of the attack was starting to set in.

Whitley rubbed her mother's back and silently mouthed, "I'm fine now, Mom."

"I had no idea. . .Of all places! In a church parking lot. . .Oh my God. What about the other person. He could still come after you, couldn't he? Well, young lady, you can bet you won't be staying another night in that awful apartment. Not one more night," she exclaimed through intermittent sobs, "and you can bet I'll be staying here until everything is packed up and you have a suitable place to live. And while we're at it, you'll be getting a safer car, too! No more of that 'Big Molly' or whatever you call that monstrosity."

Whitley's eyes were about to bulge out of her head as she held her index finger over her mouth begging for Winona to stop, while wiping tears from her mother's face.

Steve decided it was a good time to step in. "Where are you staying, Winona?" he asked as he put his arm over her shoulder.

"That reminds me, Steve, I need to call the Driskill and get a room." She reached down and pulled her bag from the guest chair to get her cell phone.

Steve gently put his hand over her wrist. "You'll do no such thing. You and Whitley can both stay at my place as long as you need to. I have two empty bedrooms that have your names all over them. Besides, it will be much quieter for Whitley, and you'll both have much more privacy there."

"No, Steve, we couldn't."

Steve pushed her purse back down onto the chair, still gently clutching Winona's arm. "I insist. Whitley is my closest friend. That means you're stuck with me by default."

"You two are just alike." Winona hugged him. "Thank you, Steve."

The very moment Whitley heard his offer, she was ready to check out of the hospital and rush directly to his house.

Winona noticed Whitley's reaction right away. Her daughter's expression was one of panic initially, then came her imploring look toward Winona while Steve wasn't looking.

Steve hadn't noticed a thing due to his lack of sleep. He had arrived at the hospital soon after EMS had brought Whitley in.

"What about your luggage? Did you rent a car?"

"No, I have a taxi downstairs waiting for me. My bag's with him."

"I'll run downstairs and take care of it. I have my company car. Plenty of room."

"Here, Steve, let me give you some money."

"No, no, we'll settle up later. For now, I'll let you two have some time alone." He walked toward the door. "I'll be back shortly."

"Thank you again, Steve." Winona broke down.

"I'll put your bag in my car and see what we need to do to get your daughter out of here. I'll be at the nurse's station if either of you need me."

"Thank you," Winona dabbed her eyes with her tissue but watched carefully as Whitley's eyes followed Steve out of the room. "He's the one, isn't he?" she said, sniffling.

Whitley stared back questioningly.

"Don't give me that dumbfounded look, young lady. He's the one, the reason you won't date, isn't he?"

A tear welled up in the corner of Whitley's eye and slid down her cheek onto the pillowcase. She nodded slowly.

"He's a good man, honey. I can tell." She kissed her own fingertips and patted her daughter's arm with them. "Oh, I'm so glad you're okay, honey."

Whitley smiled and nodded once more as she grabbed a tissue and wiped her nose. Her throat was raw and sore. Just the thought of talking seemed impossible.

After paying the cab driver and delivering Winona's lone suitcase to his car, Steve grabbed a newspaper from the gift shop and waited at the nurse's station to give the women some more time together. After about twenty minutes, he walked down the hall, looked through the window, then stuck his head back into the room. "Everyone decent?"

Winona nodded and smiled.

"Here you go, Whit. I bought you a paper so you can check your horoscope."

Whitley whispered, "Thanks, but no thanks. No more horoscopes. I'm through with all of that."

"Well! It's about time. You know how I feel about all that nonsense!" Winona exclaimed.

Whitley tried to respond, but Winona covered her daughter's mouth before anything came out. "Don't talk too much, baby doll," she warned.

Steve agreed. "That's right. I caught the doctor in the hallway, and he said it may be another day or two before you can get out of here, Whit."

She frowned and stuck out her bottom lip, jokingly.

Winona touched her lip. "Staying here is best, honey. I want you well cared for and to get plenty of rest before we take you out of here."

"She's right, Whit. Besides, you'll probably be sick of us hanging around here for the next couple of days." He held her hand as he spoke.

Whitley squeezed his hand and put the back of it against her cheek.

Steve leaned over and kissed her on the forehead.

Whitley did everything in her power to remain calm so that her response to his touch and kiss wouldn't spike the heart-rate monitor.

At that very moment Winona could clearly see the depth of her daughter's affection for Steve.

"Winona, why don't I take you to my house so you can rest a bit and get cleaned up. I'll bring you back after lunch."

"I'd like to stay with Whitley tonight."

"That won't be necessary, Mom," Whitley mouthed.

"End of discussion, Whitley."

"That's fine. I'll bring you back and pick you up in the morning."

"We can worry about logistics with cars and apartments after Whitley is out of here," Steve said. "Is there anything we can bring back for you, Whit? Magazines? Food?

"Frozen yogurt," she whispered. "Cherry Garcia."

"Anything else?" he asked.

"A T-shirt to sleep in and a change of clothes for when I'm released."

"Come on, Steve. If we don't leave now, you'll need a moving van to carry her order." Winona kissed her goodbye, promising a prompt return later that afternoon. "Get some rest, sweetie."

"You, too, Mom."

"Bye, Whit." Steve leaned over to kiss her once more on the cheek, but Whitley nonchalantly turned and the kiss landed on her lips instead. "We'll be back soon, kid," he said.

"Bye," she whispered and watched them leave the room.

Steve opened the door for Winona as they left the room.

Closing her eyes, she inhaled, wanting to catch what remained of Steve's scent. Whitley felt a surge of energy and relished the thought of repeating that kiss in earnest next time.

Walking side by side down the hall, Winona put her arm around Steve and said, "Steve, I can never thank you enough for being here for Whitley."

"It is no trouble at all, Winona. As I said, she's my best friend in the world."

"Well, she's lucky to have you."

"And I her."

"And you two have never dated?"

"No, we haven't." Steve pushed the Down button for the elevator.

"I'm surprised by that. You two seem so good together."

"That probably stems from our business relationship."

"Perhaps."

"Don't get me wrong. I think Whit is a beautiful, smart, and funny woman. It's just, we work so closely together at the office. I usually try to keep work and dating separate."

"Usually?" Winona sensed an opening.

"Usually."

"It's none of my business, but are you seeing anyone now?"

"No. I'm not." He was glad the elevator doors opened at that moment.

They stepped inside.

"I'll get you set up in one of the guest rooms and have you back here in plenty of time for dinner."

"You'll make someone a fine son-in-law someday, Steve."

"Thank you, Winona," he said calmly, sensing there was more meaning to her statement than she let on.

The doors closed, and they rode to the ground floor.

CHAPTER THIRTY-FIVE

STEVE DROVE WINONA BACK to the hospital later in the day and headed to the bath store for some "girl supplies." He needed to prep the guest bathroom for his impending visitors.

It was 2:15 P.M. on Monday when he checked his cell phone messages for the first time in two days. There was one message from earlier in the morning, and the caller was Detective Kelly.

"Steve, Kel. Listen, I just faxed you some paperwork. Nothing urgent, but I wanted to keep you in the loop until we can figure out who our friend is."

Anytime Kelly sent something via the private fax line, Steve liked to pick it up right away. He hoped that if anyone had retrieved the message from his office, it was Trent. The documents usually included classified police information that shouldn't have been sent in the first place, and Steve didn't want Amy to get to them first and unintentionally broadcast any sensitive content to the office gossip pool.

Steve made a U-turn under the freeway overpass and headed north toward the office. He parked in the circle drive and told the security guard he would be out in a few minutes. Upon his arrival in the claims area, he was barraged with questions from the staff about Whitley's condition.

Before he could answer them all and get to his office, he saw Trent with a large brown envelope in his outstretched hand.

Steve took it from him and whispered, "Kel's fax?"

Trent answered in a low voice and walked with Steve into his office. "Yep. It's the coroner's report on the dude that attacked Whitley. How is she, by the way?"

"She'll be fine. Her mother's with her now. Did you look at the report?"

"Yeah, but there isn't much to it. They don't know who the guy is, and it says that the perp's cause of death was Father Ochoa's bat-pounding to his noggin."

Steve chuckled, "Perp? You've been hanging around with Kel too much. So. Did anyone else see this?"

'No. I nabbed it before Amy made her rounds."

"Good." Steve adopted a more serious tone. "Anything else come in for me?"

"Nope. At least, nothing I can't handle. And I've got your phone forwarded to me, so I can intercept all of your calls while you're out."

"Great thinking. I'll be taking at least the next couple of days off."

"No problem."

"Call me on my cell or at home if you need anything, or if Kel sends any more info to me."

"You got it, chief. Tell Whitley we're all thinking about her.

"I will. Thanks."

"And as an extra level of security, you may also want to tell Amy that I'll be in charge of retrieving all faxes and messages from your office during your absence."

"Excellent idea. I'll tell her right now."

Steve talked with Amy, then quickly left the building and jumped in his car. He sat there for a moment, pulling papers from the envelope and scanning their contents.

The coroner had noted that three head injuries had contributed to the cause of death of the individual. One skull fracture ran from behind the left ear to the back of the skull. A second major fracture was on the crown of the skull. The third, the likely cause of death, had landed on the left temple.

Steve fired up the car's engine before turning to the last page of the report. It contained the coroner's drawings depicting the skull fracture locations. He noticed that the impact point on this man's temple had created a radial fracture. It was on the opposite side and larger, yet similar in appearance to the blow that had likely killed Miller Walker.

CHAPTER THIRTY-SIX

THE FOLLOWING DAY FATHER Alonso arrived at the hospital around 10:00 to check on Whitley. After asking directions at the nurse's station, he made his way to room 413 and tapped quietly on the door.

"Come in," Steve responded. He was sitting in the chair beside Whitley's bed.

Whitley's eyes opened wide. "Father Al!" Her voice was faint and raspy but improving. She still sounded as though she had a horrible case of laryngitis.

"How are you, Whitley?" He walked up to the edge of her bed, and Whitley stretched her arms out to give him a big hug.

"I'm okay. . .I guess."

"Good to see you again, Steve." He turned and shook hands with him, clasping the top of Steve's right hand with his left, then embraced him as well.

"Thank you so much for saving her, Father."

He stared at Steve and nodded while patting him on the back, before turning his attention back to Whitley. "I didn't want to bother you yesterday. I knew you'd need the rest. How do you feel?"

Tears welled up in Whitley's eyes. "I'll be fine, thanks to you.

Thank you so much for rescuing me. I don't remember much of what happened after that man grabbed me, but the police said you had to hit him with a baseball bat to free me."

"I am afraid it is true. I still can't believe that I broke the most serious of commandments. Even though it may have saved your life, I've been up all night thinking that there must have been something else I could have done. I am just so glad you are alright." Tears began to appear in his eyes.

Whitley took the priest's hand. "God will forgive you. You acted in self defense."

"Thank you, Whitley, but this kind of action affects you differently when you're a priest," he said, sniffling.

"We're all human, Father," Steve interjected.

"Thank you, Steve." Father Alonso looked back toward Whitley, "Do you know when you will be released?"

"At 1:00, after the doctor sees me. They wanted to keep me here for two nights, but I think one evening of Winona roaming the halls might have been all they could take," Whitley winced slightly from the pain caused by her raspy laughter.

"That's enough talk, young lady. You rest your voice now. And you make sure she does, Steve." He smiled as he shook a commanding finger at Steve.

"Count on it, Father."

"I'd like to say a prayer if you don't mind."

Whitley whispered, "Of course, Father."

All three held hands.

"Dear heavenly Father, thank you for watching over Whitley. Please help her with her healing, physically as well as emotionally. Oh Lord, bless these two friends as they will need support from each other through this trying time."

Winona entered the room just as they finished the prayer.

CHAPTER THIRTY-SEVEN

AFTER TWO DAYS OF digging, police finally identified the body of Whitley's assailant as Salvatore Pietrellas. Little was known about him other than the fact he had a Mexican passport and claimed to be an importer.

By a stroke of dumb luck, a parking lot attendant turned in the license plate of Sal's Suburban to the campus police after attempting to have the towing company haul away the massive vehicle. The campus cop had the good sense to contact APD. When they discovered during their conversation that the vehicle was registered to a Mexican company, the call had been transferred to Detective Kelly.

"Mr. Kelly, this is Hank Liles callin' from U.T. Campus Police. We just got a call from one of our parking attendants here on campus. He found an unattended vehicle, a pretty strange one at that, parked in the lot next to the Law School down here."

"What do you mean by strange, Mr. Liles?"

"It's armored."

"Really?"

"Yeah, the attendant checked to see if it was unlocked, and he got the hell shocked out of him when he touched the door handle."

"Interesting."

"Why do you say that?" Mr. Liles asked.

"Well, a couple of nights ago we had a woman assaulted just a few blocks away from that garage. The perp flat lined after a priest crushed his skull with a baseball bat."

"Yeah, I read about it in the paper."

"We still haven't found a vehicle for this guy, so do me a favor and keep everyone away from it until we get there. If it belongs to this guy, there's no telling what other surprises there may be."

Soon police swarmed into the area and sealed it off. When they finally succeeded in bypassing the truck's security system, they couldn't believe the technology they discovered inside. The Suburban was equipped with bullet-proof glass, an explosion-proof undercarriage, special run-flat tires, and an extremely sophisticated GPS system. Sealed in a compartment under the cargo area was an array of firearms that included a couple of automatic weapons, pistols, knives, and a large cache of ammo. They discovered that a company out of Ohio had made the vehicle for Mexican company that no longer exists at the location to which it was shipped only eleven months earlier. This most definitely was not the vehicle of a small-time hood.

The seizure of the vehicle eventually made front-page news.

Much to the dismay of Father Alonso, he was also news. He had become something of a local celebrity not only for saving the life of his friend but also for ridding the city of a possible terrorist.

CHAPTER THIRTY-EIGHT

BY THURSDAY AFTERNOON STEVE had all but given up on deciphering the remaining numbers. Unless he could come up with something more substantial, Detective Kelly would have nothing concrete to give his superiors that warranted reopening the case.

Then it happened.

"Steve?"

"Yes, it is."

"This is Natalie Carlson."

"Hello, Natalie. How are you?"

"Not so well I'm afraid."

"I take it you must have heard about Miller."

"On the ten o'clock news last night," she said.

"I'm so sorry you had to hear about his involvement that way," Steve said.

"Steve, it's all lies. None of that about Miller having any part in that money-laundering scheme is true."

"It seems like they have some pretty substantial evidence against him, Natalie."

She got defensive. "How things seem. . .aren't always the way they are!"

Steve changed the tone of his voice, "How do you mean?"

"I'm so scared, I didn't know who else to trust so I called you. I just had a feeling that there was no way you could be a part of this."

"A part of what, Natalie? Do you know something you haven't told the police?"

"A part of whatever Miller was involved in. And no, I haven't talked to the police."

"You knew about his money laundering? That omission alone could make you an accessory!"

"No, no, I didn't know anything about what he was doing. It's just that whatever he was doing, I know he was doing it to protect me."

"From what?"

"I don't know. He never told me."

"So what can you tell me about his involvement, exactly?"

"Perhaps nothing, but I guess, I mean, can we meet? I'd rather not discuss this over the phone."

"Certainly, but can you give me an idea as to what is this all about?"

"I'll tell you when I see you. How soon can we meet?"

"Well, I could possibly drive to Douglas Creek this evening."

"That won't be necessary. I'm in your visitor's parking lot."

"You're downstairs?"

"Yes."

Steve was already standing up from his chair. "Meet me at the receptionist's desk. It's on the first floor of the building to the left of the main walkway. The receptionist's name is Sandy. I'll be right down."

"Okay. Thank you, Steve." Natalie dropped her cell phone into her purse and put her sunglasses on. Looking around the parking lot, she got out of the Camry, half-jogged across the parking lot, up the sidewalk, and into the glass entryway.

Sandy looked up as Natalie strolled self-consciously to the desk. "How can I help you today?"

"I'm meeting someone. He's on his way down. Thank you, though." Natalie was visibly upset as she waited anxiously for Steve to arrive.

The elevator doors opened moments later, and he walked toward her.

"Good to see you again, Natalie." He extended his hand and shook hers. "You've definitely aroused my interest. Now, what can I do for you?"

"Is there someplace where we could discuss this in private?"

"We could go to my office upstairs, or we could talk in one of the rooms down here."

"Down here would be better for me, if you don't mind."

"Downstairs it is. Excuse me a minute. Sandy," Steve asked, "is there a conference room available for us to use?"

"I bet there is, Steve. Let me check." She pulled out a large binder and thumbed through the pages until reaching the last entry. "We've got an office or a conference room. Which would you like?"

"Natalie?"

"The office is fine. But does it have a computer?"

Steve was puzzled by her question. He turned and looked inquisitively at Sandy.

"Yes, ma'am." The receptionist reached into one of her drawers and pulled out a key. "Suite 103 is all yours. Available all afternoon if you need it."

"Thanks, Sandy." Steve led Natalie down a short hallway to one of several offices, closing the door behind him. "Have a seat." He walked around the desk and plopped down in an overstuffed leather chair.

Natalie sat fidgeting in her chair.

Steve paused momentarily to see if she would start the conversation.

She didn't.

"I must say, I'm intrigued by this visit. What is it you wanted to tell me?"

"I may live to regret this, but I'm afraid I wasn't totally honest with the police, nor with you. . .that is. . .when you and Trent stayed over during the ice storm and all."

"How so?"

"Here goes." She closed her eyes momentarily, then blurted it out, "The sole reason that Miller and I divorced was that he feared for my life if we stayed together."

"What? Why was he afraid for you?" Steve asked calmly and listened carefully to her reply.

"He had told me that he was being forced into some illegal activity and that if he didn't cooperate, they would hurt both him and me."

"Did he give you any details about the activity?"

"No, but he said that my life was at stake if he didn't cooperate with them. Shortly after he told me this wild story, I met him for lunch. He told me that we were going to stage a separation, so he could get me out of harm's way.

"Of course, I thought he was joking at first. Then, I thought he was having a nervous breakdown. I got very angry with him because he wouldn't see anyone about it. He was so very adamant about never discussing the topic while we were at home, which made me think he was getting more and more delusional, I mean, saying the house was bugged and all. I almost called a psychologist from home, but after all that has happened, I'm glad I didn't. At one point I even assumed he was making the whole thing up to cover up an affair. But one thing happened that solidified my belief in what he was saying."

"And what was that?"

"One weekend we went to Salado and stayed in a small bed and breakfast. After we arrived, he said he would prove the danger I was in. God, he was so paranoid, the poor thing. He insisted on whispering this story to me in bed. He said that sometime in the next two days, a woman would be found dead in a downtown Austin parking lot. Sure enough, the next morning's paper reported they had found her. And, thank God, I knew Miller didn't do it because she was killed the same night we were in Salado. Oh, it was awful. I remember particularly because the girl was missing all of her fingers on one hand and all of the toes on one foot."

"I remember that case. They said it was a drug deal gone bad."

"I felt so bad for doubting him after that."

"Did Miller ever give you any clue as to who these people were?"

"He never said a word. He never told me anything about them, other than the fact that they were extremely dangerous.

"After the Salado trip, we started the charade that eventually led to our split. In the beginning he asked me to act a certain way when we were at home in case it was bugged. This went on for several months, so the divorce wouldn't appear staged. Every once in a while, he would just show up in some out-of-the-way place where I happened to be. I never had any idea when or where it would be. I would be at the hairdresser's or at the mall or a restaurant, and he would just show up! He would give me handwritten directions from a small notepad. He would tell me when we would have arguments and what they would be about."

"Did you save any of the notes?"

"No, he insisted that I tear them into small pieces and flush them down the toilet or burn them as soon as possible after reading them. But I did receive this after he died." She reached into her purse and retrieved a flash drive from a zippered side pocket. She placed it on the desk and gingerly pushed it toward Steve.

"What's this?"

"Open it."

Steve popped it into the USB port and attempted to open the file. It was a PowerPoint file. "I'm afraid I can't see the file. The PowerPoint software isn't loaded on this computer."

"Oh, I'm sorry. I should have mentioned that to your receptionist. I'm just so scared."

"No problem. We'll find another machine. Do you know what's on it?"

"Yes."

"Where did you get this?"

"From Miller."

"I still don't understand why you are bringing this to me."

"When Miller died, his will contained instructions for the executor, his attorney, to give me two envelopes. There was a large manila envelope and a small white envelope taped to the outside of larger one. I was instructed by the attorney to go anywhere but home immediately and open them in complete privacy. So, I drove to my bank and went into the vault where my safe deposit box is, and I opened them. The large envelope contained a sweet card from Miller and a paper copy of the contents of the drive you now have. The smaller envelope contained the drive."

"Do you still have the paper copy?"

"Yes, right here." Natalie reached once more into her purse and retrieved a folder containing the documents. She handed them to Steve. "Miller asked me to keep the folder, burn his card once I had read it, and hide the flash-drive and the paper copy in the safest and most out-of-the-way place I could find. He said that once I found someone of authority that I could trust, I was to take the drive to that person. But most of all I was supposed to stay away from the police and allow whomever I gave this information to contact law enforcement. God, this thing has made me a nervous wreck for weeks."

Steve opened the folder. It contained six pages of large bold type that very well could have been printed from a PowerPoint presentation file.

"Quotations?" he asked as he scanned each page.

"Yes."

"Any idea what they mean."

"No, I don't."

The six quotations read as follows:

Truth can never be told so as to be understood and not believed. — William Blake

The hidden harmony is better than the obvious. — Alexander Pope

These are the times that try men's souls. — Thomas Paine

Behind a frowning providence he hides a smiling face. — William Cowper

For we that live to please must please to live. — Samuel Johnson

Look before you leap. — John Heywood

Steve found a pencil and started tapping the eraser on the desk as he pondered the quotations. "Well, let's see if I can find someone that has Power Point software installed on their machine so we can take a look at this." He grabbed the phone and dialed 5443, Trent's extension.

"This is Trent."

"Do you have PowerPoint software on your laptop?"

"Hey there boss. Sure I do."

"Take it down to Whitley in the basement and meet me there."

"Will do."

Natalie had a strained look on her face as Steve stood up.

He recognized her concern. "Don't worry. It's Trent."

"Oh, good." She said with a sigh of relief.

"And Whitley is one of my dearest friends. You can trust her also."

"If you say so."

She followed Steve to the front desk, where he signed Natalie in using her first initial and a false last name and asked the receptionist for a visitor's card-key. They slid the cards through the reader and walked through the large security doors to the elevators, descending to the basement location of the Information Services Department. The doors opened, and they walked across the floor to Whitley's cubicle.

"Whitley Talmadge, meet Natalie Carlson."

"Hello Natalie, so nice to meet you. Have a seat." Whitley motioned for her to sit down.

"Thank you." Natalie hesitated before sitting down. "Talmadge? Are you the same woman I read about in the paper? The lady who was attacked at St. Anne's?"

"One in the same."

Trent arrived moments later, showed Steve the laptop and gave Natalie a hug.

Natalie then looked at Steve with a fearful expression.

"Is everything okay?" Whitley asked.

Steve looked around the department, then pulled a chair from the vacant cubicle next to Whitley's, and sat down with them.

"Natalie thinks that there may be something more sinister behind her ex-husband's death."

"You mean that it wasn't accidental?" Trent asked.

Steve didn't respond. Instead, he turned and looked squarely at Natalie. "Natalie, I don't think Miller's death was accidental either. I never have."

Natalie looked shocked.

"I'm sorry I didn't or couldn't say anything before now. It's just that we had some serious reservations about the explosion being an accident. We even had to check you out," he said as he gently touched Natalie's shoulder.

Natalie smiled and began to cry, as if months of emotion had finally been released. "I knew I could trust you from the first time we met."

Whitley handed her a tissue. "Here you go, Natalie."

"So tell me." Trent asked. "What can I help with?"

"How good are you with PowerPoint?" Steve asked.

"Pretty solid."

"Good." He handed him the drive. "Open this for me, will you?" He was very serious.

Trent stuck the flash drive into the USB port. He opened up the PowerPoint program, switched to the A: drive, and clicked on the file, which was labeled "quotations."

He clicked on the slide viewer icon and the first slide appeared—*Look before you leap.*—John Heywood

"Looks like a quote to me," Whitley stated.

Steve responded, "Yeah, and I think there's a clue that Miller Walker was trying to tell Natalie in these slides." He laid the paper copies out on Whitley's desk in order to get a better view.

Trent clicked on an icon to pull up the notes pages section of the program, and scrolled through each slide. "No notes on any of the slides." He returned to the first slide in the group.

Natalie stared at the screen while Whitley and Steve examined the paper copies momentarily. "Do you think he was trying to tell me to be careful?"

"Perhaps," Steve replied. "I just don't get the cryptic delivery of these things. You know? I mean, using the attorney and all."

Whitley chimed in. "Let's go Natalie's route. Maybe there is a message in the quotes. 'Look before you leap' could be telling her to be careful, as she suggested. 'Truth can never be told so as to be understood and not believed.' What the heck does that mean? Always tell the truth?"

"There's something more to this. I just know it. I can't see anyone going to this much trouble to end up with something so simplistic," Steve said. He looked at the screen then at Trent. "Trent, is there any way to put all of the slides on the screen at one time?"

"Sure" he moved the cursor to one of the toolbars and clicked. All six slides appeared on the screen.

Look before you leap. —John Heywood

Behind a frowning providence he hides a smiling face. —William Cowper

These are the times that try men's souls. —Thomas Paine

For we that live to please must please to live. —Samuel Johnson

The hidden harmony is better than the obvious. —Alexander Pope

Truth can never be told so as to be understood and not believed. —William Blake

Whitley quickly scanned the monitor. "Hmmm, nothing new or different here I'm afraid."

Natalie gasped and covered her mouth, the tissue still in her hand.

"What is it?" Steve asked.

"Miller always liked word games."

"What are you saying?"

"Look at the first word of each of the quotes."

Steve and Whitley scanned each slide and read them aloud simultaneously.

"Look-behind-these-for-the-truth."

Steve cried out, "Natalie! That's got to be it!"

Natalie was puzzled. "But behind what. And what is the truth?"

It hit Whitley immediately. "My God, I think I know."

Grabbing the external mouse from Trent, she switched the multiple-slide view to a single-slide screen. Next, she moved the mouse over the quote and clicked on the text. A border appeared around the quote. She clicked on the border once more and used the arrow keys to move the text box toward the bottom of the screen. As she did so their eyes grew wide at what the display revealed.

"Whitley, that's it!" Steve cried and leaned over and squeezed her shoulders. "Paste the text into a Word document, then print it out so that we can examine the contents."

"Wow!" Trent exclaimed.

Hidden behind the six pages were compressed text boxes containing lists of numbers, information about the organization, and a complete account of Miller's forced involvement within it. The info was typed in a very small font. Once expanded, the document yielded organization code names and numbers, exact bank locations tied to the codes, and a thorough chronological history of Miller's collection and distribution of funds throughout the state. There was much more information here than investigators had found on the flash drive in his safe, and much more than Thor left behind in the Suburban.

"What does it all mean, Steve?" Natalie asked.

Steve tapped his finger on his lips as he continued to read the documents. "I'm not sure just yet, but if this info checks out, it means that your husband was telling you the truth."

Natalie's body quivered, and her tears flowed forcefully with the news.

"And it means it's time we got the police involved."

"But. . .Miller said not to bring the police into this, Steve," Natalie objected.

"I have one detective in the department I know we can trust. He is the person that brought your case to my attention."

Natalie seemed relieved to hear this and relaxed.

Steve looked sternly at all three. Whitley had never seen him look this way. "Not a word of this to anyone. And I mean it!"

CHAPTER THIRTY-NINE

THE SUNDAY MASS AT 10:00 was the most popular at the church. The biggest crowds always came to the "Big Ten" when Father Alonso Ochoa presided. This day, however, was to be different. Just one week after the death of Salvatore Pietrellas, Father Alonso had an announcement to make to the congregation.

He emerged from a side door with the altar boys. All were dressed in spotless white robes and took their usual seats. The priest paused momentarily in his chair as if to collect his thoughts, then stood up, and walked to the pulpit.

"Before we get started...I have a special announcement to make."

Silence spread through the congregation.

"I'm sure most of you know that a serious situation occurred here last weekend. One person lost his life and another almost lost hers. . .and I nearly lost one of my dear friends. But I am happy to say that she is recovering nicely and is in our audience today." Father Alonso looked down and smiled at Whitley as the audience broke out in applause.

She returned the smile and blew a kiss and winked at him.

Father Al remained stoic as he spoke, "Last week reemphasized an important lesson, one we should all heed. And that lesson tells us that life is a precious gift, a fragile gift, a gift that can be taken away in an instant. I unfortunately took that precious gift away from one individual.

"Regardless of the reason for my actions, I have broken one of our Lord's commandments, the most serious of the Lord's commandments. I, a person who chose to turn his life over to God, have committed a mortal sin by taking a human life. It is because of this most grievous of sins that I have come to a crossroad in my life. I must make a life-altering decision that causes me great pain and sadness, but one that I know I must meet head on and come to grips with." He paused and looked from one side of the assemblage to the other.

"Next Sunday will be my last service here. After that day, I will no longer be a priest at Saint Anne's."

A collective moan made its way across the audience.

"I will be leaving the priesthood permanently, and I will begin my return trip to my home country of Venezuela next Sunday afternoon. I have already contacted the Diocese to advise them of my decision, and they have accepted my resignation."

The audience was stunned, but Father Al didn't give them a chance to think about the announcement much longer.

"Well, then, let us begin this mass with a prayer. Dear Lord, bless this congregation of souls that have come here today to celebrate mass in your honor. Please help us to cope with the adversity we all face in our lives as we strive to make ourselves better in your eyes. In Christ's name we pray. Amen."

"Amen," the congregation responded in unison.

Many members, men and women, young and old, had already begun to cry. Whitley was sobbing, and Steve had nestled her against his shoulder, cupping her face with his left hand.

Father Alonso held his hands up trying to calm them. "Please, I don't want this to be an unhappy time. I love you all so very much. This community has been wonderful to me. You have lovingly accepted me from the day I arrived. More importantly, we've accomplished a lot together. Let me leave knowing that you will extend this same spirit to your new priest.

"Please rise and open your hymnals to page 212." He continued with the service.

CHAPTER FORTY

THE NEXT SUNDAY CAME entirely too soon as far as Whitley was concerned. She made it a point to get to the church early so that she could spend some quality time with Father Al before he left. Unfortunately, a majority of the other parishioners had had the same idea.

A large crowd had already gathered by the time Whitley arrived. All were there to bid Father Alonso farewell and give him a big sendoff to the airport. Many were lined up hugging him and wishing him well, laughing and crying, while others stood patiently waiting their turns. Several senior parishioners reminisced about the most memorable events that occurred during Father Alonso Ochoa's four-year tenure at St. Anne's. All wanted a chance to speak with him.

Whitley finally got her chance.

Father Al stood with his arms outstretched, waiting for Whitley to come to him. Softly, so the other parishioners couldn't hear, he told her, "I'm going to miss you most of all, Whitley."

"I wish you would stay. I'm going to miss you, too." Tears welled up in her eyes. "I owe you so much for what you did for me. I can't help but feel like I'm responsible for getting you into this mess."

"Now, now, you take those thoughts right out of your head. This was God's work, and second guessing why this happened won't help you heal. We have no way of knowing what could have been done to change the outcome."

"But you're leaving your true calling in life, aren't you?"

"God has a different calling for me now. I have to feel confident that in time I will find the new path he has chosen for me."

"I just can't believe I can't stop by to see you anymore. Who am I going to be able to bother at seven o'clock in the morning to have coffee with me?"

"I think I know of a certain young man you should consider," the priest said.

Whitley grinned widely, then hugged him once more. "Be careful."

"I will, Whitley."

"I love you, Father Al. Please keep in touch."

"I will, Whitley. God bless you. I hope all your hopes and dreams come true."

Whitley kissed him on the cheek, then wiped her lipstick from it and moved aside so that others could see Father Al before he left. She walked directly to her car and headed home to change clothes before driving across town to Steve's house.

One of the parishioners who owned a limousine service had arranged to take the priest to the airport. When it came time to leave, he stepped up on the vehicle's door frame and gave one final wave to those gathered outside St. Anne's before getting inside.

The driver closed the door for him, then carefully drove off through the crowd.

Alonso leaned forward in his seat and spoke loudly so that the driver could hear. "Driver, would you take us down Guadalupe Street before you head toward the airport please?"

"Sure, Father, but you don't have to yell. There's a speaker button just to your right."

"Oh, I'm so sorry."

"Don't mention it."

"As you may have surmised, I've never been in such a vehicle before."

"Well, sit back, enjoy the ride, and let me know if I can do anything else for you."

"Thank you so much. What is your name?"

"Jerry, sir."

"Fine. Thank you, Jerry."

"You're welcome, Father. And help yourself to a cold drink. We have soft drinks, bottled water, or something stronger if you prefer." Jerry chuckled.

"Club soda will be fine." Alonso reached for a small bottle, unscrewed the cap and poured the contents into a glass full of ice.

As the pearl-white Lincoln glided down Guadalupe Street, Alonso sat erect in his seat, peering fondly at the scenery out the limousine's window, while sipping his drink. He would miss the myriad of storefronts that lined Guadalupe, stacked side by side in all shapes and sizes.

Jerry made a left turn onto Martin Luther King Boulevard, then across IH-35 just past the Frank Erwin Center and University of Texas campus. He reached up to adjust his rearview mirror and looked momentarily at the priest. He knew all about recent events that had befallen the church and was examining Father Alonso's every move. It was a brief and quiet ride for the remaining distance to the airport.

Jerry had no sooner parked the limo near the airline's curb-side check-in kiosk than Father Alonso began to open the back door.

"No, no, Father. That's my job." Jerry hopped out of the driver's seat and ran around to open his door.

"If you'll show your ID and passport at the counter to get your boarding pass and give me just a minute to help check in your luggage, you'll be good to go." Jerry flagged down one of the porters who helped Jerry retrieve Father Alonso's bags.

"Whatever you say, Jerry. I just can't get used to all this attention. I feel somewhat guilty, I'm afraid." Father Alonso didn't seem to know just exactly what to do and was obviously uncomfortable as he complied, then stood watching the two men struggle with his luggage.

Jerry tipped the baggage handler five dollars and retrieved the priest's folder with the boarding slip and baggage claim tickets for his flight to Maracaibo, Venezuela. He stepped toward Father Alonso and handed him the folder. "We honestly are not trying to change you, Father. You just have a whole bunch of people that wanted to do something nice for you, to show you how much you mean to them."

"I will truly miss this place." Alonso appeared close to tears as he reached into his back pocket and pulled out his wallet.

"If you're taking that out on my account, you can just put it back where you found it. Your friends have covered everything for you," Jerry said with a grin.

Alonso hesitated, then carefully replaced his driver's license back into his wallet and slid it back into his pocket. "God bless you, and thank you for the ride, Jerry." He leaned over his briefcase and gave Jerry a hug and a pat on the back.

"You're welcome, Father."

"Goodbye, Jerry. Please give my thanks to everyone for the wonderful gift."

"I will. Have a safe trip, Father."

Jerry stood and watched as Father Alonso walked through the main terminal entrance. Once he was sure Alonso couldn't see him, Jerry looked to the right of the automatic doors at a man reading a newspaper and nodded.

The man folded his paper and walked inside.

The limo was quickly driven a short distance from the terminal where Alonso checked in and two men with briefcases climbed in, retrieved the club soda bottle and bagged it, then started dusting the interior for more fingerprints.

One of the men stated, "If he's not Father Ochoa, he looks just like him."

"Of course he looks just like him. He's Father Ochoa's twin brother Galtero. And the fingerprint on that bottle should confirm it along with the fact that he's his brother's murderer."

Ochoa went into the airport bathroom where he remained for several minutes. After he came out and scoured his surroundings, he passed through the security checkpoint only with a different boarding pass in hand; one that he had printed at home; this one going to Mexico City.

For the first time in a great while, Ochoa looked like an ordinary citizen. Gone were his priestly vestments, collar, rosary—all the insignia of his profession. He wore a simple pair of tan slacks and a black knit golf shirt. He sat calmly at gate B12, briefcase at his feet, reading a newspaper until the boarding call came for the flight to Mexico City.

He had a first-class ticket and was among the first to board the plane. He settled into a window seat. No one sat next to him. Ochoa stared out the window, watching the grounds crew but ignoring the pre-flight announcements about the plane's safety and emergency features.

The plane soon taxied to the edge of the main runway and queued up until it was time for takeoff. Once the plane was on the main runway, the pilot accelerated. No sooner had the wheels lost contact with the runway than he steered the plane to the right, and the powerful jet began its steady climb into Hill Country airspace. After continuing to climb for twenty minutes, it finally settled into its flight path and reached its cruising altitude of 31,000 feet.

A bell rang and an attendant's voice came over the speaker system. "The pilot has turned off the fasten seatbelt sign. Feel free to walk about the cabin. We will be serving beverages shortly."

Ochoa continued to stare out the window, watching as the terrain steadily changed from the hills of Central Texas to the barren flats of South Texas. Before long he pulled the shade down over the window and closed his eyes.

The man that Jerry had signaled outside the terminal was across the aisle in seat 2A. He leaned his seat back far enough so that he could watch Ochoa. Still wearing his sunglasses, he also pretended to go to sleep, so he could continue to monitor the former priest.

CHAPTER FORTY-ONE

OCHOA HAD BEEN NAPPING for forty-five minutes when the pilot's voice came over the speaker. "Ladies and gentlemen, welcome to Mexico. If you will look out either side of the plane, you will see that we have just crossed over the mighty Rio Grande River and are now in Mexican airspace."

Leaning down, Ochoa reached under the seat in front of him and retrieved his briefcase, then pulled the tray table from its place in the armrest, and rested the case on top of it. He popped the latches on each side.

A matching pen-and-pencil set fitted inside two leather tubes were part of the organized interior compartment of the case. He slipped the pen from its holder and pulled the arrow shaped pocket clasp from its top edge, locking it in place at a ninety-degree angle. Inserting the tip into a small hole on the right side of the case, he turned the pen until he heard a click. A small compartment separated from the lid of the case.

Ochoa pulled out an 8 ½" x 11" manila envelope from the case's concealed storage compartment. Lifting the flap, he slipped his hand inside and retrieved a sizable document. Carefully placing the envelope back in his case, he squeezed the pen's clasp flush, returning it to its normal state, and began rolling it back and forth in his hand as he examined the information before him.

The passenger in seat 2A was still unobtrusively watching him.

On the first page the document's header read, "THOR—Texas Operations Listing." The first line, double-spaced under the header read, "TX30dN25.44w—Saint Anne's Catholic Church." The page held a total of three columns. Each column held fifty coordinates with corresponding location names spilling down and across the page.

He shook his head in a disgusted fashion and let out a quiet, hissing sigh. He continued to roll the pen in his hand, from his palm to his fingertips, then back again.

The man in 2A continued his surveillance.

Ochoa clicked the button on the end of his pen to expose the roller-ball and made a large diagonal line across the first page, then the second, then the third. How had the Feds pieced together information that led to the seizure of so many additional accounts that weren't on the list he had planted in the Suburban? He wondered if Miller could have somehow been able to tip them off, then put that thought out of his mind. How the Feds found out didn't matter. What mattered was that this was the first black eye of Thor's career, and it would cost the organization tens of millions of dollars to fix it.

At the top of the fourth page, he wrote, "Reorg. Starts here." There were sixty-two pages left, all with just as many coordinates and locations as had been on the first four pages. He slid the papers back into the envelope, looked around, then placed the envelope back in the secret compartment. He reached into his pants pocket and pulled out a business card for a plastic surgeon located in Mexico City. He committed the address to memory, placed the card in one of the leather card slots, then closed and locked the briefcase.

He eased back into his seat and began rolling the pen back and forth in his hand, across his palm to his fingertips. He switched hands with the pen and continued the ritual, slowly, methodically.

CHAPTER FORTY-TWO

IT WAS 1:00 P.M. on Saturday and exactly one week to the day after Father Al's departure, when Whitley's new car purred quietly down Steve's driveway. Even though the Mercedes was much smaller than "Molé Grande," Whitley was surprised at how much more solid and safe the vehicle felt. Dressed in a ball cap, a white shirt tied at the waist, faded jeans, and hiking boots, she got out and followed the sidewalk to the front door. She rang the bell and waited, nervously chewing on her cuticle for a moment before she thought to adjust the brim of her cap.

"Hey you," Steve said as he opened the door. He hugged her and kissed her on the cheek, catching sight of the Mercedes out of the corner of his eye. "Wow! Somebody's been to the car store."

Whitley smiled but didn't speak.

Steve looked at the car, then back at Whitley, "Is that the car you and your mother went to look at?"

"Yep. Winona's been hammering on me for so long, I finally broke down and bought a safe one."

"That you did. Nice car. No wonder you didn't want to bring Bosco with us."

Steve locked the front door and turned to Whitley. "You sure I don't need to bring anything else?"

"I'm sure."

"Am I overdressed?" he said, looking down at his khaki pants and tan loafers.

"You look fine, you worry wart. Come along." Whitley grabbed him by the elbow, walked him to the car, and opened the passenger-side door. "After you."

Steve got inside. "Talk about service! So, where is it we're going anyway?"

"I told you that you'd find out when we got there. God, you're worse than a little kid! Besides, you're off until Wednesday. What do you care? I may just drive us to a foreign country if you're not careful."

"I always did like an adventure."

"And what's up with taking more time off? Three weeks of vacation a few months back wasn't enough?"

"Let's just say I now see the positive effects one can gain from regular time off."

She laughed, "It took you long enough. What are you going to do?"

"I'm not going anywhere. Just gonna relax at home for a couple of days."

Whitley had shut the door, walked around the front of the car, and gotten in while they talked. Now she backed out of the driveway and wound her way out of the neighborhood. Soon she was heading west on Bee Caves Road toward Highway 71.

Steve liked the feel and smell of the Mercedes' leather seating. He fidgeted with the buttons on the dash, then with the stereo.

Whitley watched him lovingly. He reminded her of a mischievous youngster with a new toy.

Crossing the bridge over the Llano River after almost an hour on the road, they continued west on 71 toward the small Hill Country town of Brady. The Saturday afternoon sun crept around into their faces as they drove.

Steve was still perplexed about the trip, still trying to deduce their final destination. He knew the area well, but with all of the

DAVID PRITCHARD

county roads in this region of the state, they could easily land anywhere from San Angelo to San Antonio in a reasonable amount of time.

Before reaching Brady, Whitley turned off the highway onto a narrow gravel road, also one which Steve knew well. Before long she pulled up to a gate. It was the entrance to the beloved ranch in the framed real estate ad on his desk.

"What are you trying to do? Rub salt in my wound?" Steve said jokingly.

"I just thought since we were in the area, we could take a look at it once more." She tossed her cap onto the back seat, got out, and walked to the gate.

"Okay, but after this where are we going?" he called out.

She didn't answer.

Steve watched from the car as her hips swayed with each graceful step. The sun silhouetted her body, and he could just make out the curve of her waist as the sun shone through the fabric of her blouse.

Whitley put one leg up on the bottom rail of the gate and placed her forearms on top of it. Her eyes followed the route of the path on the other side of it. The road was nothing more than two sandy ruts meandering down a slope to a small rustic cabin. The modest stone and timber home was surrounded by a cluster of ancient oak trees. A nice-sized pond was a short walk from the front porch; a tall windmill was spinning lazily just beside it. The sun, about to greet the horizon, cast its beautiful golden glow over Whitley's face.

Steve had gotten out of the car and walked up beside her. He mimicked her pose at the gate. They stood silently together, watching, listening to the wind blow across the gently sloping pasture. The native grasses bending to the soft breeze pointed in the direction of the cabin.

"God, this is a beautiful place, isn't it?" Steve said.

"Mmmm-hmmm, it sure is," Whitley whispered. She laid the side of her head on her arms and looked at Steve.

He was somewhere else entirely.

292

"I have something I need to tell you, Steve," she said almost reluctantly.

He turned to her.

"And while I'm telling you what I have to say, I don't want you to interrupt."

"Okay."

"This will be hard enough as it is."

"Is everything alright?"

She held her hand up, gesturing for him to stop talking. "Everything is fine. Please, just listen to what I have to say all the way through." Her voice cracked with nervousness as she gathered her thoughts.

"When you went through your divorce, I couldn't believe it. You and Connie seemed so right together, I never had a clue that she could do such a thing to you. She never came across as that type of person. You two were always so good to me, and I loved you both for it. What I hated most out of that episode was seeing you suffer because of what she did. I knew how she hurt you, and I lost a lot of respect for her because of it.

But at the same time, another part of me was ecstatic when I heard the news. I know that's a horrible thing to say, but I can't keep this inside any longer. I was ecstatic because I have always loved you. I don't mean I fell in love with you at first sight. I mean that my love for you has grown steadily over the years out of our friendship."

Steve resisted the urge to say anything, unsure Whitley was finished. He trained his eyes intently on hers.

"After your divorce, I gave you space. For the past couple of years, I've given you space. My reasoning is that I never wanted to interfere with your healing process. Then you met Michelle unexpectedly, and you seemed so happy with her. Again, my timing was less than perfect. And like you, I still can't believe she's gone. Now you're forced to go through yet another healing process.

"Understand that by my saying this, I'm not expecting you to reciprocate at all. If you don't feel the same way about me that's fine." Her lip quivered as she fought back the tears. "It's just that I had to tell you. I've had these emotions bottled up inside of me for so long that I was about to explode. I wanted, I mean, I had to find the right way to tell you, and more importantly to show you."

She paused and reached into the right front pocket of her jeans. Tears were streaming down her face as she pulled out a single key on a small horseshoe key ring. She handed it to Steve.

"What's this?" he asked, examining the horseshoe.

"It's the key to this gate."

"How did you get this?"

"It's mine. Well, actually, I guess it's yours now. I bought this place for you."

"You did what?" Steve looked down at the key in his hand, then wide-eyed back up at Whitley.

"Don't freak out. I'm not one of those stalker types that try to buy someone's love. I bought it to keep anyone else from purchasing it. I have all the papers drawn up for you to buy it back from me with no interest. Even if something happens to me, it's in my will that you alone can buy this place. And whether you decide to pay cash in two or three years or make payments for the rest of your life, it's up to you. But it's safe."

The numb, surprised expression on Steve's face said it all. "How in the world did you find out about this place, Whitley?"

"From the picture on your desk. One day while I was loading some update software on your computer, I took the number off your realtor's card and called him. He's known about this for weeks."

"Dutch was in on this?"

"Yes. It was his idea to call you and tell you it was sold. I went along with it for as long as I could. The closing took place yesterday."

"I don't know what to say." He scratched his head and paced around for a bit. "Whitley, how on earth could you afford this? Jesus! You don't make half what I do."

"Well, at work that's true. But years ago when my grandparents passed away, they left me a nice sum of money. Daddy held some of the money in trust and made some good investments for me with the rest of it."

"Whitley, this place is over eight hundred thousand dollars!

That's not just a drop in the bucket."

"I know, I know. It's just that Dad got in early with a few big high-tech companies. Awhile back before the big economic downturn, I decided to cash them out. As a result, I've never needed to continue working at Western States, or anywhere else for that matter. I had even thought about quitting so you wouldn't be able to use the 'I don't date co-workers' line on me, but I wanted to be near you. God! Now I really sound like a stalker."

Steve experienced a mix of concern and elation, but he still didn't yet know exactly how to react.

"You don't sound like a stalker, Whit," he muttered. He wiped a tear from the corner of his eye and gazed at Whitley. "I never knew how you felt. God, you've been such a good friend. Honestly, I never knew."

"I know you didn't. Again, I don't want you to feel I had any ulterior motive in doing this. I just know how much this place means to you. I wanted it to be a surprise, but it was killing me to see how disappointed you were when you found out it had been sold. After all you have been through, I didn't think I could stand to see your suffer another heartbreak if this place really had been bought out from under you."

"I can't believe I didn't see any of this coming. I can honestly say that I never could imagine or experience a greater single act of kindness in my life, Whitley. I can't tell you how much this means to me." He moved toward her, placed a short, gentle kiss on her lips and hugged her. "Thank you."

She put her arms around him and squeezed him like she never wanted to let go.

Steve rubbed the back of her head with his palm and fingertips. "I have always been attracted to you, Whitley, but with work and all, I just figured you wanted a platonic relationship. Just as I thought I did."

"Um, 'as you thought you did?' Wait a minute now. I told you don't owe me anything, Steve. Well, that is, other than the seven-hundred thousand plus for this place. Oh yeah, I got the sellers to come down about eighty thou on the asking price since it was a cash purchase, and Dutch cut some of his commission when he heard what I was up to."

They both chuckled as they held each other and simultaneously fought back tears.

"You amaze me. I feel like an idiot for not recognizing your feelings," he said.

"I didn't give you obvious clues."

"I'll get a cashier's check for the majority of it next week, and I'll start making payments next month. You don't need to have your money tied up in an interest-free loan."

"No hurry. As I said, it's not as though I need it."

Steve looked at Whitley, then at the sun, which was rapidly meeting the horizon. "Well, it's getting a little too late to take you on a tour of the property. . .and I think we should start this new facet of our relationship properly. Whitley Talmadge, would you do me the honor of joining me for dinner tonight? If we leave now, we should be able to make it back to town at a reasonable hour."

"We can't."

"Why not?"

"I haven't exactly finished telling you everything."

"Whitley, please. I don't think I can take another surprise."

"It's just that I've already made dinner plans for us tonight."

"You have?"

"I've got a cooler full of food in my trunk. If it's okay with you, we'll be dining here tonight, and we can stay for a couple of days if you'd like."

"Whitley, the electricity isn't on, and after the last time I looked at it, I can tell you the cabin really needs some cleaning."

Whitley just smiled and stared at her feet as she kicked the gravel in front of the gate.

"You didn't."

"I did; cleaned and ready for occupancy. Dutch convinced the owners to let us go in before the closing and spruce it up."

"But I didn't bring a change of clothes."

Whitley reached into her pants pocket and pulled out her keys. She flipped through them until she found Steve's house key and held it as she jingled the rest of them in the air. "I hope you don't mind me going through your dresser while Mom and I stayed with you. I got your sizes and went on a quick shopping spree at the western store. New work boots, a belt, pair of jeans, and a couple of shirts."

"Un-be-lieve-able." Steve grabbed the padlock that was dangling between the chain looped around the fence post and the gate. He unlocked it and swung the gate open without another word.

Whitley giggled, ran to the car, and started it. She pulled through the entrance. Steve closed the gate behind her, then got back into the passenger seat.

"Wait a minute. What about Bosco?" He asked.

Whitley looked at her watch, "Mom should be arriving to feed him any minute. She is also spending the night, unless I call and tell her we're coming back.

His head fell back against the headrest, "I feel like I just ran a marathon. Thank you, Whitley, from the bottom of my heart."

"You're welcome, sweetie." She carefully steered the Mercedes to keep it in the ruts as the tall grass in between them stroked the undercarriage of the car. "Maybe I should have bought an SUV."

"Please don't tell me you furnished the place, too?"

"Oh no, it's still decorated in that macho Lake Wobegon style that you loved at first sight. Some of the dust has just been blown off. By the way, the cleaning and first year's worth of electricity are my mother's gifts to you. She wanted to do a little something for all you've done for me."

"Whitley, I think your family has given me more than enough already."

"Like I said, don't feel any obligation for all of this. The last thing I want to do is change the good relationship we have. I wanted to tell you how I felt because it was stressing me out. I mean, besides, having you as a friend is still better than not having you around at all."

Steve reached across and lifted her right hand from the steering wheel. He brought it to his lips and kissed it as she stopped the car beside the cabin. "It's all I can do to keep my emotions in check right now, Whitley. Of all the things you've done for me in the past or given me today, nothing compares to your opening yourself up to me the way you have."

Another tear glided down Whitley's cheek.

Steve wiped at it with his thumb. "Of course, I want to change our relationship. But I want to take it slow, Whit." He kissed her hand again, and they got out of the car.

Whitley fumbled in her purse for a tissue and wiped her eyes. Her heart felt as though it would bubble through her chest in sheer happiness.

"You know, this weekend trip was a great idea. It will give us a chance to really get to know each other better," Steve said.

"Well, I hope I can at least get a goodnight kiss from you since this will be our first date and everything."

"I'll see what I can do, Whit. Did you bring wine?"

"Four bottles."

"Four bottles? Hmmm, I suppose anything is possible." He smiled at her and held out his hand.

She took it and together they walked up the wooden steps to the cabin door.

THE END

Made in the USA
Monee, IL
12 May 2021

67379619R00167